# Tildy's knees weakened.

She had kissed him! With a kiss that went far beyond the bounds of good taste!

"Tomorrow night meet me here before moonrise, and we'll consider ways to send Mr. Walton scurrying back where he came from. If he's still alive come morning."

Lieutenant Hull had not solved her problem, but saddled her with a new one. She had put her reputation in the hands of a soldier who would spread the story of her kiss. A sliver of light above the schoolhouse reflected off the banjo he held out to her.

"If I...promise what you want—" she hated that her voice quavered "—you'll not speak of us meeting..."

"I'll say not one word about a marvelous kiss."

She hated him, hated his blackmail with a fury new to her...!

Dear Reader,

In *The Lieutenant's Lady*, her fourth book for Harlequin Historicals, author Rae Muir begins an exciting new Western series called THE WEDDING TRAIL. This group of related but stand-alone stories begins with a quilting circle of young women in Harville, Indiana, and heads west as the members each discover their own destiny on the trail to California. In this month's story, a hard-luck soldier returns home determined to marry the town "princess," a woman who sees him as little more than a way out of an unwanted marriage.

*USA Today* bestselling author Ruth Langan is also back this month with *Ruby*, the next book in the author's ongoing series THE JEWELS OF TEXAS. *Ruby* is the delightful tale of a flirtatious young woman and the formidable town marshal who falls under her spell. And in *The Forever Man* from Carolyn Davidson, a spinster who has given up on love discovers happiness when a widower and his two sons invade her quiet life.

Sharon Schulze, one of the authors in this year's March Madness Promotion, also returns this month with *To Tame a Warrior's Heart*, a stirring medieval tale about a former mercenary and a betrayed noblewoman who overcome their shadowed pasts with an unexpected love.

Whatever your tastes in reading, we hope you enjoy all four of this month's titles, available wherever Harlequin Historicals are sold.

Sincerely,

Tracy Farrell
Senior Editor

Please address questions and book requests to:
Harlequin Reader Service
U.S.: 3010 Walden Ave., P.O. Box 1325, Buffalo, NY 14269
Canadian: P.O. Box 609, Fort Erie, Ont. L2A 5X3

# RAE MUIR
## THE WEDDING TRAIL

# THE LIEUTENANT'S LADY

## Harlequin Books

TORONTO • NEW YORK • LONDON
AMSTERDAM • PARIS • SYDNEY • HAMBURG
STOCKHOLM • ATHENS • TOKYO • MILAN
MADRID • WARSAW • BUDAPEST • AUCKLAND

ISBN 0-373-28983-9

THE LIEUTENANT'S LADY

Copyright © 1997 by Bishop Creek Literary Trust

**Books by Rae Muir**

Harlequin Historicals

*The Pearl Stallion* #308
*The Trail to Temptation* #345
*All But the Queen of Hearts* #369
*The Lieutenant's Lady* #383

---

## RAE MUIR

lives in a cabin in California's High Sierra, a mile from an abandoned gold mine. She is, by training, an historian, but finds it difficult to fit in to the academic mold, since her imagination inevitably inserts fictional characters into actual events. She has been a newspaper reporter, written and edited educational materials, researched eighteenth-century Scottish history, run a fossil business and raised three children in her spare time.

She loves the Sierra Nevada, Hawaii, Oxford and San Francisco. Her favorite mode of travel is by car, and she stops at every historical marker.

To Eric and Cathryn

# Chapter One

The clink of spurs, the plop of shod hooves in the dust disturbed the Sunday morning silence. Tildy, bent over a heap of autumn flowers, pretended to reach for a bundle of goldenrod. She twisted far enough to peek under her arm, hoping the men who rode on the other side of the town square did not notice her unladylike curiosity. Two strangers mounted on sturdy Indian ponies, leading pack-horses. They wore fringed buckskins and carried rifles slung across the pommels of their saddles. Not Mr. Walton.

She leaned the goldenrod against the corn shock and chided herself for her impatience. A lady maintained her serenity in the midst of turmoil. Mr. Walton would arrive properly, in a buggy. He had an eight-mile drive from Muncie, so two hours after sunrise would be the soonest she might expect him. At the moment, the shadow of the squat church steeple reached all the way to the west side of the square.

"Home!" shouted one of the strangers. Tildy spun about, scattering an armload of asters in the dust. "Good day, Miss MacIntyre," he called as he rode past the flag-pole. He lifted a tattered hat. Tildy stared at the creased, sun-darkened face for several seconds.

"Mr. Godfroy! We hadn't expected you—"

"You hadn't expected ever to see me again when I didn't come home to Indiana last summer. Two years gone, you supposed I'd vanished in the wilds of the Rocky Mountains."

A few early drinkers tumbled from the tavern. "Godfroy! We'd given up on you," one of the men said. "Figured one o' those grizzly bears got you."

The men clustered about the trappers. Tildy backed to the church steps, gathering asters as she went. A lady did not speak to rough mountain men, nor did she associate with men who drank whiskey on Sunday morning. What if Mr. Walton should arrive and find her in the company of...? Too bad that Trail Godfroy and his friend had arrived in Pikeston this morning. Such exciting visitors would tempt the men away from Reverend Fitch's Harvest Home service.

"This here's Jed Sampson," Mr. Godfroy said. Tildy glanced over her shoulder at his bearded companion. He had not removed his hat to acknowledge her presence. "We've been to California." She concentrated on fitting the asters between the corn and the heap of pumpkins.

"California!" marveled a voice at her elbow. Cousin Meggie held out a bundle of milkweed, its pods bursting in white clouds. She paid no heed as Tildy lifted them from her hands, but stared at the mountain men. "Imagine, all the way to California and back!"

"Ignore them, Meggie," Tildy said as she struggled to keep her attention on her work. From the corner of her eye she watched Sampson dismount and, with one quick twist, release the rope of his pack saddle.

"Here," he cried. "Here's California." He shook out what looked like a thick blanket. It materialized into a pelt, the fur dark in the morning shadow. "Feel this. Soft and tempting. This is California."

The men crowded closer, cutting off Tildy's view. She recalled herself to the church decorations and searched for a vacant spot for the milkweed.

"Let the young ladies see the otter skin," Mr. Godfroy said. The crowd parted politely; two or three men bowed and gestured for Tildy and Meggie to approach Mr. Sampson and the fur. Meggie dashed away, and Tildy noted she had not bothered to put on shoes yet this morning. Tildy cut off a public reprimand—it was not her job to discipline her cousin—and followed more sedately.

The undercoat of the pelt was black, with silver tipping the longer hairs. It reminded her of frost on a dark roof. The fur yielded beneath her hand, drawing her into its seductive thickness. She imagined the fur collar of a cloak, caressing her neck, the longest hairs brushing her cheeks. Even better, lining the entire hood, framing her face with its embrace. She snatched her hand away, but a muscle between her shoulder blades vibrated. Too seductive. Too foreign. Probably improper.

"We must finish the decorating, Meggie," she said to justify her rapid retreat. "The congregation will arrive soon, and I'm not dressed for church." Meggie backed away, but her arm remained stretched out toward the fur, as if she would draw it with her.

"When's Mr. Walton coming?" asked Meggie, breaking the stems of redhaw in an attempt to make them stand upright. "In time for the service?"

"I don't know."

"Will you really marry him? A man you've never met?"

"By the time I accept his proposal, *if* I do, we'll be well acquainted. If Mr. Walton's at all like his uncle, he'll be passably good-looking." *Handsome,* said an inner voice. "I mean, Mr. Moffett's going on sixty, and still has beautiful curly black hair. Wouldn't you fall in love with Mr. Moffett if he were a young man?"

"No. I'll never fall in love with a man who keeps a store, no matter how charming and handsome. And if my father tells me to marry a city man, even one who'll inherit the biggest store in Muncie, Indiana, I'll run off. I'd go with Trail Godfroy to California!'' She straightened up, pressed one hand to the small of her back and with the other shaded her eyes against the sunlight that reflected from windows around the square. She stared at the crowd of men, and Tildy feared she might join them.

"Meggie, put the rest of the goldenrod around the corn. You should not call him Trail,'' she added in a lower voice as Meggie bent to her task. "Mr. Godfroy's old enough to be your father, and even though his grandfather *was* an Indian, age demands a certain respect—'' She raised her head at the jingle of harness. Small puffs of dust rose from the hooves of a gray horse and the wheels of a sporty gig. Before she had managed to pull herself erect, horse and driver swung behind the growing crowd at the flagpole.

If that was Mr. Walton's gig, he had left Muncie long before sunrise! *He's anxious, too! I'm sure I'll like him.*

"He stopped in front of the store,'' Meggie said, stepping away from the church steps for a better view and making a public display of her curiosity. "Go ahead. I'll finish the decorating.''

Tildy reached for the last few stalks of milkweed, pretending to be calm. "No, it's well that Mr. Walton finds me occupied. To appear to throw myself at him would not give a good impression.''

Her hands trembled, and clumped seeds floated off the milkweed pods. She leaned forward to rescue the lacy mass, brushed the row of precariously balanced redhaw branches, bringing them down. Meggie thrust her aside.

"Let me. You're all nervous thumbs.''

Tildy's father walked slowly across the square, detouring around the fur trappers. A shorter man followed, marked by a tall hat bobbing behind her father's shoulder. Tildy stood and brushed her hands on the back of her skirt. Mr. Sampson lifted the otter skin over his head.

"In California,'' he said, "snow falls only in the mountains, and the plains blossom every month of the year.''

Tildy dragged her eyes from the fur back to her father,

and noticed his hands fluttering at his vest pockets. Her heart skipped a beat; Papa was nervous. Not a good sign. Mr. Sampson swung the fur in the direction of the church, and the sun reflected a black iridescence.

"In California, such nonsense as a Harvest Home would never be celebrated. Harvest comes every week, every day, and there's no March hunger."

The short man stepped from behind her father. His black broadcloth coat stretched across a portly belly. Her father drew his watch from his vest pocket, thrust it back without so much as opening its cover. Very nervous.

"Mr. Afton Walton, my daughter, Miss Matilda Mac-Intyre."

Mr. Walton removed his silk hat and extended a gloved hand. Behind him the otter skin undulated magically and Tildy strained to give the introduction her full attention. Even through kidskin, his hand felt clammy. He clasped her fingers, lifted them to within an inch of his lips with no bow, only a slight inclination of his head. His eyes glittered, pale blue above fat cheeks, like ice at the bottom of a hoofprint in deep, dirty snow.

"Enchanted, Miss MacIntyre."

No neck, not the slightest indentation between head and shoulders. A fold of flesh declared the presence of a chin somewhere under the fat that bulged over his tight collar. She tightened her throat to stifle a cry of protest, widened her eyes to subdue sudden tears. This ugly creature was Afton Walton? Meggie gasped behind her, too loudly, and Tildy recalled her manners.

"I...we must finish the decoration of the church," she stammered. *Don't stare. Don't shudder.* Time enough after Mr. Walton left town to tell her father there would be no wedding. Absolutely not! No. A lady had certain standards.

She focused over Mr. Walton's shoulder so he would not see her revulsion. "The service will commence in less than an hour, and I'm not suitably dressed," she said.

Tildy saw her friend Rachel enter the southwest corner

of the square, the last blossoms of her aunt's garden over-flowing her arms.

"You'll join us at our Harvest Home, Mr. Walton," Tildy continued, forcing an outward politeness, while mentally she contrasted this squat reality to the tall, handsome man her imagination had created. "The choir has practiced steadily since..."

Rachel's uncle, Mr. Ridley, walked behind her, accompanied by a stranger dressed in blue. A uniform. The sun glinted on his gold epaulets. Mr. Ridley turned to the soldier and spoke, followed his words with a laugh. The soldier tilted his face to the sun, swept off his hat, causing a knot of gold to sparkle. Young, darkly handsome, so amazingly like her shattered illusion of Mr. Walton she wondered if he might have materialized from her daydreams. But his laughter—and the slap on his thigh to accent his good humor—betrayed him as human. A blood-red stripe defined the seams of his trousers, and his long legs. Very human. The double row of buttons accented the breadth of his shoulders and the trimness of the torso beneath the coat.

"We'll leave you and Meggie to your work," her father choked. "I'm sure Mr. Walton could use some refreshment after his long drive."

"The store..." Mr. Walton said as he turned away.

"Am I too late?" Rachel asked. "I had the flowers all cut, but Lieutenant Hull called upon Uncle unexpectedly, and Aunt was in the midst of her preparations, so I had to tarry to make coffee. Who is that horrid man with your father? He reminds me of neglected yeast that's overflowed the bowl."

"Mr. Afton Walton," Meggie said with malicious relish.

"No!" Rachel cried. Tildy bowed her head, unable to speak for fear her words might collapse into sobs. If only she had not confided in her friends! If only she had kept her hopes for the marriage to herself. If only she had not bragged of her good fortune, marrying the heir to the largest store in Muncie. She studied the bits of stems and shattered blossoms in the dust, stirred the featherlike fragments of milkweed seed with her toe. Punishment! *Pride goeth before a fall,* Granny said. Punishment for her loose tongue, and the sin of pride.

"You remember the charming MacIntyre girls?" Mr. Ridley said. Tildy lifted her head to be polite, and discovered gray eyes beneath heavy black brows, a wide mouth that ended in very unmanly dimples. The stranger's cleft chin and tan cheeks glowed with the golden reflection from his epaulets.

"Margaret, and Matilda," Mr. Ridley continued. "Matt Hull left us four years ago to be a simple soldier, and has returned an officer."

"And the MacIntyre girls have grown to charming young ladies," Lieutenant Hull said, bowing.

Hull! Tildy's mind, busy with the disaster of Mr. Walton, suddenly grasped the significance of the name. Matt Hull! The filthy, ignorant son of the river woman.

But Lieutenant Hull, unlike Mr. Walton, could bend in the middle. In fact, he almost doubled himself up, and the excessive bow demanded a response. Tildy grasped the skirt of her everyday calico—why did she wish she were better dressed?—and bobbed a token curtsy. She scanned the square for her father. The scolding she'd receive, if Papa saw her greeting Matt Hull. Her father had his back turned, unlocking the store. She exhaled too loudly in her relief.

Black smudged the edges of Lieutenant Hull's gray eyes—keen eyes, curious, even as he smiled. She turned slightly away, to avoid the necessity of returning that smile. Reverend Fitch waded into the crowd in the center of the square. Beyond, her disappointing suitor and her father stood before the store.

"Pardon me, but I must go home," she said. "I...I must change before the church service." She fled, past the flaunted otter skin. The crowd forced her nearer the store—and Mr. Walton—than she wished to venture.

"Oranges—have you ever tasted an orange? Nectar of the gods! Grapes, cabbages as big as a bushel!"

"I don't open on Sunday morning usually," her father was saying as she dashed by, "in respect to Reverend Fitch, for his congregation is not always of the largest, but if you wish to see..."

Mr. Walton nodded. He obviously considered the condition of the store of greater importance than the woman who would—*would not!*—be his wife. At the corner she paused. Lieutenant Hull stood in front of the church, his hat in his hand. Gray eyes, hard beneath black brows, stared after her. A prickle crept from her neck, down her chest, until it stung her breasts. Did he see all of her? Those gray eyes stripped her modesty, and made her a harlot, like his mother. She lifted her skirts and ran down the street, rushed up the front steps, into the shelter of the hall. Up the stairs to collapse, panting, on the top step.

No, that neat officer could not possibly be odious, stupid Matt Hull. Mr. Walton. She had imagined Mr. Walton... Never would she marry Mr. Walton! Gray eyes, penetrating, exposing her... She pressed her hands to her chest to ease the sting, then to the sides of her head to control the images rattling around her mind.

Yes, marry Mr. Walton. A future for Josh, Lewis and Eddie. Her brothers expected her to marry Mr. Walton. With his backing they would open stores in Albany, Yorktown and Eaton. Her father expected her to marry Mr. Walton and bring the business of the county into her family's hands.

No!

Her boasts to the sewing circle replayed in her head. Would her friends sympathize, or would they laugh at her plight? Either pity or jeers would be hard to bear.

"Why, Matilda! Whatever are you doing, sitting here?" Her mother wore her new black silk dress and bonnet, and carried her best gloves. "You must dress immediately. The dark rose calico the seamstress delivered Friday, so Mr. Walton will see you at your best. You may borrow my rose bonnet."

Tildy stared blankly at her mother. Run away, to distant California, where a woman might wrap herself in silver-black otter skins. Gray eyes, shot with black. Not soft and seductive, like the otter skin, but hard and determined.

"I will not marry Mr. Walton," she said slowly, pulling herself into the reality of home, mother, and dressing for Church. "He's like nothing so much as a spring puffball, a slimy fungus...a poisonous toadstool!"

"Mr. Walton's arrived? So early?" Her mother's well-managed brows rose in astonishment, then lowered to join her happy smile. "He's anxious to meet you."

"I don't care how anxious he is, I will not marry him."

"When you know him better, you'll change your mind. This evening we'll go through the new *Godey's Lady's Book,* and learn what brides in the East are wearing. Perhaps Mrs. Ridley's cousins in Virginia—"

"I won't be Mr. Walton's bride!"

"Who else should you marry?" her mother asked, astonished. "I'm not aware of another suitable man. Dear, sweet innocent!" She smiled the you-can't-possibly-understand smile that Tildy hated, and patted her head. "Thrown into the world alone, dear, you'd be baffled, such a charming ignorance. A sweet little lady needs a man to stand between her and the great confusion outside her door. A deeper acquaintance—"

"I'm as acquainted with Mr. Walton as I wish to be. He's shorter than I am, and fat as a pig ready for slaughter and he cared more to see the store."

The firm words restored strength to her legs. She pulled herself up against the banister. "I'll dress and be along shortly. But I'll wear my tan dress and my own green bonnet, and tell Papa, I will not marry that toadstool."

If her father insisted, she would run away. Where? She

pulled the calico dress over her head, peeled off her dusty stockings. Indianapolis, of course. She could ask Mr. Ridley for recommendations…accommodations suitable for a single lady. He must know of a respectable boarding-house, since he had served in the legislature, and argued cases before the supreme court.

She poured clean water in the basin and scrubbed the stains of the plants from her hands. *Papa will not be such a tyrant,* she assured herself, twisting her garters at the top of her stockings. But he *had* counted on this marriage. She slid her feet into her shoes. Papa would understand her rejection of Mr. Walton. After all, he himself had been upset by the sight of the man. But there was no harm in making plans, just in case.

Matt Hull leaned against the back wall of the church, along with a dozen other young men, unmarried fellows of his own age who should have greeted a returning soldier. Instead they edged away. A muscle in his jaw quivered, letting him know he had clenched his teeth. He stared at the ceiling until the ache disappeared. Soon enough they would seek his friendship. *Time,* he said to himself. *Patience.*

The Harvest Home had drawn the entire population of Pikeston, plus the surrounding farms. The congregation overflowed the benches, so the young men stood and the children sat on the floor along the sides and before the pulpit. Reverend Fitch had disarmed his competition by cleverly cutting Godfroy and Sampson out of the crowd, and personally escorting them into the church. Their audience had followed like sheep behind goats. Trail Godfroy, on a bench near the front, stared about as if he had never attended church before. The town matrons and farmers' wives shot disapproving glances at his back. On the other hand, they nodded and smiled at Sampson, who sang every verse of "Amazing Grace" without opening his hymnal.

Mr. Walton occupied an exceptionally large part of the front bench, sitting with the MacIntyre clan. They had placed him beside Tildy. Rachel had explained Walton's presence—*Tildy MacIntyre's to marry Mr. Moffett's nephew, to provide for the future of her brothers.* Matt had dismissed the story as Rachel's fantasy, fostered by reading silly books. In the year 1847, and in America, fathers no longer dictated whom their daughters and sons would marry.

But Tildy's bleak expression told the truth. Shameful to waste such a pretty thing on a fat, middle-aged Yankee. She had not taken the man's arm when she came into church, but clasped her small hands at her waist. Matt recalled her lively green eyes, and judged those little hands sometimes strayed from propriety. Her broad face reminded him of summer flowers along the Rio Grande. And that memory brought another, soldiers singing "Flowers of Spring" on the march, the ribald words referring to a different flower, a blossom the men looked forward to plucking on the day they returned to civilization. The hymn ended.

"Heavenly Father," began Reverend Fitch, "we thank thee for thy amazing grace, the grace of harvest, which we celebrate this day."

Godfroy, Matt noticed, did not bow his head, but stared down the row at Mr. and Mrs. Ridley, and Rachel between them. Rachel had matured to young womanhood—dark hair, expressive brown eyes and a wide mouth. Her unusual beauty must invade the dreams of every swain in the county.

From what he had heard in the square, Godfroy and Sampson had given up fur trapping. They offered themselves as guides to emigrants on the overland trail. Why California? They would have an easier time putting together a party for Oregon. The British had settled the boundary dispute, and America had drawn Oregon into the fold. No telling what was happening in California. The

Mexicans balked at signing a treaty that gave most of the far West to the United States.

Even worse for Godfroy's prospects, the news of the Donner disaster had filtered east this summer, first as unbelievable rumors, then incontrovertible facts. For weeks horrid tales filled the newspapers, of men, women and children starving in the snow of the California mountains, the survivors eating the dead. Hardly an inducement to emigration.

Reverend Fitch's prayer switched from an obsequious tone to a demanding one. He lectured the Lord at some length on the people's needs, with emphasis on more responsible men at the state capital and lower taxes. Tildy's shoulder pressed against her mother's to put space between her and Mr. Walton. Matt's mind wandered in circles, skirted subjects not suitable for divine worship, finally yielded to temptation and contemplated how an obese man performed with a woman.

"Amen," Reverend Fitch said. The choir rose, a crowd of latecomers pushed in, shoving Matt more firmly against the wall. His lower back tightened, and he elbowed his way to the door before it got worse. By the time he reached the front steps the unwelcome memory danced before his eyes, flames flickering across the steamboat's deck, the men falling, his lungs heaving.

"You're leaving, Lieutenant Hull?" Meggie MacIntyre stood at the bottom of the stairs, tucking her frizzy red-brown hair under her bonnet. She wore a dress of neat blue calico that called attention to her blue eyes. The toe of a black slipper protruded from under her petticoats.

"No," he said, "I'll listen from out here. I'm not accustomed to being with so many people. Inside."

"Of course, army men live in tents," she said. "In the open."

"We did, all the way through Texas and Mexico, but in Louisiana we lived in barracks, at a regular fort." Meggie looked suddenly interested, and ceased poking at her hair.

"Real houses? Did women live there?"

"Of course. Some officers brought their families. A few sergeants were married, and every regiment hires laundresses."

"Then Tildy can run off to the army," she said with delight. "I'll go with her, but I'll put on men's clothes and become a soldier. It's awful!" she added in a whisper. She renewed jabbing at her recalcitrant curls with such violence Matt feared she would damage her bonnet.

"What's awful?"

"That Uncle Ira expects Tildy to marry that fat toad!"

"Certainly, if Tildy finds him...unacceptable, Mr. Ira MacIntyre will not insist."

"But he will! See, Moffett, of Moffett's Emporium in Muncie, has no children, so he's making Mr. Walton, who's his sister's son, his heir. And Uncle Ira and Moffett settled it weeks ago, that Tildy and Walton will marry, so the two stores are combined. Old Moffett said nothing about Afton Walton being wider than he is high. And Uncle Ira agreed, like a fool, buying a pig in a poke, for the sake of the boys."

"What does Tildy say?"

"I haven't spoken to her since she met the man. But I'll help her run off."

"Can you think of nothing less drastic?" he asked, amused by Meggie's intensity. The excitement made the freckles across her nose more prominent.

"Maybe killing him. I suppose we could do something to his gig, so the wheel fell off between here and Muncie and spilled him on the road." Matt wondered, uncomfortably, if Meggie's "we" included him. "He'd tumble out, like corn from a crib," she added.

"But he might lie hurt and in pain for hours before someone came along."

"He wouldn't starve though, would he? The man could live for weeks on his blubber." Meggie's eyes narrowed, and she reminded Matt of his colonel considering the next deployment of the flying artillery. The choir sang the final words of the hymn, "Blest be our ties of friendship true, our love of fellow men." Matt smiled at the contrast between the church service and Meggie's bloody plans.

"Grin if you want!" she snapped. "But it may be the only way. It'd be best if the accident happened at that narrow, boggy place on the corduroy. He might roll in the swamp. But now that I think about it, it's too dry to drown him, because the fall rains haven't flooded the ditch yet. I better get in before the sermon or Ma will skin me." She trotted up the steps, exposing the backs of her shoes, which she had trodden down so the heels flopped loosely.

Matt sat on the top step and leaned against a shock of corn. How long before he could talk to Trail Godfroy alone? Ridley had pumped him for news of the war in Mexico, but brushed away stories of anything other than heroism. He'd wanted to hear how the flying artillery had swung into position at Palo Alto and mowed down the Mexican infantry. Godfroy, on the other hand, would listen to the horror of it, soldiers fleeing to drown in the river, their blood turning the water red. Godfroy would not wave him to silence when he spoke of dysentery and yellow fever, gangrene and slow death, of mockingbirds so accustomed to funerals that they sang the dead march.

And Godfroy could tell him the truth about California and the long journey across the continent, instead of the glorious lies he and Sampson dispensed to their gullible audience in the square.

California? The very thought of setting out for the Pacific exhausted him. No, he would live his life right here. He would make a different kind of journey, one step at a time, to gain power over the people who had sneered at him. The people of Pikeston would eventually treat him with respect, if only because they feared him.

# Chapter Two

The Harvest Home feast covered a long trestle table down the middle of the schoolhouse. Turkeys, roast pork, squirrel stew, heaps of late roasting ears; baked pumpkin, squash and potatoes, both white and sweet; beans boiled with salt pork and turnips cooked with carrots; acres of pies. To brighten the place, and to show off their handiwork, women had hung quilts around the walls. Matt studied the patchwork nearest the door.

"You left early." His father, speaking too loudly, right in his ear. "Before I filled the jugs at the still. Ashamed of riding to town in the cart with your pa and sister, ain't ya?"

"I had to see Attorney Ridley before church, Pa. I told you last night."

"Attorney Ridley." His father sneered the title so it changed from respect to ridicule. "A cheating lawyer who's never read none o' those books he shows off. Conniving legislator! You're getting mighty big in the head, coming home a *loo-ten-ant*. You'll find out that fancy uniform means nothing in Pikeston. Ashamed of your family, sleeping in your blankets under the trees instead of in the cabin your own pa provides."

"The cabin's crowded enough—you and Ma and the children—without me moving in." He tried to make the excuse sound plausible, but he *was* ashamed of his family. And fearful of fleas and bedbugs establishing themselves in the blankets he had carefully cleaned a few days ago.

"Good day, Hull," Ridley said. "You must be proud of this boy of yours, coming home an officer." Matt's father snorted, spun on his heel and joined a group of men in the corner, who passed an earthenware jug. They paid no attention to a large quilt hanging over their heads, one cleverly pieced to resemble autumn leaves.

Ridley laid a hand on Matt's arm. "I've spoken to Mrs. Ridley," he said in a low voice. "She agrees to me taking you on as a clerk to read law—you learning to read and write while away in the army impressed her—but she expects you to sign a temperance pledge." His eyes flickered nervously to the jug.

"Of course," Matt said, making sure he spoke heartily, without the slightest hint of regret.

"And...she hesitates for you...rooming with us, with Rachel nearing eighteen...a marriageable age...the gossip."

"I quite understand." The rejection did not surprise him.

"There's a room above the office, not elegant, mind you, but adequate for a single man. Besides, a young man studying law should avoid entanglements with the fair sex, not think of marriage until his practice is well established. Then he can look for a wife among the young ladies of influential families."

Matt murmured agreement. A wife? He had not even considered marriage.

"And I'll make arrangements for you to take your meals elsewhere, perhaps at the tavern, although the temptation of drink..."

"Does not tempt me. Thank you very much. Ideal."

"Breakfast and dinner, and you might find your suppers yourself...."

Bread and cheese in the attic room above the office. He

had lived on worse during his four years in the army. One year of apprenticeship living in an attic before he hung out his shingle—Matthew Hull, Esq., Attorney-At-Law. He eyed the men passing the jug—the bottom of Pikeston society. Squatters along the river, farmers laboring on poor, stony-ridge farms. This year he would get to know them, then take their cases when richer neighbors threatened. He would accept pickles, preserves and hams in payment, and on election day send wagons to bring them to the polls. The fancy citizens of Pikeston would soon pay heed to the upstart young lawyer.

"Have you met Mr. Walton?" Ridley asked, pressing Matt's elbow as a sign that their agreement was complete. "He came recently from Massachusetts. He's Moffett of Muncie's nephew and heir. Gossip says he'll marry Miss MacIntyre. Ira's daughter, Tildy, of course. Not Jim Mac's Meggie, who's such a tomboy she's likely never to find a husband."

Shaking hands with Walton was like grasping the corner of a feather pillow. His cold eyes focused over Matt's shoulder.

"Of the Indiana militia?" Walton asked, a mocking smile deepening the crease of chin and lifting his cheeks until his eyes almost disappeared.

"No. Regular army." Matt dropped his hand to the red stripe on his trousers, the mark of the artillery, but Walton did not follow the gesture.

"The Indiana militia did not show well at Buena Vista," Walton continued. "They ran off, and General Taylor condemned them as cowards."

"I fought on another part of the battlefield so I can't comment," Matt replied evenly. Damned, arrogant New Englander!

"Walton plans to settle in Muncie," Ira MacIntyre interrupted, his hands playing nervously at the pockets of his vest. Matt smiled at the man's habit, at the verification of his memory.

"I see you agree with me on the worth, the lack of worth, rather, of the militia," Walton said. Matt realized Walton misinterpreted his smile, started to object, but Walton plunged on without regard to anyone else. "A great waste of the taxpayers' money. As to settling in Muncie, I'm currently *investigating* the situation. Uncle Moffett made an offer. Understandably, he sought a partner with business experience to aid him, and eventually inherit. To find such talent he was forced to look outside this state." He tried to look down his nose, an impossibility since he was the shortest man in the group. "The condition of Indiana's finances renders the situation uncertain. The tax rate! I may recommend that Uncle Moffett remove himself to a more settled locale."

"We'll solve the problem of finances soon enough," said Ridley in a huff. He had served in the legislature that reshuffled the state's mass of debt. "Indiana has great potential."

"If Indiana were a man, he would be bankrupt," Walton said. "The state's run out on its creditors. Foolish lawmakers, making plans for canals and railroads more suitable to wealthy eastern states. Thousands of dollars in the pockets of frauds, and no improvements. Not one. No eastern bank will ever again trust this state with a penny, sir! Not one penny. Business will suffer for years, decades—"

"Won't you help yourself to dinner," MacIntyre said, interrupting Walton's diatribe, glancing an apology at Ridley.

Matt hung back, saw Tildy and her mother in a corner, silhouetted against a white whole-cloth quilt that proved some woman's exceptional skill with a needle. Tildy's head drooped, while her mother glared and waggled a finger under her chin. Tildy shook her head violently, but did not raise her eyes. Poor girl. What would the wedding night be like?

Matt's stomach growled. He headed for the table, but when a man shoved against his back, the spasm, the shortness of breath came in a flash. He grabbed a bit of corn bread and a slice of ham, pushed his way out of the crowd, and made for the door. His earlier fantasies of Walton's sexual acrobatics no longer amused him. Not when the woman was pretty Tildy MacIntyre. Not when a man could imagine her soft little hands carried away by the lively spirit in her eyes. He sank down on the bottom step, considering the injustice of a world that bestowed such a creature on a man like Walton.

"Lieutenant," a strangled voice begged, so startling Matt that he leaped up and dropped his bread and ham in the dirt. "Here." A figure crouched against the wall of the schoolhouse. The man's hands clasped his own shoulders as if to warm himself. James MacIntyre, Ira MacIntyre's elder brother. A farmer, not a storekeeper, whom even river brats casually called Jim Mac.

"My ague's come on. Please take me home. I'd thought if I sat here in the sun for a few minutes…"

Matt thrust an arm behind Jim Mac, lifted him and led him to the steps. "I'll fetch your brother, and we'll help you to his house. Just around the corner."

"Get your father's cart and carry me home," he said.

"But your brother's house—"

"I'll not go to the house of a man who'll sell his daughter to a monster, brother or no!" Jim Mac shivered. He stiffened, trying to control the seizure.

"Let me fetch Mrs. MacIntyre."

"Don't spoil her fun. Eliza's hardly been off the farm since summer. My mother's at the house to care for me."

"Can you walk to the cart?" Jim Mac clenched his chattering teeth and tried to nod, but his head wavered as much from side to side as up and down. "Get there," Matt said, "while I tell Pa I'm taking his horse and cart. It won't do for him to raise a hue and cry that someone stole it." Matt ran into the schoolhouse, found his father sitting on a bench alone, wolfing food from a heaping plate.

"Mr. James MacIntyre feels his ague coming on, and

has asked me to carry him home. May I use the horse and cart?''

"Damn rich farmers," his father said around a mouthful of succotash, pushing fragments of corn and beans into his beard. "Don't have the time of day for a poor man, till *they're* in need." He glared around the room. "Why'd he not ask his brother?"

"Some disagreement between them," Matt said softly.

His father smiled slowly, then grinned. "Take him. If the MacIntyre brothers quarrel, a poor man can do worse than come down on the side of the farmer whose corn's already in the shock. When crows fight, they spill a quantity of food for the weasels to pick up."

Matt found Jim Mac hanging on to the end of the cart, shaking so severely he could not lift a leg to climb in. He boosted the man, mounted the fragmented board that served for the driver's seat and turned the bony horse to the road out of town.

Carrying the sick man into the house proved difficult, for the shakes had him firmly in their grasp. The ground floor bedroom seemed to belong to Mr. and Mrs. Mac-Intyre, judging by the scattering of hairbrushes and a nightshirt hanging on the back of the door. Matt pulled the appliquéd coverlet away before he dumped Jim Mac on the bed. He emptied a chest of blankets to cover him, for the man shivered so violently the bedstead creaked and the mattress moved on the leather straps.

"Water," Jim Mac quavered.

Matt ran through the sitting room, figuring the kitchen must be at the rear of the house. It turned out to be a large room, the log walls betraying its origin: the first cabin built on the farm, where the whole family had once lived.

He filled a kettle from the water pail and poked at the dying fire in the cookstove. Tea. Hot tea, to bring on the sweats and end the ague sooner. But the painted tea caddy was not only locked, it seemed to be nailed to the shelf.

He poured out a cup of tepid water just as the kitchen door opened.

"What are you doing in my kitchen? Who are you?"

The woman carried a basket of eggs over her arm. She had the wrinkles of age and gray hair peeked from around her mobcap, but she did not stoop and seemed not a bit frightened at finding a stranger fussing around her stove. Matt realized with a start that he had pulled himself to attention.

"Lieutenant Hull, ma'am. I brought Mr. MacIntyre home with the ague, and thought to make him some tea." He should have sought out Granny MacIntyre first thing. Jim Mac had said his mother was at home.

"James!" cried an out-of-breath voice. "Oh, Lieutenant, your father told me you'd brought James home with the ague." Eliza MacIntyre's chest heaved and her face flushed. She must have run the whole quarter mile from town.

"He's in the bedroom." Matt pointed to the front of the house. "I meant to make him some tea, but—"

"I'll take care of it," Granny said. "You go to him, Eliza." She placed the basket of eggs in the middle of a round table, reached a box down from a high shelf and removed a packet of silver paper. Mrs. MacIntyre disappeared without a word, her hurried footsteps echoing in the silent house.

"Shave a bit of ash bark," Granny said, as if recalling some long-past direction, "steep in boiling water for as long as it takes to say the Twenty-seventh Psalm. 'The Lord is my light and my salvation, whom shall I fear?'" Matt stepped toward the door, thinking she had forgotten his presence, but she said, "You'll find a sieve hanging in the pantry." Matt obeyed her pointing finger, through a curtained door, into a small room with cool stone walls.

"Who are you?" she asked when he returned.

"Matthew Hull."

"Emma Callom's oldest boy?"

"Yes."

"Where you been all these years?"

"In Mexico, with the army."

"Many's the day your mama thought you dead. Came here crying to me that you were dead. Why didn't you send word?"

"Ma nor Pa, nor any of my brothers and sisters can read."

"Can you?"

"Yes."

A flicker of respect widened the pale eyes. "She might have carried the letter here, and my son would have read it to her."

Matt nodded, feeling more abashed by Granny MacIntyre's reprimand than his mother's whining complaints of last evening.

"I hadn't expected that Ma and Pa would notice I was gone, except that it made life easier. Ma was always readier with a cuff than a kiss."

"Mothers hunger for news of their children, even the troublesome ones."

"And I was a troublesome child?"

"Indeed you were! Troublesome to the whole countryside, always turning up where least needed. I hope you're better behaved now, if you intend to stay about."

"Better behaved," he said, to reassure her and convince himself. "I'll read law with Mr. Ridley, and try very hard to be an upright citizen. You tell me if I step out of line."

Granny smiled, but her bright blue eyes warned him he had met his master, one who would see through both jests and lies. "Has that New Englander arrived, the one who's to marry my granddaughter, Tildy?"

"He arrived. Quite early."

"And?"

"A fat Yankee, with indoor-colored skin, who harps on Indiana's debt and tax rates."

"So you've already formed a bad opinion of him. But

you're the troublesome one. Other men, what do they say?''

"I carried Mr. MacIntyre home because he wouldn't ask his brother. He said he'd ask no favor of a brother who expects Tildy to marry a monster."

Granny busied herself straining the tea, so he could see no change of expression on her furrowed cheeks.

"His chills are easing," Mrs. MacIntyre said from the doorway. "He'll soon be in the sweats. He said you carried him into the house, tender as a nursemaid. Thank you, Matt…uh…Lieutenant."

"Soldiers nurse one another," he said to explain, to ease her awkwardness at how to address him.

"He asks to speak to you, Lieutenant." Matt followed Mrs. MacIntyre through the sitting room, noticing on this second, less hurried trip the plainness of the furnishings, except for a mirror with a heavily carved frame.

Jim Mac waved his fingers weakly over the pile of comforters. "That fur trapper, Sampson, he says there's no ague in California. He says once a man with the shakes turned up in California, and people gathered around to watch, because they'd never seen ague before, and he made a fortune charging admission."

"Godfroy and Mr. Sampson tell tall tales to seduce people into traveling with them. For money," Mrs. MacIntyre said.

"Is Sampson telling the truth?" Jim Mac asked, his eyes on Matt.

"I can't say. I wasn't in California. I was in Mexico with General Taylor."

Jim Mac sighed, disappointed. "I hoped you'd been to California. You might tell me the truth."

Mrs. MacIntyre waved her hand and mouthed, "Go." She followed Matt into the sitting room, stopped him right in front of the mirror. He concentrated to keep his eyes on her, not the reflection of the tall officer. He had not seen a mirror since the day the tailor fitted the uniform.

"Mother MacIntyre and I can care for him, so you return to the party, before the food disappears and the dancing commences. I have another favor to ask of you, Lieutenant."

"Anything." His father was right. When crows fight, the weasels may grab a morsel. As a boy he had come often with his mother, bringing herbs to Granny, and been left standing on the back stoop while she fetched the small coins to pay. He had never before been past Jim Mac's door.

"Please, see Meggie home. I left her at the dance alone. Her brother—you remember Peter?—he's busy with some sudden job, and the dancing will go on past moonrise. Make sure she's safe home."

"My pleasure, Mrs. MacIntyre." He bowed deeply, and was pleased to see, from the corner of his eye, that the officer in the mirror had a military bearing.

See Pikeston's tomboy home? The other young men would probably tease him, but Meggie *was* a MacIntyre, no matter that she went barefoot in town. Did she still gallop about on her pony with her skirts up? Not a bad day, he thought, as he urged the horse back to town. Not bad for the son of Hector Hull and Emma Callom, who had never bothered to marry. Not bad for the boy Ira MacIntyre had thrashed at any opportunity.

He had approached Ridley with some trepidation, carrying the old fear of the tramp child, whom Ridley had more than once ordered off his property. Was it the uniform, or the learning he had gained in four years? The mannerly behavior and the cultivated speech Major Linder had demanded? Whatever, the attorney welcomed the opportunity to take on a clerk.

And the bad luck he had suffered on the steamboat—the panic that made it difficult for him to bear constricted crowds—that misfortune had borne good fruit, and he was now the benefactor of James MacIntyre. One side of the MacIntyre family owed him a favor. And Eliza MacIntyre entrusted her daughter to him. Not bad for a boy born and reared in the squatters' swamps along the White River, a boy who had depended on a French and Indian trapper to be father to him, a boy who had never sat in the school-house where the dancers would soon square off.

He had never expected to come back to Indiana. The army offered a good life. Until the day he gained the right to wear the gold epaulets of an officer. On that day he decided to return, to show Pikeston what a child of the river might accomplish if given half a chance.

"Where's your pack?" Godfroy asked.

"On Ridley's back stoop."

"Get your gear and come down to the river. Sampson's hanging about here, to polish off the pies and then sashay with the ladies."

"I thought to do a bit of sashaying myself."

"The evening's young. You'll have a better chance when the mamas doze off."

"Mrs. Jim Mac asked me to see Meggie home, since she's taking care of her husband and can't be here her-self."

"Plenty of time for both dancing and sparking," God-froy said.

Godfroy made a small fire to chase away the bugs. It cast moving shadows of tulip poplars on the buffalo hides of his tepee. "So, where did the army send you?"

"To Mexico, with General Taylor."

"The war's over. Where next?"

"I'm not staying in the army. Mr. Ridley's willing for me to become his clerk, and read law with him."

Godfroy's head came up. "Read?"

"I worked my way to Louisiana on a steamboat. I met an army captain, he convinced me I should join up, and he said I'd be sure of promotion if I learned to read and write. He taught me. It's easier than I thought. The letters stand for the sounds we say when we talk, although mostly the way Yankees say them, because that's where the men live who write most of the books.''

"You talk different than you did before. Sort of like the Yankees who trade on the river. This captain, he came from New England?"

"Pennsylvania. Anyway, when we got to the fort on the Sabine River, the Army promoted him major, and he made me his aide, a fancy name for servant, and I learned to work the guns. Flying artillery, they call it, because we moved so fast the Mexicans never knew where we'd turn up, and they had no light guns to oppose us.''

"So you had a good war?''

"Except a damned Mexican sharpshooter killed Major Linder. But by that time I could do any job around a gun, and when Lieutenant Burton died of fever, the colonel put me in charge.''

"Why don't you stay in? The army will be sent to the new lands we're taking from Mexico.''

"Because there's no future for an officer who hasn't gone to the army school in New York. I'd live and die a lieutenant. And after four years I wanted to see the White River again. The trees down south don't turn like fire in October. They just turn brown and the leaves fall off. The winter there is nothing but cold wind and rain. About Christmastime, I'd feel to see a snowflake was worth two years of my life. And…I thought it would be fun to show these Pikeston bumpkins that a man may be a Hull, but he's not born to be kicked and pissed on.''

"So you'll be a lawyer?''

"That's my plan. Maybe someday I'll win election to the state legislature, like Mr. Ridley.''

"Ridley didn't do such a fine job at the capital, I understand. You planning to marry that gal who lives with the Ridleys? Rachel?''

"Mrs. Ridley won't have me in the house. But in two or three years, I'll have my pick of the females of Pikeston.

I might even marry a MacIntyre.'' He followed the words with a short, deprecating laugh, to disarm the brag.

Godfroy coughed. ''I don't see Meggie MacIntyre making a very fine wife for a lawyer.''

''Who said Meggie?'' Matt squared his shoulders, surprised at the sudden revelation. Tildy. The MacIntyre princess. Raised in a brick house, with maids to sweep the floors, a piano and a dearborn coach. Wouldn't Ira MacIntyre kick and burn if Matt Hull took his daughter?

''Watch your step,'' Godfroy warned. ''Ira MacIntyre'll kill the man who touches Tildy. He's selling her to Moffett's nephew for a stake in that enterprise. As I understand, Walton's the only boy born in that family, so he inherits from his father *and* his uncle. Keep your seductions to girls from the river.''

Seduce? No, marriage. So MacIntyre had no choice but to accept him; Sunday dinner around his shining table...on the front bench with the family at church. MacIntyre, behind his counter, saying to visitors, ''Have you met my son-in-law, Matthew Hull?''

Marriage, with the groom so polite and proper beforehand, MacIntyre had no choice but to bring the preacher and guests into his own house. Wearing out his parlor carpet, pacing in despair that he could not prevent his daughter going to a Hull. Shredding his vest pockets with his nervous fingers.

''Why are you boosting California?'' Matt asked, his mind still busy considering how he could get even for all the beatings Ira MacIntyre had given him by mating up with Tildy.

''The beavers are gone.''

''They've been gone for years.''

''Everyone hoped they'd come back. But a winter in the Rockies don't buy a man's groceries. We're better off here, trapping muskrats and mink on the White River. But California! Out there they don't count farms in acres and quarter sections. They talk about miles and Spanish leagues.

And the Californios don't lift their noses and sneer that I'm the grandson of François Godfroy of the Miamis, nor do they call me a half-breed. It's no lie, winter never touches that land. A bit of rain, the hills green up, and spring in February.''

Matt remembered his anxious desire to see snow, and decided eternal spring offered little encouragement to start on a rugged, three-thousand-mile journey.

"But getting to California! I read the newspapers this summer, how people died in the snow on the mountains, eating each other to keep from starving.''

"Fools!'' Godfroy exclaimed. "That's why emigrants should join with me and Sampson. We've made the trip both ways. We know the path and the water holes, and won't go wandering off into salt plains and dry *journadas* of a hundred miles that kill all the stock.''

"Found anyone in Pikeston interested in the trip?''

"A few headstrong boys, who'd be of no use except to herd cattle. We need men with families, men who have the ready cash to buy proper gear.'' He leaned back, at his ease. "But we got in only this morning. Jim Mac might consider California after another attack of ague,'' he added lightly.

Matt nodded. "He spoke to me of that. No ague in California. Is it true?''

"True as the stars.''

"What's the trip like?''

"Hard, but we don't speak so plain. We say men, women and children, with good wagons and animals, and a proper guide, can make it through to California without suffering.''

"Too much,'' Matt said, laughing.

"You should consider. Read law with Ridley this winter, then set out west to hang your shingle. No one in California cares that your pa's as honest as a fox, and your ma made food for her youngsters by cuddling half the men in the county. Here, in Pikeston, you'll fight and push, and never be let into Ira MacIntyre's front hall. In California, you'd have the best front hall in town.''

"What town?"

"Monterey, the capital, right on the Pacific. Or San Jose. Yerba Buena, on the big bay. Now there's a town with promise, sitting on a harbor as big as some oceans.''

Matt stood, stretched and thought of Tildy at the dance. If he got in her set, he would have her on his arm occasionally, and grasp her little, soft hands in passing. "I'd best get back to the schoolhouse, so I can see Meggie home.''

"Talk up California to Jim Mac. And that son of his, Pete. He's set himself up making wagons and carriages. He'd make a fortune in California. And when you have the chance, tell Rachel—''

"I'll not have the chance. Mrs. Ridley won't let me in the house.''

"Young men of parts make their own chance. Rachel'd be a fine lady in California. The Ridleys can't say much against her going, because she'll be eighteen in March, and by rights, she's not their child.''

"Mrs. Ridley's her aunt, and her mother's dead, so who else would have a say?''

"Her father.''

"Her father's disappeared, or dead.''

"No, he isn't.''

Matt sank back down on his heels, sensing a new story, one that might be important to his future. He waited for Trail to fill his pipe.

"Caroline Williams,'' Godfroy began, "who's Mrs. Ridley now, had a fine little sister, Belle, who behaved a lot like Meggie MacIntyre does, running with animals, collecting plants in the woods. She married a man by the name of Barman, who bred and traded horses. They lived on a farm down by the river bluff. She didn't particularly want the marriage, but a girl of that type doesn't have many choices.''

Godfroy took a small branch from the fire and lit his pipe. Matt had heard all this before, but remained quiet, sure Godfroy would add some new permutation to the story.

"Many's the time Barman took horses down to the Ohio, leaving Belle alone. The second summer after they married, I met her in the woods and we lay together, those times when her husband had gone," Godfroy said, embarrassed, but also slightly boastful.

This new twist so startled Matt that he fell off his heels and dirtied his hand catching himself. A respectable, married woman giving herself to a French-Indian trapper?

"Lest you think too hard of me, Matt, the first time I took her, she was a maiden. Barman had never lain with her as a husband."

"After being married a year?" he asked, incredulous.

"Nearer to two. She said he couldn't do it. Anyway, Barman came home for a few days, and told her of a big horse fair down about Madison, and he set off with the best mares and geldings, and the breed stallion."

Matt knew the rest of the story, the haunting jest of his childhood applied to any impossibility: "That'll happen when Barman comes home."

"Belle had a child on the way, and we decided to tell Barman the truth when he came home. I got things together for us to light out for the Rockies. But weeks passed, and Barman didn't come. The leaves turned, and he didn't come. The man who held the mortgage on the farm demanded his money, but Belle had nothing, no horses to sell. I had no place for her, just a shack here on the river. We decided she'd go to her sister, and pretend the baby belonged to Barman, and we'd head west the next summer."

"But she died," Matt whispered.

"Yes, of a cough, just a month or two after Rachel came."

"You never said anything to the Ridleys?"

"A baby gal I thought best with Caroline, who'd raise her like a white child. I thought I'd forget Belle and get another woman, and have a family. But it's never happened, and Rachel's my only child, and she'll come with me to California. Because of Rachel, I never stayed year-round in the Rockies, nor hired out to a big fur company. Every spring, I must see how she'd grown... how beautiful she'd become. Coming home from California I swore a vow—this winter I'll break it to her that I'm her father, and she'll go west with me."

Matt grinned, imagining how Pikeston would vibrate with gossip when it learned the Ridleys had cared for the daughter of a half-breed for nearly eighteen years! Matt supposed Godfroy wanted to talk more about Rachel, but he needed information, and now was the time to get it. He cleared his throat.

"When Barman left to take his horses to Madison, did any other man from Pikeston go south? Did any other farmer have horses to sell?"

Godfroy puffed on his pipe. "Not that I can think of, for at that time, in this country, only Barman was breeding in a big way. And the townsfolk quizzed any man who had been away, you know, for Barman left some debts behind. I remember that summer Ira MacIntyre traveled to the Wabash River to meet a boat stuck by low water, and Belle inquired of him, had he seen her husband, but he'd heard naught of Barman."

Matt controlled his face, but let his heart grin broadly. He ground the fist of his right hand into the palm of his left, a silent, unnoticeable signal of triumph. Godfrey's account verified everything he suspected about Ira MacIntyre.

# Chapter Three

"I will *not!*" Tildy cried, glaring at her father, hoping he saw all the fire in her soul. "You can't make me! I'll run off!" She sensed movement at the open front door, slid her eyes in that direction without turning her head, for fear her father might suppose that her determination faltered. Meggie leaned on the doorframe, tapping her foot impatiently.

"You'll be rich. You'll have piles of silk dresses, and diamonds in your ears, and shoes with high heels," Josh said. Her brother slouched against the wall, his shoulder rubbing on the new flowered paper, and Mama did not reprimand him. Tildy thrust her banjo into Meggie's hands, because she was tempted to smash it in her brother's face.

"You're not thinking of me," she cried. "You're thinking of a store in Albany or Yorktown."

"Why not?" Josh asked with a shrug that caught a seam in the wallpaper and started a small rip. Still her mother did not order him away from the wall. Boys got such extreme privileges! "You have to marry someone, so why not Walton?"

"Because he's…he's not a nice man," she said, putting her hands on her hips to show her determination. "Faith nearly cried because he said her autumn leaf quilt showed how poor the Toles must be, that she couldn't buy new goods. Did you see him eat at the Harvest Home? Like a hog! He has no table manners at all. And he didn't leave at four in the afternoon because Mr. Moffett expects him in Muncie before dark. He left because he didn't dare be around when the dancing started."

"Walton can't 'bow to your lady and promenade,'" Meggie said, "because he can't bend in the middle—"

"*Mr.* Walton, Margaret," her mother said. "Let us maintain the use of proper address."

"And Walton's partner would leave him behind," Meggie continued, intentionally contrary, Tildy knew. "Do-si-do with him, the lady would find the trip around so long, everyone else'd be doing 'grand right and left' by the time she finished."

Tildy smiled her thanks at Meggie, took off her bonnet and flung it over the knob that topped the finial post. "Now, I'm off to the dancing, and I never want to hear Afton Walton's—"

"I'm not ordering you to marry him, Matilda," her father said, stepping between her and the door. "But I ask you to consider. And think of the advantages."

"What advantages?" she inquired sweetly. "Besides to you and the boys?"

"Well, one thing," Meggie said, "he'd kill you straight off, crush you to death on your wedding night climbing on top of you, so you don't have to bear with a husband or children."

"Margaret!" Tildy's mother cried. "I don't know what your mother and father allow to be said in mixed company, but in my house, you'll watch your tongue!" Tildy saw the bright warning flush on her mother's cheeks, frowned and shook her head at Meggie. No sense angering Mama. She might ban Meggie from the house, and Tildy was counting on her support.

"I'm sorry, Aunt Ravania," Meggie said, catching Tildy's hint. "Can we get back to the schoolhouse now?"

She smiled her engaging smile, her head bent meekly so her chin nearly touched her collarbone.

Tildy's father stepped away from the door, but his hands fluttered at his chest. "Go ahead," he said, and Tildy spun to stare at him, startled by the roughness of his voice. "You've always been a good girl, Tildy, not head-strong—" his eyes shifted to Meggie "—willing to be led in the right way. You've never before objected—"

"So it's time I did stand up for myself," she said. She ran past Meggie, onto the porch, between the two columns supporting the veranda roof, and down the steps.

"I'll be down shortly," her mother called after her, "to take my turn as chaperon."

Tildy held her tongue until she and Meggie rounded the corner into the square. "Meggie, stop a minute. We've got to talk before we get to the schoolhouse."

"I'll help you run off, Tildy. You come to my house."

"You only live a quarter mile out of town!" Tildy said. "I'm thinking of more significant running off than that!"

"Pa and Uncle Ira had words about Walton before Pa went home with the ague," Meggie said. "Pa will help you. And I spoke to Pete about doing away with Walton, and he said there *are* tricks to be done to a gig—"

"No!" Tildy said, drawing away, frightened by the ease with which Meggie's skillful brother could arrange an accident. "Killing's infernally wicked. Tell your father I may need his help." She lowered her voice. "I'll need money, because if Papa won't listen to reason, I'm going away. I'll find a gentleman to escort me—"

"A man!" Meggie cried, excited, bouncing up and down and clapping her hands. "Which man?"

"You'll see, but don't tell a soul what I'm up to."

"That mountain man, Sampson?" Meggie asked fearfully.

"You'll see."

"But Tildy! I mean to flirt with Mr. Sampson, so he'll

take me with him come spring, when he leaves for California.''

''Meggie! You can't mean it!''

''Of course I mean it. Do you think I'll stay in Indiana my whole life, and never see mountains, or buffalo, or the Pacific Ocean? Captain Frémont says the mountains of California are loftier than the Rockies, and the deserts of the West rival those of Asia.''

''I can't think that deserts rival each other. They're perfectly useless.''

'''In our eight months' circuit, we were never out of sight of snow,' Captain Frémont says. Imagine. Mountains so high, snow stays through the summer!'' Her eyes sparkled, reflecting the last glow in the western sky.

Tildy doubted that summer snow, like deserts, had any earthly use, but did not say so out loud. She contemplated her frightening situation, and wished she had a more practical cousin. Casual inquiries through the afternoon had failed to turn up a single citizen of Pikeston who planned a journey to Indianapolis. No one had business with the governor or the legislature, or a case before the supreme court. That left only one man who would, as a matter of course, be leaving. Lieutenant Hull, going back to his regiment.

Filthy, stupid, baseborn Matt Hull.

Tildy hesitated just inside the door of the schoolhouse. Men and women, boys and girls, but no blue uniform. The room stilled as people turned to stare at her, friends sympathetically, others simply curious. Goose bumps sprang out on her arms. Some of the young men grinned at her with wicked delight, men whose courtship she had rejected. She lifted her banjo against her chest.

''Have you been waiting for me?'' she cried, her gaiety ringing false in her own ears. She would not let them see how much she hurt. But where was Lieutenant Hull? Tom Riding lifted his fiddle and bow. She joined him and busied herself in tuning the banjo.

"Not dancing?" asked Tom.

"Not at first. I'm too full of pumpkin pie and apple cake."

He drew his bow across the strings to announce the first dance, and from the aimless gatherings squares emerged as if by magic. All the girls had a special fellow, except for her.

Balance one and balance eight, Swing 'em on the corner like you swing 'em on the gate.

Rachel danced with Cousin Pete. Meggie and Mr. Sampson promenaded behind them. They separated to their corners, and as Pete passed he winked at her.

Esther Hull—her dress far too large—spun on the arm of a gangly farm boy. Where was Esther's brother? In the morning Lieutenant Hull had accompanied Mr. Ridley, but now Mr. and Mrs. Ridley sat against the opposite wall, alone. What if the lieutenant didn't come dancing at all? She *must* find out when he would be leaving. And within the next few minutes, before Mama came, for if her mother saw her in his company, she'd never hear the end of it!

Cage the bird, three hands round; birdie hop out, and crow hop in.

"Stop the caterwauling!" came a yell from the door. "There's a hurt man out here." Tom's bow skidded to a jarring cord, and stopped. "Found this fellow four, five miles out of town, on my way from picking the missus up at her sister's in Muncie." The men headed for the door. Pete, who had been swinging Rachel only a few feet away, stepped to Tildy's side.

"Maybe your troubles are all solved, Tildy."

She dropped her banjo and dashed after him. Pete's killed Mr. Walton! The marks would be on the gig. She elbowed two men aside, and threw herself against Pete's back.

"What have you done?" she whispered. Pete did not answer, but by clinging to him, she managed to get down the steps, into the street.

"Bring a lantern," said a very practical voice, and Tildy saw her mother standing by the side of a flatbed wagon. A great black hump occupied the center, and a woman clasping a baby sat with her skirts hanging over the end.

"He has a big lump on his head," the woman said, "and a cut on his forehead." A raised lantern revealed Mr. Walton's sagging face, distorted and bloody. Dead?

"He's still alive," the woman continued, "but not got his senses. Someone lift him off the wagon so we can get home, for my baby's like to take the croup in this night air."

"To our house," Tildy's mother said without hesitation. Tildy stepped forward, holding up her hands in protest. But the owner of the wagon was already tugging at the horse's bridle, and he led the procession around the corner. Tildy trailed behind, her head spinning, her heart thumping with fear. She stopped to watch a tall man and three boys lift rails from a nearby fence.

"Who's got strong rope?" Lieutenant Hull's voice commanded in the dark. Tildy slid into the shadows. Now was her chance, while everyone else followed the wagon. He wove a length of rope about the two poles, knotting every loop. He worked skillfully and quickly, bending over, squatting. Not awkward, as tall men so often were. *Graceful, as tall as I expected Mr. Walton to be.*

They rolled Mr. Walton onto the litter, and ten men, five to a side, trotted toward the house. The rest of the crowd muttered among themselves, then turned back to the school. All except the tall shadow, which remained in the street as the wagon rolled away. He faced her, and even in the dark she knew his eyes saw all of her.

"Miss MacIntyre," he said, the words not her name, but a tense invitation. She should run into the house. The prickling started on her collarbone. She had to ask him. Now, more than ever, she needed his help.

"Yes."

"Mr. Walton is your betrothed?" He spoke in a way

she had never heard before. The drawl of Indiana, overlain with precision, an almost ceremonial diction.

"No, he is not my betrothed," she answered with equal formality.

"I was told that your father arranged a marriage between you and Mr. Walton. Perhaps I heard wrong."

"What my father decides and what I'll do are two different things."

"Do you wish to go to Mr. Walton's side?"

"No. Sally, the maid, she's accustomed to tending injuries. I'd but be in the way."

"Your aunt, Mrs. James MacIntyre, asked me to see Meggie home. Would you care to accompany us?"

"I think Meggie would rather walk out with Mr. Sampson."

"Her mother asked me, and honor binds me to keep my word." He held out a hand. "We might search for Miss MacIntyre and Mr. Sampson at the schoolhouse."

"I—"

"Matilda!" Mama stood in the doorway, peering into the dark. "Are you there? Come and help me."

Tildy happily remembered her banjo. "I left my banjo at the schoolhouse."

"Fetch it, and come directly home. What in the world possesses you to stand in the night air? Worse, all alone. It's not proper. Mr. Walton will need watchers by his bed all night."

"Yes, mother." So the fall hadn't killed him, and disappointment claimed her. An evil feeling, letting the devil into her heart. Nevertheless, she wished Mr. Walton was dead.

"May I escort you?" Lieutenant Hull asked, stepping to her side. She laid her hand upon the sleeve of his jacket. Starlight reflected flatly from the double row of buttons down the front of his uniform, and their lines drew her eyes downward, suggestively.

"So nothing's settled between you and Mr. Walton?" he asked.

"No…yes. I'll not marry him, if that's what you mean to ask."

"No wedding?" A wry pleasure in his voice?

"Absolutely not. Mr. Walton has nothing to recommend him but money."

"How pleasant to meet a young woman whose heart is magnetized by love, not wealth."

Magnetized by love? Hardly. Fear. Fear would drive her to rely on Lieutenant Hull, if no one else could help her out of this scrape.

"There you are!" Meggie called. She stood beside Mr. Sampson in front of the schoolhouse, holding the banjo. "You left this behind." Tildy jerked her hand off Lieutenant Hull's arm and stepped away from him, lest anyone in the schoolhouse notice.

"Your mother asked me to see you home," Lieutenant Hull said, bowing to Meggie. The army, Tildy thought grudgingly, had taught him a rough sort of manners.

"But I don't want to go home yet! The dancing's beginning again," Meggie said. "All the beaus have come back and the fiddler's waiting for Tildy. Although I suppose, with Walton hurt, it's not proper for Tildy to appear. Carry this to Tildy's house," she said, thrusting the banjo at Lieutenant Hull, who managed to grab it as it headed for the ground. Meggie skipped up the stairs, followed by Sampson.

"No!" Tildy cried, grabbing at Lieutenant Hull's sleeve. What would Mama or Papa do if he turned up on their doorstep? She stood on tiptoe to reach his ear. "I wish to speak to you," she whispered, "but not here. Out of sight."

Lieutenant Hull seemed not to pay attention. He strummed the banjo, twisted the pegs. What was he doing?

"Stop that! You'll spoil the tune! You don't know anything about banjos!" But he fingered the cords expertly, and after an introductory melody began singing, "Down along the Rio Grande—"

"Quiet!" she snapped, frightened that he called attention to them standing together. "We must go where we can talk alone."

He grasped the banjo by the neck, took her hand and pulled her out of the lamplight that spilled from the open door of the schoolhouse. Down a narrow passage between the school and the livery barn, a faint illumination from light seeping through the cracks in the clapboard walls. He stopped behind the stables. A glow on the eastern horizon showed where the moon would rise in just a few minutes. He leaned the banjo against the wall.

"Yes, Miss MacIntyre?"

"I'm in dreadful trouble."

"Mr. Walton?"

"Yes. Everything gets worse and worse. Now Mama will expect me to tend him. And I know who did this to Mr. Walton, and what if he should die?"

"Did this? But Mr. Walton had an accident, no surprise, truly, for the gig he drove was too light a vehicle to carry his weight."

Tildy put her hand over her mouth, wishing she could unspeak her thoughtless words. Naturally everyone would conclude that Mr. Walton had had an accident. She had nearly betrayed Pete to this man!

"Lieutenant Hull, I can't bear to even *think* of marrying Mr. Walton. When do you leave?"

"Leave?"

"To go back to the army?"

"I'm no longer in the army, Miss MacIntyre. Tomorrow I enter Mr. Ridley's office as a clerk, to read law."

"No!" She beat her fists against her forehead, protesting everything that had happened since sunrise, since the gray horse pulled the gig into the square. Why couldn't this man be leaving town? The pent-up tears rolled down her cheeks in a sudden gush. She must leave right now, before she ruined her reputation being seen alone with Matt Hull. She stepped blindly into the dark, into a sharp depression, staggered, and as she fell, wondered, *How do I explain the filth on my dress to Mama?*

But his arm grasped her waist, caught her, and there was no filth to explain away. He pulled her closer than she had ever stood to a man not her kin. Her eyes came to his shoulder, and his height and strength took her breath away, almost as frightening as Mr. Walton's bulk.

"Say, 'Matthew Hull,'" he ordered. Was this some sort of new game? Tildy wondered. She whispered his name, and his mouth found hers wide open. She had kissed a boy before, a smacking kiss during a play-party, half in fun. But nothing remotely like this wet, energetic combining. His tongue stroked her upper lip, and the texture of otter skin wrapped about her, a velvet blackness.

This could not be proper! She pushed with her tongue to fight him off, points of silver light exploded, and instead of breaking away, she clutched his arms to remain on her feet. Lightning, in the midst of a clear, still night. He drew away slowly, first his lips, then his tight embrace, but the velvet dark remained.

"Say, 'Mrs. Matthew Hull,'" he whispered, his mouth so close to her cheek that she closed her eyes against his hot, damp breath.

"What?" *Fly! Escape his dangerous heat.*

"Will you marry me, Miss MacIntyre?" The dark fantasy fell away with this nonsensical question.

"Of course not! What a ridiculous idea! You're not an appropriate suitor." She imagined Matt Hull standing before her father, asking for her hand. The boy Papa had once chased away from their chicken coop with his blackthorn cane. How the whole family had laughed when Matt screeched and sprawled in the dust! She tilted her head to see the wary eyes of the boy, but instead saw the determination of the man. "What I need," she said softly, "is an escort to Indianapolis, to escape Mr. Walton."

"Escort? Indianapolis?" He laughed. "Escape? Indianapolis is less than fifty miles away. Besides, you don't solve problems by running away from them. We'll get rid of Mr. Walton, and then we'll be married in your front parlor."

His strange accent gave the words very hard centers. Each shaped of stone, never to be withdrawn. She drew back and he let her go, except for keeping her right hand in his. The calluses across the top of his palm were hard, like his words.

"I intend, within one year, to open my own law office," he said, speaking very quietly. "For the next few months, resist your father's orders. Don't marry Walton. Let your father imprison you, beat you, set you to doing the scrub-woman's work, but say no. Next year we'll be married."

"We will not!" she said. She recalled the wicked pleasure in the eyes of her rejected suitors. How much greater their ridicule if she settled for Matt Hull? "I'll find someone else to run away with," she said with exaggerated calm. "Mr. Godfroy, or Mr. Sampson."

He laughed, drawing her once more into an embrace. The vibrations from his chest flowed into hers, and she hated the sense of being connected to him. "Godfroy and Sampson have no use for women with parlor manners, piano playing and fine dresses, Miss MacIntyre. Their women work like squaws, butchering deer, tanning hides, cooking over an open fire, repairing the tent, packing the horses. And at night they satisfy the lusts of their men on the ground, beneath a buffalo robe." Tildy wondered if she might faint, hearing a man use such dreadfully improper words.

"There's no room on a packhorse for banjos or straw bonnets. And no marriage certificate. May I walk you home, Miss MacIntyre?"

She had not fainted, so she decided to be very stern with him. "I don't want to go home. I want you to take me to

Indianapolis, where I'll find a room in a respectable board-inghouse until Papa comes to his senses."

"No, Miss MacIntyre. Taking you away would destroy *my* future. A law office, and a respectable marriage."

"We can't be married. Why should you even think it?"

"We fit together rather well, don't we?" He gave her a sudden squeeze. "And as a young lawyer, I should take a wife who's accustomed to fine society. Who better than you, raised in the luxuries of the brick house of Ira MacIntyre?"

"Fine society?" she echoed, astonished. "You want me to be your wife, so everyone in town will say 'Good morning, Mr. Hull,' and think you're someone to be reckoned with? You're no different than Mr. Walton. He doesn't want me! He wants Papa's store! He doesn't love me, and neither do you!"

"And do you respect me, asking me to sacrifice my future? If we ride to Indianapolis together, both our reputations end black as soot. There's an easier way to get rid of Mr. Walton. Simply say you won't marry him." His arms opened and the sudden freedom chilled her. "I believe we're two of a kind," he whispered, so to hear him she had to remain close. "Both determined to have our own way, both selfish. Our marriage will be interesting."

"Don't think you'll ever see me standing by your side," she snapped, but she longed to feel his arms again. When he made no move to restrain her, she slid her feet along the ground carefully, so she did not fall into the hole a second time.

"You forgot your banjo."

His hand found her in the dark and she felt the cold imprint of the strings on the back of her hand.

"You know how to play," she said. "How?"

"In the army everyone carried a rifle, but half the men toted a banjo or fiddle as well." Her knees weakened. She reached out to the wall for support. He was a soldier. She had kissed him! And his tongue...that must extend far beyond the bounds of good taste! Soldiers had notorious morals. He would gossip, in the tavern, in the law office.

"Tomorrow night, meet me here before moonrise, and we'll consider ways to send Mr. Walton scurrying back where he came from. If he's still alive come morning."

She had put her reputation in the hands of soldier who would spread the story of her kiss. A sliver of light above the schoolhouse reflected off the banjo he held out to her.

"If I...promise what you want—" she hated that her voice quavered "—you'll not speak of us meeting...."

"I'll say not one word about a marvelous kiss."

She hated him, hated his blackmail with a fury new to her. "And you'll help me get free of Mr. Walton?"

"Yes. That is a solemn vow. You can't marry me if Walton takes you to wife."

She grabbed the banjo. "I'll be here tomorrow evening." She ran to the door of the schoolhouse, but at the very foot of the stair changed her mind about returning to the dance.

Had his kiss left a mark on her lips? She made her way home through the back lots and cooled her hot face at the kitchen washstand. She scrubbed her numb lips twice before she presented herself to her mother.

# Chapter Four

Matt heaved his pack onto his shoulders and made his way into Pikeston by the red light of dawn reflected on a band of clouds. He would be waiting at the office when Ridley arrived.

He leaned his pack against the wall of the law office facing the alley, near a crude bench that served as a washstand. He had washed and shaved on the riverbank, put on the best of his civilian clothes. Nothing to compare with his uniform. Actually, the cheapest things he could buy in St. Louis. Trousers of jean cloth, coat and vest of linsey-woolsey. The coat and vest covered most of his shirt, of the cheapest unbleached cotton. He had been afraid to spend money on clothes, not knowing if Ridley would demand a fee to teach him, or if he might be charged room and board.

"Put your gear upstairs, right off," Mr. Ridley said when he arrived, eyeing the pack. Matt looked around for a stairway, then realized the horizontal boards nailed to the exterior of the building were foot- and handholds. They led to a squat door tucked under the peak of the roof.

"There's a couple of trunks stored up there, old papers of mine, but it's a sizable space, and they shouldn't be in your way." Matt gritted his teeth to steady his resolve, shouldered his pack and climbed the makeshift ladder.

He could stand upright only in the center of the windowless attic. Peeled poles lay side by side on the rafters, making a floor with the texture of a corduroy road. They had not been nailed down, and rolled slightly beneath his feet. At the far end of the narrow space, against the front wall, stood two battered trunks. Matt shoved his pack under the eaves. He gingerly stepped off the length of the attic. The slender poles bent beneath his weight. Dust covered everything, so thick it obscured the brass bindings of the trunks. By testing with his feet, Matt found the most stable part of the floor, and unrolled his blankets there.

Mrs. Ridley considered this hovel appropriate to his station. He thought of shouldering his pack and walking away from Pikeston immediately. Within a few days he would surely find a friendlier community.

He remembered the sweet taste of Tildy's mouth, and the sensation—shaken by a giant hand—when their tongues collided. Frost lay heavy upon the lower meadows this morning, and in the woodlots underbrush shone red and yellow. Late in the year to be on the road, with no destination in mind.

"Accept what's dealt out," he whispered to himself, "until the day comes when you're the dealer." The boy who had left Pikeston four years ago, that boy would have roared in anger, and laid out with his fists to avenge the insult of this attic. The memory settled him. He *had* been a troublesome child. Yesterday he had changed that image in a few minds, and every day of the coming winter would change a few more. The army years had beaten a new philosophy into him. Accept what you cannot change, but keep your head high. No matter what another man says or does, you do your best.

He must buy ticking for a mattress, to cushion the ridged floor. And find straw or corn shucks to fill it.... He remembered the corn leaning against the church door, ready for the taking. In fact, he would be praised for cleaning up the debris of the Harvest Home. Fine ladies like Tildy

MacIntyre might spread flowers about, but would be insulted if asked to clear them away. That was servants' work.

No lock on the door. Another expense. He drew the leather bag from the bottom of his pack, scattered the silver coins on his blankets, and counted them for the hundredth time. Ninety-four. When he began his trip home, there had been more than a hundred. Now, each penny must do the work of two, so the money lasted until spring, with enough left to meet the expenses of opening his own office.

The chill of the silver always surprised him. Money obtained by violence should burn the hands. The largest coin seemed to bulge before his eyes. *Carols IV*. The letters arched in heavy relief above a man's head.

The attic metamorphosed into the dusty road. The stench of the mortifying wound filled the air, the agonized face materialized in the floating dust motes, pleading for help and life.

"Forget it," he whispered to himself. "It was war. You had no choice. You were the only officer." His mouth dried. He tried to cover the coin that triggered the vision, but his hands trembled, as they had trembled when he checked the loads of his revolver. His legs cramped in agony, as they had cramped when he knelt in the road, praying for an easy answer. But no divinity had spoken then, and none did now. He could not risk the gun the captain had left in his charge. Could not load a dying man on the spent mules. Not with water still ten miles away. He could not order men with swollen tongues and closing throats to carry a litter.

Dust rose as the troop marched away, leaving him, the man in charge, to make the decision. His gorge rose, he heard the agonized plea for a quick death. He saw himself put his canteen to the polluted lips, say a final prayer...and pull the trigger.

Matt's fingers scrapped convulsively at the irregular

floor. He scrambled to his feet, stretched and grasped the rough ridge pole to draw himself out of the past.

"God forgive me," he whispered.

How could the memory stay so clear? He fought against the echo of the man's final words. "She is the death of me." He saw the clawed hand point to the knapsack. So clear he might have this moment holstered his revolver, snatched up the bag, and plunged after his troop.

That night he drank his fill, wallowed thankfully in the brackish water before he opened the knapsack to learn the man's identity. And discovered more money than he had ever seen in one place. In an instant everything became clear—the money, the knife wound, the final words. The man had stolen a family's wealth, raped a woman, probably killed her, but with her last strength, she had dealt a mortal stroke.

Matt knelt to put the coins away. He touched the engraving on the largest. Carlos. With no other name, the dead soldier had become, in his mind, Carlos.

"Carlos paid for his crime," Matt whispered, the sound of his own voice helping to break the spell. "It's only right that his executioner get something for his work." Death for one. A chance for a new life to the other.

*My greatest crime,* Matt rationalized, *would be to squander the opportunity.*

He scooped the coins into the leather bag, keeping out a small one, which he slid into his pocket. He studied the rafters close above his head, and with his knife carved out a space, just beneath the shingles, and stuffed in the bag.

"Satisfied?" asked Ridley, as Matt climbed down the ladder.

"Fine."

"Sweep out the office." Ridley pointed to a broom leaning near the back door. "I've arranged for you to take your meals with Tole, the blacksmith. After the cleaning's done, go there and Faith'll give you some breakfast."

Matt nodded, accepting the menial assignment as a test.

If he reared back and shouted he was no man's servant, he gave Ridley good reason to send him on his way. He swept the floor carefully, more thoroughly than it had been cleaned for several months, for he found two dead mice behind the bookcase, and a pile of peach pits under Ridley's desk.

Ridley saved money by sending him to eat at the Toles' instead of the tavern. Faith Tole, the daughter, hardly more than a child herself, was housekeeper for the motherless family. Matt contemplated a winter of badly cooked bacon and beans, gray biscuits tasting of salt and saleratus, sour butter and adulterated coffee.

He pounded the doormat on the front stoop to dislodge its load of dust and gravel. Godfroy and Sampson had once more taken a place near the flagstaff, and attracted a new audience with the otter skin and their California tales—men who had not come to church, but on Monday morning sought a dram of whiskey. Ridley stood on the outskirts of the small crowd.

"The mercury as it stood this morning—six degrees below freezing—has never been seen in California," said Sampson. Matt stepped behind Ridley.

"I'm done, sir."

"Go get your breakfast," Ridley said, without taking his glowering eyes off Sampson.

Matt stared at Faith Tole, startled out of courtesy by the demonstration of how many years he had been away. Not a child, but a woman, carrying a woman's burdens.

"You come for breakfast every morning after I've fed the boys," she said. "I doubt you'd want to be at the table with them."

"Thank you." Did they snatch at their food like wolves? More likely, Tole feared Matt Hull would corrupt his sons.

"Dinner, I'll carry to you at the office, at noon."

"I can come here. No need for you to bother."

She shook her head and bent over the hearth, where eggs simmered in a skillet balanced on three legs. Her stance and rigid face said the less time he spent in her house, the better. Eggs and biscuits, light and fluffy, coffee and fried potatoes.

"I'll have meat for tomorrow's breakfast," she said, "but Mr. Ridley only asked early this morning, and I had no bacon or ham in the house." She sighed, the sigh of a thousand women struggling to carry out the whims of the men who governed them. Faith cooked and cleaned for her father and four brothers. Now, at her father's orders and for the pittance Ridley paid, she fed another, a man she neither liked nor respected. Faith did not rebel against her father's orders, as Tildy did.

As the unknown Mexican girl had rebelled against Carlos. She must have attacked him as he lay satiated after the rape, for the knife had slashed the part that ravished her.

"She is the death of me." Matt blotted the complaint from his mind by thinking how good Faith's biscuits were and taking another.

He concentrated on spreading molasses. He liked Tildy, who rebelled, and the vengeful Mexican girl better than Faith. Which was just as well, since he would marry Tildy. And that thought recalled Walton.

"Have you heard anything of the condition of Mr. Walton?" he asked. "When I left last night, he was still alive."

"My father went early to the MacIntyres, and Sally told him Mr. Walton's senses returned in the middle of the night. He sat up and ate a great breakfast. As if he needed it," she added wryly. She smiled. Perhaps not so timid as he supposed.

"Since he didn't reach Muncie last night, he'd had no supper," Matt said, smiling back at her. Tole inquired after Walton's health, Matt thought cynically, just in case the metal fittings for a coffin were needed.

"You never know with a knock on the head," he said. "Some soldiers in Texas tried to drive a boar from the bushes by tossing rocks. They hit a man on the head. He walked around fine for the rest of the day, and keeled over dead that evening."

"So you suppose Mr. Walton will keel over this evening?" she asked, rather too eagerly.

"I said, you never know with bumps on the head. Do you hope Mr. Walton will keel over?" he asked, concealing his smile by holding his cup near his lips.

"No, but I do wish Mr. MacIntyre would send him packing, and not put Tildy through such misery."

Through an open door he could see part of the sitting room. Homemade settees and a rough table. Color flashed from a braided rug and a quilt draped over the back of a chair. The patchwork glowed in the tones of autumn. Faith Tole had pieced the magnificent quilt that drew everyone's eyes at the Harvest Home.

"Do you suppose Mr. Ridley could help Tildy?" Faith asked. "There might be some bad thing in Mr. Walton's past. Mr. Ridley could write a lawyer in Massachusetts, and inquire after Mr. Walton's reputation. Mr. MacIntyre wouldn't ask Tildy to marry a man without principles."

"I'm sure Mr. MacIntyre will ask for references," he said, forking up the last potatoes. Faith smiled, seizing the slender hope. "But Mr. Moffett certainly knows his nephew's history, and took that into account before inviting him to Indiana," he said, ruthlessly changing Faith's smile to a frown. "Miss MacIntyre must be comforted, her friends rallying around in a time of trouble."

"We hope it teaches Tildy a lesson," Faith said. "The past few weeks she's been difficult to abide—prideful, boasting that she'd marry a rich man from Muncie, richer than any husband Rachel and I might find, and she'd live in a great house. Out at the forge this morning the young men laughed, and called her 'Mrs. Yankee Lard.' They say she's getting what she deserves, because two of them courted her, and she laughed at them for their trouble. She said she'd never marry a farmer and work herself to death keeping chickens and pigs and digging in a garden.''

Matt occupied himself with a third golden biscuit. Tildy had rejected honest farmers. Prideful, like her father.

The pride made her more desirable, more suitable to be his wife. The first time he came to her, he would use the gentlest of caresses, until she returned them, the way she had joined in the kiss. Tildy had the strength of mind of the Mexican girl, and roughness might send her searching for a knife.

"I heard the men talking to Pa this morning." Faith's voice faltered in shame at this confession of eavesdropping. "They made crude jokes about...what it would be like for Tildy...having such a husband."

More than one man in Pikeston wondered how Walton managed sex around that protruding belly. Wherever men gathered today, the ribald conjectures would form the main topic of conversation. But not the thing to discuss with a woman, if a man wished to establish a good reputation.

"Will Miss MacIntyre make a good wife?" he asked.

"Oh, yes, for the right man. She's very skilled. Did you see the white quilt at the harvest feast? She made it last winter. She does the tiniest stitches, smaller than any of us. Of course she's accustomed to servants and riding behind fine horses, but she knows how to embroider with silk ribbon, and she plays the piano and the banjo, and the dress she wore Sunday—the tan one—she made the pleated flounce with the lace edge herself."

A wife worthy of Matt Hull's brick house, broad garden and strong teams. He let his mind play with a fancy of that marriage. A passionate wife. When their tongues met, every part of her convulsed. He would treat her with respect, furnish her every mark of position his income could provide, eventually win her respect. To his surprise, the plate was clean. No time now for fantasies. "Thank you."

"I'll bring your dinner." She stood near the table, eyes

down, hands fidgeting at her waist. "Why—" almost a whisper "—why has Mr. Ridley taken you on? Pa refused to believe it, until Mr. Ridley came this morning, asking us to board you, and the men at the forge speculated—"

"Mr. Ridley was once a poor boy himself," he said, repeating the words Ridley had used to justify his decision. "A lawyer in Kentucky gave him his chance."

"Oh."

Matt wended his way among the sheds and rail fences of the back lots to avoid the gathering in the square. Ridley would never reveal why he accepted Matt Hull as his clerk. In return, Matt Hull would banish the "incident" from his mind. He would never speak of finding Rachel, no more than three years old, wandering along the river, scratched by briars, crying pitifully. He had led her home, to be greeted by Mrs. Ridley's curses. She refused to open the door, even though he came submissively to the rear, and hung back, pushing Rachel ahead of him. Matt had finally taken the little girl to the law office, cringing, expecting a beating for intruding upon the business of respectable men.

One day in Louisiana, while he and the rest of the soldiers hooted at a staggering laundress, a sudden rush of recollection told him the truth: Mrs. Ridley had been drunk.

Matt leaned against the wall of the schoolhouse, listening to Pikeston settle down for the night. The shuffling of hogs at their trough, the rustle of chickens settling upon the roost, the slamming of doors, the dying squeal of a mouse that had failed to spot the cat lurking in the shadows. Distant voices. Men pulled canvas over wagons, commenting upon the bank of clouds that might hold the first rain of autumn.

Matt did not hear Tildy's footsteps in the dusty street but saw her cloaked figure outlined against the faint light in the square.

"Lieutenant Hull," she whispered.

"Here." He tugged on her cloak, turning her to face him. "What's happened with Walton?"

"Mr. Moffett came this morning." Matt had heard that gossip from the men who loafed about Ridley's office. "He was terribly angry. He blamed Mr. Walton for damaging his gig, said he'd driven too fast over the corduroy. The axle broke near the hub of the right wheel, and when the wheel collapsed, it skinned the horse's leg, so it's lame."

"It was an accident then."

"I don't know," she whispered, misery underlining her words with a sob.

"And Mr. Walton?"

"He hurts all over. He's scraped and bruised from head to toe. He whimpers for ice, but there's none in the ice-house at this time of year. He expects someone to sit at his side every minute. Mr. Moffett refused to take him back to Muncie, for he says he'll not spend good money to hire a nurse, when I can take care of him. Mama told me to read to him this evening, but I'd promised Meggie I'd help her put together her double-ax patchwork, so I ran off and stayed at Uncle Jim's for supper."

"From now on, sit with Mr. Walton as often as he asks."

"Why?" she cried. "I despise him."

"Talk to him. Learn about his life in Massachusetts."

"He's disgusting! Where he's not black-and-blue, he's white, whiter than a baby, like a grub in a rotting log. I never thought the first man I'd see, I mean like that, in bed, would be so ugly!"

"If he mentions names, write them down," Matt said, grabbing her arm to make her listen. "Find out where he lives, and everything about his business. Does he have a partner?"

"I don't understand."

"Would your father ask you to marry a dishonorable man? A man who's been in trouble with the law?"

"Mr. Walton's never been in trouble," she said, adding a snort, plainly exasperated by his suggestions. "To break the law, a man must move, be quick on his feet, and Walton sits and does nothing."

"Even sitting, he must do something. Reads, or writes letters, or—"

"Sunday, he did nothing after church but sit and eat. He carries the most disgusting molasses candy about with him, in a tin box, with sifted sugar over the top, and the sugar sticks to his lip, like a mustache. He finished all his candy this morning, and he's fretting to Mama for more, but Sally's sister's lame, from dancing in tight shoes that raised a big blister, so she must sit with her foot in salts. Sally's gone to stay with her because there's a baby to care for, and the last apples haven't been hung to dry, and if the cold stays another few days, Papa will have the hogs butchered, so there's little time for making candy."

"You make his candy."

"He'll think I'm courting him! Besides, I don't know how to make molasses candy."

"Learn! And you *are* courting him. Courting him to betray himself. Listen to me. If Walton has a thriving business in Massachusetts, why should he bother to come to Indiana? Imagine how uncomfortable travel is for someone his size. Who paid the fare for the steamboat down the Ohio? For the stagecoach all the way to Muncie? Find out, and write the answers down so you remember."

"You're already sounding like a lawyer," she sneered. "Have you learned so much in one day?"

"So far, I've swept up peach pits, moved a table from Ridley's house, hauled a load of firewood and stacked it in the alley and copied a letter for Mr. Ridley, who complained of my handwriting. I'm to practice writing every day after work, but without costing him extra by lighting a lamp or candle. I thought I wrote well enough, but I learned without a book, just copying Major Linder, and it's not to a lawyer's copperplate standard."

"Copying who?" A gusty wind, laden with moisture, eddied through the narrow passage.

"The officer who taught me to read and write. You'd best go home now. Rain's coming."

"Why did he teach you?"

"Because he was kind, and didn't care that my mother and father hadn't gone to a preacher." She stepped into the dark, so quickly he might have threatened her with a raised fist.

"Will you marry me?" She turned her back on him.

"Will you marry me?"

"Yes," she said.

"You're lying." Her father would one day order her to accept Matt Hull's proposal. Ira MacIntyre would have no choice, once he knew of the ammunition Matt had gleaned from Major Linder's diary.

"Yes, I'm lying. But I need your help to get rid of Mr. Walton."

"Someone else attempted to rid you of Walton, and did you no favor, for the 'accident' ended with him in your house. Isn't that true?"

"Yes." The single word came after a long hesitation.

"And that's why you ran to Jim Mac's house this evening. Not to help Meggie with her patchwork, but to warn your cousin Pete not to make another attempt on Walton's life."

She spun about, the hood of her cloak fell, and her pale face reflected the moonlight flickering through the scudding clouds. "He didn't! Why should you think—"

"Not difficult to figure out. Who in Pikeston has the skill to weaken an axle, without the least damage showing? Pete MacIntyre. Any other man would simply cut a few spokes, so the wheel collapses after a mile or two. But when that's done, the wood shows the mark of the saw or the hatchet. Mr. Moffett blames the accident on his nephew's carelessness, so Pete did something rather clever."

"Please, don't say!"

MacIntyre pride. The whole family—except perhaps Granny—assumed they might do anything and escape the consequences, because who in the township dared challenge them?

Another gust of wind, stronger, whistling round the corner, raising stinging dust. A sudden high shriek, the sound of a banshee battle with witches, funneled through the passage, almost swept him off his feet. He grabbed at Tildy in panic, blinded by dust, frantic to protect her. Her arms reached for him. The dust blotted out the moon, and gravel stung his legs. He shoved Tildy into the fragile protection of the livery barn, fought with her cloak as it streamed behind her, a loosened sail. Monstrous thunder joined the shriek, a hundred furious bulls bellowing in concert, and in this tumult, a crash, tumbling in declining echoes about the square.

She clung to him, her chest rising and falling against him. The squall, cyclone, whatever had ridden on the face of the clouds, passed, leaving roiling darkness overhead. Boots pounded in the square; men shouted from every direction, searching for the building that had gone down. No need for him to crush her so tightly, but his spirit said to hold her close. He slid his hand beneath her chin, lifted her face and laid his lips upon hers.

No friendly reaction this time! She twisted in his arms, slid from his grasp, ran down the narrow alley and vanished in the dark tangle of backyards. Matt leaned against the wall, willing his breath to deepen, his heart to slow. Lanterns bobbed in the square like large fireflies.

"The store!" someone yelled. Matt eased out to join in the search. Men congregated on the west side of the square, behind MacIntyre's store. The wind pelted them with icy raindrops, and he sought the shelter of the north wall. Lanterns illuminated a pile of wreckage.

"Here's the roof!" The man raised a lantern to show a tangle of shingles and rafters twenty feet away. The whirlwind had lifted the roof off a small shed, tossed it aside, and the walls, without its weight and strength, had fallen in. The lantern light turned the raindrops into slanting silver daggers. Ira MacIntyre waded into the wreckage, tossing planks aside to expose boxes and barrels.

"Help me, boys!" he yelled. "Help me get this under cover."

The men formed a line from the ruin to the back door of the store, tossed boxes hand to hand as quickly as MacIntyre pulled them from the wreck. Others rolled barrels under the eaves. Matt plunged into the tangle and discovered long parcels wrapped in brown paper. Dry goods of some sort. Rain rattled on the paper. Unseen hands snatched them as he wrenched the bundles free.

"Get that lantern away!" MacIntyre screamed almost in Matt's ear. "That cask's powder!" Hands drew back, men sank into the shadows. The pool of light shifted from the wreckage to MacIntyre's face. Under Matt's gaze worry and panic turned to fiery hatred.

"What are you doing here?" MacIntyre snarled, his voice more furious than the whirlwind. His words carried the weight of the rod he had once laid across a bastard boy's shoulders. Matt cast about for a suitable answer to the question, found nothing, and had time to consider that a lawyer must be quicker on his feet.

"Fancy yourself something, don't you? Uniform doesn't alter a bastard. If you mean to parade as a gentleman, pay your father's bills, beginning with what he owes me. Unless, maybe Hull's not your father." He did not speak softly. Every man had to have heard.

The man holding the lantern laid his hand on MacIntyre's arm. "Not now, Ira," he said in a low voice. "Hull's trying to help."

"Callom. That's his rightful name, his mother's name. That's what a bastard carries. I can do without help from sprouts of the swamp." He bent and pried a box from beneath a shattered plank.

Matt swung his feet tentatively to find a route out of the

tangle, his toes pressed against another soft bundle, and he picked it up to give himself more room. The paper peeled away beneath his fingers, sodden and cold. Damaged goods; icy hatred. He stared at the wet sleeve of his coat, expecting to see steam rise from the heat of his resentment. One day, soon, he would have Ira MacIntyre crawling at his feet, MacIntyre's pride shattered like the timbers amid which he stood.

Only three or four lines in Major Linder's diary, but enough to tie Ira MacIntyre to the long-ago disappearance of Hiram Barman. A patient lawyer could dig out more, enough to convict.

# Chapter Five

Tildy could not bear to sew on the oak-leaf appliqué of her bridal quilt; every stitch conjured up thoughts of Mr. Walton, or the fear of a jeering comment. She dug in Meggie's sewing bag and helped her piece her double-ax quilt top. She kept her eyes on her work, smoothly matching each of the curved seams, hoping her friends saw nothing but a sedate lady. Internally every nerve strained, fearing to hear Mr. Walton's demanding call from upstairs.

Were Meggie and Faith and Rachel unnaturally quiet, or was it her imagination?. She wished they would chatter and exchange gossip. Then, if Mr. Walton did call, she could pretend she hadn't heard. But the click of Faith's bone knitting needles was the loudest noise in the parlor, and Tildy could clearly hear the faint sigh of her own thread passing through the cotton.

"Aunt Caroline wrote out the temperance pledge yesterday," Rachel said. Everyone looked up eagerly. "She took it to the office and Lieutenant Hull signed without a murmur. I had supposed he would resist, that army officers couldn't live without whiskey."

Couldn't Rachel find something more interesting to talk about than Lieutenant Hull? The shameful kiss still lingered on her lips—on her tongue. She lowered her head, pretending the curved seam did not fall into place. Just in case she blushed. At least last night she'd had the presence of mind to run away when he tried to kiss her.

"Lieutenant Hull's very much a gentleman," Faith said. Tildy disagreed, but said nothing for fear Faith would demand details. "Father told me to carry his meals to the office, not wanting him in the house, but I explained that breakfast—with eggs—is difficult to tote around, so he comes after I've fed the boys."

"Your brothers are the wildest boys in town," Meggie said in her blunt fashion. "I can't see how associating with Matt Hull could possibly make them wilder."

Faith looked hurt. She cast off the stitches for the thumb of the mitten she was knitting. She always took it hard when her brothers got into trouble, but her father gave her no authority over them, so why should she blame herself?

"How's Mr. Walton?" Rachel asked.

"Complaining," Tildy whispered, glancing toward the stairs. "He's got a raw place on his chest, and his legs hurt when he moves them."

Meggie laughed. "He could barely move his legs before he crashed. Does he expect a tumble on the road to fix them?"

"Hush!" Tildy said, glad Mama had gone to pay a call on Mrs. Ridley.

"How long do you suppose Lieutenant Hull's hands are?" Faith mused aloud, holding up the incomplete mitten. "While I'm knitting for the boys, I might as well make a pair for him, as a surprise, if I can figure how long his hands are."

Long enough to cover the back of my head! thought Tildy. Long enough to reach halfway around my waist. The prickling sensation began where his arm had crushed her, and crept upward. Did Faith have designs on Matt Hull? Faith, even at twenty-one and almost an old maid, could do better than Matt Hull. Tildy laid her sewing in her lap and stretched her fingers, as if grasping the small needle caused a cramp.

"When will Mr. Walton go home?" Rachel asked.

"I have no idea." Her friends looked at her, expecting more, curious about her unwanted suitor. "Mr. Moffett made no arrangements for a carriage, which is the only way Mr. Walton can possibly travel to Muncie. I wish he'd leave today, for he complains and complains, about how Mrs. Weeks is not a good cook, and the bed's too hard, and how everything's so poor, compared to what he's accustomed to in the East. I made him molasses candy, and he said the sugar didn't suit, although I pounded it and pounded it in the mortar, as fine as for the best cake, Mrs. Weeks said."

"His family must be very rich for him to think your house poor," Faith said.

"If his family's rich, why did he come to Indiana?" Tildy heard Matt Hull's voice ask the same question. He had planted his ideas in her head, along with the tingle wherever he had touched her. "Why did Mr. Walton make that exhausting trip if he inherited a fine business from his father?"

"I suppose," said Rachel, "a man with money will do anything to get more."

"Lieutenant Hull has no winter things," Faith said. "I told him, if he purchased the goods, I'd make him a coat."

Tildy stared at Faith, completely abandoning any pretense at sewing. Faith Tole must want a husband desperately if she would settle for Matt Hull, and allow him the intimacies a woman must yield to a husband. Tildy flushed suddenly hot despite the chill in the parlor.

"I should expect Lieutenant Hull's mother to—" she began sharply, but the front door opened and she closed her mouth.

"Hello, girls," her mother called from the hall. "Busy as bees, I see. Matilda, you should be working on your oak-leaf appliqué." Her voice turned sugary when she spoke of the wedding quilt, letting Faith, Rachel and Meggie understand the destiny of that piece of work. She removed her bonnet.

"I hope, Faith, your father is not offended by Mr. MacIntyre's protests, but offering board to that Hull boy affects the entire community. Your father did not reflect adequately upon the matter."

Faith murmured into her knitting, like any well-reared young woman, shy about contradicting her elders.

"Uncle Ira's quarreling with everyone these day," Meggie said. "My pa, his own brother, won't speak to him, and—" she turned to Rachel "—I understand when Uncle Ira complained to Mr. Ridley about his new clerk, Ridley told him to mind his store and leave the law to those who understand it! Why should he be upset that Matt Hull's come back to town, and wants to read law? What difference does it make?"

Tildy looked at her mother, alarmed at what her reaction might be to open opposition.

"It makes a difference because the Hulls are thieves and drunkards," her mother said. "It's bad enough having the father around, without a grown son who—"

"He sighed a temperance pledge," Rachel said quickly.

"Meaningless to a Hull. They're so accustomed to lying they'll tell a lie when the truth would do just as well, simply because the truth is beyond them. And think of what's happened since that boy returned to Pikeston! Mr. Walton's accident. And the shed behind the store completely wrecked. Mr. MacIntyre is sure he caused it, not the storm."

"No!" exclaimed Tildy, then bit her lip hard. If she spoke of the gig, she might implicate Pete. And she dared not explain that at the moment the shed blew down, she and Matthew Hull stood together near the schoolhouse. She picked up the patchwork, and smoothed the curved edges with uncertain fingers.

"What is that you're sewing, Matilda?"

"Meggie's double-ax patchwork."

"I forbid you," her mother said. "Go get your appliqué. After all the expense to Mrs. Ridley of having her cousins send the oak-leaf pattern from Virginia... Margaret, I can't imagine that your mother is aware you are piecing such a common thing. Double-ax has never appeared in *Godey's Lady's Book,* and only the lowest of women, those with very common tastes, make it. Faith, knitting is not a graceful occupation. So clumsy." She did not wait for a response to either of these declarations, but turned to Tildy. "Have you looked in on Mr. Walton?"

Tildy shook her head while keeping her eyes on her stitches.

"He's asleep," Meggie said, not at all abashed by the denigration of her choice of patchwork. "Can't you hear him snore?"

"I must reassure him that we've not forgotten him. He'll understand, surely, that Matilda's engaged in a worthy pursuit. Sewing, proper sewing, is a ladylike occupation." Tildy sighed as Mama sailed out of the room and up the stairs. Footsteps overhead, then back on the stairs. Voices in the kitchen. Her mother must be ordering some tasty tidbit for Mr. Walton. She spoiled him! He might end up staying for a month!

"Excuse me," Tildy said. "I think, Meggie, that Mama's right. I should be working on my appliqué." She tiptoed up the stairs and into her room so she would not draw Mr. Walton's attention. She searched through a heap of old books at the bottom of her cupboard, until she found her tattered penmanship book. Sitting at her table she wrote a hurried note, thrust it deep against the binding and folded the book inside her appliqué.

Mrs. Weeks, looking very harried, came into the parlor with the tea tray. Her mother would be close behind, Tildy knew, so she had but a moment. As her friends laid their work aside, Tildy edged near Faith and slid the book under her knitting.

"This is for Lieutenant Hull," she whispered. "I understand Mr. Ridley complains his handwriting's poor."

Matt crawled out of his blankets at the first sign of gray light around the door. He dressed, climbed down the ladder and went into the office. He huffed three times, but could not see his breath. Warmer than the past few mornings. His new schedule worked well. Sweep the floor and take out the ashes in the dawn twilight, so he could use the hour of sunrise to practice his handwriting. And now read. Yesterday Mr. Ridley had piled four large leather-bound volumes before him.

"This—" his hands had touched the books reverently "—is Blackstone. Sir William Blackstone. *Commentaries on the Laws of England.* You'll read these books until you know them by heart. You'll breathe Blackstone, eat Blackstone, until any sentence uttered in your hearing, you parse for its meaning to Blackstone." He tapped the top of the heap. "Of course, the sections on the powers of the kings of England and Parliament, rather meaningless to an American, but the rest...absorb it until it's engraved in your brain."

Matt bent over to scoot the spittoon out of the way of his broom. He doubted that he could find room to engrave four huge volumes of law on his entire body. He had not expected legal studies to be exciting, but the mass of four volumes...

"Matt." A moment's tremor of fear and hope. Tildy? He straightened up, found his sister Esther standing in the open back door. What was she doing in town at daybreak? "Pa said you'd help me."

He grasped the handle of the broom tightly, in a spasm of concern. "How?" The single word was curt and unwelcoming, but if his father suspected the silver coins hidden in the attic, he would have no peace until Hector Hull had laid claim to them all.

"I need a dress." He looked her up and down. She wore

a brown dress, made of the goods called bombazine, the same one she'd had on at the Harvest Home feast.

"That looks fine to me." Too big, and the style unsuitable to a young girl.

"This is Ma's. We only got the one respectable dress between us."

He nodded, recalling that at the cabin both his mother and Esther had worn calico shifts.

"I want to get married, and I need a dress."

"Who's the lucky man?"

"I ain't found one yet because I got no dress," she said, sarcastic, accusing him of ignorance. "Pa said you got money, or could sell the buttons off that fancy uniform. You could get me a dress. He wants I should marry soon and get out of the cabin. If I don't, he says I'll have to take over Ma's work, because few men pay to lie with her anymore."

"How old are you?"

"Fifteen."

She had been a child when he left. Still a child. The gathered bodice of the dress sagged over her narrow chest.

"Has any young man come courting? Or walked you home from the dance?"

She shrugged her shoulders. "I'm not aiming for any boy. Pa said Tildy MacIntyre won't have that gent her father brought from Muncie, so I thought I'd flirt with him. I'm not so picky as Tildy."

Walton? She would marry Walton?

"How do you plan to flirt with Walton? He's in bed, hurt, in the MacIntyres' house."

"He'll get well, and the MacIntyres always go to church, and if I had a blue calico dress, I could go, too. And to the socials, and the spelling bees. He'd see me."

Matt nearly burst out laughing at a mental picture of his illiterate sister at a spelling bee. "Come in," he said. He closed the door, resumed his work, and as he lifted a chair aside an idea came with it.

"Are you good at nursing a sick man?"

"I've nursed the children," she said, sitting down in Ridley's high-backed chair and wiggling her hips to estimate its comfort.

"You go around to the MacIntyres' house, to the back, and speak to the woman who answers the door. The cook or the maid. Say you're looking for work. Mrs. MacIntyre might take you on, for Sally, their maid, her sister's not well." Esther nodded, but her eyes showed no agreement. "You do anything they ask of you, but especially be kind to Mr. Walton, who loves molasses candy, with well-pounded sugar sifted over the top."

Esther smoothed the dark skirt with both her hands. "Ma wouldn't want me to cook and scrub in this dress. It's her only one."

"Then you must ask to borrow an old dress from Mrs. MacIntyre or Tildy. And if they're satisfied with your work, they might give you a dress to keep."

"You won't give me the money?" Her eyes told him he was selfish. By damn! He was selfish, and to improve himself he'd stay that way.

"Did Pa say I had money?"

"He said the lawyer fellow must pay—"

"Mr. Ridley pays me nothing. I'm lucky he'll take me on without a fee for tuition. Every cent I have, including my buttons, I'll need to live through the winter."

Her shoulders sagged, making the bodice pouch out even more over her flat chest, but she still seemed unconvinced. "Pa said—"

"Are you too proud to be a serving girl? You'd rather sell yourself to whatever man Pa brings down the river path?"

"Shut your foul mouth!" She jumped out of the chair and stood before him, her green eyes snapping with a fire he had never noticed before. "Pa *is* truly your pa, Ma told me, but my pa—" she held out her hand as if inviting a kiss "—Ma says he's a real gentleman."

Matt managed not to smile at her ridiculous pride. He searched for words to soothe her. "If your father's a gentleman, you should marry a gentleman, and if Mrs. MacIntyre hires you, you might succeed. Gentlemen like kind women. You might have the chance to take care of Mr. Walton while he's feeling bad." Not likely would Walton marry such a beanpole, he thought, watching her flounce to the door, swinging her nonexistent hips. And Moffett would not turn his store over to a nephew who showed such bad judgment in selecting a wife.

"Watch yourself with Walton," he called as she lifted the latch. "Don't let him seduce your virginity, if you still have it. Men pay extra for that."

"You think I was born yesterday, you dumb bastard!" she said over her shoulder.

He rushed to finish the sweeping, for near the window the light streamed in, strong enough to read. He opened the first thick volume.

*Law signifies a rule of action. It is a rule; not a transient sudden order, but something permanent, uniform, and universal.*

He translated this from his own experience. Law was not an order given by a spiteful sergeant, but was the principles laid down for the conduct of the entire army. He felt an unexpected pride. A lawyer studies the universal rules.

He was deep in page ten when he heard footsteps in the alley, heard Faith call his name. The morning sun flooded the square, harness jingled on the street, and boots tramped on the boardwalk. "Aren't you coming for breakfast, Lieutenant Hull?" she asked.

He followed her to her kitchen, where the coffee stood simmering at the side of the hearth, and his breakfast warmed atop the skillet. On the table, next to the fork and mug, lay a thin book. He touched it with the tips of his fingers, questioning its presence.

"Tildy sent it," Faith said. "She thought you might find it helpful."

"Give her my thanks." He would thank her himself, except that Ira MacIntyre caused enough trouble for his daughter without knowing she spent time with Matt Hull. Faith turned to the fire and he ruffled the pages, which fell open at a paper covered with minuscule handwriting. He closed the book.

"Mr. MacIntyre has a new bolt of heavy wool that would make a fine coat. If…if you need one," Faith stammered. Matt remembered the bundles he had pulled from the ruins. The thought of patronizing Ira MacIntyre's store stuck in his craw, but it must be done. MacIntyre owned the only store in town. Besides, MacIntyre would gain a sense of security if Matt Hull's money passed over his counter. MacIntyre must never suspect until the final, fatal moment that Matt Hull carried a stick to punish him. Destroy him.

When he returned to the office, Matt climbed to the attic to scan Tildy's note in private.

Mr. Walton comes from a town called Braintree, but he does not say much about his life in Mass. I don't think he has a store, for he called my new shantung hat a bonnet. When I inquire, he will not tell me of his store, but says that women do not understand business, and he manages his mother's affairs. He's not a brave man. He moans in pain, and worries that he is badly hurt and will not get well. He says a horse threw his brother some years ago, and he was in bed an invalid for half a year, and limped forever after.

Wise woman, Matt thought with approval. Not all young ladies would notice that a shopkeeper should know the difference between a hat and a bonnet. Matt pulled a small account book from his scanty pile of possessions. The book fell open to the well-fingered page where he had copied the lines from Major Linder's diary.

> August 11. Visited the pasture and arranged with Barman for purchase of his string. Gave him half the cash. Fine horses.
> August 12. Note from Barman, to meet a Mr. Mack today for delivery, as he is called away. Detail sent for horses with balance of payment, returned with useless, bony nags, not the string Barman displayed. Rode immediately to pasture, and found it empty. Sergeant Watson said the man called Mack is my height, and clean shaven, very nervous, for his fingers played at his vest pockets while they spoke.
> August 28. Corporal Hendricks discovered the stallion from Barman's string on a farm fifteen miles out of Madison. Farmer says he bought the horse more than a week past, his description of the man resembles Mack, particularly fingers playing at vest pockets.

Matt folded Tildy's note and shoved it into the account book. Ira MacIntyre. Eighteen years ago last summer, when the army sent young Lieutenant Linder to the Ohio ports to buy horses, Ira MacIntyre had cheated him. He'd stolen Barman's horses.

Once he hung out his shingle, he would correspond with a lawyer in Madison, or perhaps the sheriff. Linder would have reported the matter to the sheriff, perhaps put a notice in the newspaper. Matt climbed down from his attic.

"Floor looks better for regular sweeping," Ridley said as he entered, "but the stove needs blacking before winter truly sets in. Today might be good. Feels like Indian summer intends to settle in for a few days."

Matt regarded his black hands with dismay. No matter how hard he scrubbed, the blacking would not come off.

He shrugged his shoulders. It would wear away of its own accord.

A grizzled man came in the office, sat on the bench by the front door, eating apples that he pulled from a capacious pocket. He tossed the cores onto the street, where a waiting pig gobbled them up.

"What do you think of this California business, Ridley?" he asked.

"Foolishness," said Ridley, without turning away from his writing.

"Why foolish?" asked the man.

"The war's not over. If the Mexicans should gather even a small army, they could chase every American out of the province. They'd kill the emigrants as they came over the mountains. Men weakened by that trip would have no chance at all against an army."

"Hadn't thought of that," grumbled the man, who had obviously been caught up in the excitement generated by Godfroy and Sampson.

"Ask Hull what that country's like," Ridley said. "Desert and mountains, fit only for savages."

"That true, Hull?"

"I wasn't in California," Matt said. "I crossed into Mexico at the Rio Grande. From Texas."

"They must be quite the same," Ridley said, "being in the same country."

"There's more distance from the Rio Grande to California, than from here to New York," Matt pointed out. The men stared at him, the apple eater astonished, Ridley unhappy at having his ignorance exposed. At that moment Faith walked in carrying a basket.

"Take that outside to eat," Ridley said. "Crumbs and such bring in mice this time of year."

Matt nodded, took the basket from Faith and went out the front door and sat in the sun on the edge of the boardwalk.

"Well," the apple eater said behind him, "Sampson

mentioned it was a far piece, and that jumping off from the Missouri River in May, we'd not arrive until September.''

"Foolhardy," Ridley said.

Never correct or contradict, Matt told himself silently. Some men find new information a threat. He munched on the barely warm roast pork, and Faith's delicious corn bread. A wagon drawn by a trotting team came down the street, and Matt hunched over to shelter his dinner from the dust.

"Thought I'd find you here." Pete MacIntyre looked down at Matt from the seat of a wagon. He shoved his hat to the back of his head. "Pa asks you to join us for supper tonight."

Supper at Jim Mac's house! Three good meals today! "Tell him thanks for the invitation, and I accept. Any particular reason he wants me there?"

"He's asked Godfroy and Sampson to come out and explain about California, but Ma says you should come, too, as a corrective to their lies."

"I've not been to California."

"But you've been farther west than most. And know something about traveling." Pete jumped down from the wagon. "Look at this wagon, now. I think it's fine for just about any hauling, but Sampson says it won't do for a California trip. Mule killer, he calls it. He wants me to build a light wagon, but still strong enough to take the beating of rough roads. What wagons did you use in the West?"

"Army wagons. And they're mule killers."

"What sort of wagons do they drive in Mexico?"

"No wagons. Carts." Pete looked disappointed. "But you don't need suggestions from me," Matt assured him. "Knowing what a wagon's to be used for, you can certainly design one to fit. Light and strong, convenient for a long trip."

"That's what Sampson and I talked about this morning,'' Pete said, ''but got interrupted by Cousin Josh, bringing a message from Uncle Ira, asking me to look at the plans he's drawn for a new shed. He wants to replace the one that collapsed while this fine weather holds. Of course—you gonna eat those beet pickles?—he expects me to do the work for nothing, being his nephew.''

Matt offered Pete the beets, even though he was still hungry. Dinner would make up for them.

''He doesn't consider that I'll miss two or three paying jobs while I'm putting up that shed,'' Pete continued. He leaned closer. ''And when I finish, Uncle Ira'll give me some bit of trash from the store as payment, something no one will buy. Last time, it was a silk reticule embroidered all over with beads, 'for my sweetheart,' he said. I gave it to Granny.'' He jumped back on the wagon, rubbing his beet-reddened hands on his pants. ''See you for supper, then.''

Matt gulped down the last chunk of corn bread and returned to the small table that served as his desk.

''Is Jim Mac seriously considering emigrating to California?'' Ridley asked, letting Matt know his conversation with Pete had been overheard.

''I don't know,'' he said.

''If he's asked Godfroy and Sampson out there...''

''Maybe he just wants the entertainment of listening to tall tales,'' Matt suggested.

''If Jim Mac should decide to head west, farmers with smaller places—and men with trades here in town—might be tempted to sell out and move,'' Ridley said, worry plain in his voice. ''It's always bad when a man with money and reputation leaves, the whole township comes unbalanced, the smaller fry trying to step into his shoes.''

''Ira MacIntyre would still be around,'' Matt said. ''His shoes are big enough to serve for both.''

''You think so?'' Ridley asked. He pursed his mouth in thought. ''It could be, taking all this land from Mexico isn't a good idea. Emigration drains money and good men from the older settlements. You're not thinking of any such nonsense?''

"No. I intend to stay here."

"Good. Very good. You see, Pikeston needs more than one lawyer. Right now, a man comes to see me, says his neighbor's bull got into his corn, and he wants damages. The other fellow, he must go to Muncie to find a lawyer to represent him. See the problem?''

Matt smiled to himself. "So with two lawyers, we can keep the litigation right here in Pikeston, between ourselves."

"Exactly, so you see, I don't look upon you as competition, but as a—'' A thump from the back door interrupted him.

"That awful man! That awful man!" Mrs. Ridley cried without greeting. She wavered from one foot to the other, looked wildly around the room, surprised, as if she found everything out of place. She staggered, grabbed for the back of a chair, but missed and crumpled on the floor, a heap of petticoats. Matt smelled the whiskey before he reached her. Ridley waved him away, and heaved his wife into the chair.

"Get some fresh water," he ordered.

Matt grabbed the bucket, ran out to the well in the alley and cranked the windlass. The chilly water spilled over his boots as he filled the bucket.

When he returned to the office, Mrs. Ridley was crying and blubbering. "A half-breed! Belle would never have done such a thing, so it can't be true, even though Rachel's eyes are dark, not like anyone in my family, but I can't remember Mr. Barman's eyes, so perhaps he was dark, too."

"Leave us be," Ridley ordered harshly.

"If there's anything I can do, sir, to help Mrs. Ridley home, perhaps a buggy—"

"You know Trail Godfroy?"

"Yes, sir."

"Find him, and tell him if he ever again upsets Mrs. Ridley this way, I'll be after him with a rifle." So much for friendly litigation, thought Matt. He detoured to his table to get the first volume of Blackstone.

"He seduced Belle," Mrs. Ridley said between hiccups. "He'll take Rachel away, to California! He shouldn't even be in Indiana. Why wasn't he made to leave when they sent all the Indian tribes across the Mississippi?"

"Hush," Ridley said, watching Matt's progress in such a way as to tell him to hurry. "Rachel has been a dutiful daughter to us," he whispered. Mrs. Ridley groaned, gagged and vomited down the front of her spreading skirts.

"Hell and damnation!" Ridley yelled, springing away from his wife. "Get some water, Hull!"

"I did, sir. Right there..."

"Clean up this mess!"

"She'll leave," Mrs. Ridley muttered thickly. "Do you know what Rachel said? Do you?" she demanded.

"Hush!" Ridley said, but she paid no attention.

"Rachel said, 'I often wondered. It explains so much.' My daughter! My girl as good as my daughter said that! Oh, if only we'd gone to our cousins in Virginia!" She leaned back in the chair, blubbering again, while Matt sponged at her skirt.

"Leave it be," Ridley said. "I'll take her home." He thrust his arm around her back and heaved his wife out of the chair, none too gently. "If anyone comes, tell him I'll be back directly. I'd be most grateful if you said nothing of this."

"Of course not."

"Mrs. Ridley's...been taken sick with a fever, and says crazy things," he stammered.

"Of course, sir."

With her husband's arm supporting her, Mrs. Ridley managed to waver down the alley. Matt dashed to Ridley's desk, extracted a sheet of clean paper from a cubbyhole, and checked the nib on the pen.

Dear Finlay,

You are home by now, I suppose, and I hope your journey was pleasant as mine. I returned to my birthplace of Pikeston, Indiana, to be met with a strange situation bedeviling friends of mine. A gentleman of your state has arrived to claim the inheritance of Mr. Moffett of Muncie, Indiana. This gentleman, Afton Walton by name, hails from Braintree, or says he does, but I have reason for doubt. He is two or three inches over five feet tall, and nearly as wide, with pale skin. It would be a great favor to me if you would investigate this gentleman's situation, talk to his friends and business partners, etc. to see if he is what he claims to be.

You may address me in care of Mr. L. Ridley, Esq., in aforementioned town of Pikeston.

Matt folded the sheet into thirds, dug into the drying paste pot to seal the letter. He should mix more flour and water into paste, before Mr. Ridley even thought to ask. Tonight he would hand the letter to Pete, to mail next time he visited a nearby town. That way, it would not pass through the postbox at MacIntyre's store.

# Chapter Six

Tildy pronounced the words of Prescott's *History of the Conquest of Mexico,* without paying the slightest attention to the meaning of the sentences.

Papa was dreadfully angry, and Tildy did not know what had started the argument between him and Mama. They had retreated to the unheated parlor, but even from that isolation their voices filled the house. Something about the girl her mother had hired to help in the kitchen, although the girl's arrival had been a gift from heaven, what with Mrs. Weeks down with a fever and Sally still tending her sister.

After the argument her father had confronted Tildy still in her morning robe, railed at her because Mr. Walton lay alone in his room.

"It's time, young lady, that you understand your responsibilities," he had shouted. So now she sat beside Mr. Walton, blankly reading Prescott, wishing her father were dead.

But if her father died, it would be even more necessary that she marry Mr. Walton. Light-brained Josh could not run the store, and Lewis and Edward were too young.

Mr. Walton grew livelier every day, his mental confusion clearing rapidly, until today he could understand Prescott. Too bad his memory had improved. Her father wouldn't expect her to marry a dim-witted man, and Mr. Moffett wouldn't turn his business over to a nephew who couldn't add a column of figures.

Tildy had never seen a crazy man, but she had seen steers plunging about after eating jimsonweed. Perhaps men, too, she thought wickedly. Granny would know.

Tildy slowed her pronunciation of the words, dragging them out in a monotone. Paragraph after paragraph, all the time trying to imagine Mr. Walton's antics after a cup of jimsonweed tea. She must talk to Granny, alone, and learn where she could gather the herb. Mr. Walton's eyelids drooped. Once he jerked himself awake, and tried to concentrate on the advance of Cortés on Mexico City. Tildy turned the page easily, making not the least rustle, lowered her voice and watched him fall asleep. She read on and on in a whisper, until a deep snore set the flab of his face quivering.

She crept away to her own room to wash her face and hands. But the dirty water of morning had not been emptied from the basin, and she remembered Sally would not come until her sister's babe took its nap, and Mrs. Weeks had sent a message that she was sick, and some strange girl helped down in the kitchen, and Papa shouted in irrational fury.

She found Mama bent over the cookstove, struggling with a pot of string beans. A slight figure sat on the porch, quartering apples, and stringing them on a long, stout thread.

"Here, help me," her mother said. "Sally will come before dinner and fry pork chops and make gravy, but some things must be done beforehand." Tildy took the long fork from her mother and poked at the beans, wondering what she was expected to do.

"It's Emma Callom's girl, Esther," her mother whispered, twisting her mouth to point at the girl on the back steps. "Your father agreed to let her stay, but she must not enter the house. He raised such a fury, I would have sent her away, but the apples must be hung to dry. Men don't understand the work...."

Tildy shielded her face from the heat of the stove.

"That basket's done, Miz MacIntyre." Esther wore one of Tildy's mother's discarded day dresses, far too large for her skinny frame. "I think you got that fire too hot, Miz MacIntyre."

"But it was nearly out...." Esther shoved the beans to the cool side of the range, opened the firebox, and with the poker separated the flaming brands. She cast two dippers of water on the fire. "That'll be just about right for corn bread." She grinned her contempt for women so clumsy in the kitchen. Tildy stepped back in confusion, remembering the same expression on the faces of the young men at the dance.

Esther returned to her exile on the porch, but leaned in at the door, her green eyes radiating triumph, not subservience. "That basket's all done, Miz MacIntyre," she repeated, and smiled a superior little smile. Why didn't Mama order her away for such insolence?

"Peel the potatoes for dinner." Her mother handed Esther a kettle. "You'll find them in the shed out back." Esther's narrow hips swayed as she crossed the yard.

"She shouldn't be here, but we'll have to make do until your father hires another servant. I don't believe Mrs. Weeks is ill at all. She just resents being made to help around the house. And this is the second time Sally has abandoned us for some petty problem of her sister's."

Tildy considered how to ask permission to spend the evening with Meggie. Right now seemed a bad time to make any request.

"How is Mr. Walton?"

"Asleep. He complained about his breakfast. He doesn't like eggs except well cooked, he likes corn bread soft, and from now on wants maple syrup, not molasses, on his flapjacks."

Her mother sighed, but then perked up. "We must expect him to be picky. He's a gentleman, accustomed to fine things.''

''I promised Meggie I'd help with her patchwork, for she wants to put her double-ax top on the quilting frame next week.''

''Quilting?'' her mother asked. ''A quilting bee? With Mr. Walton so bad, it hardly seems suitable—''

''Just the four of us—Meggie and me, and Rachel and Faith. Faith says we can set up the frame at her house. This will be the first top we've quilted for Meggie.''

''Seventeen, and only one quilt!'' Her mother shook her head. ''You must offer to loan her copies of *Godey's*, so in the future she will choose a more suitable pattern. I'm afraid your aunt and grandmother haven't paid proper attention to Margaret's rearing. Without the tastes of a cultured woman, she'll not marry well. Her mother and her father have allowed—''

Esther leaned in the door, holding out the kettle for examination. ''This enough?''

''Yes, yes, that's quite enough, but you should not put the dirty potatoes in the kettle. You should carry them in your apron. Pile the potatoes on the porch and rinse the kettle at the well.'' Her mother shooed Esther out the door. ''I understand, Matilda, that you feel bound by your promise to help Margaret, but circumstances change, and women must subdue their own desires. Mr. Walton needs your attention.''

''I'll sit with Mr. Walton, if it's a watcher you need,'' Esther said, still leaning in at the door. ''I've cared for hurt people before—my brother, and Pa when he comes home sick, you understand.''

Tildy held her breath. Would Mama even consider such a trespass?

''Don't think you'd need to pay me extry,'' Esther added hastily. ''You give me this dress, and I should do more work for that.''

''Mr. MacIntyre will not be home until late this evening," Mama mused. "The lodge meeting..." Tildy allowed herself a shallow breath. "I see no reason why Esther could not amuse Mr. Walton for an hour or two." She turned to the grinning girl, who had grown so bold she took a step into the kitchen. "Can you read, Esther?"

"No, ma'am." She was not in the least shamed by the confession.

"I suppose it will do, as a temporary measure. Now, peel the potatoes."

The stove had cooled and the beans needed far less attention. Tildy dropped the fork and, following her mother's gesture, went into the dining room.

"Don't mention Esther to your father," she said. "For the moment I can see no other solution, for you must keep your word to Margaret." She leaned closer. "You understand your father and uncle have quarreled?"

"Yes. About Papa wanting me to marry Mr. Walton."

"Your father's most upset, for Granny seems to have turned against him, too. She says no woman in the family has ever been made to marry against her will, and she would do anything to see that you...of course, you're better acquainted with Mr. Walton now, and see the wisdom...but that his own mother should doubt his decision bothers your father terribly, and he's sure his brother talks against him. You must speak to Granny, and convince her to move here, with us. She's too old to spend another winter on the farm."

*Granny opposed her marriage to Mr. Walton.* That information cheered Tildy. Granny would give her the jimsonweed to drive Mr. Walton into fits.

"Once you've gone to Muncie with your husband, Granny can have your room, and Ira says he'll build a shed for her herbs, although I believe she should give that up. She's much too old to be bothering with sick people. Now, set the table for dinner, then go check on Mr. Walton, and if he's awake, read to him."

* * *

Matt joined the MacIntyre men, Godfroy and Sampson on the benches at the rear of the house. Overhead the evening breeze stirred the scarlet leaves of the maple tree, and periodically a leaf detached itself and rattled to the ground.

"Good planning gets you to California with time to spare before winter," Sampson was saying. "Hello, Hull. Glad you're here. You explain to Jim Mac how careful planning can make even the longest of journeys safe."

Matt shook his head, and laughed. "I never was part of a well-planned expedition, Sampson. I was with the U.S. Army." This set everyone to guffawing, except Jim Mac, who did not seem to find it funny.

"The Indianapolis papers had a piece last month," Jim Mac said. "A number of families have settled in a town on the Bay of San Francisco. They've taken up land and started farming, regardless that the treaty with Mexico hasn't been signed."

"And such land you've never seen!" Sampson exclaimed, but Mrs. MacIntyre cut off his praise of California real estate by calling everyone to supper.

To Matt's surprise, Tildy sat across the table from him, beside Meggie. If Tildy was visiting her aunt and uncle, he decided, Ira MacIntyre and Jim Mac had settled their quarrel. For a long moment his eyes met hers, until she bent her head and studied the table settings. Three extra people crowded the round table, and twice Matt looked over his shoulder to assure himself that the room was otherwise empty, and a route of escape led straight to the door.

Granny passed a bowl of potatoes, and behind it came thick flour gravy, fried pork, sliced cucumbers and applesauce. Tildy wore a dark dress with white lace about the neck. She had no cap on her reddish-brown hair, and when she turned to speak to Meggie, he could see the coil of braid pinned to the back of her head.

Mrs. MacIntyre rose to refill the gravy bowl; a few minutes later Granny shoved away from the table to fetch a pan of fresh corn bread. Godfroy's knife scratched on the empty butter dish. Mrs. MacIntyre prepared to stand up.

"Let Tildy go," said Granny. "It's her turn to fetch. Then Meggie."

Tildy's brows shot up, and her fingers tightened on the fork poised above her plate. Her mouth opened as if to protest, then her face relaxed in obedience. She took the butter dish into the pantry. Meggie sniffed, and Matt thought she stifled a giggle. When Tildy returned with the heaping butter dish she smiled weakly at her grandmother, frowned at Matt, and he shifted his eyes guiltily when he realized he had been staring.

"Now," Jim Mac said as Meggie poured the coffee and Mrs. MacIntyre lit two candles in the middle of the table, "the whole county knows I've spoken to Godfroy and Sampson about joining the party they're organizing for California. Two neighbors stopped at the gate today to tell me there's nothing beyond the Missouri but certain death. Reverend Fitch visited to say that a man who takes his family across the plains should be convicted of murder before the fact.

"On the other hand, Godfroy and Sampson—" he pointed to the men "—have been there, and they talk of no sickness, of crops year around, of fine harbors never closed by ice, and cities certain to grow, and farms that stretch for miles. All this sounds grand, and persuades me that a man who takes his family to California before the main rush of emigration will settle a fortune on his sons and daughters."

"Amen," Sampson said. He looked much encouraged by this speech.

"But everyone in the family must speak. Going to California cuts us off forever from family and friends. I'll force none of you on such a trip against your will." As he spoke, he looked directly at Tildy, and Matt understood Jim Mac offered her support in resisting a marriage to

Walton. She could join his family on the trip to California. The brotherly quarrel had not been settled.

"My dear?" Jim Mac asked, turning to his wife.

"Whither thou goest," Eliza MacIntyre said, not bothering to complete the biblical phrase in this group of Bible readers. "At fourteen I made the trip to Indiana with my father, and I can't recall an unpleasant day on the journey. In fact, it seemed more like a long picnic."

"You'll not find the trip to California a long picnic," warned her husband. "I want your honest opinion."

"If there is no ague—" she looked at Godfroy, who nodded "—if you might be relieved of that burden, one difficult summer would be a small price to pay. And if they speak the truth of life in California, that it's much easier than life here, the hard work of getting there will be repaid."

"Meggie?" Jim Mac asked.

"Can I take my pony?" Meggie not only smiled, she beat lightly on the table with her fist.

"Of course."

"I'll ride him, all the way to the Pacific Ocean!"

"Peter?"

"You're ignoring me!" Granny protested. Every head swiveled in her direction.

"We'd not thought, Mother," Mrs. MacIntyre said, "that you'd want to consider...particularly since Ira stays here and offers you a place."

"But I should have my yea or nay," Granny said. Everyone fell into respectful silence, waiting for her verdict.

"If what these men say is true—" she pointed at Godfroy and Sampson with a gnarled finger, and Matt had the ridiculous notion that she bewitched the truth out of them "—California is the earthly paradise. I turned fifty-nine last summer. Before I die, I should like to see the earthly paradise. If you go, I go." She silenced a chorus of protest with a wave of her hand. "How old are these mountain men who guide the emigrants across the plains?'' she asked Godfroy. ''Some as old as I?''

''More than one,'' Godfroy said. ''Some older, I think.''

''Then, I see no reason to stay in Indiana. Growing old will be easier in California, with no snow in winter.'' Jim Mac looked at his wife with distress; Pete grinned at Meggie. Granny's part in the expedition would be long debated, Matt thought. But come spring, Granny would be perched in the wagon as it headed out of Pikeston.

''May I give my answer now?'' asked Pete. Jim Mac nodded. ''Here there's dreadful competition, dozens of wagon builders between Fort Wayne and Indianapolis. In California, from what Godfroy says, men'll crowd my shop, for the natives build nothing but crude carts. Sampson's helping me design a wagon particularly for the trip across the plains, and Granny, I'll make one for you elegant as a palace, so well sprung, you'll think you ride in a steamboat to California.''

Sampson threw back his head and let out a whoop of approval. Godfroy smiled, but shot a worried glance in Granny's direction.

''You'll declare in public, you're going with us to California?'' Sampson asked, looking from Pete to Jim Mac.

''It's settled,'' Jim Mac said. ''Now, Tildy's turn. You'll join us! Walton can't follow you over two thousand miles of trail, for even Peter couldn't build a wagon sturdy enough to hold him.''

Tildy stared at her uncle, eyes wide and lips moving in frustrated speech. She turned to Godfroy and Sampson, accusing them with her eyes, then to her grandmother. ''Granny,'' she cried. ''You can't think to go! You'll die on the plains! You must come live with us, in town. Those people who suffered in the snow, the Donners, they tried to take an old lady along, and she died!''

''She was much older than I,'' Granny said. ''I read the papers too, you know.'' Matt felt rather than saw the similarity between the two women—the young and the old.

Not so much a physical resemblance...the same determination. The same wisdom, but at nineteen, not so developed in Tildy.

"When do we need to leave for Independence, Missouri?" Pete asked.

"No need to go to Independence," Sampson said. "That's the best-known jumping-off place, but from Indiana you waste days traveling so far south. Where's the map?" Jim Mac fetched a small pamphlet from the sitting room, and opened it to the center.

"See!" Sampson jabbed at the map. "Directly west from here lies St. Joe, on the Missouri River."

"Saint Joseph," Mrs. MacIntyre read, bending over the booklet.

"West through Springfield, Illinois," Godfroy said. "Cross the Mississippi at Hannibal." He did not glance at the book. He carries the map in his head, Matt thought. A map of the continent from Indiana to California.

Jim Mac offered the book to Granny, but she waved it away. She stood, and disappeared behind a curtain. Not the door leading to the pantry. Matt heard the faint sounds of her movements in the room beyond.

"What weapons do we need for the trip?" Pete asked eagerly. "A rifle, I suppose..."

Jim Mac laughed in Godfroy's direction. "For two years Peter's searched for a reason to buy a Colt's revolving pistol."

"Never used one," Godfroy admitted. "Matt, in the army you carried such a weapon?"

"A fine pistol. I bought one in Louisiana, to carry on my trip home." Matt braced himself for a request from Pete to buy the pistol. He did not want to sell it. Granny saved him from having to refuse in company by returning to the table carrying a small bag that glittered with embroidery and beads. She shoved her coffee cup to the center of the table, brushed the crumbs off the cloth without sitting down, so Matt got to his feet out of courtesy. She loosened the drawstring and carefully poured objects in a line across the cloth. Matt leaned forward, and saw she had laid out a trail of seeds, some large, some small, of different varieties of flowers, vegetables and trees. Granny sat down and studied the seeds. The family fell silent, their eyes on her. Mystified, Matt backed into the shadows.

"Each plant," Granny said to no one in particular, "has a place in this world. Some kill. Some cure. Some seem to be useless, but that's only because we're ignorant of their uses. This—" she pushed a dried berry at the head of the line "—comes from the cypress, and since we plant cypress trees near graves, you might suppose it stands for death. But in truth it's a seed of life, for cypress stops bleeding." She ran her finger the length of the line, her mouth pursed, her brow furrowed.

"Cypress trees grow in California," Sampson said.

"I thought as much. The berry fell from the bag first of all. The lemon and orange seeds, they came next, and they stand for fertility, because those trees bear fruit and flowers at the same time. And the golden seal, the most useful of plants, lies with them."

"So you say the trip will be fortunate?" Jim Mac asked, and Matt found no skepticism in his voice. Did the family believe this strange sort of fortune-telling?

"I say nothing of the trip. But whatever trouble we face, California will be worth the struggle." She swept the seeds into a pile at the edge of the table, then into the beaded bag. Once more she spilled them upon the cloth.

"Now we'll seek Tildy's future, for she's distressed and the unhappiness shows in her face. Too thin. But see, the seeds say nothing about a wedding. They show a productive life, but nothing of a husband."

"I'm to be an old maid?" Tildy asked. She laid a hand on her cheek, a dainty hand, and Matt remembered its softness and wished it lay on his face, not her own.

"You might or might not marry. Perhaps you haven't

yet met your husband. Perhaps he lives in California,'' Granny said mischievously.

"Me!" Meggie cried. "Read my future."

Granny once more poured the seeds in a practiced stream.

"Ah, there he is!" said Granny, pointing to a clump midway in the line. "You'll not marry this winter, but when you do, your husband will be a storekeeper."

"He will not! I'll never marry a boring storekeeper, and if Pa should try to force me, like Uncle Ira's doing, I'll run off to the army!" Everyone but Tildy laughed merrily.

Tildy stared at her hands, folded in resignation on the table. No, not resignation. Tildy's fingers closed tightly, until the ball of her hands was scarcely larger than a duck's egg. She lifted her head, and Matt saw not her green eyes, but the flames of the reflected candles. She stared at him, and the burning entered him, flowed through every vein.

*Resist your father and Mr. Walton, until the day I ask for you,* he wanted to cry. He concentrated on the thought, and hoped the message slid into the mind behind the dancing flames.

"Meggie, fetch a paper and pencil," Jim Mac said. "We'll start a list of things we need for the trip, things we must do over this winter, before we leave.... When do we leave, Godfroy?"

"March. To reach the Missouri before the end of April."

Matt leaned against the wall in the shadows, barely aware of the family's chatter. Tildy's hands had relaxed and now lay flat on the table. Perhaps they trembled slightly, but that might be the flickering of the candles.

The wagons, the mules, the bedding, the cookware. None of it to do with him, unless Tildy should be caught up in the excitement. Granny left the table, heading for the curtained door. Her fingers grasped the sleeve of his coat as she passed, and she drew him behind her. She lit a candle stub, illuminating a small room crowded with bundles of drying plants hanging from the ceiling. A bed filled one corner. Another lean-to, similar to the pantry, built against the sturdy log walls.

"Don't worry," she whispered. "You'll marry her, as your heart desires."

How did she know about his plans to marry Tildy? Had Godfroy talked out of turn?

His heart? His heart had nothing to do with his desire for Tildy, he told himself. He would take her as his wife to crush Ira MacIntyre's pride. To avenge himself for the blows from a blackthorn cane. To cement a new lawyer's position at the top of the township's society.

Granny eyed him from under furrowed brows. Did she fear he would seduce her granddaughter? Of course not. He had known from the first thought of her. Ira MacIntyre must know the moment when his daughter's flesh yielded to Matt Hull. Play out the ritual of the wedding night, with the bride's father aware...cruelly aware as he paced his carpeted floor, knowing he had no power to stop the insult of Hull sex pollinating the MacIntyre flower.

"She's poorly prepared to be a useful wife, I'm sorry to say. Her mother encourages fantasies of money and servants, and reads magazines from the East with city notions of a woman's duty. Even Tildy's sewing is a foolish waste of time and money. Flounces and fancy quilts! Patchwork is a great waste unless it uses such scraps as are in the house. Imagine buying new goods to cut up and rearrange into patterns!"

"Some of the quilts are quite beautiful," Matt protested.

"Be that as it may, patchwork wastes hours better spent on plain sewing and darning. I spoke to Tildy earlier this evening, told her she must train herself to wed a man of moderate means. I meant a young lawyer, but didn't say so directly, for right now Tildy would resent any suggestion that you'll be her husband."

"No fit husband for a lady," he said wryly.

Granny nodded, amused. "How do you enjoy reading law, Lieutenant Hull?"

"Fine. I'm reading Blackstone's *Commentaries,* four volumes." He laughed quietly. "I'd expected them to be dull as dishwater. But instead, every paragraph points like a sharp arrow to his meaning. Mr. Ridley forbids me to burn a candle or lamp in the office once he's gone home, so I snatch my reading in short bursts."

"Sup with us, and bring your Blackstone. Learning the law won't hurt anyone, man or woman. I'd like to hear you read this Blackstone aloud of an evening. Now, we'll join the others. If you would be so kind as to walk Tildy home, it would save Peter the trip."

## Chapter Seven

Tildy looked back toward the house, nervous at being alone with Lieutenant Hull. Perhaps Pete…but the light in the kitchen window faded as the last member of the family departed for bed.

"Good night," said Mr. Godfroy, and he and Mr. Sampson turned their horses onto the road to the river.

Lieutenant Hull would try to kiss her. When he stood in the shadows he had stared at her, and the tingling sensation remained on her shoulders, her breasts.

"Thank you for the writing book," Lieutenant Hull said. He pulled the gate shut and led her onto the road. For a few moments Tildy depended upon his guidance, until her eyes adjusted to the starlight. "I've written a letter to a friend of mine in Boston, and asked him to inquire after Afton Walton."

Matt Hull had friends in Boston? Impossible! Then she remembered the army, and the blue uniform, the epaulets he had worn on Harvest Home Sunday. And the glowing reflection of the gold on his cheeks.

"Thank you." He alone took sensible action to relieve her of Mr. Walton. Her friends commiserated; Pete had probably done something to Mr. Walton's gig that only made matters worse. Uncle Jim could think of nothing but California. Granny, instead of discussing the matter, had made her sit in the kitchen, among the cooking and cleaning, and practice casting on stitches to knit stockings. She had laughed when Tildy repeated her mother's opinion of knitting.

"Have you learned more of Mr. Walton's life?" Lieutenant Hull asked.

"He talks about a store, but when I ask what he sells, he says women don't understand." A shadow loomed ahead, and Lieutenant Hull stepped in front of her, his hand catching at hers. The shadow resolved into the old spotted dog that wandered from door to door, begging scraps. He sniffed at them, decided they had nothing to offer, and moved on. Lieutenant Hull again presented his elbow for her hand.

He did not wear gloves on this warm night. For an instant her fingers had traced the line of calluses across the top of his palm, and the suggestion of intimacy brought a faint shiver. His hands were warm, and gentle in their strength.

"I wanted to get some jimsonweed from Granny, and give Mr. Walton tea to make him crazy. But Granny said the frosts have cut the plants down, and she doesn't pick such a dangerous herb to dry for the winter."

Lieutenant Hull laughed, and laid his hand over hers. Rough, seductive in its warmth. She should have brought gloves. Ladies always wore gloves.

"Keep madness as a last resort. Some other young woman in Pikeston might be willing to accept Walton."

She opened her mouth to ask who, but they had rounded the corner, and the double pillars of the brick house reared up, white ghosts in the starlight.

"I'll walk by myself from here," she said, removing her hand from his arm, surprised at the sudden chill. Papa must never see them together. His anger already had the house in an uproar. It would be foolish to make it worse.

"Good night, then. I'll trail behind in the shadows, so you're not alone."

She waited for him to try to kiss her, but he stepped back. She hesitated for a few seconds, a few more, but he made no attempt to embrace her.

"Goodbye, then," she said. She turned and ran down the middle of the street, toward the lamp lighting her own door stoop. Why hadn't he tried to kiss her? He might at least have bent over, and let her have the pleasure of shoving him away.

The only light filtered down from the upstairs hall. Her mother must have gone visiting. She heard laughter, a high, girlish giggle, and a chortle Tildy did not recognize. Had her father brought company to meet Mr. Walton? She crept up the stairs, and as her head cleared the floor, she glimpsed the tableau through the rails of the banister. Esther sat on the edge of Mr. Walton's bed, her skirt pulled to her knees and her hands between them in the manner of a coachman heavily involved with his teams.

"Then those old horses, scared to the edge of death by that witch—" She swallowed the rest of the words in a burst of giggles, but demonstrated what she meant to say by somersaulting onto the floor, her skirts above her head. Mr. Walton roared.

"So you see," Esther gasped, untangling herself from her petticoats and climbing back onto the bed, "you ain't so bad off. You didn't break your head going ass over teakettle off the front of no stagecoach, and skin your hair off like you was scalped, being drug half a mile. Shall I rub more liniment on that bad place on your chest?"

"Yes." Mr. Walton flopped down, spread-eagled, his nightshirt unbuttoned to his breastbone. The tail of the garment lumped about his fat knees. Esther slid her hand in the open placket; her whole body undulated with the motion of her hand, massaging him gently.

"Am I pressing too hard?" she crooned, leaning over him. "That's a horrible bad place."

"It's much better. You're a good girl. Do you know how to make molasses candy?"

She made a sound halfway between a snort and a laugh. "Only fine ladies don't know molasses candy. I've made it for my brother and sisters."

Tildy backed down the stairs and lit the lamp in the sitting room. She unfolded the oak-leaf appliqué, but restlessly tossed it aside. If Granny's seeds told the truth, that she would be an old maid, she should learn to knit. Hats, mittens and shawls served more purpose than whole-cloth quilts and appliqué to be used only on special occasions.

Granny *was* right. Mama had told her the truth on the day Mr. Walton came, and she had not listened. No other suitable man lived in Pikeston, the entire township, for that matter. If Mr. Ridley had a son, he might come courting...there were prosperous men in Muncie, but none rode to visit her. She would end an old maid.

*If only I lived in the city. If only we had relatives in Virginia, like Mrs. Ridley! I could visit, and meet crowds of men.*

Uncle Freddie, her mother's brother? Richmond, Indiana? His tavern on the National Road made a fine living, Mama claimed. But would the prominent men of Richmond, the kind of man she meant to marry, pay attention to a tavern keeper's niece?

California? The Spanish had built towns there, and Mr. Godfroy and Mr. Sampson spoke of rich storekeepers and wealthy landowners. Tildy paced the length of the sitting room twice. She spread out the completed blocks of the oak-leaf quilt. If she went to California it would be of no use, for Mr. Godfroy made it clear, emigrants to the far West could take nothing but essentials.

"Sell everything," Mr. Sampson had said. "Money is of greater importance in California than gewgaws."

If she went to California, she would fold her new rose calico dress in the bottom of a trunk, so she had something decent to wear when they arrived. Who knew what great landowner might be waiting at Sutter's Fort, at the end of the trail? She would take her sewing basket, and ask her father to bring knitting needles from the store. Secretly, so Mama did not see.

Tildy wished she had someone to talk to. Too late to walk back to the farm and discuss this with Meggie or Granny. Rachel or Faith? But they might mention the conversation to other people, and the town gossip would circle back to her parents. She opened the front door, looked carefully up and down the street to make sure no one was walking out on a late errand. She ran to the square, hugged the building fronts, then slipped around the law office until she stood beneath the door to the attic.

"Lieutenant Hull," she called. The door swung open.

"Miss MacIntyre?" She heard the surprise in his voice. He twisted through the door, catching his toes on the boards that served for a ladder, and slid down like a squirrel coming down a tree. He made no noise when he hit the ground, and she saw he was in his stocking feet.

"What are you doing here?"

"I must talk to someone. I think...perhaps going to California with Uncle Jim would be best for me. I'll not marry Mr. Walton, under any circumstances, and in California I'll meet men of business and great farmers."

He lifted the latch and shoved her into the office, pushed her against the wall, his fingers tight on her shoulders. "California?"

"Here I haven't a chance of meeting a man of means," she said, trying to explain her problem while he held her in a very uncomfortable position. "Except Mr. Walton. But you heard what Mr. Sampson and Mr. Godfroy say, that emigration to California will grow larger every year, and the cities, too, and my acquaintances would be much wider—"

His hand covered her mouth. "You're mine," he whispered into her hair. "My wife. You'll marry me."

She stiffened. How silly she was to come to him for advice! If he knew she meant to go to California, he'd not help her get rid of Walton! She'd have to marry him, and for the rest of her life hear him sneer that she was a Hoosier, while he came from New England...a vision of his nightshirt caught up so high she had seen the thickness of his thighs, like tree trunks, and open disgustingly far at his neck, so Esther could...

"Did you send your sister to my house?"

"Yes."

"She'll seduce him!" she cried, understanding now. "You sent her so Papa might catch the two of them... together, and certainly he'd not ask me to marry—"

"Esther wants to marry Walton. Since you've rejected him, she supposes he's fair game for any woman."

The hand gently massaging Mr. Walton's chest, the hips sticking up in the air, waggling obscenely, and Mr. Walton's contented sigh. The cheap linsey-woolsey of Lieutenant Hull's vest scratched her palm. She jerked her hand away, shocked to find herself imitating Esther's motion.

"Before you decide for California, consider how fitted you are for such a trip. Will you wear sturdy boots and skirts hemmed up so they don't sweep the ground?

"I'll ride in the wagon," she said. "I won't need ugly boots—"

"You'll refuse to walk, even when the mules are tired, and the road steep? In camp, you'll let everyone else fetch water and wood? Can you cook over an open fire? Can you patch your own petticoats?"

"Many women have crossed the plains," she said, hurt by his accusations.

"Few, I wager, as helpless as you. Go home, or your father will discover you where you shouldn't be."

He caught her wrist before she was aware that she'd drawn back her arm, aiming for his mouth. She ran across the square without checking for late-night wanderers. She would show him! The lamp burned low in the empty sitting room. No one had filled it today. She wadded the oak-leaf appliqué into an untidy bundle, jammed it into her sewing basket.

She would show Lieutenant Hull what a woman could do! She could learn all the things she didn't know and go to California!

Matt stood in front of the church, watching the Mac-Intyre family parade across the square in their Sunday best, Mrs. MacIntyre plump and petite in black silk, on her husband's arm; Tildy, poker-faced, bright as spring in rose-colored calico. She walked beside Mr. Walton, but did not take his arm. She gave Matt one sidelong glance, then looked away. Behind marched the three boys, Josh and Lewis gangly in new growth, Eddie still a child. Behind them trailed Esther, wearing a gown of faded blue, and carrying a bottle and a tin box. Matt fell in beside his sister.

"After the service, meet me at the law office," he whispered.

Esther nodded. "Got news for you," she said, smiling broadly.

Mrs. MacIntyre stopped in the rear of the church. "You will sit here, Esther."

Mr. Walton shook his head. "I need her beside me," he said with a grandness that eclipsed Mrs. MacIntyre. Esther stepped to Walton's side and marched down the aisle, her head high. The family milled about to determine the seating arrangements. Finally, Esther took her seat on one side of Mr. Walton, with Tildy on the other. Tildy managed to leave a space of several inches between them.

*Esther's done very well,* Matt thought, greatly amused. And Tildy would furnish every opportunity for the serving girl to wiggle her way into Walton's heart.

A bustle at a side door heralded the arrival of Reverend Fitch. Matt left before the preacher saw him. He dared not waste a bright day that offered hours for study. He settled on the bench by the front window, Blackstone propped on his knee.

Faith scurried toward the church, herding her unwilling brothers. At the bottom of the steps the two eldest managed to evade her grasp. They ran across the square and took refuge behind the livery stable, leaving her to push the two youngest, protesting and crying, up the stairs. Rachel and Mr. Ridley appeared, and waited in front of the church to greet Jim Mac and his family, whose wagon had just rounded the corner. Matt turned his eyes to Blackstone.

*Law is a rule of civil conduct prescribed by the supreme power in a state, commanding what is right and what is wrong.* He sank to the floor, his back against the bench, the heavy volume resting on his chest. *It is necessary to have recourse to reason to discover what the law of nature directs in every circumstance of life.*

And the lawyer is the instrument of that reason, Matt thought. The lawyer and the court. He had known that lawyers wrote out deeds and wills, that they represented people charged with crimes. But he had never before considered the importance of the law to society, and the responsibilities of the men who applied it. Right and wrong. The whole foundation of civilization, and it lay within this book. He turned one page, and the next.

"Brother?" Matt sprang to his feet, found Esther standing over him. He had not even heard the door open. "I don't have time to chatter. Afton says his back hurts from sitting so long on that hard bench, and wants a rub." She smirked.

"Afton?" he asked. "What do you know of Walton that you call him by his Christian name?"

"I know no woman ever flirted with him before, or called him Afton, or cared enough to tend his hurts. His uncle's driving a carriage out after dinner to take him home to Muncie, and—" she tossed her head "—I'm going with him, for he's not well." She leaned closer. "'The nursing only a gentle woman can provide,' that's what Afton said to Mr. MacIntyre."

"Mr. MacIntyre's loath to let you go?" he asked facetiously.

Esther laughed. "Old MacIntyre has fretted his fingers raw on his vest pockets because I'm in his house. He's only let me bide because Afton insists. Old MacIntyre's ruled by anything Afton wants, for fear he'll go home to Massachusetts and not marry his useless daughter."

"Tildy's useless?" Matt asked, then wished he could retract the question. He did not want to hear his sister's opinion of Tildy.

"Yesterday she came to me with her knitting, a mess because she didn't know the difference between a knit and a purl, and doesn't see when she drops a stitch. And she stood by with paper and pencil while I made Afton's molasses candy. She knows nothing of cookery, and must write down what she sees, or she forgets. A mind like a sieve. Now, I got to go," she said.

"Esther, has Walton asked you to come into his bed?"

"No, but he quite probably will, once we're out of MacIntyre's house."

"*Don't*. Until he offers marriage, nothing but the most chaste kiss."

"Is that what you offer me? A chaste kiss!" Tildy stepped into the room, removed her rose satin bonnet and swung it about as a boy would twirl a sling. "Mama asked me to find you, Esther, and tell you she needs you at the house. Mr. Moffett's expected directly."

"I'll say goodbye to my brother as I please," pouted Esther.

"Then say goodbye, and be done with it."

Esther snatched up the bottle and tin box she had put on the table, and walked to the door, slowly, to show her disgust with her young mistress.

"So Esther expects to marry Mr. Walton," Tildy said.

"Are all Emma Callom's children ambitious to marry above their station?"

"I believe so."

"You need do nothing more in the matter of Mr. Walton," she continued loftily. "He's leaving the house, and I expect Papa to forget the entire matter, because Mr. Walton's been a difficult guest. And in case Papa shouldn't forget, I'll go to California with Uncle Jim."

"You're sewing a wedding quilt?"

"I was. Granny told me to give it up, that appliqué's nothing but nonsense, and I've packed it away, because I can't take such a thing to California."

"Finish it. You'll need it before another year's gone by."

"You? Or Mr. Walton?" she mocked.

"Me. When did your father build the brick house?"

"What?" she asked. She caught at the back of a chair, and Matt decided she was not quite so confident as she pretended.

"When did your father build the brick house? I remember the masons laying the walls, but when?"

"Before I remember, when I was quite small. Two, perhaps three years old. Why should you want to know that?"

Matt shrugged his shoulders. "Curious to know when your father's business became so prosperous."

"I remember now, the summer Josh was born."

"And he is...?"

"He just turned sixteen. Why should it concern you?"

"Because knowing these things makes you my wife. I pile up little facts, each one so simple it means nothing by itself, but in the end, because of them, your father will be my father-in-law." He stepped toward her, offering his hand; she backed away, her eyes cautious.

He lusted after her. Granny's private words had released the specter of sex, an impulse he had thought shut away in a closed place in his mind. He burned for her, kisses, caresses, and the extreme of intimacy. He dropped his hand, stepped back. He must resist, so Ira MacIntyre suffered when it happened. But the pink across her cheeks...he wished to stroke....

"Godfroyyyyy!" The high-pitched yell came from the square, and Matt dashed to the front window, his heart clogging his throat. Mrs. Ridley!

"You come out, Trail Godfroy!" she shrieked. "Come out, you dirty bastard!"

Matt flung open the door, hurled himself down the boardwalk, abandoning Tildy to her own devices. Thank heavens for Mrs. Ridley! She was making a spectacle of herself, but she had saved him from a dreadful mistake.

Curious men circled Mrs. Ridley, but no one came too near, for she held a rifle pointed in the general direction of the tavern door. The rifle wavered whenever she swayed, and the crowd surged one way, then another, to avoid the gun. Like water in a jostled basin.

"I know you're in there, Trail Godfroy," Mrs. Ridley cried. "You can't escape. I'm not leaving you alive, telling folks that my dear girl is your bastard!"

Matt pushed into the crowd, stepping on toes and jamming his elbows into ribs, asking the pardon of men without looking at them, because he kept his eyes on Mrs. Ridley. *Stay behind her.*

"Come out, Trail!" Drunk as she was, she might shoot the first man who walked through the door. "Come out, or I'll come in!" Mrs. Ridley took three tenuous steps toward the door.

"Get out of the way, you men, for it's only Trail Godfroy I'm killing," she said in surprisingly level tones. "He claims he seduced my dear sister Belle, and that Rachel's his child, and he'll carry her off to California. I'll kill the liar!" She reached the door, swung the rifle from side to side as she peered into the dim interior. Matt crouched, then sprang at her as she turned her head away from him, but instead of Mrs. Ridley, he collided with three men who were crawling out the tavern's only window. He rolled in the dust.

"Grab her!" he yelled. "Someone grab her, for God's

sake!'' He untangled himself from the knot of legs and arms, crawled in her direction, heard the blast of the rifle when her dark skirt was still five or six feet away. He lunged, grabbed at her petticoats. She struggled so violently he felt and heard the fabric rip. He grabbed again, caught an ankle.

"I killed him! I killed Godfroy!'' she cried as she teetered. Mrs. Ridley and the rifle thumped on top of him. The smell of whiskey sickened him. She reeked, as if she had used the stuff as cologne. "I killed him,'' she muttered, and Matt prayed she was wrong.

His prayers were answered. Godfroy stood over them, reached down, pried the rifle from Mrs. Ridley's fingers. The crowd, seeing the danger ended, rushed in, so close that a foot kicked Matt's shoulder. He loosened his grip on Mrs. Ridley, got to his knees and searched for a way through the wall of men. Mrs. Ridley tried to get to her feet, but fell again, this time sitting on the ground, her skirts up, her bare legs stretched in front of her. She stared at Godfroy.

"The ball went through the roof,'' Godfroy said. "No one's hurt.''

"Is this true, Godfroy?'' someone in the crowd yelled. "What she says? You fathered Rachel Ridley?'' A threat behind the question? Matt gave up trying to bull his way through the crowd and looked back at Godfroy with concern.

Godfroy glared at the crowd, swinging his head from side to side, his lips pulled back, his teeth clenched. He held the empty rifle by the barrel, as a club.

"Yes, it's true. Barman was no man. He couldn't bed a woman, and Belle came to me. I meant to take her and the babe to the Rockies, but Belle died.''

Men on the fringe of the group nodded. A few went back into the tavern. Godfroy seemed capable of handling the situation himself. Mrs. Ridley groaned and doubled up so her head touched her bare knees.

Where in hell was Ridley? If he didn't turn up soon,

Mrs. Ridley was his responsibility. Matt gritted his teeth, got to his feet, clasped her arm and pulled her up.

"It's time you went home," he said. Where in the devil did the woman find whiskey, when both she and her husband claimed to be temperance? *Hector Hull,* sneered an inner voice. She must have a quiet arrangement with his own father.

Matt pushed Mrs. Ridley ahead of him, steering her with a hand wrapped about the back of her neck. Someone materialized at her side, and Matt shook his head to clear the dust from his eyes. Rachel took her aunt's hand, guided her. He took his hand away.

"Come, Aunt Caroline," Rachel said, as one would speak to a child in a temper. "We must go home, for Uncle will be there soon, expecting his Sunday dinner. I'll wash your face and hands with lavender water." Rachel turned to Matt. "She's fine now. She'll come with me." He trailed behind, an unnecessary guarding, for the two women made their way slowly down the middle of the street, between lines of curious onlookers.

Mrs. Ridley had exposed her secret sin. The whole town now knew she drank, and she had revealed Belle Barman's adultery, and Trail Godfroy's seduction of a white woman. The girl they called Rachel Ridley, whom they treated with the respect due the daughter of a legislator, had been fathered by a French-Indian fur trapper.

Rachel and her aunt turned into their own dooryard, and Matt retreated to the office. Empty! Thank heavens Tildy had gone home. He retrieved Blackstone from the floor, pushed a chair into its proper position at the table and wondered if he should sweep and straighten a bit, to have it done for Monday morning.

"Good, you're here!" Ridley exclaimed, bouncing in the alley door. "We have business tomorrow, for Jake Sales and Bill Richie are at sword's point about a calf that disappeared, and I met with Sales and believe he's ready to enlist the services of the law." Sales lived more than a mile out of town. Ridley was obviously not aware of his wife's performance in front of the tavern. "Don't be off tonight, by the way. I need you at my house."

Something to be done at Ridley's house? Wasn't it enough that he kept the office clean, and blacked the stove, and rescued drunken Mrs. Ridley?

"Tonight's Holy Eve," Ridley said, as if that explained his need. "October 31st."

"And?"

"You'll guard my outhouse. Last year a gang of boys tipped it over. Find a sturdy cudgel, or a whip, and drive them off. But not a pistol. No bloodshed. Be there at dusk."

No fine supper at Jim Mac's, no reading the section of Blackstone on the laws relating to the rights of individuals. "Yes, sir. Sir, Mrs. Ridley came to...the tavern while you talked to Sales, and she said things I believe you meant to keep private."

Ridley sat down heavily. "Where does she get it? Rachel and I searched every cubbyhole in the house, and concluded we'd found all the whiskey she had hidden." He dropped his head in his hands and spoke to the floor. "Whenever she's upset or worried...she can't bear uncertainty, to lose hope...this is the worst it's ever been. Damn Godfroy!"

"Rachel took her home, calmed her."

"Do you remember bringing Rachel here? She was a tiny thing, and you not more than six or seven."

"Yes, sir. I remember."

"Did you guess my wife's weakness then?"

"Not then, but later. After I'd gone to the army."

"She'd been in the family way. The only time in all our marriage when the natural order of things...and the babe came at six months, a boy, dead of course. And that's when it started. God knows where it'll end."

# Chapter Eight

Matt sculpted a length of firewood with the ax, a thick club with one end shaped to fit his hand. He trudged, supperless, to take his position behind Ridley's house, half amused, half annoyed. Through uncounted centuries boys had tipped over privies on Hallowe'en, and they would do so for centuries to come. And the citizens who complained the loudest about vagrancy and vandalism, they had tipped over privies in their youth. They'd probably been the worst.

He tucked himself into a clump of leafless lilac bushes and watched the stars come out. The moon hung in the western sky, a narrow sickle, and it slid down, pulling the evening star with it. A few thin clouds stretched from horizon to horizon, perhaps heralding a change in the weather. He regretted the end of Indian summer, but November arrived tomorrow, and no sane man could expect winter to hold off much longer. Matt thought of the roll of heavy wool in MacIntyre's store, and Faith's offer to make him a coat. Soon. The sooner the better.

Shouts echoed somewhere north of the square. Perhaps another man had kept watch and seized the gang of boys. If so, Ridley's outhouse was safe for this year. Matt hugged his shoulders against the chill, and waited. The clouds thickened in the west, and the streamers of mist became solid, blotting out the wheeling constellations. How much longer must he wait, cold? And now that he thought about it, hungry?

A sniff. Matt tensed. Someone else felt the cold, and that person stood quite nearby. The smallest shuffle in dry leaves in the neighboring yard. Three figures crept near the lilac, the fallen leaves crunching faintly beneath their feet. The boys had been smart enough to don moccasins for their clandestine work. For a moment the three boys stood very still and examined Ridley's dark house. The tallest gestured in the direction of the outhouse, and with exaggerated stealth, they rounded the lilac bush. Matt rose to his feet, the cudgel at the ready.

"Do you have business with Mr. Ridley?" he asked.

The tall boy drew in his breath with a squeal that became a scream, spun about and started to run back the way he had come. His foot caught on a new sprout the lilac had sent out over the summer. He sprawled on the ground. "Oompf!"

His companions paid no attention, but streaked down the side yard, toward the street. The boy on the ground slowly got to his hands and knees, but with one well-placed kick, Matt tipped him onto his back. He shoved an ankle against the ground with his boot. The face of Josh MacIntyre, scared, panting, reflected the starlight.

"Is this being neighborly? How would your mother feel tomorrow morning, to find her outhouse tipped over?"

"Can't. It's brick," he said as he recovered his breath. Josh scooted backward to shake off the weight of Matt's boot, but gave up after a few seconds. "If you hurt me, Pa'll call the sheriff and have you hauled to the jail in Muncie."

"Undoubtedly. And tipping over privies? That deserves no punishment?"

"We don't do no harm. Except last year, when we didn't know one of the Tole boys was inside when it went over."

"Who's there? Who're you talking to, Hull?" Ridley called.

"A trespasser. Would you care to come and identify him?"

"No!" Josh cried, struggling again at the weight on his ankle. He sat up and grabbed Matt's leg; Matt shoved the cudgel into his chest and pushed him down. Ridley opened the shutter of a lantern to illuminate the boy's face. "Josh MacIntyre!" Josh closed his eyes and twisted away from the light. "I'd thought so. Your father will hear about this in the morning, and—"

A thud, the report of a cannon. Enemy fire, and quite close by. By the time Matt had the sense to consider where he was, that no artillery company could possibly be attacking Pikeston, he found he had backed into the shelter of the lilacs, his boot far from Josh's ankle. He sorted out the loud noise from across the street, and concluded—amazing!—that what he heard was the roar of tumbling masonry. Ridley lifted the lantern, futilely attempting to penetrate the distant darkness.

"I believe," Matt said, addressing Josh, who still lay on the ground, frightened and resigned, "that some boy in town has solved the problem of bringing down a brick shithouse."

Tildy. He snatched the lantern. Tildy! What if Tildy was in the outhouse? He plunged toward the labyrinth of sheds and pens. Josh pounded beside him. The boy had overcome his terrorized paralysis.

"Wait!" cried Ridley. Matt skidded to a stop in automatic obedience to the voice of authority. "No need to hang on to Josh. I'll speak to his father tomorrow, and the families who lost their privies. They might want to sue."

Tildy *must* be in bed at this hour. No self-respecting woman would be in the privy in the middle of the night. Women of the MacIntyre family had chamber pots. Matt sagged against a fence, ashamed of his unreasonable panic. Ridley reclaimed his lantern, and Matt followed him back to the house, glad for the darkness that hid what must be his very red face.

"A cup of tea?" Ridley asked. "To take away the chill?"

"Yes," Matt agreed, aware now that he could barely feel his hands and feet.

Rachel welcomed them. She was completely dressed, so must have waited with her uncle for the Hallowe'en attack. A kettle simmered on the back of the range, and she lifted it over the fire to renew the boil.

"I'd better check on my wife," Ridley said.

"Sit down," Rachel said after her uncle left the room. "Thank you for rescuing Aunt Caroline. I didn't have a chance to thank you before."

"No need. Any man—"

"No, not any man. All the other men stood about, enjoying the spectacle of Aunt Caroline far gone with drink. She asks them to sign a pledge of temperance, she has signed one herself, but when trouble comes..." Rachel's voice faded, and Matt had the impression that her words dissipated like the steam of the kettle. "You heard what she said?" she whispered.

"Yes."

"Aunt Caroline assures me that Mr. Godfroy's lying, and I pretend to agree with her, but I know he's telling the truth. He's my father. Aunt Caroline, more than once, said my mother didn't want to marry Mr. Barman. The family forced her to it." Rachel spread her hands on the table. "Look at my hands! No one in my family has hands like mine." Long and narrow. Matt thought of Godfroy's long nimble fingers, skinning a deer, carefully preparing the tinder to receive the spark of flint and steel.

"Deep in my heart I've known, forever. I try to do what Aunt Caroline says is proper, try very hard do behave as she and Uncle expect, but my wild soul envies Meggie, that she can be so daring." She pulled her hands into her lap. "He wants me to go to California with him."

"I know. He told me."

"And my heart, my spirit says go, but I can't forsake Aunt Caroline, who has been a mother—" Mr. Ridley appeared. Rachel rose, and her long, agile hands lifted the kettle and poured the water into the teapot in a steady stream. The lamplight cast shadows across her face, and Matt saw the profile of Trail Godfroy, feminized. The blood of old Chief François Godfroy of the Miamis, whose coureur de bois father claimed descent from the French king of Jerusalem. A princess. From both races, a noble woman.

Matt gulped his tea, pointed at the clock to explain his departure. At the corner of the square he stopped under the protection of an ancient maple tree, listened to the silence of Pikeston. Rather than cross the square, he detoured to the passage between the school and the livery barn. Ira MacIntyre's extensive property reached all the way to the pens behind the barn. Fifty feet beyond stood the ruined privy. The wall that faced the livery had collapsed, bringing the roof down on one side. The MacIntyres' chicken coop stood between the house and the privy, furnishing concealment to any vandal who wanted to dig under the foundation, lay a charge and string a short length of fuse. Hidden behind the coop, he might have prepared the charge in daylight. Matt's boot kicked an oblong shape that shone in the failing light. A jackknife, open. He closed the blade, dropped it in his pocket.

His hands slipped on the crude ladder as he climbed to his loft. Fatigue, when it finally came, descended with the swiftness of a hawk. He did nothing more than pull off his boots before he crawled under his blankets. The jackknife pressed uncomfortably when he shifted onto his right hip. He wiggled, finally drew it from his pocket and tossed it on the floor at the head of his bed.

Matt carefully wrote out the charges Mr. Sales leveled against Mr. Richie. Richie had tempted a Sales calf into a cornfield by lowering the rails, then slaughtered the animal. Matt eyed the dinner basket Faith placed on the corner of the table, decided he should finish copying the statements of witnesses before he ate his dinner. Nearly done, only one last long paragraph...the crash of the door...his jolted pen...an inhuman roar. Two words blotted! Damn!

The curse caught in his throat. Ira MacIntyre stood before the open door, glaring at Ridley, pointing at Matt with an arm that seemed, from Matt's perspective, six feet long.

"Ridley, get rid of him! He's to leave town and stay out, or I'll get men together to run him out!"

"Can't spare him," Ridley said laconically, leaning back in his chair and swinging his feet onto a bench.

"The whole town can spare him! Since he's come, Mr. Walton's gig fell apart, my shed—a well-built shed—tumbled in a wind hardly more than a breeze, and now, my privy, blown to bits."

Ridley made no response to these charges, but smiled slightly and drew a small knife from his desk. He began paring his nails. MacIntyre's arm dropped to his side, his fingers curled into fists, and Matt decided it was time he spoke in his own defense.

"We heard the explosion clearly, Mr. Ridley and I, because we were outdoors, behind his house, questioning Josh about his intentions toward the Ridley privy."

"That's a damn lie!" MacIntyre said. "Josh and his brothers were home, as any boys should be at midnight. You—" he shook his fist in Matt's direction "—set the powder under the privy. Who else in town knows how to lay a charge to bring down a building? Who but an army man?"

"Any man who's blown a stump," offered Ridley with exaggerated calm.

"He's to get out of town!" MacIntyre yelled. "No one wants him here. Camp down by the river with that scoundrel mountain man and half-breed Godfroy, that's where you belong."

The man's face twisted, his nostrils flared. His voice sputtered along the edge of self-control. Why did MacIntyre hate him so much? He did not suspect the paper in the attic, the lines from Major Linder's diary that convicted him of horse stealing, if not murder. Matt Hull had never chased Ira MacIntyre with a stick, or beat him on the shoulders and called him a bastard.

There was no reasoning with a man in such a temper, Matt knew. He looked at Ridley for help, found him so relaxed he might be napping. Ridley was hinting, Matt realized. Stay calm. Matt dipped his pen in the ink and laid a finger on the line he was to resume copying. He scratched out the two blotted words, crudely, for the muscles of his arm remained tense.

"Ira," Ridley said softly. "Lieutenant Hull caught Josh and his brothers behind my house last midnight. Josh admitted to being the author of the outhouse destruction of last year."

"You forced him to speak," MacIntyre said, but with less certainty.

"So you admit he wasn't at home," Ridley said, showing too much pleasure at catching MacIntyre in a misstatement. "You've been too easy on the boys, Ira, pulling them out of scrapes, so they think anything's permitted to a MacIntyre."

"That's a damn foul lie!" MacIntyre shouted, newly aroused to anger by the need to defend his sons. "Other boys in town are jealous, they spread accusations, to shift the blame from their own shoulders."

"Lieutenant Hull spent the evening in my yard, at my request, and we were together when your privy went sky-high."

"He set the charge earlier, then skulked through the back lots to light the fuse," MacIntyre said, his arms swinging about as wildly as his voice. "Hull wasn't at church yesterday morning, like a Christian should be, and my whole household attended, so no one would see...."

So that was how it had been done! Matt thought. The blacksmith's elder sons escaped their sister just before the services, and the MacIntyres had already entered the church. Until Pete replaced the shed behind the store, the cask of powder sat under the eaves. A very tempting sight! No trouble for an enterprising boy to scoop up a sackful. Two nearly grown boys could make quick work of digging a hole under the privy foundation. Only one boy need slip out a window to light the fuse at midnight. If he used slow fuse, he might have been home in bed before the charge blew.

Revenge, for the younger brother trapped last year in a toppled privy. Perhaps for Josh MacIntyre's bullying? For the pressure Ira MacIntyre brought on Tole to cease feeding Matt Hull? Ira MacIntyre's tyranny had gone on too long.

Matt turned his head just far enough to see the man from the corner of his eye. Why? What was the source of MacIntyre's fury? He flung down the pen and pushed his chair away from the table with a rasp that sounded much like the warning rattle of a snake. MacIntyre jumped a trifle, giving Matt the opportunity to take two long steps unopposed, to push his nose within twelve inches of MacIntyre's.

"Why the hell do you hate me? What have I ever done to you?" Matt felt his right hand closing into a fist, and he forced it open. No violence.

"You're alive, God damn you!" MacIntyre shouted.

"So's every man out there," Matt said, lowering his voice to ease his own tension, gesturing out the open door to the crowd drawn by MacIntyre's shouts. "Alive and breathing. Do you hate them?"

MacIntyre swung. Matt ducked just in time, managed to grab MacIntyre's wrist before he could recover and aim another blow. Ridley dropped his languid pose, sprang to his feet and grabbed MacIntyre by the shoulders.

"Let's go to the tavern, Ira," Ridley said. "Let's have

a drink together and use calm reason to figure out who blew up your privy. Maybe some of these men out there have a notion, for it's not everyone who has powder and fuse handy...." He led MacIntyre with an arm laid gently across his shoulders.

Matt considered following them to the tavern and confronting Ira MacIntyre with his question a second time. After one breath he thought better of it. Let the men beyond the window see Matt Hull lawyerlike, unruffled and secure. He reseated himself at the table, picked up the pen, but didn't bother to wet the nib. So easy to pull MacIntyre down, like boys playing king of the hill. MacIntyre had made no friends among townsfolk or farmers by flaunting the money he made in the store. On the contrary, they resented his wealth, accused him of inflating his prices. Josh, Lewis and Edward made enemies among boys who were just edging toward manhood; MacIntyre's insistence that Tildy marry Walton alienated his brother and mother. Ira MacIntyre stood alone, and did not yet know it. When Matt Hull finally spoke, no defenders would come forward.

Matt imagined stepping idly into the tavern one spring night. He would bring up the topic of Barman's disappearance, casually reveal what he knew, and the rumor would flow out faster than water over a wheel. Ira MacIntyre, a thief and a murderer. With only a bit more information—the information a lawyer could gather—MacIntyre might be arrested and hauled off to Jefferson County, to stand trial for killing Barman.

Then again, Matt mused, he could visit MacIntyre privately, late at night, lay out what he knew and name his price for silence. Tildy.

The barest thought of Tildy brought a flush of anticipation and a heat that warmed his jangled nerves. He dipped the pen in the ink, and set about finishing the witness statements, conforming as much as possible to the model handwriting in Tildy's book. His laid his fingers on the book and imagined her warmth emanating from the pages. He leaned over, sniffed. Yes, a bit of scent. Rose, perhaps?

After eating his cold dinner he climbed to the loft and found the knife he had so carelessly tossed aside. The owner had scratched his initials in the brass handle. K.T. Christopher Tole, the eldest boy, who was called Kit. Matt piled his dinner dishes in the basket, strolled around the corner and paused briefly before the wide-open door of the forge. The blacksmith hammered iron into shape, gestured to the boy who leaned against the wall. Kit flung himself upon the huge bellows and the fire flared.

Matt walked on to the house, to the kitchen garden, where Faith knelt, picking pods of dried beans from almost leafless bushes.

"Thank you," she said, jumping up. "There's no need for you to interrupt your work to bring the dishes back."

He handed her the basket with one hand, the knife with the other. "Tell your father to take down the coil of slow match hanging on his back wall. Put it out of sight. I'll give MacIntyre money to cover the cost of wool for my coat. You pick it up next time you're at the store."

He walked down the street, jingling silver in his pocket. He whistled as he entered the general store. Two men played checkers on top of a barrel, and two more hung over their shoulders, watching the game. They stared at him, then at MacIntyre behind the counter. The game stopped as they waited for the fireworks.

Matt bowed his head politely, as if addressing a superior. "One tin candlestick, please."

"Candles?" MacIntyre asked, gruff and ill at ease.

"No, I'll buy dips from one of the ladies about." He pointed to the roll of gray wool. "Six yards, and wrap it for Miss Tole, who'll pick it up next time she calls."

He turned to the men in the corner. He made his voice hearty, curious. "You know, I've been gone four years. Has any news of Hiram Barman ever come? I always wondered what happened to him."

From the corner of his eye he saw MacIntyre freeze, the bolt of wool halfway between shelf and counter. Fear and astonishment fought with his resolve to remain unmoved. He slammed the fabric on the counter.

"How much did you say?" The words were so strangled Matt barely heard them.

"Six yards. Beautiful weather, lucky the clouds of last night passed without wind or rain. But we can't count on it lasting, for today's November 1st." He waited to grin until he passed the tavern. Verification of all he suspected. Not the sort of evidence to stand up in court. But that would come, with a lawyer's steady investigation.

Tildy stirred on the bare, uncomfortable settee, the best seat in the Toles' front room. When the sewing circle met at Faith's house, her bottom hurt within an hour. But a lady did not insult a friend by bringing a cushion from home. Tildy remembered there would be no settees, even bare wooden ones, on the road to California. Was she too fine a lady to make the trip? She hated to think that Lieutenant Hull might be right.

"You're not working on a quilt today?" asked Faith, eyeing the muslin in Tildy's lap.

"No. I need aprons." She did not elaborate, dared not elaborate, but the frilly aprons her mother selected for her would certainly not be suitable on a trip to California. To her relief, neither Rachel nor Faith seemed to find it unusual that she should be making plain aprons.

"Rachel, what's this about Trail Godfroy claiming to be your pa?" Meggie exclaimed from the door. She dropped a basket on the floor and spilled a cascade of miscellaneous scraps. Tildy dropped the apron string with a stitch half complete. Faith's needle tangled within the folds of a thick seam. Only Rachel continued her tiny stitches; the ticking of the clock on a high shelf filled the room, and Tildy held her breath.

"My mother did not want to marry Mr. Barman," began

Rachel, speaking softly but firmly, "but when her father died the family insisted, for he was the only man who'd asked her. A year later she met Mr. Godfroy, while she walked along the river, and they fell in love."

Meggie sighed and began sorting her scraps. Tildy arranged the strips of muslin in a neat pattern on her lap. A woman caught in a loveless marriage, a man who carried her memory in his heart for eighteen years. The possibilities hung in the air, almost visible. Tildy imagined herself mistress of a fine house in Muncie, married to repulsive Mr. Walton. A dinner party assembled at her polished mahogany table. One of the guests, a tall gentleman remarkably like Lieutenant Hull, bowed over her fingers.

She picked up the apron string and her needle with steady hands, certain now. She had no choice. Adultery was a fearful sin, and marriage to Mr. Walton would make it inevitable. Someday she would fall in love.

"How cruel," Meggie said, "to force your mother to marry a man she hated."

"I don't know that she hated him. At the time it seemed the only solution," Rachel said with practical acceptance. "No one in the family felt they could take her in, although, in the end, Aunt Caroline gave Mother shelter...and me. I'm most grateful."

"Perhaps," Faith said, "it's not true. Perhaps Godfroy made up the whole story. Being alone in the mountains for months on end, that can touch a man's mind, and he starts believing his fantasies."

Rachel shook her head violently. "No, something inside me always knew the truth, even before Mr. Godfroy told us. Tildy, remember how I admired the feathered star patchwork your mother brought from Muncie? I wanted to borrow the pattern, although it's very difficult, and everyone said—"

"I don't see what that has to do with Mr. Godfroy," Tildy said.

"Mr. Godfroy told me, the night I was born, a great

fireball hung in the sky, a star with a tail like a feather. He wanted my name to be Falling Star, or something like that in the language of the Miamis, but of course Mother couldn't give me an Indian name, for if Aunt Caroline should guess I wasn't Mr. Barman's child...she'd order her out of the house if she knew the truth.''

"Pshaw!" said Meggie. "Just because he saw a star, and you like star patchwork—'' she shook out a rather crumpled, unbalanced nine-patch "—doesn't prove a thing. I like mother's Queen Charlotte's Crown quilt, but that doesn't mean a bandit stole me from the nursery of the queen of England, or that my name's Charlotte.''

"The star seemed to be me," Rachel said, her face and voice troubled, and Tildy thought it cruel of Meggie to mock her. "Or me as I'd like to be. Not living in hard lines, like inside a fence, but running off about the edges. Daring to do, well, the things you do, Meggie.''

"Will you go to California?" Meggie asked eagerly. "Pa has said most definitely, we're leaving in March.''

"I'd like to. To see the prairies and the mountains that Mr. Godfroy loves! But Aunt Caroline would take it dreadfully hard. She's...she's not well.''

Tildy came within a thread's width of saying, "I'm going to California." She forced the words to stay in her throat. Sturdy boots, cooking over a campfire. Perhaps that life would not suit her. Besides, she dared not mention the possibility to anyone in town. It must be a total surprise to Mama and Papa when, on the morning in March, she stuffed her bundle in Uncle Jim's wagon and climbed in after it. No one must know her intentions, or they would try to stop her.

"I expected you to be working on your oak-leaf appliqué, Tildy," Faith said.

"I've no need of a wedding quilt," Tildy replied. To finish the oak-leaf appliqué seemed to make marriage to Mr. Walton a certainty.

"Your father told my father the matter was settled,"
Faith pressed onward. "You and Mr. Walton, I mean."

"My father's mistaken." She looked from Meggie to
Faith to Rachel, asking for their belief, and support. "I
*will not* marry Mr. Walton. I don't love him. I'd never
learn to love him. After what Rachel's told us, about her
mother, would any of us marry a man we didn't love?"

"I'll never marry, whether I fall in love or not," Faith
said, jabbing her needle into the wool with great force.
"There's nothing in marriage for a woman but hard work
and grief. After the boys leave home, I'll keep house for
my father, and be a quiet old maid."

"I intend to marry a man like Mr. Sampson," Meggie
said. "A man who'll take me to the mountains, and we'll
have great adventures."

"Is that why he's about your house so much? Courting
you?" Faith asked.

"No." Meggie shook her head and dropped the nine-
patch on the floor. "Mr. Sampson confessed, he has an
Indian wife and three children in the Rocky Mountains.
He'll find them as we pass through next summer, and take
them on to California."

"I'll marry only for love," Rachel said. "Wherever I
am, here or in California, I'll never marry except in a
*grand passion.*" Her emphasis upon the final two words
made everyone laugh, even Rachel. Tildy knew all eyes
had turned to her, expecting her thoughts on marriage. She
concentrated on making neat stitches.

"Come, Tildy," Meggie begged. "Tell us what husband
you intend to catch."

"I don't know," she choked. "I'd counted on Mr. Walton being tall and handsome, rather like I—rather like his
uncle. I thought he would be pleasant and gracious, a real
gentleman, and that I'd fall in love the moment we met."

"Love at first sight?" Faith asked, sarcastic. "I think
you put too much faith in the silly stories printed in *Godey's.* Getting a husband doesn't solve a woman's problems.

Look around you. Who laughs and flirts at dances? Women without husbands! Marry, and the burdens come piling!''

Tildy walked home slowly, swinging the sewing bag that concealed the muslin aprons from prying eyes. If her father had told Mr. Tole the matter was settled…her only chance lay in postponing the wedding. Could she put Mr. Walton off until March, when the wagons headed west?

She retreated to her room, and in the next hour hemmed the second string and attached both to the apron. She tried it on in front of her mirror, spun about, and was delighted to see how the long apron swung away from her dress. Much more graceful than the useless organdy and lace her mother thought proper for a young lady. Might there be dancing on the road to California? She imagined herself on the arm of a young man—grand promenade, swing your partners, all hands round. She reached her hand to the reflection in the mirror. No, it would be a man. She turned away from the mirror. A vague ghost of Lieutenant Hull waited, hand outstretched. Callused, certain, definitely a man's hand, and his shadow clasped her waist as she twirled.

## Chapter Nine

"Matilda."

Mama! Tildy tore off the apron and thrust it beneath a pillow on her bed. A soft knock.

"Matilda. Your father wishes to speak with you in the sitting room."

Tildy jerked open the door. "I was resting," she lied, breathless. "Just a moment, let me arrange my hair."

"Your hair's fine. After all, it's only your father who's to see you, not Mr. Walton." The words warned her. Her father had decided; she would marry Mr. Walton. She walked downstairs, and in her imagination, Lieutenant Hull's tall figure accompanied her. She lifted her hand to rest it in the crook of his elbow. He looked down at her and his words rang clear.

*Say no. Let them lock you in your room, do the work of the maid, but say no.*

She left the sitting room door ajar, but her father rose from his chair and shut it. "Sit down," he ordered. He did not take a chair himself. "I've received a letter from Mr. Walton," he said. Tildy wished he would not stand over her.

"I hope he's formed a bad opinion of me." If Mr. Walton rejected her, she would hug him and kiss his repulsive face.

"On the contrary, he finds you quite attractive."

"But I don't find him attractive."

"He's anxious for the wedding to take place, but he's also aware that young ladies have preparations to make for such an event. He suggests December 31st, in the afternoon. Your mother assures me if the ceremony takes place soon after dinner, there would be an hour to serve refreshments to your friends, and still leave time for the journey back to Muncie before dark. Mr. Walton's found a house that will do for the first few months."

"I'll not marry Mr. Walton on the last day of the year, or any other day." Her father walked to the window overlooking the barren side yard and said nothing. Tildy stood up. "I hope that settles the matter," she said.

"Sit down," he said, and when he turned around, his dark visage told her she had no choice. "It does not settle the matter. Has brain fever seized you, made you contentious and wrongheaded? Mr. Walton has made an honorable offer. A better offer than you have a right to expect. I've accepted his proposal for you."

Tildy held on to the back of the chair, feeling somehow that if she sat down, she agreed to the marriage. "I have no choice?" she asked.

"Of course you have a choice. Your choice is Afton Walton. Every young woman in Pikeston envies your future, the wife of a wealthy man. All your friends wish they were a bit younger, so they might attach their affections to Josh, or Lewis, who will—"

"Who will be wealthy, too." She completed his sentence, and didn't bother to conceal her bitterness.

"Yes. And give contentment to me and your mother. Once you have children of your own, you'll understand the happiness that comes from seeing your offspring well settled and prosperous."

"Married to Walton, I will certainly *not* be well settled! Look what happened to Belle Barman, married off to a man she didn't love. Is that what you want for me?"

"You've spent too much time with Meggie," he said, his lips pinched, his fingers busy at his vest. "My brother's allowed her to become strong-willed, completely unwomanly. From now on, you may see Meggie only at church, or at such social functions as…" Tildy stopped listening. Her only escape lay through Uncle Jim. She must keep that contact open.

"Mother asked me to visit them often, to convince Granny to move here," she said hurriedly.

"That's unnecessary now. Mother has no choice but to come live with us, for today Pete told me the whole family's resolved to pull up stakes and follow Godfroy and Sampson to California. A foolhardy decision. They'll end up dead, all of them, in the plains or on the mountains."

"Granny intends to go with them." Her father sneered, and for a moment her heart failed. If he could be so contemptuous of his own mother, he would have no sympathy for his daughter.

"A woman her age! Don't talk nonsense. Even my stupid brother wouldn't be *that* stupid, to—"

"Pete's making her a wagon like a palace, built to run so smooth she'll think she's on a steamboat."

"Peter humors her," he said, but Tildy heard the uncertainty bordering each word. "Have you spoken to Matt Hull?" he asked, the question catching her unprepared.

"When…when…" How to tell the truth, but not rouse his anger? "When Mother sent me to fetch Esther, she was telling her brother goodbye, so out of necessity we exchanged a few words." Could Lieutenant Hull's letter reach his Boston friend in time? No. Impossible for a reply to come back to Indiana before the end of the year.

"Did Lieutenant Hull ask you about Barman? Rachel's…legal father?"

"I can't recall Lieutenant Hull mentioning Mr. Barman, although I believe he and Mr. Godfroy are good friends, so perhaps he knew of the…Rachel's circumstances."

"Hull and Godfroy are birds of a feather. Half-breed

and river trash. If you hear any gossip about Barman, tell me, for someone's spreading lies.''

"But Mr. Barman's dead, has been dead for—" she calculated from Rachel's age "—eighteen years."

"We don't know that," he said. His pulled his watch from its pocket and it slipped from his uncertain fingers, swung on the chain. "Barman may be alive. Perhaps he went to California to escape the shrew he married." His mouth, for a moment, stretched out in a grim line. "Now, girl, I expect you to do your duty to your family. Write a sweet letter to Walton, accepting his proposal."

"I will not."

"Then go directly to your room. I'll not bear any more of your nonsense. A few days alone will change your mind."

Tildy marched out, head high, surprised at her own confidence. At least now she knew where she stood, and what she must do. She paused, looked back over her shoulder. "You may imprison me, you may set me to doing the maid's work, but I will still say no. And remember, the longer you keep me shut up in my room, the more likely that Granny will go to California. I'm the only one who might dissuade her."

Not true, of course. Granny wanted to go to California, and when Granny had her mind made up...

The slam of her door echoed throughout the house, informing everyone—she hoped—that the threat of imprisonment would not weaken her. She sat in the twilight, too exhilarated to need light. She examined the walls. She had heard of people driven mad by imprisonment. No, she would keep her hands busy and her mind firm. Shut away in her room, what a fine opportunity to sort her clothes and prepare for the trip. She would shorten the tan dress, and rip off the flounce. In March, with Mama and Papa complaisant about their willing prisoner, she would slip away.

Of course, staying in one room might render her too soft

for the journey. She took four steps from the bed to the door, four steps back. Eight or nine feet. How many times must she pace from bed to door to walk a mile? For two minutes she traced figures in the air, dividing 5,280 feet by nine; 586, plus a fraction. Every day she must walk from the bed to the door, then back again, at least 587 times.

*I'll find a way to send secret messages, like the heroines in novels who are shut away by evil uncles.* She remembered, unhappily, that these heroines usually had the services of a cooperative maid. She could not imagine practical Sally participating in an intrigue. Besides, she would read the notes, and she talked too much. Tildy regretted that Esther had gone to Muncie with Mr. Walton. Esther, she suspected, had a romantic streak in her soul. And she could not read and write.

Matt staggered a bit when Faith grabbed his arm, slammed the door behind him and pressed a hand on his shoulder. She shoved him toward his chair, snatched the coffeepot off the hearth and poured his coffee so erratically that he took the pot from her. She leaned against the table, her face only inches from his.

"Mr. MacIntyre has sent Tildy to her room, and won't let her out until she agrees to marry Mr. Walton," she gasped.

"How do you know?"

"Sally came by on her way home last evening, so I ran to Rachel, and she went to see Tildy after supper, and Mrs. MacIntyre ordered her away. My father says Mr. MacIntyre must be in dreadful straits to do such a thing!"

Imprisoned! He must rescue her. Denounce MacIntyre publicly for murder and horse stealing? But that was his trump card, not yet ready to play. Would people believe a few lines from an old diary, words that did not even mention MacIntyre by name?

Faith put his breakfast on the table and sat down facing

him. "I almost forgot, my father asked me to give you his thanks, about the fuse, that is, and will you join us at dinner?"

"Tildy will resist," Matt said, so distracted that he heard only half her words. "She'll say no, and say no until her father gives up."

"I hope so. Mr. Ridley will let you be absent?"

Matt stared at her, knowing she had said something important, something that had slid noiselessly around his worry about Tildy. "For dinner?" Mr. Tole admitted him to the family's midday meal? "My thanks to your father, and Mr. Ridley won't object if I leave the office for dinner. In fact, he worries about the crumbs attracting mice."

Matt hurried with his breakfast, for he had not swept the office. He did not taste the food, too preoccupied with Tildy. What desperate circumstance would lead a father to imprison a daughter? Money seemed the only explanation. What had Faith said? "Desperate straits."

Faith stopped him as he rose to go, holding a mass of dark gray fabric in her hands. "Please, try this on, so I know there's room across the shoulders."

The wool she draped over him only vaguely resembled a coat. She murmured to herself as she circled, holding the fabric taut. "There'll be a cape across your shoulders, of course, and a band at the wrists to keep out the cold."

"If you see Tildy, or can get a message to her—" the corners of Faith's mouth twitched into a hint of a smile "—tell her to hold firm to her resolve, and I'll do what I can."

He ran to the office, grabbed the broom and made a sketchy business of sweeping. Could a man do this—force his daughter to marry for his own profit? He grabbed the first volume of Blackstone. The duties of parents to children. Maintenance. Protection. Could MacIntyre be charged with not protecting his daughter?

*The consent of the parent to the marriage of a child*

*under age is directed by our law, to protect children from
the snares of artful and designing persons.*

Matt shoved the book away. Could he be classed as
"artful and designing"? But Tildy's own father shoved his
daughter about like a checker on a board, to increase the
profits of his store. Moffett and Walton, too, had business
plans, "artful and designing."

"Poor Tildy!" he whispered as he stood to welcome
Mr. Ridley, and behind him Jed Sampson. In the square
stood two horses, one saddled, the other packed with
Sampson's gear.

"You're leaving?"

"Yep, on to Ohio, where I have kinfolk. I expect to
bring them to Missouri in the spring. But I wished to bid
you goodbye, and remind you a young lawyer has more
opportunities in a new country."

"Indiana is plenty new," Ridley said.

"In California, Hull would be a judge right off," Sampson said.

"He's not yet a lawyer, and won't be admitted to the
bar for at least a year, at the earliest," Ridley said. He
turned his back on Sampson and unlocked his desk, plainly
indicating he had more important things to do than spar
with an ignorant trapper.

"Now, how does he go about doing that? Becoming a
lawyer?" Sampson's eyes sparkled.

"Why, he presents himself to the judge at the county
seat in Muncie, when the circuit court sits. I testify that
he's of good character, and that he's spent time in my
office, studying diligently. The judge examines..."

"So this is no United States judge?"

"Of course not. The circuit judge accepts new lawyers
at the bar, and registers—"

"Then you just come on with us to California," Sampson said, grinning at Matt. "I'll stand before the California
judge, if such there be, and testify to your good character,

and that you studied hard for ever so long as the law requires.''

"But he doesn't know California law!" Ridley said.

"There's no law in California," Sampson scoffed. "He'll know California law 'cause he'll write it. We'll arrive in September or October, plenty of time for any man in our party who has political inclinations to get elected to the territorial legislature. This boy here, why everyone can see he's meant to sit on the bench—he looks like a judge—so we'll push him—''

"You..." Ridley's interruption failed because he gasped for breath.

"—at least for justice of the peace, if not for the territorial court.''

"You don't understand," Ridley finally blurted out. "A man must have years of experience as a lawyer, pleading cases, before he's qualified as a judge.''

"Not in California," Sampson said. "It's *you* who don't understand. In California, a man's what he says he is, until his actions prove otherwise. If he strides down the Sierra carrying a shingle in his pack, why he's a lawyer in that country without a court saying yea or nay, and studying makes no difference, for it's all in books, and he can carry the books in his wagon. I'll personally see to them books arriving in good order.''

Ridley flung up his hands and returned his attention to his desk, pulling papers from a cubbyhole. Sampson finally took the hint that he had wasted enough of the lawyer's valuable time, and tramped out the door.

"Now you consider this, Hull," Sampson called as he checked the knots on the pack saddle. "You can partner with Godfroy on the trip, for a wagon's able to carry provisions for three or four, and the only other person Godfroy will have to feed is Rachel.''

"He will not have Rachel along!" Ridley yelled, leaning out the door. "This is insane! Godfroy takes Rachel out of this town over my dead body. Jim Mac and his family, I'll lecture them every chance I get, telling them the truth about this mad endeavor. Reverend Fitch has already spoken to Granny—I mean the elder Mrs. MacIntyre—telling her of the dangers.''

"Yep. Granny understands the dangers, and already's putting up the herbs to treat such ills as we're like to meet. Goodbye, Hull. See you in Missouri, end of April. St. Joe's the meeting place. Just ask for me or Godfroy at the ferry." He swung his hat around and spurred his horse.

Ridley stared after Sampson as the horses trotted out of the square. "You're not thinking of joining this fool emigration?" He still held the papers he pulled from his desk. Unread.

"No. I got home less than a month ago. My feet aren't cured of that journey, so why should I consider two or three thousand more miles of walking?"

"You don't believe what Godfroy and Sampson say?"

Matt shrugged his shoulders. He did not want to be drawn into the controversy over California, for neither argument had irrefutable facts on its side.

"You've heard of what Ira MacIntyre's done to Tildy?" Matt asked nonchalantly, then stiffened when he realized he had used her Christian name and betrayed too close an acquaintance.

"Yes. Rachel begs me to take some action," Ridley said. "She can't believe a father has a legal right to imprison a child, or force a daughter into an unwanted marriage."

"Does he? I looked it up in Blackstone, but..."

"A girl of nineteen? I can't say the law's particularly clear. I hope MacIntyre's doing it out of concern for the girl, not for..." Matt didn't like the look on Ridley's face, pale and drawn.

"Would a father who's truly concerned for his daughter's welfare, a father who loves her, would he force her to marry a man like Walton?" The words carried more emotion than was suitable in a legal conversation.

"What is love?" Ridley asked, no longer bothering to conceal his anxiety. "Trail Godfroy says he loves Rachel, so he comes to us and says she's his daughter—an illicit connection, but his daughter. He wants to take her to California, a journey that a strong man can bear, but one that most likely will kill a woman. What has Godfroy's love accomplished?" He tossed the papers on his desk. "He's thrown my household into turmoil, my wife into intoxication. Rachel cries she's known all along that Godfroy's her father, and babbles about fireballs and patchwork patterns. I'm afraid her mind...finding she's kin to a Miami half-breed has damaged her good sense. Love!" he snorted.

"Love *is* a rather selfish notion," Matt agreed. He searched his memory, and was relieved to find little trace of love in his life. Not between his mother or father. Not in any treatment they meted out to him. Unless...the way he'd felt about Trail Godfroy as a youngster...the ties with his gun crew. After he'd been made an officer, he had fretted over the men in his command, looked out for them, even justified shooting Carlos so they would not be burdened....

"If Rachel says she's leaving with Godfroy, will you lock her up to keep her home? Because you love her?"

Ridley made a noise that reminded Matt of the snarl of a cornered cat. "There'll be no trip to California. I'll do everything in my power to discourage those poor deluded souls. Godfroy's peddling a fairy tale. Pete MacIntyre's been talking to Tole. Can you imagine? A man with four boys, the youngest only ten.... We'd best get to work."

Matt uncorked the ink, and proceeded to copy the statements of new witnesses brought forward by Mr. Sales. His stomach growled. Faith should be coming soon with the basket...and then he remembered.

"Mr. Ridley, I'm to take my dinner with the Tole family, to save Faith the trouble of carrying it here."

Ridley smiled broadly, and nodded. "So, the townsfolk

begin to accept you as a man, and not a filthy boy from the swamps. Another year or two, they'll forget you're Emma Callom's son." He leaped out of his chair. "By Jupiter! Could you convince your father and mother to emigrate to California? If they'd leave the country, in a year no one would recall that your birth had questionable..." Matt appreciated Ridley's circumlocution, omitting such damning words as bastard and illegitimate. He dismissed the idea with a smile and a shake of his head.

"It takes money to travel to California, and the talent to plan ahead, months and months ahead. I'm afraid Pa's idea of the future is limited to remembering when to put mash in his barrels." Ridley nodded, unhappily agreeing with Matt's assessment of his father.

When Matt walked through the back door, Mr. Tole and his sons were washing up for dinner. The tallest of the four boys—Kit—moved stiffly and sat down gingerly. The culprit had been thrashed.

"Good day, Lieutenant Hull," Tole said. He looked sternly from one boy to the other.

"Good day, Lieutenant Hull," they mimicked.

"I want to talk to you, no legal matter, but about this California trip. Pete MacIntyre's ladling out great raw lumps of praise for California—the boys are quite convinced—and I thought you might counter him with something more digested."

"I've never been in California."

"But you traveled to Mexico—"

"Half a continent away from California."

Tole leaned across the table, his wide elbows endangering the cups and tableware. "Don't spread this about, young man, but I tell you for your own good, Pikeston's finished. County seat, they said. The county's too large, it'll be split and Pikeston the seat of the new one. Do you see a courthouse in that square? Of course you don't. Then they promised the Fort Wayne turnpike, but do you see it running past my door? No! Then a canal, the legislature even passed the law, but the spur to Muncie, will it ever be built? No! For the state wasted that money, and there's no canal to have a spur from. Now I hear talk of railroads, but the closest? Indianapolis! I made a great mistake settling here, believing promises of men in tall hats, promises that proved nothing but lies. There's barely trade enough to keep my family, and when Faith leaves to be married—''

"I'll not be married!" Faith said.

"You say that now, girl, but look at you! One day a man will ride by and catch your eye, and in a quarter of an hour you'll be shaking the dust of Pikeston off your feet. But, as I was saying, Lieutenant Hull, when Faith leaves, the forge doesn't make sufficient income to hire a housekeeper to cook and clean for me and the boys.''

"So California sounds promising?" Matt asked.

"It does. And it should for you, too. What if they should build a railroad? The ladies would catch the morning train to do their shopping in Muncie. Fewer horses needing shod, fewer tires to be fitted. Pikeston's finished! Two, three more years and grass will grow in the streets. You and Ridley will be bringing each other to court, for there'll be no one else left to sue. By the heavenly saints! Now that I hear myself talk, what's to keep me here? Boys, Faith, let's go to California!''

Faith stood rooted, halfway between table and hearth. She held a huge bowl of potatoes and could not spare a hand to cover her face, to conceal her appalled anguish.

Tildy heard voices in the kitchen. Loud enough to convey excitement, but not so loud she understood the words. She dropped her sewing, threw up the sash and stuck her head out. No better here.

She closed the window, had picked up her needle when a scream echoed in the hall, bounced from stair to ceiling. She threw the fabric on the bed. Closer, pounding feet on the stairs, the shriek now definitely her mother's, finally interrupted by sensible words.

"Margaret, don't! You don't know what you're doing!"

Tildy jerked open the door, and Meggie fell into the room.

"Get a bundle together. I'm rescuing you," she said, not even out of breath.

She must be joking. But the pistol in Meggie's hand, the largest pistol Tildy had ever seen, was no joke.

"Come on! Don't stand there like a ninny. My pony's waiting behind the livery barn!" Tildy grabbed the unfinished apron, stuffed it in her sewing bag.

"I don't have shoes on," she objected.

Meggie stooped, grabbed a pair of shoes that peeked from under the bed and handed them to Tildy.

"Make a bundle," Meggie cried. Tildy stuffed the shoes on top of the aprons, looked about, vaguely wondering what should go in a bundle. Meggie snatched a pair of undarned stockings off the bedside table.

"That's enough! Come on!" Meggie jerked impatiently at her arm. "Before Uncle Ira gets here from the store." She swung the pistol around, and Tildy decided she should stand behind Meggie.

"Where are we going?" she asked, grasping at the banister to keep from falling, trying to stay close to Meggie, who took the stairs two at a time. The pistol swung in a wide arc, pointing from floor to ceiling.

"To the farm. Pa'll figure how to spirit you out of Walton's reach."

Tildy looked for her mother in the front hall so she might explain the necessity of humoring Meggie, at least until she got the pistol away from her. No one in sight. Perhaps Mama had gone to fetch Papa. Through the kitchen, past Sally and the cook, whose eyes bugged out, reminding Tildy of a frog. Past the ruined outhouse and the frame of the new one, along the snake fence of the livery.

"Climb on," Meggie ordered as she jerked the pony's reins free of the top rail.

"There's no saddle."

"Throw your leg over and get on!" Meggie yelled, shoving so violently that Tildy stayed on her feet only because she landed against the pony. Meggie boosted her, Tildy threw her leg over, and had time to note that her skirt pulled up and displayed her ankles. More than her ankles. She made one useless grab at her skirt before Meggie kicked the pony and it leaped into the square. Men ran toward them, coming from all directions like chickens who see corn being scattered. Someone—one of her brothers—had spread the alarm. Papa ran in the middle of the pack, shouting.

"Stay back or I'll shoot!" Meggie called. The men skidded to a dusty halt, except for one who kept on coming, legs and arms pumping. "Why's he after you?" Meggie asked.

"Who?" Tildy looked over her shoulder just as the pony rounded the corner. She caught a single glimpse of Lieutenant Hull pounding across the square. Out of sight now. No. Here he came around the corner, running like a boy runs in the foot races on the Fourth of July.

The broad curve on the edge of town flashed by. He'd give up now. A tan field and corn shocks. No, he still pursued them, his hair standing up in the wind. The gateposts of Uncle Jim's barnyard.

"You get to the house, while I close the gate," Meggie gasped. Tildy slid off the pony, and only in her dash for the house noticed that raindrops rattled among the bare branches of the maple tree, and glistened on the leaves beneath her feet.

"Tildy!" Aunt Eliza said, popping up out of the rocking chair beside the kitchen window. Granny's head poked around her curtain.

"I've rescued Tildy!" Meggie said, slamming the door, still waving the huge pistol. It bulged in the middle, a revolving pistol. "Granny, hide her in your room. Uncle Ira won't dare go in your room without permission."

Warm blood flooded Tildy's veins, bringing with it a surge of rationality.

"Rescued?" she said. "Meggie, I'm only a quarter mile from home! Papa will be here in five minutes!"

"And we've got a rifle—" Meggie pointed above the kitchen door "—and this fantastic pistol. Six shots, without reloading!"

"Where did you get that thing, Margaret MacIntyre?" Granny asked, eyeing the pistol with distrust. A great banging at the door interrupted Meggie's reply.

"Tildy!" Lieutenant Hull's voice. "Tildy! Are you all right?"

Granny gave Meggie a scornful glance. "Five minutes!" she snorted. She marched across the room and opened the door, and the breathless lieutenant fell in. He wore no hat, no overcoat or cloak, and raindrops sparkled in his dark hair. Meggie held out the pistol.

"Here. You can manage this better than I can, I bet." He grabbed the pistol, examined the bulge, spun it around, and his shoulders sagged in relief. "If that crowd had kept on coming," Meggie said, "I would have laid out six men."

"No, you wouldn't," Lieutenant Hull said. "It's not loaded."

"Not loaded! What kind of man keeps a gun about without loads?"

"You took this pistol from Lieutenant Hull?" Aunt Eliza asked in shocked surprise. "That's stealing!"

"I borrowed it," Meggie said, only a trifle abashed. "Lieutenant Hull left his place unlocked when he went to dinner, so after Ridley went home, I just climbed up." The window rattled. Raindrops borne on the wind smeared the windowpane and pattered on the roof. "Good, rain's coming like the great flood, so Uncle Ira'll be slowed down because he'll have to lift the cover on the buggy. Where's Pa?''

"Your father and Peter went into town, something about ironwork for the new wagons," Aunt Eliza said.

"Then we'll hide Tildy until Pa comes home. He'll know where to take her, safe from Walton," Meggie said.

Granny grabbed Tildy's arm, and she felt a flash of relief that Granny had taken command. "Please, go to the sitting room," Granny said. "Lieutenant Hull, if you would be so kind, start a fire in the stove there. Kindling's in the box." Lieutenant Hull thrust the pistol in his belt and headed for the sitting room, as Granny had ordered. "Tildy, do as I tell you," she warned. "Go with him."

Tildy followed Lieutenant Hull uncertainly, noticed a thump against her leg and discovered her sewing bag still hung over her arm. She sat on a chair some distance from the stove—and Lieutenant Hull—pulled out her shoes and the pair of stockings, found the apron she'd been hemming, not too much dirtied by its abuse and resumed her work. When her father turned up, he must find her composed, and not at all excited by being alone with Lieutenant Hull.

# Chapter Ten

Lieutenant Hull knelt in front of the stove, blowing on an ember within the ashes of the morning fire, feeding tiny scraps of wood into the glow.

"Why did you run after me?" she asked.

"I was afraid Meggie had loaded the pistol. Someone might have been hurt."

"Exactly why I came with her. I decided the safest place was behind her."

He laughed, took a deep breath and blew upon the tiny flame. He laid on a larger twig. "Where do you go now?" he asked.

"I don't know. This fracas is Meggie's idea. She thinks Uncle Jim will whisk me to safety."

"You're not tempted to say yes to Walton?" The flame caught on the twig and Tildy heard the first satisfactory crackle of burning wood.

"Absolutely not! No matter what Papa does to me, I'll refuse to marry Mr. Walton."

Another bit of kindling and he abandoned the fire to lean over her. "Good. Our time will come."

*I must tell him the truth, that there's never a time for us. But after he kisses me.*

His hands carried the heat of the new fire as they framed her face. She touched his damp hair, and wondered how a tall, strong man could possess silken waves that any woman might envy. The run through the rain had chilled his lips, so it was only right that she warm them. A tap at the door, and he returned to the fire.

"Tildy, your mother's here."

"Say no," he whispered, "until you say yes to me."

"I already said yes to you."

"But you lied. The next time, you'll mean it."

She shook her head. "Papa won't allow you in the house. What makes you think he'd agree to a wedding?"

"He will," he said, his hand trailing through hers as a farewell. She snatched the fallen apron, and pretended to be hard at work when her mother erupted into the sitting room.

"What was he doing here?" she asked, forgetting her manners and pointing at Lieutenant Hull's disappearing back.

"He laid the fire, so I might warm myself after the chill of the ride."

"You might have warmed yourself in the kitchen."

"Granny told me to come in here."

"How did you and Margaret plan this?"

"*We* didn't plan it. Meggie simply burst in and said she meant to rescue me."

Her mother blew through her nose to show her disbelief. Tildy raised her eyes from her sewing. Her mother's hair bulged around the sides of a summer bonnet, and the bonnet sat askew. Her black fringed Sunday shawl covered her everyday dress; she wore house slippers. She had left the house in a panic.

"I did not feel myself in need of rescue," Tildy said, speaking as she imagined the ladies in *Godey's* spoke. "I'm quite content in my room. But I judged everyone in town would be safer if I trailed after Meggie. That great pistol frightened me."

"Home," said her mother briskly, pointing toward the door.

"Polite ladies do not point," Tildy said. Her mother's arm dropped, and she blushed with embarrassment. Tildy saw she had her mother's attention. "Mama, listen to me, while Papa isn't here to interrupt. No matter what you and Papa do to me, I'll not take Mr. Walton as my husband. You best make up your minds to that, and get on with business."

Her mother sank into a chair. "But Tildy, that's the problem. The business. We've said nothing, not wanting to upset you, or the boys, but the store—" she removed her bonnet and ran her hands through her hair, frowned at discovering her bun had dropped to the nape of her neck "—no longer pays its way."

"Pays its way?" Tildy asked, baffled. The store made them the richest family in Pikeston.

"Times are hard, Matilda. Fewer people shop in the store, and when they do, they don't buy so much. Months go by, and they don't settle their accounts. Your father tried to explain to me, something about the state legislature, refusing to pay off the improvement bonds, which I don't pretend to understand. It's not a woman's business. But many people lost money."

"But that can't have anything to do with me, or who I marry!"

"But it does. Unless a man with ready cash, like Mr. Moffett, steps in and helps your father... He has debts, you see and the bank will not loan...." She reset a few pins in her bun, patted the back of her hair, satisfied. She settled the bonnet into place. "Do you understand bankruptcy, Matilda?"

"Bankruptcy? Having no money?"

"Not enough money to meet your debts. Without help from Mr. Moffett, your father faces bankruptcy, and we'll be turned out of the house." Her chin quivered, but she squared her shoulders and organized her face to a frigidity that matched the rain on the window. "When our families re connected, Mr. Moffett will be sure to help, and the onnection is you, dear."

"Me, married to Mr. Walton?"

"Exactly."

"If I refuse?"

"Your father must settle with his creditors, else they'll ake the store. We'll sell the house and rent a smaller one. f the house doesn't bring enough money, then the store nust go. In that case, we'll be forced to move to the only property left, a cabin a mile beyond James and Eliza, and et about clearing the eighty acres of wood your father eceived as his inheritance."

Tildy knew the cabin. She and Meggie often walked here early in the spring to find violets of such a light avender they appeared white. A tumbledown, filthy place, with an earthen floor and no proper chimney.

"Is that what you would have us come to?" asked her nother. The frigidity changed to stern accusation. "Starting over, cooking in pots hung in the chimney, you and ne, for there'd be no money for cookstoves, nor for Sally or Mrs. Weeks. Sleeping in a loft that lets in the snow, clearing land, with nothing to offer Josh for his future but hard labor—"

"It wouldn't hurt him!" Tildy snapped. "He's never done a lick of useful work in his life."

"Your father, at his age, grubbing stumps, when with one word—*one word*—you might ease his life, not to speak of enriching yourself, wearing silk and diamonds every day."

Tildy buried her face in her hands, stopped her ears with her thumbs. She saw her father, bent and exhausted in a poor cornfield planted among skeletal trees. Her mother grinding corn on her knees in the dooryard. She took her thumbs out of her ears, jerked upright when she heard sobs. Tildy stared, appalled. Mama crying? She laid aside her sewing, sat primly, her feet close together, her hands folded in her lap, and observed her mother's tears dispassionately. Mama, but in this despair, a stranger. A woman accustomed to running her household with an iron hand now a frightened waif.

The wind shook the window in its frame. Some greater force moved in the room, and Tildy sensed a reversal. For the first time she noticed her reflection in Aunt Eliza's elaborate mirror. Her own stern face, her mother's bent shoulders. She the powerful one. Not Mama. Matilda MacIntyre held the fate of the family in her hands. Power! Tildy experimented by tightening every muscle, her shoulders, her arms, her legs. A new strength.

"Why haven't you told me this before?" she demanded.

"We feared it would upset you."

Tildy laughed, and noted that her laugh had changed. Not a girlish titter, but a mixture of mirth, mockery and bitterness. Not upset her! They'd give her to a vile man, without considering how *that* upset her.

"Go away, Mother," she said. "Go talk to Granny and Aunt Eliza, while I think this over."

"Don't say a word to anyone, about the money, I mean," her mother begged. "If the town should hear of your father's plight...demands, demands from every side. Men who owe would wait, until the bankruptcy...he'd lose everything!"

Tildy nodded curtly, anxious to be alone. After the door shut she experimented once more with her muscles, then relaxed. The rain streaming down the window blocked her view.

Blocked? No way out? Even if Uncle Jim or Lieutenant Hull offered her escape, by accepting she doomed her family to poverty. To suffering winter storms in that desolate cabin. She could not remember glass in the window. Shutters, closed against icy rain, fire the only light, crouching over the hearth for a bit of warmth.

What would her friends advise? Meggie? Run away. Rachel? Marry only for love. Faith? Take no husband at all. All three would accept poverty rather than Mr. Walton.

But all three were better suited than she to a life without money. They could cook and keep house.

Granny? What would Granny tell her to do, if she knew about Papa's need for money?

Granny's money! Tildy tightened her fingers around her legs. Her father wanted Granny to live with them, but not out of love. He wanted Granny's money. Everyone knew she had money, although no one was sure how much she had, or where she kept it.

"I wish I had someone to talk to," she whispered to the reflection in the mirror.

She walked to the stove and extended her hands, but the sheet iron top held no warmth. She gingerly opened the door of the firebox. The kindling had fallen into ashes, the fire nearly dead. She studied the woodbox, selected the smallest bit of kindling and laid it carefully across the last flame. The flame flickered once and went out. Tildy studied the smudge of soot on the bottom of her sleeve.

The woman in the mirror looked at her wrist, distressed. Not the face of confident power Tildy had seen before. She knelt in front of the stove, selected tiny slivers, laid them on the coals and blew. Over and over again. The ashes smoked. Billows of dark smoke. She took a deep breath, filled her lungs with the smoke, and fell back coughing. She was useless, unable to do a simple thing like light a fire and keep it burning.

Mama was right. Her destiny—her ignorance—led of necessity to a man like Afton Walton. She sat back on her heels and glared at the smoking mass of wood. *Light, blast you!* At that moment the flames exploded. She fed in larger splinters, finally added the piece that had put out the fire. By the time the flames licked around the largest chunk of wood in the box, she had made up her mind. She opened the kitchen door a crack.

"Lieutenant Hull, would you please come here? I wish to speak with you."

"Matilda! No!" Her mother tried to throw herself in

front of Lieutenant Hull, but he very agilely stepped around her, and slid through the narrow opening.

"Lieutenant Hull," she said before she even sat down, "do you have any great secret that you've never revealed to any other human being?"

He looked at her suspiciously. "Why do you want to know?"

"I want to know if you can keep my secret."

"Yes, I have a great secret."

"This secret, is it a matter of life and death?"

"If generally known, it would destroy a man."

"Fine. I'll tell you my family's secret, and why Papa insists I marry Mr. Walton, and you swear you'll carry this knowledge to your grave." He swore, then listened intently as she briefly explained the situation. His close attention gratified her. Papa and the boys paid no heed when a woman talked. Lieutenant Hull nodded in understanding, and his gray eyes fastened upon hers. *Men with gray eyes look very wise.*

"What shall I do?" she asked at the conclusion of the story.

"What you're saying, you and your family will be reduced to the level of other people in Pikeston. Are you afraid to work like other women?" he asked. No mockery in the words. Simply an inquiry after the facts. She stared through the isinglass windows, into the fire, and found confidence in the flames.

"Mama tells me I'm innocent and helpless, but I'm not sure I believe that anymore. She raised me to marry a man of some wealth."

"But you don't like the man fate provided?"

"No. I suppose I could learn to cook and clean, and the prospect doesn't frighten me terribly. I mean, I haven't burst into tears at the thought," she added, thinking of Mama, remembering she was stronger than Mama.

"Simply refuse to marry Walton, and accept the new

situation. You might find work, as my sister's done, and send your wages to your father to help pay the debts."

"Go out to work? But if I refuse to marry Walton, Papa will shut me up in my room again. How do I learn to cook and clean when I'm a prisoner?" He had not thought of that, she could see by the startled expression on his face.

"If you agree to marry Mr. Walton, will your father let you go free?"

She laughed at him. He did not understand her new power. "I believe I might demand the moon, Lieutenant Hull, and my father, to hear me say yes, would try to pull it from the sky."

"Then say to him, 'I will marry Mr. Walton,' but don't write to Walton yourself. Tell your father to do that. Never write a letter of your own, ever!"

"You sound like a lawyer, Lieutenant Hull! But if I say yes, I'll be lying."

"Lying bothers you now? You lied to me—you said you'd be my wife, so I'd ride to your rescue."

"But lying to Papa—"

"Is different than lying to a river brat?"

Tildy stared at her fingers, at the stain of soot on her wrist. She had never thought of herself as a liar, but she supposed...little white lies when necessary...

"Say 'I will marry Mr. Walton,' only those words, and it's my firm belief you won't be lying. Never speak of Walton as your betrothed, never write a line to him. And the less you say in his presence, the better."

"He never visits, and doesn't seem inclined to. But I don't understand the purpose of all this mendacity."

"How many brothers does Walton have?"

"Why none, of course. He's the sole heir of Mr. Moffett's sister's husband." A light flashed that could not be the fire. "His brother, injured by a horse! When he was so sick he told me he had a brother!" she shrieked, clapping her hands.

"Exactly. His brother. And this supposed storekeeper hasn't the slightest notion of ladies' hats."

"Hats!" Tildy jumped up. "Mr. Walton calls his tall hat a 'beaver,' Matt. *Godey's* says no man of fashion wears a beaver hat any longer. Only silk."

"I can't help but think Walton isn't...Afton Walton."

She sat down, sobered by the implications. "This does nothing to help my family," she pointed out. "We might end up in that cabin, clearing eighty acres of wood, more than a mile out of town."

"Would that be a great disaster, Miss MacIntyre, to be more than a mile from town?" This time he did mock her. A friendly tease, a sparkle in his gray eyes that made them far less wise. Stress laid upon her name, Miss MacIntyre! Heaven help her! She had called him by his Christian name! Matt! She turned away, hoping he ignored the red that must accompany the warmth on her face.

"A mile from town means nothing," she said to the reflection in the mirror. That woman blushed. "Think how far Uncle Jim and Aunt Eliza will be from any town on the trip to California." She gripped her fingers around the chair to keep herself seated. "We can go to California! Papa could open a store, and the boys would have opportunities...."

"If your father sells both house and store, will the money settle his debts?"

"I don't know. Papa might tell Josh the exact amount, for Josh is nearly a man, but he'd never tell a woman. I don't believe Mama knows how much money he owes."

"Tell your father you'll marry Mr. Walton, but bargain with him. Tell him you want complete freedom to come and go as you please until the wedding, and put off the marriage until spring, so there's time for Finlay's letter to come from Massachusetts."

"Finlay? He's your friend?"

"Yes. And if Walton visits, talk about his life in Massachusetts. Gather up every little clue, beaver hats, poke bonnets, moiré taffeta."

Tildy laughed at his serious face. "I doubt Mr. Walton will visit. Winter's coming." She pointed at the window.

"The longer you delay, the more likely that a passing stranger will recognize Walton. Indiana isn't so far from civilization as he believes. Stage lines pass through Muncie. New settlers will come in the spring. Now, I shouldn't be with you any longer, alone, for you're another man's betrothed."

"But we're conspirators. You're my lawyer." She lifted her face to him, pursed her lips for a kiss.

"Leave messages for me with Faith," he said, and backed to the door.

Mama burst in the moment the door opened. "No one must hear! Absolutely—"

Tildy raised a hand to silence her. "I agree to marry Mr. Walton, but until the wedding, I must have freedom to come and go, meet with my friends, and you and Papa must never question me, where I've been, or who I've seen."

Her mother dropped on her knees and grabbed her hands. "Dear girl! Dear girl!"

"The wedding will be in the spring. I can't possibly finish my wedding quilt by the end of December. A spring wedding's every girl's dream. December!" She dismissed the season by waving at the rain that now spread in granular blobs. Soon it would change to snow. "How would my friends dress in their best, if they had to wade through snow?"

"I'll consult your father."

Tildy dashed to the buggy and wrapped a woolen rug about her legs. Her mother gathered up the reins.

"Your father was wild to come after you, but I truly feared he might kill you, so angry—"

"Killing me kills any chance of a wedding and a son-in-law rich enough to pay off the debts," Tildy said, relishing her new status. "I have no sister to be sacrificed."

"It's not a sacrifice. You'll see. You've spent too much time with Margaret and Faith and Rachel. Too many hours gossiping about love. You're nineteen, old enough to understand that women must be practical in choosing a husband. I told your father I'd bring you home, told him you would agree to marry Mr. Walton. But you must never say anything that so much as hints at his money problems. Men are very proud, and your father would take it hard that you know how he's failed in his responsibilities."

Tildy examined the snowflakes drifting onto the lap robe. Men were strange creatures. She'd given Matt Hull the chance to kiss her, and he had rushed away, like a frightened deer. She must never say a word about bankruptcy, to protect Papa's pride. Weak, indecisive men, and women lying to protect them. Perhaps women had to lie, to commit a sin, to relieve men of the necessity. Was it really necessary to marry and put up with an unpredictable man?

If Granny read the seeds correctly she would be an old maid. Men made nasty remarks about old maids, but perhaps old maids were simply women who refused to lie to get a husband.

"Granny said I would never marry," she said. "She saw it in her seeds."

"Granny's seeds are a bit of nonsense. And all women must marry. Particularly girls like you, so innocent, who can't care for themselves."

Tildy smiled at the snow. Her mother and father would see who couldn't take care of herself!

Matt woke to utter silence. No slow drip of water from the eaves, no clank of harness chains from early teams in the square. The rain had turned to snow. He opened the door, viewed the smooth whiteness, snow at least a foot deep. He pushed the powdery heaps off the rungs of the ladder with his feet. He lit a fire in the stove, and after fingering his stubbly chin, put water on to heat. He dug the broom from a drift and swept the office. The same drift that covered the broom buried the wash bench. No way he could shave there. He hoisted the bucket of water into the attic with a rope, propped his mirror on one of the dusty trunks, poured the water in a basin and hung his candle holder from the rafter.

He examined the hand that held the razor, and to his surprise found it steady. He had slept badly. The news that Ira MacIntyre was hell-bent for destruction on his own, with no interference from Matthew Hull, had kept his mind circling busily through much of the night. Before the end of winter Pikeston would know MacIntyre as a profligate bankrupt, of no more worth than a pig herder or a wandering tramp. Ira MacIntyre's daughter would be of no particular value as the wife of an ambitious young lawyer. Meggie would be a better choice, but Meggie would not give up California.

Matt paid careful attention to the depression in his chin. If Tole was right about Pikeston's future, MacIntyre's bankruptcy could pull down the whole rickety edifice. The most prosperous farmer, Jim Mac, and the blacksmith, heading off to California. No telling how many other men Godfroy might convert by March, and their savings would go with them, hidden in cunning hidey-holes in their wagon boxes. He must face the fact that to be even moderately successful in law, he might be forced to leave Pikeston. He'd go to Muncie, or perhaps Indianapolis. No triumph over Ira MacIntyre, no impressing the locals, for what men would remain in Pikeston to impress?

After he had established a practice in a larger town, he could court the daughter of a circuit judge, or an officer in state government. Years and years, before he could think of a wife. And that thought brought the stab of need in his loins, a sensation he had noticed more frequently in the past few days. A woman. But he dared not risk his reputation.

Water slopped over the edge of the basin; he grabbed

his towel. The water spread down the curved lid of the trunk, carrying the dust with it, exposing a square of paper. He blotted quickly; his towel came away black with wet grime and the stain of ink.

*Contained within, papers relating to:* His heart skipped a beat. *James MacIntyre, Sr. Hiram Barman.* Barman's papers might show some business agreements with Ira MacIntyre. The mirror reflected a half-shaved face. A clown. He laughed at himself, relaxed and went back to shaving. No need to search for evidence against Ira MacIntyre. MacIntyre's star flickered even now, and would blink out before spring.

Now, more than ever, Tildy must not give in and marry Walton. Walton wanted the store. A man who marries for property, and discovers in the harsh morning light that there's less property than he imagined, he might take out his disappointment on his bride. In that dawn after the wedding night, MacIntyre would present his bills to his son-in-law. But it would be Tildy who would pay.

Matt wiped his face, looked in the mirror and found his mouth turned down and his eyes drooping. Sad? Just a bit unhappy, he assured himself, that Tildy would not be his wife. She *was* a pretty little thing. He dressed and waded down the alley toward his breakfast. Early yet. Perhaps a cup of coffee in the warmth of the kitchen.

"Lieutenant!" A gang of boys tramped through the snow, Kit Tole at their head. One of the boys trundled a barrow filled with lumpy snow. Snowballs.

"The snow fight starts as soon as the forts are built. We need your advice," Kit said.

"We was skunked last year," a younger boy said.

Matt fell in beside Kit. On the far side of the square, another gang of boys piled up snow.

"What're the rules?" Matt asked.

"First snowfall of the season, north side of town against the south." The younger boys started heaping snow into a long wall.

"Wait!" Matt said. "Don't make it straight." The boys

eyed him dubiously. "Put a point on it." He traced a long shallow angle in the snow with the toe of his boot. "And build some little extensions on either side."

"That's a lot of building," Kit said.

"The walls don't need to be high, just two or three feet, to protect your ammunition. Put your sharpshooters on the ends, so when they—" he jerked his thumb across the square "—attack, they'll be hit from three sides, not just one. Use your time and the snow to make snowballs, not a massive fort."

Kit pulled him aside as the boys set to work. "We could attack them first," he said.

"You say they won last year. They're confident. Let them attack, but stand firm and drive them off. Your sharpshooters, tell them to aim at the faces of the biggest boys. Have the small boys make snowballs for the best shots. And when the enemy retreats, send three of your men running as fast as they can, across the square."

"No one's gonna want to look like a coward, running off."

"They're not cowards. They'll circle in back of the fort, and when the enemy tumbles in, thinking they're safe, those three mount an attack from behind."

"By jingo! You're one great general!"

The opposition fort stood at least five feet high and fifteen feet long. Building it had consumed all the snow for twenty feet in every direction.

"You'd better send a spy behind the lines," Matt suggested. "Hide a cache of snowballs over there. They've used up all the raw material." Kit nodded.

In the dim shadows of the livery's roof Matt noticed another spectator. A teamster perhaps, preparing a wagon for an early customer. Skirts. A shawl pulled over the woman's head, but he knew Tildy's erect carriage. The south side had their general, too.

## Chapter Eleven

"Lieutenant Hull," Tildy muttered to no one, squinting at the activity across the square. "He's a bit old to play at snow fights."

"Look at that puny fort!" Josh yelled. "Come on! Let's attack before they get it higher!" He balanced a dozen snowballs in the crook of his left arm and led his men at a trot across the square.

Josh's attack, Tildy noticed sadly, had taken the other side by surprise. The north-side boys spread in a thin line, not massed in the shelter of their fort.

*Josh will wipe them out again this year, and for the next few days he'll be impossible to live with.* She stamped her feet to warm them, but also in frustration.

"Wait," Josh yelled, turning to his troop. "Not until you see the whites of their—" His head jerked back, his cap flew in the air, and his face disappeared in an explosion of white. He hunched his shoulders, wiped the snow from his face and, in the process, dropped his snowballs, exactly the wrong time to be disarmed, for the battle erupted around him.

Josh shouted for a renewed assault, but another face full of snow sent him staggering blindly. Two small boys slipped away and took shelter behind the plinth of the flagpole. One, Tildy noticed, was her brother Eddie.

The battle became a silent, grim struggle, everyone's energy devoted to grabbing, aiming and throwing. Another south-side boy defected, his head and shoulders a heap of white. He huddled at the flagpole. Then another, and suddenly the square filled with speckled figures lurching back to the fortress in front of the livery stable. Three boys hurtled over the northern fort, and headed for the path beside the school.

"Cowards!" Tildy shouted, and in her excitement she ran from under the protection of the barn. "Cow—" Faith's three younger brothers. They scooped up heaps of snowballs concealed behind the schoolhouse steps.

"Brilliant!" cried Tildy. "Beat them! Beat them!" The retreating army tumbled into their fortress, followed by a volley so intense the air turned white. Tildy threw her shawl aside and ran to the schoolhouse, picking up the ends of her long apron as she ran. "Pile some in here," she said to the boys. "I can carry more...."

"Git out of here. You'll get hurt. This isn't for girls."

"I'll walk behind you, so you have plenty of—" The boys shoved her aside, galloped to the front of the livery and methodically fired at the figures cowering behind the fort. Tildy knelt in the snow, held the apron over one arm and loaded the snowballs with the other hand. She dumped the load at the feet of the Tole boys, did not stick around for thanks but scampered back to the steps. A shout of triumph. Three boys, with Josh at their head, pounded across the square toward the unoccupied fortress. They would destroy the frail fort!

Kit Tole rose from behind the barricade. Three perfectly aimed snowballs, one after the other, and Josh and his friends wandered aimlessly about the flagpole, shaking snow from their hair, rubbing their eyes and searching for their hats.

"Hooray!" she screamed. She filled her apron and dashed back to the barn. Hands grabbed her skirts, her arms, and dragged her into the open. Boys kicked at the high wall of snow, demolishing in seconds what had taken half an hour to erect.

"We've captured one of them. She's a spy," said a squeaky voice behind her. "She should be executed."

"No," another boy said in an assumed dark baritone. "Captive women are given to the officers. Don't the Indians always give women to the chief? General Hull!" he yelled.

He stood at the foot of the flagpole, laughing, his head thrown back, and Tildy remembered her first view of him, on Harvest Home Sunday, with the balmy breeze of October stirring the flag, and the sun on his epaulets.

No sun today, but the gray morning flared in unexpected heat. The snow turned to white fire, the crystal breath of his laughter threatened her with scalding steam. She struggled against the hands that grasped her, fought her hot desire, but both propelled her to Matt Hull.

"General Hull," Kit said, "my men have captured their woman. You may...you may...do..."

"Do with her as I will?" he asked, grinning so widely he had a hard time speaking.

"But have mercy," Kit continued, drawing himself erect in imitation of a soldier addressing an officer. "She brought ammunition to our men."

"Let me go!" Tildy said, snatching her skirts away from the boys. "I'm trying to get to Faith's, because we're quilting Meggie's double-ax patchwork today, and you silly boys have made a mess of the square—look at this mud!—and a person with serious business might be hit by a snowball, and you'd never know or care!"

"We're bound in the same direction," Lieutenant Hull said, suddenly serious, very polite, "for I haven't eaten my breakfast." He offered his arm.

"I can't...I can't...what if Papa should see us together?"

"Your father dare not say a thing," he said, grabbing her hand and pulling it through the crook of his elbow.

"He would pull down the moon, remember, to hear you say you'll marry Walton. Besides, you must obey my orders, for you're spoils of war, my captive."

She took a deep breath and let it out in a huff that turned to ice and blinded her. She dug her heels into the remaining snow. His gray eyes shone, not with amusement, not with the pleasure of winning, and certainly not with wisdom. Prickles spiked across her shoulders, her breasts. Her lungs and heart froze, while a part of her lower down rose to the melting point.

"My shawl," she whispered. "I dropped it in front of the livery stable."

A maelstrom of boys jammed the kitchen, slurping coffee and snatching flapjacks as fast as Faith lifted them from the griddle. Matt plastered himself against the wall. He might bear the noise, but not the loud, congratulatory circle crowding around him. Fire glowed on the back of the hearth, brightened and threatened. His back ached, and he wondered if he could move his legs. His heart pounded, his lungs weakened. He slid around the wall, sidled into the front room. Chairs and settees had been pushed aside to make room for an expanse of colorful patchwork stretched on a frame. Tildy sat alone. She paid no heed to him, but focused on her needle and thread. She stabbed unsuccessfully at the hole, sharpened the thread by touching it to the bud of her tongue, moved thread and needle to bring them into focus. The spasms in Matt's back sank lower. The demons frolicking in his chest had nothing to do with the shouts in the kitchen.

Standing in the snow, under the curious stares of half the town's boys, he had hidden his lust beneath exaggerated courtesy. But the glow in her green eyes had reflected his desire, and proclaimed her own. A magnet between them, the mutual frenzy of copulation, exaltation, the easing of the ache in the loins. He had led her through the torn snow, not even touching her hand, but had yearned to pick her up, carry her to the livery barn, toss her upon the bedding straw and fall upon her.

The ice of good sense triumphed over seething passion, because of ambition, because of the presence of lads just feeling their own urges. But in all the long two blocks from the livery to the Toles' house, he had feared the fire would break through. *Never!* his mind had ordered. *Now!* his heart cried.

The front door opened. Rachel stopped on the threshold in surprise, staring first at him, then at Tildy. Did a visible thread of energy connect them?

"Good morning, Lieutenant Hull," she said, with one last curious glance. "Good morning, Tildy." She placed a dainty basket of sewing equipment on the quilt top, took off her hat, shawl and gloves.

Meggie, disheveled, smelling slightly of her pony, popped in without ceremony and grinned in the direction of the kitchen. "I guess the north won this year," she said, pointing with the hand holding an overstuffed sewing bag.

"Yes," Tildy said, stiff and formal. "And the jubilation keeps Lieutenant Hull from his breakfast, unless he wants to fight a second battle for flapjacks."

"Second battle? You tossed snowballs?" Meggie asked. "No wonder the north won! You didn't get enough of snow fights when you were a boy?"

"I never fought as a boy," he said. "I wasn't a town boy, remember?"

"That's right." She threaded her needle with the first jab. "You lived down by the river."

Tildy managed to twist her face into an expression of disgust, but her pose held no conviction.

"A very lovely quilt," Matt said. The multicolored scraps intertwined in the shape of double-headed axes.

"It's Meggie's," said Rachel. "The first we've quilted for her."

"Aunt Ravania says the pattern's common," Meggie

said lightly. "It's not been in that lady book she gets in the mail."

"*Godey's,*" Tildy said, pulling too firmly on her needle, leaving the thread to pile like a snake on the patchwork. "*Godey's Lady's Book* is a genteel source—" Her chin quivered, her hands shook as she tipped the thread on her tongue. "Standards for behavior..." Every nerve in his body stretched out to her, and his reluctant flesh burned with the agony.

The school bell saved him, brought him rushing back to reality while the younger boys spilled out the kitchen door. Kit clattered through the sitting room, heading for the forge. Matt retreated to the kitchen, weak with relief. He collapsed on a chair, heedless of the fragments of flapjack and drops of molasses on the seat.

Her eyes were green—the green of new leaves in the spring. Her small mouth pouted, a bud, tightly furled against a cold spring wind. But her lips opened to point her thread, and brought the memory of their sweet kiss. A harbinger of other tastes, of the blossom spread for the man who married her.

Faith flipped the last pancakes onto his plate, along with a rasher of bacon and three eggs. Coffeepot in hand, she leaned through the door to the sitting room.

"Have you heard about the Christmas Fair?" she called.

"Christmas Fair? No," said Tildy's voice, strong, recovered now in his absence.

"A man stopped by yesterday, a huckster, to have his horse shod. There's to be a Christmas Fair in Muncie, in a great tent on the edge of town. The middle of December."

"I've never been to a Christmas Fair," Meggie said. "But it's no use to buy trinkets this year. We're leaving for California, and we couldn't carry them along."

"There'll be a Christmas tree," Faith said, gathering her sewing things from the sideboard. Abandoned, Matt ate slowly, and wondered what Tildy looked like beneath her corsets and voluminous petticoats. He liked his women buxom, breasts firm. Hers looked adequate, but the fullness of her bodice made it impossible to say with certainty.

"Josh says you walked across the square with Mat Hull." Tildy met her father's eyes, forced her own wide open, unblinking. He put down his soupspoon, staining the tablecloth. "You'll stay away from him."

"I'll not marry Mr. Walton if you keep telling me what to do, like I was a child," she said.

"Allowing you freedom to come and go doesn't mean you can disgrace your family," he said in a rising voice. He picked up the spoon and waved it about. "I'll not have you walking with that man!"

"He escorted me across the square to Faith's house because the boys had torn the snow up so my feet slid this way and that!"

"I don't want you visiting Faith while Hull's there." He held his spoon upright while his other hand fidgeted about his vest pockets.

"I won't marry Mr. Walton," she said. Josh giggled. Tildy pushed back her chair, stood up and walked to the hall door.

"Matilda, please," her mother begged.

Tildy stopped in the doorway, but didn't turn around. "Papa said I could do as I like before the wedding. He promised."

"But the Hull boy, Matilda! No one, except for Mr. Ridley, associates with him. Everyone knows that his mother…Mr. Walton might have second thoughts if he should hear gossip…about you…that man…a soldier. No respectable young lady is *ever* seen with a soldier!"

"He's an officer, a lieutenant," Tildy said, "not a soldier." Soldiers ravished women, that she knew, but officers were gentlemen. Except that his smoky eyes had looked as if they might explode. A real gentleman would conceal crass physical desire.

"Come sit down," her father said after two heavy sighs. "We'll discuss this."

She returned to her chair and conveyed her contempt of the family by staring out the window. Snowing again. Sally dumped a platter of fish on the table. Salt fish. Tildy hated salt fish. Why couldn't Josh and Lewis go fishing in the river, like other boys, and bring home fresh?

"This fish has been boiled!" her mother accused, poking at the offending creatures with a fork.

"'Twasn't me!" Sally cried. Tildy retreated into her own world, knowing from experience that the argument would occupy ten minutes. Lieutenant Hull wanted to ravish her, and she was not quite clear about the process. Something like what a man did on the wedding night, but far worse. Painful, a disgrace that made a woman unsuitable for marriage except to her ravisher. She must find out how bad it would be. Rachel or Faith? They probably didn't know.

Granny? A year ago Tildy had sat tongue-tied while Granny described what her husband would expect of her on their wedding night. Very embarrassing, but now she must discard her modesty long enough to ask the details of ravishment.

"...unless you take better care in the kitchen," her mother was saying to Mrs. Weeks, who had been called to the dining room, "you must go, for we cannot afford to waste in this fashion." Mrs. Weeks flounced out of the dining room.

"Granny says I'll never marry," Tildy announced in the vacant moment before the door closed. Everyone stared at her. "I'm to be an old maid."

"Quit saying foolish things like that!" exclaimed her mother, distracted from the fish.

"She saw it in her seeds. And Meggie's to marry a storekeeper." Josh whooped in disbelief.

"That's the tales of an old woman. Her mind's wandering," Papa said. "More reason than ever that she live here with us. She might lose herself in a storm—'' he gestured toward the window where the snow piled on the sill ''—and die not knowing her way to the house.'' Tildy smiled at her plate. She would rather be lost in a storm with Granny than anyone else. Unless maybe Lieutenant Hull, who would be sure to find shelter in an abandoned cabin, or in a thicket where he would build a lean-to. Where he would ravish her.

''I'll visit Granny after dinner,'' she said. ''I'll tell her how cozy she'd be in our brick house.''

''Not in this storm,'' her father said, but she pretended she had not heard him.

''Sleds have come into town all morning, and packed the road quite hard. It's only a quarter mile,'' she said. She smiled her most winning smile. Maybe she should warn Granny about Papa needing money. Just in case Granny truly did have money of her own.


Granny handed Tildy a knife, and demonstrated how to carve out the center stalks of the dry burdock leaves.

''Soak them in warm vinegar to make a poultice for the feet. They bring on perspiration,'' she said. Tildy glanced past the curtain, swagged back to let in the warmth radiating from the kitchen stove. The dinner dishes had been cleared away, and Meggie and Aunt Eliza had disappeared into the loft to sort through a trunk of outgrown clothing.

''Granny, you must tell me, what happens…when a man ravishes a woman?''

''Has someone threatened to ravish you?''

''No, but I can tell he wants to, and…Granny…what I didn't know is that I want him to do it! I wanted to roll on the ground, except the boys had stirred it to mud, and if he'd taken me into the barn, I'd have let him…ravish me.''

Granny smiled. ''You're growing up. It's time you got married. What man are you in heat for? Not Mr. Walton,

I guess.'' Granny tried to sound serious, but Tildy heard pleasure in her words. She bit her lip rather than answer.

"Lieutenant Hull?" Granny asked.

"Yes," she whispered.

"And he did nothing, beyond look at you?" A serious question. No amusement now.

"He took my hand on his arm, and walked with me across the square, where the boys had made a mess in their snow fight. Granny, if I let him do this, and Mr. Walton finds out, he'll not want to marry me. But I can't marry Lieutenant Hull, and disgrace the family. Your seeds were right. I'll be a shamed old maid."

An old maid, struggling along in the poverty of her parents' house, helping in the store, if the store survived the debacle of their fortunes.

"But if I go to California," she mused, "no one there would know I'd been ravished."

"That you could," Granny said. "Perhaps California men aren't so fussy about the chastity of their women." She stood up and lifted a bundle of dried stalks from a hook in the ceiling. "This is tansy, which relieves sunburn. According to Mr. Sampson, the sun shines much hotter on the plains and mountains than it does here, so we'll lay in a good supply of tansy for the trip."

"Papa wants you to move into town, with him and Mama and the boys."

"What would I do in town?" Granny scoffed. "Besides, I'm leaving for California—" she counted on her fingers "—in three months and a bit more. March, they say, so we arrive at the Missouri River with time to spare, to rest the animals."

Tildy heard footsteps above. Aunt Eliza and Meggie would be downstairs soon. "Granny, what…when he ravishes me, what happens?"

"For a man to ravish a woman, she must be unwilling, so when you go with Lieutenant Hull, you want him, it won't be ravishment." She sighed. "I thought he'd wait, since he's straining so to be proper, but perhaps that's too much to expect of young blood.''

"Wait? For what?"

"Until you married."

"I'll not marry Lieutenant Hull!" Tildy cried.

"A woman marries the man she'll dash into the fire for," Granny said. "The day comes when you can't bear the pain of being separate, and in some private place you make yourselves one. Wedding or no."

"Did this happen to you?" Tildy breathed.

"Oh, yes! I saw Jimmy MacIntyre driving an ox down the road one spring day. He strutted past the cabin. He knew I saw him, and the next day he came by again, this time with a pig and a bitch dog. And our old hound ran out into the road, howling, and covered that bitch. Jimmy grinned at me, so I knew what he wanted. The next Sunday we walked out together, into the woods, to a place where the mayapples bloomed, and we mated, not like the dogs— that's what I'd expected—but face-to-face, kissing and loving. That sundown, he told Ma and Pa we should marry."

Tildy tried to concentrate on shredding the dry stems of tansy onto a cloth, but she flushed hot all over, like just before she broke out with the measles. And a faint cramp tightened muscles in her thighs, one after the other, in pulsing rhythm.

"He was true to me, Tildy, from that day, because we always lusted after each other. I've known men and women marry for other reasons, money usually, thinking the lust would come, but it seldom does. Not like that. Then one day the man sees another woman and feels a stirring, and soon he slips away. Perhaps the woman does, too. Belle Barman did."

"I cannot marry Lieutenant Hull," Tildy whispered.

"He's your natural husband. I saw it the first time he supped with us. Your mother's tongue-tied when it comes to telling you the truth, so I'll speak plainly. Mr. Walton's too fat to give you any pleasure in his bed, unless he loves you, which he does not. Marry Lieutenant Hull. The two of you will try every way of coming together except falling through the air like larks.'' Granny had a faraway look in her eyes, as if she saw beyond winter and snow to an ancient spring. Tildy dropped the half-shredded tansy stalk and pressed her arm against her stomach, where the cramps now spread. She blinked to ward off tears, tightened her throat, but one sob broke through.

''Now, now!'' Granny said. She took a bottle from a high shelf and fetched a spoon from the kitchen. Tildy leaned into her grandmother's kneading hand, a touch that had comforted her through the ills of childhood.

''What must I do, Granny?''

''You take one spoonful of this syrup every day, for it relieves your melancholy. Put the tansy in this box—no, first line it with brown paper, so the herbs don't touch the tin. And then we'll start supper. With this storm, you'd better stay overnight. I'll sleep upstairs with Meggie, and you use my bed, closer to the kitchen stove, for you're accustomed to a warmer room.''

Tildy swallowed the sweet syrup. ''What is it?'' she asked.

''Sarsaparilla.''

''And if I take this every day, I'll be more content, and want him less?''

''No, dear child.'' Granny laughed. ''Sarsaparilla excites the nerves. You'll want him more.''

''Then why?'' She thrust the bottle into Granny's hands.

''Your father has a stubborn streak a mile wide. He said you would marry Walton, so he's blind to any alternative. He thinks he'll be less a man if he changes his mind. Walk out with Lieutenant Hull, encourage his desire and let it rule you. The gossip—I'll see to that,'' she said, and Tildy could not miss her triumph.

''You don't understand, Granny. I promised Mama I would never, never say a thing, but Papa...he has debts, and Mr. Walton or Mr. Moffett will satisfy them. Mother said if I don't marry him, the house will go, and perhaps the store, but I don't want...."

Her grandmother's face hardened. She shoved Tildy backward, until she collapsed on the bed in the corner. "Why hasn't he consulted his mother?" she hissed. Tildy shook her head, frightened at the stern determination, the unexpected consequence of her words. "He'll sell my granddaughter to keep his pride."

Meggie walked into the kitchen, opened the door of the stove and added two sticks of kindling. Granny jerked down the curtain between the kitchen and her room. "You'll stay the night because of the storm," she whispered to Tildy. "You'll sleep in my bed. I'll take Lieutenant Hull aside—"

"Lieutenant Hull will be here?"

"I asked Pete to bring him, so he could read more from his law book. Pete will suggest he sleep over, rather than walk back to town in the snow and dark, and I'll let Lieutenant Hull know where you lie."

"Mother said if I don't marry Mr. Walton, we might end in the old cabin, on the eighty acres of wood beyond this farm."

"Is dishonor easier to bear than honest work? You let your father suffer the evils of his own poor judgment." She took a jar of milk-white glass from her shelf. "This is tincture of pond lily in goose grease. When you and Lieutenant Hull are at peace, after the first coupling, ask him to spread this, very carefully, where he entered you."

Tildy grasped the cold glass. "To ease the pain?"

Granny shrugged. "It may not hurt. It's different for every woman."

"You?"

"Why, Jimmie and I rolled in pleasure from the very first time. Women without desire suffer more. Ira and Ravania must have a dry time of it."

"Mama and Papa?" Tildy whispered.

"Why, haven't you figured, child, at your age? He married her for the money. Her father gave him a thousand dollars, so he might open a store. Now, come and I'll teach you how to make biscuits."

# Chapter Twelve

The idlers left the bench behind the stove early, confused by the twilight of the afternoon. Ridley looked at his watch. "Only four," he mused, half to himself, "but the wife will worry in this storm." He corked his ink and blew out his lamp. A gust of snow entered the room as he left, and glistened in the candlelight. Matt shoved aside the form book and the papers he had been copying, and opened Blackstone. His candles would burn for at least two more hours, perhaps three.

*Our law considers marriage in no other light than as a civil contract, valid where the parties are, in the first place, willing....*

Willing? Tildy's marriage to Walton, should it occur, would not be valid unless both partners were willing.

"It must not come to that," he said to the candles. The flames wavered under the force of his breath. Unwilling or not, Walton would demand that she occupy his bed...before a court could hear her protest, Walton would...Matt could not bear to let his mind dwell on that eventuality, but the image forced its way past his defenses. He shuddered.

But to whom did Tildy go to complain of her unwillingness? Matt had never before considered the weak position of women under the law.

The door opened a crack, the wind seized it, flung it with a crash against the wall. The visitor, wrapped around with scarves so only his eyes showed, snatched the door and slammed it, but not before snow had blown into the farthest corner.

"Mr. Ridley's not here," Matt said. The first muffler fell away. "Oh! Hello!" Pete unwound a second, longer scarf, and shook his snow-covered hat over the stove, so the flakes sizzled into steam.

"Hull, Granny says this snow's not to prevent you coming to supper. If Ridley will let you go now, you can ride with me in the wagon. Granny's itching to hear more on the law of husband and wife."

"I've been studying on my own. I've reached the law of parents and children. What are you doing in town in the middle of this blast?"

"Finishing the roof on Uncle Ira's new outhouse. Not so elegant as his old one, nothing more than planks. But I guess he figured it's cheaper to set a wooden outhouse back on its feet after Hallowe'en than call the mason from Muncie. And you can bet, from now on no boy in Pikeston will think he's done his best until he blows up a brick privy." Matt blew out the candles, swept the snow off his ladder and fetched a bit of blanket to wrap the volume of Blackstone.

"What did MacIntyre give you in payment this time?" Matt asked as he climbed into the wagon.

"An air-proof bust improver," Pete muttered into his muffler.

"What?" Matt assumed the muffler had obscured a word or two, and when he heard Pete's entire statement, it would make sense.

"An undergarment for a lady lacking in chest development. She inflates it to match her ambitions. Uncle Ira said I could give it to my special sweetheart, but I've not acquired that item yet. And when I do, she'll not need a bust improver!"

Matt thought back to the embrace behind the livery, and decided Tildy did not need a bust improver. But he'd had no experience with inflatable bust improvers. Did the garment mimic the real thing so closely that a man could be fooled? Until he had his bride naked beside him on the wedding night?

"Tildy's at the house," Pete said, as if he read Matt's thoughts. "She drove a hard bargain with Uncle Ira. Before the wedding she does pretty much as she pleases. Uncle Ira's not in a position to quibble, so long as she keeps her promise to marry and doesn't ruin her reputation. But I can't imagine Tildy yielding to seduction before her wedding day."

Matt could imagine Tildy yielding. In fact, tonight before he went to sleep, he would imagine exactly that, the sweetness of her mouth, the weight of her breasts, free from the restraints of her corset. Matt did not see the gate through the driven snow, but Pete turned the team with a sure hand. A square of yellow light marked the house.

"Come see the wagon I'm working on. A California wagon." Matt helped Pete brush the snow from the horses' backs, and cover them with coarse blankets. Pete led him to a stall where the naked running gear of a wagon lay on a bed of straw.

"Aged oak," Pete said, "with straight-grain hickory for the axles. Every piece as fine as can be planed and still keep its strength. I'm making four, three for the family and one for Godfroy. But if you order soon, there's time to build five."

"I expect to make my home in Pikeston. There's a future here for a lawyer."

Pete shook his head doubtfully. "That's not what Tole says. Did you know he's thinking of joining us?"

"Yes." *And Faith is appalled at the prospect,* Matt nearly added.

The wind flung the snow in eddies about the barn and outbuildings, and the yellow light marking the kitchen window dimmed and brightened. A low drift already arched against the back stoop. The hot air of the kitchen hit Matt like the blast from a cannon. His legs still wavered from battling the erratic wind, and now his head pounded and his vision blurred in the sudden heat. Tildy kneaded a mass of dough. She wore a plain dark dress protected by a long white apron. She extended her lower lip to blow away the hairs that strayed into her eyes.

*No woman in everyday dress wears a bust improver.* This stray bit of logic prompted Matt to blink his fog away and take a second look. A satisfying bulk changed shape with the motion of her arms. She lifted her head, smiled at him, and Matt stepped back, collided with Pete, who was beating snow from his coat. He saw something different in her smile, slow, dreamy, a twitch in the dimple at one corner of her mouth. Matt used the excuse of the snow on his coat to turn away from her and imitate Pete.

Seductive. Even more blatant than the glow in her eyes after the snow fight.

"Pa's in the sitting room," Pete said. Matt followed with an alacrity he knew came close to insult. But he must avoid Tildy.

"Look at this," Jim Mac said, holding out a folded newspaper.

"A private letter from California…'a most miserable godforsaken country…flagrantly misrepresented…the fog so heavy that water drips from the roofs…overcoats and flannels are worn the year round…how the emigrants who come here will be disappointed!'"

"Godfroy and Sampson must have visited a different country," Pete said, reading over Matt's shoulder.

"Someone's lying," Jim Mac said. Matt congratulated himself on having resisted the California excitement. "You take this to Godfroy," Jim Mac continued, "read it to him, and ask him why he talks of eternal spring and oranges and figs, while this man writes of a damp, cold hell! What crops grow in a fog bank? A farmer would starve to death."

Matt nodded. "I'll find Godfroy. Might take a while, for he'll be busy with his traps."

"If this story's true, Godfroy's wasting my time, and Peter's. Building California wagons that no farmer here would want to buy."

"Supper's ready," Meggie's voice sang from the door.

Matt took the chair he had occupied before, next to Granny's. Tildy leaned over his shoulder, placed a platter of biscuits in front of him and sat down. Another smile, this time bolder, but the same hint of nervousness in the dimple. Granny took a seat beside Meggie and dished up a pie filled with pork and hominy in thick gravy, onions simmered in milk, apples boiled with rice. And Tildy's knee swung too close and briefly touched his. She smiled, not an apology. Once more her knee, but this time she did not pull away. He shifted in his seat to separate their legs.

"I'm staying the night," she announced. "Aunt Eliza says the storm's much too nasty for me to go home." She lowered her voice. "Granny says I can sleep in her bed." She nodded toward the curtain. Matt gulped down an apple so hot it burned his gullet.

He *had* considered the possibility of curling up behind the kitchen stove, delaying the struggle back to Pikeston until morning. Impossible, with Tildy not twenty feet away, and the rest of the family asleep in the front of the house or in the loft.

Tildy's leg trespassed into his territory, this time more than a knee. Her foot, clad in a soft slipper, edged over the top of his boot. *Shove her away!* commanded the rational part of him. His sex surged, and he could think of nothing but her eyes glowing in lustful acquiescence. She was inviting him to join her in Granny's bed!

"Uncle Ira gave me an air-proof bust improver," Pete said. "Any of you women want it?" Meggie howled, Tildy broke into nervous laughter.

"I told Papa not to put the thing in the store," Tildy said. "What girl would buy a bust improver in Pikeston? Everyone would know! Girls with any sense go to Muncie, so the tale doesn't spread."

"You know someone who wears a bust improver?" Pete asked.

"Yes," Tildy said, "but I'll not say who, for she married last winter, and I fear her husband was disappointed." Pete let out a sigh of relief.

Matt stared at Granny, wondering if she noticed Tildy's behavior. She smiled indulgently at him, shifted her gaze to Tildy. *The old lady's not surprised at all! She's conspiring to shove me into Tildy's bed!* She probably had it all arranged that Jim Mac would *accidentally* pay a visit to the kitchen at the vital moment. Tomorrow morning Jim Mac and Pete would visit the blacksmith, get the gossip going, then go to Ira MacIntyre, who would grab his rifle.

After suffering a moment of inchoate terror, Matt found himself admiring Granny's logic. Tildy, openly bedded by Matt Hull, was damaged goods, unacceptable to a gentleman like Afton Walton. But Granny did not consider the consequences of seduction to a law clerk. Mrs. Ridley would hear, and raise a hue and cry against him. Ira MacIntyre had every right to bring suit, demanding compensation for the violation of his daughter. Ridley could not honestly testify to his good character, not after he'd seduced the most prominent virgin in Pikeston. Perhaps been marched at rifle point to a wedding. Matt Hull would not be admitted to the bar in Indiana. No matter now hard he studied.

Tildy's knee explored in his direction. Jim Mac shifted one of the candles to bring the dish of apples within his reach. The light glittered upon Tildy's banjo leaning in the corner. Matt jumped up, grabbed the instrument and made a great display of strumming and tuning. Singing gave him an excuse to stand up, out of range of Tildy's tempting knee, but what decent song? His entire repertoire had come from the army camps.

He had once visited the camp of the Indiana militia, to borrow the newspapers sent from home. He had learned a song that, if he left out a verse or two... He swept his hand across the strings to announce his readiness, and at the last minute shifted into a minor key to make the song plaintive and sentimental.

> Mississippi gals put on airs,
> Sabine River gals dance daily,
> Rio Grande gals have dark brown eyes,
> Monterrey gals are ladies.

He raised his voice on the chorus.

> But none of them equal the girls of the Wabash,
> Wabash gals who are blushing and brave;
> The girls of the Wabash excel all the others,
> Away to the Wabash, away.

The song had meant nothing to him, sitting at the campfire with the homesick Hoosiers. He had left no girl behind on the Wabash, or the White or the Mississinewa. But Tildy *was* blushing. And very brave in her struggle against her father.

*The girls of White River excel all the others.*

If no other solution presented itself, if the December wedding became inescapable, he would satisfy his lust with her. Make love to her. In this house, so everyone knew. But not tonight. And he would not marry her.

"Another! Sing another!" Granny begged, and Matt saw a tear glint on her cheek. He leaned the banjo in the corner.

"It's important that I study tonight," he said "Rights of parents and children." He went into the sitting room to find Blackstone, took his place next to Tildy but extended the large volume in her direction, so she had to move over, out of foot and knee range.

*Children are of two sorts; legitimate, and spurious, or bastards.*

Matt closed his eyes, gripped the edges of the book, and took a deep breath before continuing.

*A legitimate child is he that is born in lawful wedlock, or within a competent time afterward.*

Hard as it was to keep a steady voice, Matt congratulated himself on the selection. Blackstone reminded Tildy of the circumstances of his birth. Recalling the bastard, she would not want him. He glanced at Jim Mac, anxious to see his reaction. Would he have second thoughts about allowing Matt Hull in his kitchen? He plunged ahead, into the duties of parents to their legitimate children—the duty of protection, of education—and discovered none of these privileges extended to bastards.

If he lay with Tildy, and conceived a child in her womb, he must marry her. No matter what her father's condition—bankrupt or respected storekeeper—he would be honor bound to marry her. If, to prevent the wedding to Walton, he must seduce her, he'd use the lambskin sheath. Major Linder had assured him it prevented conception as well as disease. Matt struggled on, through the legal verbiage, knowing he was not understanding, and must read it all again tomorrow.

"I must be going," he said as he finished the section. He slammed the volume shut.

"Why, you'll stay the night, of course!" Granny said. "Listen to the wind!"

"Peter's bed is plenty large enough for two," Mrs. MacIntyre said. She had been kept ignorant of the plot.

Matt blindly pulled his coat from the peg by the door, wrapped his muffler around his hat and clutched Blackstone in its protective blanket. He glanced over his shoulder to say goodbye to the family, but he saw no one but

Tildy. Her outrage filled his eyes. The fire in her eyes would melt the snow; her jaw stuck out, and her chest rose on a deep inhalation. She didn't wear an inflatable bust improver!

The snowdrift covered the stoop, but he felt his way down without slipping. He ran into the rail fence, and had to follow it to the gate. Snow lay two feet deep on the road, and where wind had piled drifts, to his hips. Once in town, he cut blindly across the square, and only by accident found himself in front of the law office.

He started a fire in the stove and huddled over the tiny blaze until the numbness in his hands and feet eased away. He dug an armload of wood from the snow-covered pile, for morning, used the broom to once again clear his ladder, climbed to the attic, pulled off his damp clothes and curled under his blankets. The heat from below sifted through the gaps in the floor and lulled him to sleep. At the very last moment of consciousness, he remembered Tildy's breasts, and snapped awake.

Maybe he should leave town. But if he left Ridley's office, would another lawyer take him? He did not want to give up law. He had expected his studies to be dry and boring, a necessary evil to suffer before reaching his goal. A month ago he had seen law as nothing more than a path to power, a weapon to use against Ira MacIntyre. But Blackstone's eloquence and logic concealed a trap, and he had fallen in. He could not leave.

He lifted himself onto his elbow, looked around, but found nothing in the dark except a vision of Tildy. He must avoid her, for he was not sure he could resist her blandishments forever. Not even for a week or two. Just the thought of her brought his sex up. And the thought of her with Walton throttled him with sickness.

What a mess he had walked into. He felt like a rooster who discovered a fox in the chicken house, and ran about aimlessly, somehow missing every chance at escape. He must make definite plans for his own future and stick to them. And forget Tildy. Let her figure a way to escape the fox without involving Matt Hull. Marry Walton, if she must. His gorge rose, and he beat it down by forcing himself to remember everything Blackstone said about the duties of parents, and the legal position of bastards.

Tildy pulled Meggie's spare flannel nightdress over her head. The chilly air of the loft did not moderate the heat of her anger. She crawled in the bed, next to her cousin. Not the way she had planned to spend the night. She stared into the darkness, listening to the faint hiss of snow blowing beneath the eaves.

"Matt Hull is a low, common man," she said.

Meggie turned over, raised herself on her elbows, letting in the cold. "I thought you liked him. Why else did you flirt with him this evening?"

"I didn't flirt with him," Tildy said, unhappy that Meggie had noticed. "I was merely pleasant to him."

*I flirted. I did more than any respectable woman should do, and he rejected me.*

"Maybe he thought courting improper, with so many people looking on. Maybe he'll call on you in town and sit in your parlor."

"Papa won't let him in the house."

"I wouldn't mind Lieutenant Hull calling on me," said Meggie, "except I'd tell him flat out, I wouldn't marry him because he's to be a lawyer, and live in town, which I couldn't abide."

She had not thought about the law office! Matt might entertain the men loafing about the stove by telling how she had pushed her knee against his, and put her foot on top of his. Within a few days, every man and boy in Pikeston would know! She should never have confided in him, especially she should never have told him of Papa's money problems. Matt Hull only wanted to marry her to become Ira MacIntyre's son-in-law. He would find little prestige as the son-in-law of a bankrupt. The future took shape in the dark, young men turning away from Ira MacIntyre's daughter, or taking liberties without mentioning marriage.

"I've got to stop dashing about like a hen who finds a fox in the chicken coop," Tildy said. "I've wasted time thinking ever so many ways to dump Mr. Walton, when I should have concentrated on just one."

"What?" Meggie reared up again.

"Stay down, Meggie. You let in the cold. I'm running away. Would you please ask your father, could I borrow twenty dollars?"

"I've got twenty dollars. In fact, I've got more than thirty."

"Where did you get thirty dollars?" Tildy asked. When she wanted something, she asked Papa. She had no need for money. Ladies did not fret themselves with money, because money was…masculine, and slightly dirty.

"I have my own chickens. I've sold my eggs and hens since I was nine years old. Why do you need twenty dollars?"

"Stagecoach fare. I'll ask Pete to take me to Muncie, and there I'll catch the stage to Indianapolis, and from there to Springfield. You're coming through Springfield on the way to California, and can pick me up in March."

"Springfield! You don't know anyone in Springfield!"

"I'll go to the first church I see, and tell the preacher that I'm an orphan, making my own way, and would he please recommend me to his congregation for cooking and sewing. And I can give piano lessons, too."

"Cooking and sewing! You don't know how to cook and sew!"

"That's what I'll learn, in the next month. I won't run away until the middle of December. I'll let Papa keep on believing the wedding will be on New Year's Eve. The Christmas Fair gives a fine excuse to go to Muncie. You, me and Pete. Everyone in town will think it wrong of me, I know, running off when Papa has such desperate problems—"

"What problems?"

"Can you keep a secret, Meggie? A dreadful secret?"

"Of course."

"Papa owes money, and can't pay the men he borrowed from. He's nearly bankrupt."

"Hmm," murmured Meggie from under the comforters.

"He'll ask Mr. Walton's help, after we're married."

"Hmm," Meggie said again.

"Don't you understand?" Tildy lifted a shoulder as she turned, and let in the cold in her turn. "Papa'll lose everything. The house, maybe even the store. Unless I marry Walton. But Granny says I shouldn't let Papa's problems sway me. That Papa got himself into this mess, so let him get himself—"

"Pete and Pa wondered. I heard them talking in the barn, when I went gathering eggs, and they didn't know I overheard."

"They suspect?"

"Pete says Uncle Ira hauled planks from the sawmill for the outhouse, and not even good ones, but the first cut of the log that they give away free. With the bark still on."

"It's only temporary," Tildy said, "until he gets the mason from Muncie."

"Then why did he ask Pete to take the bricks from the old privy as payment for putting it up?"

Tildy scooted down and pulled the comforter over her head. Papa's situation was as bad as that? He couldn't afford to repair the outhouse. All winter they must use that shanty with planks so rough the wind blew through? But not all winter for her. She would be in Springfield.

"We're leaving for California on Monday, March 6th," said Meggie. "Just postpone your wedding until—"

"Papa insists, the last day of this year. I told him I wanted a spring wedding, but he won't hear of it. I think it's something to do with the loans coming due. Lieutenant Hull wrote a friend of his in Boston, asking him to find out the truth about Afton Walton, but the reply can't arrive before the end of the year, especially with winter coming so early. When I get on the stagecoach, I must be in disguise, because Papa will inquire, and I don't want the hostlers to remember me."

"Granny still has her mother's wig. The moths got in one side, but with a bonnet on, it looks fine."

"A black bonnet," Tildy said. She imagined herself in the gray wig, in a black bonnet and shawl. Even a black dress.

"Does Granny or Aunt Eliza have an old black dress? One I could remake to fit me, one that Papa wouldn't recognize?"

"We'll look in the trunks tomorrow," Meggie said. "Ma says they must all be emptied before we leave for California. I'll help you. Oh, Tildy, how exciting! I wish I could go with you, but there's too much to do here. It's what I said on Harvest Home Sunday, you must run away. But will you travel alone, without an escort? A lady—"

"From now on I'm not a lady. What has being a lady ever got me? I'm so stupid I can't—"

"You're not stupid, Tildy. You made delicious biscuits for supper."

"And if Granny hadn't stood over me, I'd have put salt in twice. Mama's quite right when she says I need a man to take care of me. But I'll show them. I'll learn to take care of myself!"

"In the wig and a black dress and a deep bonnet, I suppose no man will make advances, so you'll be safe."

"Of course I'm safe. Besides, what if a man should make advances, what if he ravishes me? I'm going to California, and the men there need never know."

"Tildy, you're finally talking sense," Meggie said. She clapped her hands under the comforter, taking care not to let in the cold.

"We'd better go to sleep. I'll get up early and help Granny cook breakfast. I'd better learn to fry eggs."

She would do this on her own, in her own way. She would ignore all the advice her mother had given her, and never read *Godey's* again. And never again would she ask a favor of Matt Hull, who was a low, common man. She hated him. She had never been so insulted in her life.

She rolled over, her back to Meggie, so she could wipe away the tears secretly. She had so looked forward to him beside her. Just once.

## Chapter Thirteen

"Why did you wrap up that book?" Ridley asked as Matt unwound the bit of blanket from the first volume of Blackstone.

"For protection. I carried it out to Jim Mac's place last night."

Ridley gulped and gasped as if he'd swallowed boiling coffee, but Matt knew for certain the mug on the edge of his desk had been sitting there for twenty minutes.

"To Jim Mac's!" Ridley said after he quit choking. "You're never to take those volumes out of the office! Do you have any idea how much a set of Blackstone costs?"

No, Matt realized. He hadn't the faintest notion how much the books cost.

"I'm sorry, sir. It hadn't occurred to me—"

"It's plain you've never purchased books of quality. Blackstone costs five or six dollars a volume. Leather bindings, marbled endpapers, gold-edged—"

"I'm sorry, sir. It won't happen again."

"I hope not. The matter of Sales versus Richie needs attention immediately. The circuit judge arrives in Muncie two days from now."

Matt uncorked his ink bottle, stifling a sigh. No more nights reading by the light of candles paid for by Jim Mac. He recalled the family sitting around the table. Tildy's foot sliding over his. On second thought, Ridley's objections were a blessing in disguise.

"Going to Muncie, take everything you'll need to stay three, maybe four days. Sorry to be so abrupt about the Blackstone, but when you buy your own set, you'll learn how precious they are."

His own set. Fifteen or twenty dollars. Could he afford to take the plunge? Before he hung out his shingle he must own a copy of Blackstone.

"I hope this weather clears and the roads are passable day after tomorrow," Ridley mused, half to himself.

"Yes, sir." MacIntyre did not carry books in his store, except for almanacs, but he could certainly put in a special order with some stationer in Indianapolis.

Before dinner Matt walked through the slush to the general store. The early-season storm carried a warm wind at its back, and it brought a quick thaw. A trotting horse splashed icy mud on his legs. He had forgotten about slush. In Texas and Louisiana his memories had been of the virgin snow. Virgins, with green eyes that begged... Hell!

"Blackstone?" MacIntyre asked. He turned to the men playing checkers at the stove. "Can't pay his old man's grocery bill, but can squander money on law books." He laughed, a short, deprecating laugh. "You intend to stick to this lawyer business?"

"Yes." Matt swallowed the "sir" he normally would have added to the single word.

"I don't order in such things without a deposit," MacIntyre said, his tone implying that Matt Hull could not be trusted for the money. "And your pa's cost me too much. I won't carry a second man named Hull on my books."

"Of course not." Matt spun on his heel, heading for a dramatic exit. The door opened and he had to step aside for Tildy and Granny. Granny nodded and smiled. Tildy surveyed the population of the room with one glance, turned her back on everyone, but particularly on Matt. She pulled off her right glove, examined a blister on the side of her hand. She put her lips to the red spot.

"Ira, this daughter of yours hasn't the start of a necessary wardrobe," Granny said. "She's staying with me until we've done some sewing." She pulled a scrap of paper from her reticule. "Dark gingham, dark calicos as won't show the dirt—"

"Ravania's seeing to her trousseau," MacIntyre protested. Tildy's pink tongue touched the blister, and Matt wondered what parts of his body she would be willing to...he should leave. His boots had suddenly acquired leaden soles.

"Silk dresses and fine stockings! That's what Ravania's planning. Tildy's marrying a storekeeper, Ira, not an idle gentleman. She'll be managing a house, and she won't do that in silk dresses." Walton's wife, in Walton's bed, and her pink tongue darting to Walton's orders.

MacIntyre shrugged in the face of his mother's determination. "Ravania has the seamstress coming next week. Move into town while the weather's fine, and you can help her get Tildy's things ready. And not suffer another winter in that drafty house, without even a proper bedchamber."

Granny laughed, a knowing laugh, a private laugh, which Matt found a bit embarrassing. Like viewing an argument between a married couple. "I'm quite content," Granny said. She smiled at Matt. "You'll be joining us for supper, Lieutenant?"

"Not this evening. Circuit court convenes in Muncie in two days, and all the cases must be—" Tildy took off her left glove. A narrow bit of muslin was knotted around her third finger. What had she been doing to herself? "—must be ready to file."

His feet moved, not to the door, but in Tildy's direction. He swerved under her hostile glare, and hit the boardwalk running, aware of the laughter behind him.

The blue sky promised clear weather, and the wind was drying the roads. He would find the books in Muncie. And within a few weeks, the men behind the stove would laugh at Ira MacIntyre, because he had passed up a big sale out of spite. Clouds right now, but silver linings in the future.

Matt tried not to think of Tildy, standing passive while her grandmother selected the goods for her dresses. Everyday dresses, appropriate for the wife of a prosperous merchant, overseeing the operations of her fine house.

"My fault," he muttered. If he had crept into Tildy's bed last night...he should never have suggested that she agree to marry Walton. Why couldn't the wedding wait until spring? Because MacIntyre needed the money. Tildy would give in and save her family.

By the time he entered Faith's kitchen, all the silver lining had dimmed, and the clouds hovered in a dismal mass.

"We've decided," Mr. Tole said as Matt sat down on the bench beside Kit. "We're joining Godfroy and Sampson."

"Ho for California!" Kit said.

"Ho for California!" yelled his three brothers.

"Will we see buffalo?" asked the youngest.

"No shouting at the table," Faith said. Her face had the stolid, fixed look of a person coping with bad news, determined to show no emotion.

"How long will the quilt frame be up in the front room?" Mr. Tole asked. "We'll need the space for arranging our loads. Jim Mac gave me a list of things we'll need on the journey."

"Until Meggie and Tildy come for another day of quilting. They're busy making clothes for Tildy, who hasn't appropriate everyday dresses." She turned to Matt. "Can't you or Mr. Ridley do something? Must she marry that horrid man?"

"She can refuse to go through the ceremony, she can refuse to sign the certificate." *I can go to Jim Mac's and bed her, and let the hue and cry carry me straight to a wedding.* Then what? No money, no profession. He and

Tildy would be forced to join Jim Mac and head for California, he thought with a shrug.

Except that it cost money to travel to California. Would Jim Mac be that generous? Granny? She must have money, for MacIntyre wanted her to come live in town.

Matt climbed to his loft and studied the trunk with the streak across its lid, where his shaving water had washed it clean. Locked safe from prying eyes. He touched the hasp of the lock, and it fell open.

The papers relating to James MacIntyre, Sr. lay on the very top. A will, granting to son James, Jr., sixty acres with outbuildings, equipment and cattle. To son Ira, eighty acres of uncleared land. "Fully confident of her talents and fairness, so she may not in her age become dependent, to my wife, Margaret, all assets in cash and investments at interest."

Matt flipped through the papers, looking for the final settlement of the estate. "To Margaret MacIntyre, the amount of $2,345.72."

A young fortune! What had happened to the money? Perhaps Granny had invested in state improvement bonds. If she had more than two thousand dollars, she could certainly help her son pay his debts, and thus buy Tildy's freedom. Instead, she had schemed in Tildy's seduction.

The money had vanished, Matt decided. Frittered away in foolish purchases, or unwise investments. Yet, old James MacIntyre had been "fully confident of her talents and fairness." And Matt could think of nothing in that lean-to chamber that betrayed one rash purchase.

A dais lifted the judge's bench six inches above the floor. To one side sat twelve armchairs for the jury; below the bench a great curved table furnished plenty of space for lawyers and their clients. A carved railing isolated the dignity of the court from the public, who made do with benches so crude that Matt could see the splinters sprouting from the edges of the planks. Ridley led the way to the front bench.

"Sit here, on the aisle," he said, "in case the oratory becomes like a widow's ax. Dull."

The sheriff let the attorneys and parties to the first case through the gate, and they took their places at the table. The clients glared at each other.

"Osburn," whispered Ridley, nodding at a tall, skinny fellow a few feet in front of them. He wore a coat with exaggerated tails and a very tall hat, which he removed with elaborate care. He drew a sheaf of papers from the hat.

Men crowded onto the benches. The muscles in Matt's lower back contracted. He stiffened to regain control, reminding himself that a lawyer must put up with crowds when representing a client in a sensational case.

"Oyez, oyez, the Right Honorable..." The racket of two hundred men scrambling to their feet—and fighting for the few remaining spaces on the benches—drowned out the rest of the ceremonial phrase.

"Judge Simon Stanley," Ridley muttered as they resumed their seats. Upon sitting down, Matt found only a few inches for his backside. In the confusion of the judge's appearance, another man had shoved onto the bench.

Judge Stanley glanced from one lawyer to the other. "You ready?" He did not wait for an answer, but pointed to the man standing guard at the railing. "Call the jury."

The spasms in Matt's back inched upward. He looked over his shoulder, and discovered latecomers jamming into the aisle. His heart lurched. Someone on his bench wriggled to gain more room, six or eight men slid sideways, and Matt lost another two inches. He swung his shoulders, preparing to shove back, then realized the impudent man in the middle had done him a great favor. He stood up.

"Let me give you more room, sir," he said to Ridley, and stepped into the aisle. He inched toward a side door, dodging hats and hands of the men sitting on the floor, and leaned against the doorframe.

The attorney for the plaintiff embarked on his preliminary speech, sometimes addressing the jury, and at other times talking to Judge Stanley's boot soles. He outlined the contract between the two men, and called the opposition an assortment of vile names. The judge leaned farther back, and Matt noted that the distance between the chair legs and the edge of the dais narrowed every time the judge shifted.

"We shall prove, beyond all doubt, by presentation of documents, that the agreement between my client and this blackguard was signed before witnesses, agreed to with full formality...."

Osburn, Esq. unfolded himself like a cat from a sunny windowsill, and Matt realized his deliberate movements called attention to his height. He did not speak immediately, but studied the opposition, the audience, the judge and finally the ceiling.

"I believe that learned counsel for the plaintiff confuses a mere discussion of possibilities with a contract, and fails to distinguish between a contract and a covenant," he began in a quiet voice.

"Confuse the opposition," whispered a man leaning on the other side of the door.

"And, we must admit, after a study of Blackstone, we believe this entire case should be dismissed, for there can be no breach of contract where no contract exists. My learned friend—" Osburn wriggled his shoulder in the direction of the other lawyer "—might have filed a writ of covenant, and this court might rightly address that issue, for does not Blackstone say, 'if a man covenants to be at York by such a day, and is not at York at the time appointed, this is a direct breach of his covenant....'"

The quiet voice trailed off. Osburn studied the ceiling again, and clasped his hands behind his back, beneath his coattails.

"But," he said so suddenly and loudly that people jumped, "since we're here, we might as well proceed, although the case is fatally flawed. We shall show that no contract existed, no verbal covenant, not so much as a promise to arrive at York—or Muncie—on a specific day." The audience tittered. "We shall show nothing existed but a discussion of potentialities, nothing at all like a promise to be at York. More like, 'I'll be there if nothing breaks or comes untwisted.'" The audience stirred, a murmuring laugh at the homely aphorism.

"To accuse this respected gentleman of breach of contract wastes Your Honor's time—" a nod at Judge Stanley "—and wastes the time of every man involved." He waved a hand at the jury. "Here you sit, gentlemen of the jury, hog-tied to a case that should never have come before this court. Why, I'm reminded of the agony of an elderly lady of my acquaintance, who complains of the inordinate amount of time wasted upon leaving church, at the very instant when her kettle and skillet should be laid to the fire, if she's to feed her hungry family a Sunday dinner. 'Why,' she asks, 'why cannot all the gossip be announced from the pulpit, so's to let a woman get on with her work?'"

The audience laughed and sat up straighter. No one cared about the breach of contract, Matt realized. They had come to see Osburn perform. To hear a man quote Blackstone without so much as a scrap of paper in his hand, to tell humorous, homely stories that quietly ridiculed his opposition.

"Can always count on Osburn for some fun, even if it's no more'n a sheep stealing," Matt's neighbor whispered. "And he gives value for his fee. Every time a man threatens me, I say, 'Osburn's my man. Who's yours?' and he turns the color of a spring toad and I hear no more about the matter."

A good lawyer. A great lawyer. Matt decided to buy his own copy of Blackstone.

Osburn praised his client as a man who helped widows and orphans, a man who put out scraps for puppy dogs. The audience roared, the judge snorted explosively. The force just sufficient to send the back legs of his chair skittering over the edge of the dais. A crash and a startled roar from the judge. The jurymen in the front row leaped out of their chairs and ran to the bench, cutting off Matt's view.

"Damn," said the man leaning on the door. "If the judge's hurt—" But at that moment the judge's head peeked over the edge of the bench.

"Osburn," he yelled, "you're in contempt of court!" Judge Stanley rubbed the back of his head. Osburn reared in astonishment. "You knew I'd fall off this damned platform when you mentioned puppy dogs."

"I retract puppy dogs," said Osburn. "Kitty cats." The audience howled. "Canary birds."

Judge Stanley gaveled for silence. "This court's adjourned, until the judge determines how bad he's hurt."

The crowd dashed for the doors. Matt stepped outside and took refuge behind a pillar. When Ridley walked by, he fell in beside him.

"There you are! We'll take the opportunity to pay a call. There's someone you should meet." To Matt's relief, Ridley ignored the crowded taverns near the courthouse, and set off down a side street. He turned in at the gate of a white house with a high peaked roof.

"Stanley's," he explained. "We'll pay our respects to Mrs. Stanley, who plays mother to all the young lawyers following the circuit."

Matt was prepared for a stout, full-busted woman. Mrs. Stanley proved to be rather tall, and as skinny as a top rail. "I'll make tea," she said after the introductions.

"What was all the uproar about puppy dogs?" asked Matt, after Mrs. Stanley bustled out of the sitting room.

"Why, everyone knows the defendant shot Judge Stanley's best coonhound, because the dog howled. Why'd you run off like that? A man stands up for what's his. We had that bench first. You should have knocked the ingrate onto the floor.''

"I don't like crowds.''

Ridley stared, his jaw working. "Well, you've picked a hell of a profession if you don't like crowds. That's the idea of the law. Public debate, public trials, public verdicts. A good lawyer like Osburn, he draws crowds who come for the fun of it.''

"I'll be fine when I'm sitting at that table in front, not being elbowed and my feet stepped on.'' *If the aisles are kept clear,* he said to himself. "Right after I left home, I was on a steamboat that caught fire, down on the bottom deck with quite a mob. I jumped over the side just ahead of the flames. Being in a crowded room, with no path open to the door, sets my nerves tingling.'' Not to mention drying his mouth and tightening his back.

"Get over it,'' Ridley said without the least show of patience. "The last thing a lawyer needs is nervous tics.''

"Yes, sir.''

"Hanging on to a memory like that, that's a coward's way. Blights your life. Forget it.'' Ridley turned over the pages of a leather-bound Bible resting on a table next to his chair. "What you do, you force yourself,'' he said in a low, stern voice, flipping the pages. "You walk into crowds. Go to church and sit up front. Sit in the very back of the tavern and beat the fright down with whiskey.''

"I signed a temperance pledge.''

Ridley waved the pledge away. "Mrs. Ridley's fancy. You draw that memory to you. Right here.'' He tapped the Bible. "'Take hold of shield and buckler...draw out the spear.' Remember the fire, until it's of no more consequence than recalling what you had for breakfast.''

Breakfast? Should he remind Ridley that he'd had no breakfast, because they had left Pikeston long before he could politely show up at Faith's kitchen?

"Yes, sir. I'll forget it,'' he lied, to end the conversation because Mrs. Stanley walked in carrying a tray. A clock somewhere in the house struck eleven, and Matt's stomach growled. The tray held only the teapot, cups, the cream pitcher and sugar basin. No plate of cakes. Not even buttered bread or cold biscuits.

He drank two cups of heavily sugared tea, while Mrs. Stanley chattered on about the Christmas Fair and the quilt the Methodist ladies would raffle to raise money for lightning rods for the church spire. "Not that I'll see them," she said sadly. "Judge Stanley insists, after the spring circuit, we're moving to Indianapolis."

"Leaving?" Ridley cried.

"We should have moved years ago, for the good of my husband's career. Living in the capital offers much more opportunity. Judge Stanley hopes—" she lowered her voice "—for the supreme court."

"Is there truly a chance..." Ridley leaned toward Mrs. Stanley, and Matt had the feeling that his presence hampered an exchange of legal gossip.

"If you'll excuse me, ma'am, sir, I have some errands—"

"Watch to see when Judge Stanley heads for the court," Ridley warned. "I'll meet you there."

Matt made two wrong turns before he discovered Moffett's Emporium on a corner of the main street. To his surprise the store was empty, except for Walton, sitting behind the counter. Walton glared at the tingling bell set trembling by the opening of the door. He heaved himself to his feet.

"Good day, Walton," Matt said. Walton's eyes dropped from the bell, and Matt felt the man's stare rather than saw it. He could not determine if Walton's gaze was friendly or hostile, and he found no readable expression on his countenance. "Matt Hull, of Pikeston," he prompted. "We met at the Harvest Home."

Walton nodded. Matt waited for Walton to inquire about Miss MacIntyre. Walton leaned his elbows on the counter to take some of his weight off his feet; he tilted his head to show impatience.

"My sister, Esther." Walton nodded slightly. "She's well?"

"You expecting to visit with her?" Walton asked. "This time of day I don't allow callers. She sits and chats if I'm not there to watch her."

"Of course. But is she well?"

"Well as can be." Was that a glower of disapproval in his eyes? He looked back at his chair. "Anything I can get you?"

"A set of Blackstone, four volumes. I'm afraid I must make do with the cheapest edition—"

"Books. Across the street. Stationer's." Walton backed to his chair in the bent huddle he had assumed at the counter. He collapsed rather than sat down. The chair creaked.

Dismissed, by God! Matt turned in his smartest military style, strode to the door. No wonder the idlers had deserted the place. Walton had all the charm of a snake at a salt lick.

He walked around the corner, stood behind a fence, hesitating to cause Esther more difficulty with her employer. The back door opened, Esther carried a bucket to the well. Her face showed no distress. If anything she had gained a bit of weight. After she had gone inside he walked back to the main street.

Matt stated his business to the stationer's clerk, who pulled a catalog from under the counter. He ran a well-tended finger down a list of authors.

"Blackstone, Sir William. Commentaries, et cetera, et cetera. Cloth bound, $4 per volume; gold-edged and embossed title, $4.50; finest leather-bound, $5."

"Cloth. Plain," Matt said. Plenty of time to buy leather-bound books after he had a well-established practice.

"None closer than Cincinnati," said the clerk. "Four weeks if the snow holds off. Bad weather—" he shrugged

"—might be spring." Matt nodded. "Fifty percent deposit," the clerk droned, pulling a ledger book from a shelf. "That'll be eight dollars." Matt counted out the money and slid the coins across the counter slowly, bidding them goodbye.

"Send a note to me when they arrive. In care of Mr. Ridley's office, Pikeston."

He found a dinner of bacon and beans for ten cents. Even the knowledge that he was half owner of a set of Blackstone did not cheer him. Tildy must not go to that overstuffed swine. First, because Matt Hull could not bear the thought of her physical intimacy with Walton. Second, because Walton would not, in the long run, be the owner of the biggest store in Muncie. He had already driven Moffett's customers away.

Dregs fouled the last half inch of coffee. Matt looked into the cup. Did he want to strain the stuff through his teeth? His worried face reflected in the black liquid. If, by Christmas, the wedding seemed certain, he would abduct Tildy. He would seduce her in a place where discovery was certain, to the ruination of both their reputations. She could join her uncle on the road to California. And he would stick around—if Ridley would allow him to stay after such a dastardly deed—and in the spring sling his pack on his back and head for some other state, where people didn't know or care. Arkansas, or Texas maybe.

# Chapter Fourteen

Tildy scrunched down beside Meggie in the narrow protection the wagon box offered from the cold west wind.

"I hate wind," Tildy said. "I'll find myself a husband rich enough to buy a closed carriage."

"It's only a quarter mile in to church," Meggie said. "Besides, you won't need a closed carriage in California."

Tildy tucked her hands beneath her arms, then realized her thick mittens made that cold-weather gesture unnecessary. She pulled her hands from beneath her cloak and held them up to admire her handiwork. The very first things she had ever knitted.

"There's a loose string on this side," Meggie said, deflating her pride. Tildy pulled her hands under her cloak.

"I'll take the horses over to the livery," Pete said, his voice muffled by his clothes. Meggie stepped over the side of the wagon, showing too much ankle.

"Why thank you, Lieutenant," Tildy heard Meggie say, and she was facing him, his extended hand, before she had a chance to go to the other side of the wagon. She did not want to accept anything from a man who had rejected her, a man who had probably spread gossip of her indecent advances all over Pikeston. She struggled to find a toehold on the narrow ledge outside the wagon box. She grasped the edge, put her weight on her hands to balance while she lifted her other foot.

"Ouch!" She shifted her hand to take the pressure off the burn on the edge of her palm, teetered on the toe of her left foot and would have toppled backward, except for two strong hands about her waist.

"Good morning, Miss MacIntyre," he said gravely as he set her on the ground. She dared one glance into his gray eyes, and flushed hot. She turned and bounded up the church steps. She felt his eyes upon her as she walked up the aisle, to the front bench where her father and mother and brothers had already taken their accustomed place. At the very last minute she remembered the mittens, hastily pulled them off, rolled them up, and shoved them in her reticule. Mama was sure to ask who had made them. Tildy smoothed the gloves she wore beneath the mittens.

"Good morning," she announced her presence.

"I'm so glad you're home," Mama exclaimed. "You've stayed out on the farm for far too long, and the seamstress says she needs a second fitting on the wedding dress before she takes another stitch. Josh, move over so Matilda can sit beside me. Mrs. Ridley's cousin in Virginia sent a pattern for a—" her mother leaned close "—nightdress. I have imagined it in cream silk."

"Not now, Mama."

"Has your grandmother come with you?" asked her father.

"No, Granny stayed at home."

"People gossip that she's a heathen," Mama said in a low voice. "Herbs and seeds, and not coming to church. She'd be far better off living with us. What's he doing sitting up here? People of his sort stay in the back of the church." Tildy knew whom her mother was talking about even before she looked down the row. On the other side of the aisle, Lieutenant Hull had taken his place on the front bench.

*I won't so much as look at him.*

Pete scooted onto the bench directly behind Matt, and leaned forward to say hello. Kit Tole plopped down beside Matt—no Tole had ever before dared to sit on the front bench! Kit whispered in Matt's ear and stifled a laugh. Had Matt told him how she had pressed her knee against his? How they had kissed behind the livery?

*I won't so much as look at him.*

"Kit's sniggering to Hull that we're not going to California because we're scared," Josh whispered. "Thinks he's better than me, just because his old man's decided."

"You want to go?" Tildy asked in astonishment.

"First he wins the snow fight, and now, California."

"Do you want to go to California?" she whispered, more determined.

"Yes. I don't say I'd stay, but it's bad to be mocked by Kit Tole."

Tildy shook her head, amazed at the silly things men do for ridiculous reasons. She looked over her shoulder to see who had come to church. The cold wind would keep the congregation small. Lieutenant Hull also twisted his head to look over his shoulder, warily. He shifted uncomfortably on the bench. What was he nervous about? Perhaps he feared Mrs. Ridley, who had just now arrived. Maybe she would order him off the front bench, back to where he belonged. Mrs. Ridley and Rachel took seats directly behind Tildy.

"Look who has come to church," Rachel whispered, leaning forward.

"Yes." *I won't so much as look at him.*

"You should tell him to move," Mama said to Mrs. Ridley. "You always sit in that spot."

"Not always. And today, I prefer being closer to the stove. How the wind howls!"

Reverend Fitch preached on a text from Ezekiel, and elaborated upon the evils of the far West, and his duty to warn his congregation against prophecies spoken by swindlers. Uncle Jim looked grim. Pete smiled, and Kit mocked Reverend Fitch by imitating his mannerisms.

Lieutenant Hull mopped his brow with a kerchief. Again and again he looked to the rear of the church, not at the people behind him. *He's expecting someone,* Tildy thought. *He keeps looking at the door.*

Hinges squeaked. Lieutenant Hull's head swiveled. Tildy turned just enough to see the latecomer from the corner of her eye. Trail Godfroy. He walked halfway down the aisle and took a seat on the warm side. Lieutenant Hull showed no interest in Mr. Godfroy, but glanced again at the door. What would make a man so nervous? *A woman,* thought Tildy. *He's expecting a woman. Matt Hull's expecting a woman, and he will take her to a private place, and...and do things with her I wanted him to do with me!*

*I won't so much as look at him.*

*He's a vile, common man, not fit to...I hate him!*

Tildy seethed through the final hymn and the benediction, and instead of turning down the aisle, where she risked coming face-to-face with him, she made her way to the wall and ran to the exit.

"Tildy, do wait," Mrs. Ridley said. "You must see what my cousin in Virginia sent. Rachel, you have the package."

Rachel produced a roll of white muslin tied about with a length of yarn. As she unrolled the fabric, Tildy saw a glitter that intensified in the sunlight flooding through the open door.

"A yard," Mrs. Ridley whispered. "An entire yard of gold cloth."

"A yard!" Tildy heard Mama whisper behind her. Her mother stepped forward, stripped off her glove and touched the amazing fabric with the tip of a finger. "Just feel it, Tildy, like the petal of a rose." Tildy dared not take off her gloves, lest her mother see her damaged hands. She extended one finger.

"It belonged to my grandmother, and my cousin sent it as a gift to Rachel."

"Margaret's already left," Mama said. "Let me fetch her back to see it." She bustled to the front steps. Tildy took the opportunity to remove her right glove and barely touch the gold with a roughened finger. A man stepped beside her; she lifted her eyes. Lieutenant Hull. He did not return her glance, but stared at her hand. She snatched it back, struggled to pull on the glove without tearing the collapsed skin of the blister.

"What have you done to your hands?" he whispered. She saw the concern in his eyes.

"I'm learning to cook," she said, making her tone as severe as possible while whispering. "And you'll say nothing about it! To anyone! I hope you enjoy your new doxy, and that I never see you again!"

She expected him to drop his eyes in shame that she had guessed his immoral secret. Instead, he stared at her, puzzled.

A tint of pale lavender spread across the horizon where the sun would rise. A cold color, suitable to a morning with the mercury only a few marks above zero. Matt tested the snow and found the crust would bear his weight. He pulled his hat down on his head, tightened the belt of his coat—saying a silent thanks to Faith for the weight of it—wrapped his muffler so it covered the lower part of his face and set off down the street that became the road to Muncie. The fierce cold struck through his wool mittens, so he thrust his hands in his pockets. He wrapped his fingers around the silver coins, and the note from the stationer's that informed him Blackstone, in four volumes, had arrived. Sleds and sleighs had packed the road without turning it to ice. He stretched his legs, walking fast enough to raise a trifle of sweat under his coat and wool shirt.

Beyond a thin stand of saplings a crescent of sun lifted over the horizon, turning the icy crust to diamonds, as far as he could see. He slowed down at the corduroy, picked his way carefully through the churned, frozen snow. A rugged landscape, like the desert of Mexico in miniature. Smoke ascended from the chimneys of roadside houses, and the smell of burning oak and hickory gave a suggestion of warmth. On the outskirts of Muncie smoke gathered in a little hollow, creating an aromatic fog that obscured the road. And suddenly he walked among houses, then on boardwalks, with horses and wagons struggling along the streets churned to sticky mud.

The stationery store had just opened when he arrived. The only warmth lay in the immediate vicinity of the stove. "Can I help you?" asked the clerk, each word marked by a puffy ice cloud. Matt laid the note on the counter.

"Matt Hull, of Pikeston. My Blackstone's in."

The clerk studied the note in the same way he would examine a suspicious banknote, then vanished into a back room without a word. Matt backed to the stove and lifted his coat to warm his legs and rear end.

"He's asked you, too?" asked a man huddled on the opposite side of the stove. Matt wondered if this curious question had been addressed to him, but upon turning around, discovered a second gentleman briskly chafing his hands over the fire. Matt pulled off his mittens, and held his hands close to the stove.

The second man nodded, frowning, then shifted the motion of his head to a negative shake. "Two thousand dollars is a heap of money to loan on property I know nothing about. And how he'll manage the mortgage, I don't understand. After all, he'll be only a son-in-law."

"Did I hear right?" asked the first man, now definitely looking at Matt. "You're from Pikeston?"

"Yes."

"What's the situation of property there? Selling well?"

"I really can't say." Tole's gloomy assessment of Pikeston's future should not be spread to strangers. Particularly since Tole was presently negotiating the sale of his forge. "I own no property."

"I'm Swab," the first man said, "this here's Boyd."

Matt introduced himself and shook hands. "I'm reading law with Mr. Ridley," he added, to explain his unpropertied state.

"A man here in Muncie's to marry the daughter of your storekeeper," said Boyd. He stopped, looked at his companion, as if seeking advice on how much to say. Matt controlled the impulse to grab the man's coat and shake the gossip out of him. "It seems after the wedding he'll control his wife's property, which is considerable, and he's asked us to take a mortgage, two thousand dollars, on the house and store. He says the house is substantial."

Matt made a pretense of toasting his backside again, and used up half a minute loosening his coat. He searched for innocuous words that would give minimal information, but keep the men talking.

"The house is substantial," he said. "Brick. The only brick house in town."

"And the store?"

"I know nothing about storekeeping. I can't say if it's a substantial business or not."

"You have no idea how much trade—"

"Not at all."

"How old's the heiress?"

Heiress? Tildy was no heiress. She had three brothers, and tradition gave all of them a better claim to both store and house. And Ira MacIntyre showed no symptoms of ill health. Did Walton expect to take over MacIntyre's property?

"A pert girl," Matt muttered. "Not yet twenty."

Boyd shook his head again, slowly and seriously. "We need more information before we commit ourselves."

"I vote against it," said Swab. "I don't like Walton. He's snobbish about being born Yankee, talks bankruptcy, bankruptcy every chance he gets, like a babe on a hobbyhorse, and treats businessmen, no matter their age or experience, like unwashed innocents.''

"He knows railroaders..." began Boyd, but he let his voice die when the clerk reappeared behind the counter. Matt opened the top blue-bound volume. Not nearly so elegant as Ridley's copy, but the pristine pages crackled as he turned them. He fished about in his pocket, and counted out the money. The clerk piled the books on a sheet of brown paper, wrapped them and bound them with string. He twisted the ends into a carrying loop.

Matt glanced at Swab and Boyd, who waited expectantly. He stepped toward the door, glanced again. They stared as if they might gain information from the way he walked or the expression on his face.

"Don't," he muttered from the corner of his mouth. He bolted out the door, fearful of being drawn into more personal gossip that would betray his feelings. He had not seen Tildy since the Sunday morning when he had sweated through church. Tortured by her presence as well as by the crowd. Still tortured.

The smell of coffee drifted from the hotel's front door and drew him up short. His mouth watered, for he had sacrificed breakfast for an early departure. He felt in his pocket, touched the few extra coppers and dimes he had allowed himself in case he must buy dinner. If he walked home as fast as he had come, maybe caught a ride with a farmer, he would arrive in Pikeston in time for dinner with the Toles.

A board at the entrance to the dining room advertised coffee at five cents. But with a fifteen-cent breakfast of bread, butter and beans, coffee came free. He ordered the breakfast.

The cream on the table had turned slightly, the butter was too salty, but the beans had been simmered with molasses and side pork. He wolfed them down, but his stomach remained unsatisfied. Four hours, at least, getting home. The sun softened the icy crust, whether it warmed the air or not. In spots he would sink up to his calves. He thought about another plate of beans, then decided to set off immediately. By pushing, he might yet get his dinner.

Icy branches creaked, a nippy breeze had come up and blew dead in his face. The wind had blown the smoke away from the low spot, and he could see a clear half mile down the road. Even with that visibility, he heard the bells of the sleigh before the horses appeared. A quarter mile closer and he recognized the gait. Pete MacIntyre's team. He must need some vital part for the California wagons, something he could buy only in Muncie.

Matt watched the team, not where he stepped, and found himself wallowing up to his hips in soft snow. He staggered, struggled to right himself. He had wandered off the road into the side ditch, and floundered about with no predictable footing, hampered by the heavy package in his hand.

"Hull!" Pete yelled. "Whoa!" The vehicle was not a sleigh, but a small wagon fitted with runners. Behind Pete, snuggled beneath a buffalo robe, sat Tildy and Meggie. Tildy pulled the robe to cover her mouth and nose, but Meggie popped out of the nest like a hungry bird.

"Lieutenant Hull! Get in! We're going to the Christmas Fair."

"I...I shouldn't," he stammered, and was embarrassed because he caught himself looking at Tildy, rather than at Meggie, who had spoken to him. Tildy wore a plum-colored hat. Enough of her cheeks showed above the robe to reveal her blushes. Blushing and brave.

"If I stay on the road—" he pointed to the cavernous hole he had left in the snow of the ditch and smiled wryly "—I should be in Pikeston in time for dinner."

"There's food at the fair," Meggie said. "We'll leave at—" she turned to Tildy "—when?"

"Two in the afternoon," Tildy said in an undertone. She had ceased to glare at him, and glared at Meggie. She laid a mittened finger across her lips, as if stating the time of departure had violated some great secret.

"He can keep a secret," Meggie said to Tildy. "He won't blab it all around town, and he won't guess where you're—" Tildy sprang out from under the robe, and slapped her mitten over Meggie's mouth. She twisted from side to side, staring suspiciously, as if the woodlot on one side of the road, or the flattened cornstalks on the other, had overheard.

"Do join us, Lieutenant Hull," she said flatly, sinking back onto the seat.

She did not want him along, he saw that in her unwelcoming eyes, but Meggie's loose tongue made it necessary to keep him away from Pikeston until something happened at two in the afternoon. The mystery—and Tildy's eyes—drew him toward the sled.

"They've put up a Christmas tree," Meggie said. "I've never seen a Christmas tree."

"The eastern newspapers say bringing a tree indoors for Christmas is all the fashion," Pete said.

Matt lifted his parcel into the box behind the seat, and carelessly brushed a rug. It covered one sizable carpetbag, and a smaller one. He tucked the rug back into place and climbed upon the driver's seat next to Pete.

"I've never seen a Christmas tree either," he said. The carpetbags were of fine tapestry, much finer than Meggie probably owned.

"Sounds crazy to me," Pete said. "Why should anyone want a tree in the house?" Two in the afternoon? The stage from Fort Wayne to Indianapolis. Matt smiled to himself. Tildy would not be a passenger in the sled when Pete drove back to Pikeston.

Wild objections, wild relief jostled to seize his heart. Tildy, dear Tildy! He'd never see her again and thankfully, neither would Walton! He could resume supping at Jim Mac's house and, with his own copy of Blackstone, read by the light of Jim Mac's candles, and draw Granny's questions and sharp commentary.

Pete turned off the road and circled the town. Columns of smoke rose beside a large tent, and as they came closer, Matt saw ranks of parked vehicles and a crowd of people. Pete stopped the team some distance from the festive ground, where the snow still lay heavy on the ground. Matt sprang down to assist Meggie and Tildy. Tildy wore a black woolen dress that made her look older than her years. A young matron. The wife of a successful businessman. He remembered the carpetbags and was glad that at least it would not be Walton.

The smoke rose from fires beneath caldrons. Seething broth smelled of sausages and onions, of potatoes and pork. Sawdust and wood chips covered the ground. Odors of coffee and cider drifted by, hominy and spices. They passed a rough table covered with pies, some steaming through half-moon vents in the top crust. Beyond the food sellers, one wall of the tent had been rolled up to reveal the booths set up inside.

"Cider?" asked Pete.

"No," Matt said, remembering he had only twelve cents in his pocket. "I breakfasted in town." Tildy and Meggie reached for mugs of cider. Matt walked toward the tent, for fear Pete might suspect his poverty and offer to pay.

In the tent the crowd promenaded clockwise, with little eddies here and there as people hesitated at the booths lining the walls. In the middle stood an evergreen tree about fifteen feet high. Someone had cut bits of gold and silver paper into cunning shapes and hung them on the branches. They moved in the faint breeze, covering the tree with glittering points of light. So that was a Christmas tree! His imagination had been unable to conjure up anything more decorative than a sycamore with its ball seeds still dangling. He stepped into the tent, and the resinous perfume of the tree overwhelmed the smell of food. He understood why Christmas trees had become popular so quickly.

High above the tree, at the peak of the tent, hung a gaudy rosette, and from it fanned colored streamers more varied than a rainbow. Each of the streamers draped to the point of a tent pole, where a smaller rosette held it in place. Matt allowed himself one glance over his shoulder before he stepped into the crowd. He had managed to sit through a church service. In the front row. Today he would walk completely around the Christmas tree.

He stopped at a booth selling pens and inkstands, nibs of varying width, gold, silver, steel. He pretended to study the display while he concentrated on relaxing his back. If he had more money, he could buy his own pen. He passed silver thimbles and needle cases. Knives of all shapes and sizes. The knife seller had set up a grinding wheel, and offered to sharpen knives for three cents, scissors for five.

Hanks of silken floss, some spun with threads of gold. He remembered Rachel's cloth and Tildy's hands, and her stern dismissal of him. What doxy? Maybe, if he found her alone, he could ask her what she had meant. Today he and Tildy might be seeing each other for the last time. The spasm came, not in his back but in his chest.

Matt looked back at the tree and beyond that to the wide opening. A sea of bobbing hats and bonnets. He closed his eyes and gritted his teeth, determined to follow Ridley's advice and win out over his fear. Tension in his thighs. A gust of wind around his legs distracted him for a moment, and he opened his eyes. The decorations on the tree danced, and the reflections reminded him of sunlight on water. Sawdust rose from the floor, and a few women turned their backs to the wind. Across the tent, two men lowered a section of the wall.

Matt ignored the jeweler, the toy seller, the tinsmith selling new pots and mending old ones. He gave no more than a nod to the vendor of copper weathervanes. He must get out of the crowd, beyond that narrowed opening. He stopped where he could see the sky, pressed himself against a tent pole, out of the way of the people jockeying to get in and out. He had a view of the Christmas tree, but by turning ever so slightly, he could see the food sellers' alley, and beyond that the open countryside.

The plum hat leaned far over, to protect the black dress from the juice of the sausage she was eating. Then a piece of pie, sketchily wrapped in paper, devoured in the same fashion. Tildy would fill her stomach before she climbed on the stage and whirled away to Indianapolis. Did she have someone to meet her? Where would she take supper? Certainly, some friend of the family… He did not like to think of her on a stranger's arm.

Meggie selected a second piece of pie, and Pete stood beside her, holding out coins. Tildy shook her head—the broad brim of the plum bonnet dipped and wavered—and now she walked toward the tent. Matt sank behind the folds of canvas, in no mood to offer his arm and suffer further rejection.

The peddler of thimbles and needle cases bowed to her. Tildy's hand rested on the reticule hanging from her belt. He had not noticed it before, lost within the pleats and gathers of her skirt. She shook her head, and stepped away. A silver thimble would be of no use to her in her flight. She wandered past the knife sharpener, the toy maker, until all he could see was the brim of her bonnet. The bonnet hesitated before the display of colorful threads, disappeared as Tildy bent over the table. If she carried embroidery in her carpetbag, she might buy some thread. Embroidery to pass the time until her father agreed she need not marry Walton. Matt imagined Tildy in a rocking chair beside the fire with her embroidery spread in her lap.

A gust of wind chilled his legs. He inched into the tent, and leaned against a pole topped with a yellow rosette. Seeing it close, just above his head, he noted it was of paper, not calico or gingham.

An excited shout, a thin feminine scream pulled his attention from the bunting. A rustle of activity at the knife table—a pickpocket? He could see the brim of Tildy's bonnet at the tinsmith's bench, far from danger. Another shout, and a cry that chilled his bones. *Fire! Fire!*

On one side of the Christmas tree the silver and gold ornaments reflected streaks of orange. Behind the knife seller's table a flame like a tall candle. It wavered in an eddy of wind, and in the next instant sprang to life, a great beast gobbling the red rosette hanging at the tip of its tongue. Livid orange, a devil's stream that despised gravity, flowed to the peak of the tent. A roar, and Matt told himself the sound came from a hundred throats, not the fire. But some primal spot within him said *dragon,* said *sacrifice.* And Tildy stood at the tinsmith's stall, and in an instant the evil beast flared between them.

He fought against the sudden surge of people, elbowed men and women aside, and his foolish mind imagined fish swimming upstream, and at the same time he had sense enough to note that the plum bonnet moved as fast as possible away from the tinsmith's. Snow fell languidly from the expanding, red-gold rosette in the peak of the tent—snow as it might look on a sunny day, glittering, fiery.

Matt hugged the stalls, crawled beneath the coppersmith's table and gained a quick six feet. The smith snatched his vanes from the table and piled them into a disorderly heap near the wall of the tent, clasped an awkward bundle to his chest, his eyes squinting and his cheeks wet with tears.

The bonnet bobbed momentarily behind a broad shoulder, close to the tree. Tildy had tried to cut directly across the tent rather than follow the sweeping circle. She staggered toward the tree. The branches glowed with the debris of fallen stars. Matt caught one glimpse of the bonnet before it disappeared in a downward arch, and in the same instant the tree exploded. Men clambered over tables, pulling women behind them, both sexes shouting and screaming. In that chaos one man had the presence of mind to straddle the black bundle curled on the sawdust.

Her arms wrapped over the plum bonnet, in the automatic attitude of self-protection. Matt grabbed her ankles, with no clear memory of how he had reached her. He pulled her from between her protector's legs, aware that her skirts hitched up and revealed long, plain muslin drawers. In the seconds he needed to bend over, lift her, a haze of sawdust blended with smoke. A blind hell, the only certain direction marked by the flaming tree.

"The tinsmith's," he gasped to the man. He wished Tildy would wrap her hands about his neck to take some of the weight, but she kept them arched over the top of her head. Matt staggered through the gloom, searching for what his heart knew existed. The tinsmith would cut the canvas with his shears, an escape from the inferno. Ears, not eyes, led him to safety, a clashing of tin as the smith threw his pots and pans out the opening, heedless of the dings and dents they suffered.

"Through! Through!" Matt cried to the men battling for precedence before the strip of daylight. "A lady! I have a lady!"

The tinsmith disappeared through the slashed canvas, but his hand reappeared, offering help, which Matt could not possibly seize. Cold air on his face guided him. He tripped on the rope threaded through the bottom of the tent, and nearly went on his face. The tall central pole of the tent would collapse when its support ropes burned through. What direction? He slipped on muck, half ice, running but not running, her weight dragging him down, her heavy skirts tangling about his legs. And sticky moisture on his face that slid into his mouth. The taste of blood.

"Stop, Hull! For God's sake, stop! Meggie's getting the sled." Pete's voice, and Pete's hands grabbing at his coat. And clean snow beneath his feet. Matt sank to his knees, his arms crying out against the weight, while he steadfastly held Tildy above the snow.

"Tildy, put your arms down," Pete ordered. She obeyed, and crimson flowers blossomed in the snow.

"Hurt," Matt croaked. Crushed bonnet, tattered sleeves soaked with blood that turned the black cloth purple. Her face, smeared with gore. "She's terribly hurt!" he said, but his voice was of no more consequence than the silent meow of a newborn kitten. "Don't die, Tildy." He'd go with her, wherever she meant to go. If she died, the dark river that had seized Godfroy's heart would capture his own.

Horses snorted, so close he felt the warm moisture of their breaths. Pete shoved him against the solid side of the sled, and took Tildy from his arm. Cold seared his cheeks, and when he touched them, he found a coating of ice. Meggie wiped Tildy's face with a handkerchief, a job Matt felt was his. He climbed onto the sled, pulled Tildy onto his lap. Meggie's handkerchief scraped harshly over his own cheeks.

"I'm not hurt. It's Tildy's blood." Meggie exposed Tildy's arms by ripping away her shredded sleeves. Long, ragged cuts. Matt had seen such injuries before, when hobnailed boots raked across human flesh. The hard fact cleared his world and brought his senses into wobbly balance.

"It's not her face," Meggie said with relief. "Her arms."

"I rolled on my face and put my arms over my head," Tildy said, her voice so calm and practical Matt took his first normal breath, and it set off a fire in his lungs. He struggled to exhale.

"We'll go into town and find Moffett and Walton," Pete said, climbing upon the driver's seat.

Tildy must not go to Walton. To anyone but Walton. Matt wiped his sleeve across his eyes, and added sawdust to the half-frozen slime on his cheeks.

Half-frozen. The sled could not get close to Moffett's store. "Don't!" he tried to yell, but his lungs still heaved to get rid of the smoke. He reached for Pete's sleeve. "To the right, a side street. I've met the woman. Mrs. Stanley."

He flinched at a flick of white. "Hold still," Meggie ordered. "Let me wipe your eyes." Her ministrations cleared his vision, and he spotted the Stanleys' house in time for Pete to halt the team at the front gate.

"Don't die, Tildy," he whispered. Later he would find the words to tell her how much he loved her. Tell her she need not run away alone, that he would be with her, whether or not she would marry him. Sacrifice anything, for of what use was life if he must live with the nightmare that Tildy had been sold to Walton?

Sold? The significance of the conversation in the stationer's store washed over him.

"I can walk," Tildy said as Matt lifted her from the sled.

"I'll carry you. Until we're sure it's just your arms."

Walton needed money! Ira MacIntyre needed money! If he could manage a calm conversation with Ira MacIntyre, Tildy need not run away.

# *Chapter Fifteen*

Tildy watched Mrs. Stanley cut away the rags that had been her sleeves. Nothing too bad, hardly more than scratches, until Mrs. Stanley bared her right arm, and Tildy saw the deep slash from wrist to elbow, still seeping blood. She leaned back in the chair, ready to faint, but she did not feel the slightest bit giddy.

"Someone should fetch the doctor," Mrs. Stanley said.

A doctor? In Tildy's experience, doctors were called only in desperate cases. And if she were dying, wouldn't Meggie be crying, and an angel choir be hovering...?

"It's just a cut," she protested. "I want Granny. She'll know what to do."

"The doctors in town will be busy with hurts worse than cut arms," Pete said.

"My God!" Matt exclaimed, right in her ear. Hearing his voice, she realized his arm rested lightly on her shoulders, and that the wooly pillow behind her neck was the sleeve of his coat.

"How many people were hurt or killed?" he asked. "I didn't look back. Did the whole tent go up in flames?"

"It did," Pete said grimly.

*He loves me. He thought only of me. Not of that other woman.*

She had known instantly whose callused hands grasped

her ankles, and had not been the least surprised. Who else but Matthew Hull would risk fire and pounding feet to drag her away?

Mrs. Stanley filled a basin from the kettle. "How did it start? The men who planned the fair were very strict—all the cooking fires must be outside. Can you hold your arms out, dear?" Tildy lifted her arms, and for the first time saw the full damage to her dress. Rips, all the way to her shoulders.

"I think sparks from the grinding wheel started the fire," said Matt beside her. "I really hadn't thought about it, but that's where I saw the first flame. If a spark fell into the sawdust, it could lay there for hours, until the breeze came up in the middle of the morning."

She could not wear the dress in public now. "I can't go on the stagecoach."

"You're leaving on a trip?" Mrs. Stanley asked.

"Yes." She looked at Matt, to see his reaction to the news, and his wise eyes told her he had known all along, since Meggie's hasty words, or perhaps even before. His clever mind ferreted out all her secrets. "But now I'll go home. Granny—my grandmother—she makes poultices and teas to cure anything."

Tildy bit her lips when Mrs. Stanley touched her arm with a wet rag. Matt's arm tightened on her shoulders, rather like Granny's comforting touch. Except Matt's hands carried a little extra spark. She leaned into him while Mrs. Stanley bandaged her right arm.

"That should do until you get home," Mrs. Stanley said, adjusting a knot. "But your poor dress. And your bonnet." She picked it up from the floor, smashed beyond repair.

Matt draped her shawl over her head and pinned it beneath her chin. He extended his arms to lift her.

"I'll walk," she said. He kept his arm about her waist, needlessly, for her legs were quite steady. She had not fainted; she was strong enough to go to California.

Once on the sled, he pulled her onto his lap, wrapped the buffalo robe around her until she could not see and could barely breathe. She gave up protesting. He was bound to wrap her like a baby. She had no idea where they were until Pete slowed the team at the bumpy corduroy. Cushioned by Matt's legs, encased tightly in his arms, she hardly noticed the rough road. What she *did* notice was the hard shaft pressing against her hip. In a moment he would shift her off his lap, onto the seat. Instead, he lowered his hands, drew her closer. Like her grandparents, she and Matt would make love in the open air. But spring and mayapples were a long way off.

Pete chirped the horses into a trot on the long, flat stretch into town. "I'll take you home," he said over his shoulder. "Then I'll fetch Granny, and while I'm at the house, I'll take a little load off the sled."

"Thank you," she whispered. If her parents saw the carpetbags, they would know she meant to run away. She had two and a half weeks before the last day of the year, still a chance to make her escape. As soon as her arms mended.

Matt lifted her from the sled. She should walk to the front door, but she enjoyed the warmth of his attention. She glimpsed her mother on the steps, wringing her hands.

"Where's your room?" Matt asked.

Strange, Tildy thought, that he didn't know her room. All the best people in town—and some not the best—had visited in her house. "Up the stairs, to the left."

"I'll take care of her," said her mother. "Lewis, go to the store and fetch your father!"

Matt lowered her onto the edge of the bed and knelt beside her.

Mama would wonder about the strange black dress. Perhaps if she got it off quickly, she would not notice. "Lieutenant Hull, unbutton my bodice. The wool scratches my arms." Not a very good excuse, since the sleeves were nearly gone, but the first one she thought of.

He nodded, smiling, turned to Meggie to ask her help. Meggie's surprise lasted for only an instant, before she set to work at the buttons.

"Lieutenant Hull!" Mama cried. "Leave this instant! It's not proper—"

"No, it's not proper," he agreed, not turning his head for an instant. Meggie pulled the bodice down, carefully detaching the remains of the sleeves where they caught on the bandage.

"Water and rags?" Matt asked, looking at her mother for the first time. "When the bandage comes off, the bad cut on her arm will probably start bleeding again."

Mama turned very pale and leaned against the door. She did not react to the noise in the downstairs hall, Papa's boots pounding on the stairs, taking them two at a time. An exclamation of worry, a hasty description by Meggie of the disaster at the Christmas Fair...

"What the hell are you doing here?" His brows came together, and the way he lifted his arm, Tildy thought for a moment he meant to hit Matt.

"He saved her life!" Meggie cried. "He carried her out of the burning tent!"

"Ira, this is no time or place for a display of temper," Granny said from the door. She shoved Papa aside and he looked startled. "Is it just your arms, or do you hurt other places?" she asked Tildy.

"Just my arms. Actually, just my right arm."

"I'll get you out of your clothes and check," said Granny. "You men, leave the room, you're nothing but in the way."

Matt scrambled to his feet, but before leaving he laid his hand on her shoulder, and leaned over in the possessive manner of a new husband.

"I'll stay close by. Don't you die on me," he said.

She shook her head. Die? She hadn't the least intention of dying! At least, not until he made love to her, the way Grandpa had made love to Granny where the mayapples bloomed. Down by the river. But snow drifted high along the riverbanks, and waiting until spring...too long. Maybe Matt's room above the law office. She remembered the ladder, and her injured arms. A part of her heart tore away as he walked out the door.

"The wind's picking up. I'd better move the horses under cover," Pete said. He slammed the front door rather more briskly than necessary. Matt waited in the shadow under the stairs. He was in no mood to argue with MacIntyre. If he could not be with Tildy, he would rather be alone, mulling over the consequences of being in love. The slow footfalls on the stairs mimicked the pace of his heart. For Tildy's sake he must break through MacIntyre's anger, have one sensible conversation. He stepped to the foot of the stairs.

"Sir, I must talk to you, privately." The darkness concealed MacIntyre's face, but Matt could imagine his scowl.

"Meggie told me how you saved my daughter's life. I thank you. Beyond that, we have nothing to talk about."

"Yes, we do, but it must be in private."

"No, you may not call upon my daughter. That ends the conversation."

"The news I have doesn't concern Tildy, except indirectly. Her engagement to Walton."

"So, tell me." He leaned against the finial post, where a shaft of light from above outlined his hand caressing the silken finish of the ball.

"In private, sir. With Tildy hurt, Pete at the livery barn, everyone in town will hear the news in the next few minutes, and might burst in on us."

"Muncie rumors, I suppose. Gossip. You're in league with my brother, bound and determined to blacken Walton's name. I should never have allowed my daughter to spend so much time on the farm. You've visited, and corrupted...get out of my house!"

Matt considered blurting out what he had learned from

Swab and Boyd. But wrapped in his stubborn anger, would MacIntyre understand the significance of the news? He stepped toward MacIntyre, into the patch of light at the foot of the stairs.

"If you refuse to speak to me, I'll go directly to the tavern," he said firmly. "I'll climb upon a table, announce I have a great tale to tell, how eighteen summers ago Ira MacIntyre went to the Ohio River, with a string of bony horses. He lied when he said he'd been to meet a stranded boat on the Wabash."

Instinct told him to retreat; he stepped back into the shadow, feeling hollow, as if he had expended a great treasure. Holding the secret, nursing it in his bosom, had given him more pleasure than revealing it. MacIntyre's hand lay still on the polished ball. Matt waited, not daring to breathe.

"Come into the sitting room," MacIntyre said, and Matt let out his breath through his nose, slowly, so MacIntyre did not hear his sigh. MacIntyre lit a stick in the stove, touched the flame to the wick of the lamp. The light, coming from below, threw the shadows of chin, nose and eyebrows upward, suggestive of a devil. His left hand fluttered about his vest pocket.

"How do you know about the horses?" he asked. He did not sit down, did not wave Matt to a chair.

"We'll talk about that later." Matt pulled a chair into a shadowed spot by the wall. "Sit down, MacIntyre, this will take some time." MacIntyre backed up to the stove and lifted his coattails, let one fall as his hand fluttered at his chest. "Are you listening?" MacIntyre nodded.

"Today, in the stationer's store in Muncie, I met two men. When they heard I came from Pikeston, they introduced themselves as Swab and Boyd. They asked about property values in Pikeston."

"Nothing in that," MacIntyre snorted. "Boyd's famous for buying and selling property, so why shouldn't he make inquiries, when he has the opportunity?"

"But the inquiry was not about property in general, sir, but very specific. About this house, and your store. About the mortgage value of the property, and the business carried on by the store. And they named the person who had inquired. Afton Walton."

MacIntyre sat down, without grace or conscious intent, for he sat on his coattails. "He can't do that! In a mortgage, the owner must sign—" He stopped abruptly. It had taken several seconds before the implications unveiled themselves to MacIntyre. He did not complete his thought, so Matt put the frightening possibility into words.

"Walton expects to own both your store and house by the first of next year. Or hold such control over you that you'll sign a mortgage."

"No! That's a lie!" MacIntyre came up so fast his chair might have been lined with nettles. Matt stretched out his legs, thrust his shoulders against the back of the chair to ease his muscles. He had not realized how cramped he had become, holding Tildy all the way home. He had ignored the aches, because his every thought had focused on the woman in his arms.

"I hope you've not given Walton a written statement, nothing to imply that he'll control your property after he's your son-in-law," he drawled, consciously imitating Lawyer Osburn. "It might be construed as power of attorney—"

"The young lawyer," MacIntyre sneered. "I haven't suggested any such a thing to Walton. Do you take me for a fool?"

Not a fool, but a man whose mind was clouded by fear and anger.

"A curious situation, a marriage for money, particularly if there's no contract ahead of time, both parties believing their own vague assumptions. What happens if, after the ceremony, the groom discovers the bride's not an heiress? When the bride's father learns the groom's poverty-stricken? Not a happy situation, I wager."

"You keep your mouth shut, and if you go yammering at the tavern I'll see your bloody carcass thrown in the river."

*Stay calm.* "Not tonight. The river's frozen. I would recommend, not as a lawyer, but as a friend—"

"Hell will freeze over before you're my friend!"

"As your friend, that you might investigate what Swab—curious name, isn't it?—and Boyd have to say." MacIntyre muttered something unintelligible. "My personal observations lead me to believe that Moffett's business suffers from Walton's presence. His opinion of Hoosiers hasn't changed, even though by now he might be said to be a Hoosier himself. He fails to leap up with alacrity when a customer enters the store, and there's a curious lack of idlers around the stove. Moffett might be happy to send his nephew back to Massachusetts."

MacIntyre sat down again and dropped his head in his hands. *Good. The words had sunk in.* But he jerked upright, newly aggressive.

"You're a lying bastard. I went to the Wabash. I never took horses to Madison."

Matt unfolded and paced between MacIntyre and the stove. "Who said Madison? I said, you took horses to the Ohio." MacIntyre gulped. "The young officer in charge of purchasing horses was Lieutenant Linder, later Major Linder, my commanding officer. He was killed in Mexico, and the colonel assigned me the task of returning his personal effects to the Linder family. Major Linder kept a very extensive diary. He wrote about a man who called himself Mack, who nervously played with the pockets of his vest." MacIntyre's hands dropped heavily into his lap. "I copied the excerpts from the diary, and they lie sealed in a protected place, and will be opened if anything happens to me." *Beginning tomorrow morning,* he added to himself, *they will be in a protected place. Ridley's locked desk.*

"You bastard!"

"Exactly. I've been a bastard since the day of my birth, and after all these years the accusation fails to sting. Will you consult with Swab or Boyd? If there's any way I can help, ask. But from this moment on, remember, I'll do anything to prevent Tildy's marriage to a fraud, a man who's only after your money."

MacIntyre gnashed his teeth. Matt had heard the expression, but had never actually seen a man so overwrought that he gnashed his teeth.

"I must check on Tildy, in case Granny MacIntyre discovered any injuries we overlooked. I would feel everlastingly guilty if—"

"You stay away from my daughter!"

"You gave your daughter permission to do as she likes until the end of December. As her protector, the same leisurely discipline applies to me." More gnashing of teeth.

Matt turned back from the hall door. "Why do you hate me so much?"

"You're a river bastard!"

"When I was young you chased me out of your backyard with a stick. You threw rocks at me when I wandered close to your fishing hole on the river. My younger brother and sisters are bastards, too. Worse than bastards, for their looks suggest Hector Hull fathered none of them. Yet you've never given them any special attention."

"Ask your mother!" The words exploded with the force of a blow. MacIntyre stood over the lamp, and the shadows of his brows sprang up like the horns of a grinning devil. Once more the aggressor, and Matt the victim. Matt shut the door quietly, then bounded up the stairs to leave the specter behind.

Granny answered his soft knock. "Come in. She's fine."

Tildy lay propped on pillows, her bandaged arms outside the coverlet. Matt leaned over and kissed her forehead, before he considered how the kiss would be interpreted by the women in the room.

"Thank you for saving my life," she said. "I didn't thank you before, did I?"

"I didn't save your life. One man didn't run in panic, but stood over you, protecting you. I simply pulled you from under him, and carried you out of the tent. Are you certain there's nothing hurt but her arms?" he asked Granny.

"Nothing. A bruise here and there," Granny said. "I did the best I could on her arms, but that bad gash, she'll have a scar."

"Long sleeves," Mrs. MacIntyre said, and her words ended with a curious, hissing wail. "She must forever wear sleeves to the wrist! I'll ask Mrs. Ridley to write her cousin in Virginia. She might have faced such a tragedy before. Two weeks! Only two weeks for the seamstress to replace the sleeves on the wedding dress. Perhaps a trifle of lace, if some can be found of the right color and rich enough...texture...." She was crying. Matt leaned over Tildy so he would not see. He kissed her on the lips, but kept his mouth closed against temptation.

"You sleep well," he said. He managed to sidle out of the room without looking at Tildy's mother. He peered down the stairs, into the shadows, hugged the wall, cautious. The door of the sitting room opened when he reached the final step.

"Come in," whispered MacIntyre. Matt followed him, took a chair next to the stove, and sat motionless through a long silence. MacIntyre regarded his hands, tense on his thighs.

"I didn't kill him, if that's what you think. I bought horses as I traveled south. I camped near Barman, for the grass was best in that spot. The army man came, but he didn't see me, because I'd gone off into the trees to clean up. Shaving. The first chance I'd had since I left home."

No beard, Linder had written. Clean shaven. MacIntyre slid off the chair, onto his knees, carefully selected two splits of wood and placed them on the fire.

"That night Barman took sick in his bowels. I'd never seen anything like it, and didn't know what to do. Holy Jesus! I hope I don't die that way. Cramps and vomit. Have you ever seen a man—"

"Yes." Matt could do without a detailed description of such a death. He had seen too many in Texas.

"I did what I could, which wasn't much. He died before dawn."

"Yes." Nothing more to say, for Matt knew the rest. The temptation of Barman's horses had been too great, for MacIntyre had a wife and a daughter, whom he loved, and a man did strange things for love.

Matt leaned over, clasped his hands between his legs. "In Mexico, I shot a man. Not in battle. A...a dying man we couldn't carry along," he began, and he sensed the first bond between himself and this man he hated.

Tildy held her arms away from her sides, kept her hands in her lap, one on top of the other. Using her bruises as justification, Meggie had carried a pillow to cushion the Tole settee, so at least her tailbone didn't hurt, too.

Faith, Rachel and Meggie draped the black dress over the unfinished quilt, huddled around it, cutting out a segment of the skirt to replace the sleeves.

"I'll sponge the bloody spots," Faith said. "Tomorrow you won't know it from new."

"Two weeks from today," Tildy said, counting by raising her fingers slightly. Even that caused her right arm to hurt. "The stage leaves only on Mondays and Thursdays. Could Pete take me to Muncie next Monday, Meggie? I'll tell Mama and Papa I'm staying the night at your house, so they won't come looking for me directly."

"You'd better wait until you're healed," Rachel said. "Thursday's soon enough. Besides, if you arrive in Springfield at Christmas, the spirit of the season will lead some proper family to offer you shelter."

Tildy shook her head. "The sooner the better. What if

a storm comes, and the snow makes it impossible to travel for weeks?''

''If we can't drive to Muncie, Walton can't come *from* Muncie to marry you,'' Meggie said. ''The moment the roads are hard, Pete will take you away. Even though he's busy with the California wagons.''

''Don't forget, if there's room in the wagon, bring my banjo,'' Tildy said. ''And scraps aplenty, so I can while away my time on the trail with patchwork.''

''Keeping the mending done will use up any spare time a woman's likely to have,'' Faith said, the tone of her voice expressing all her doubt and objections. ''Between watching the children all day, and cooking, and keeping the wagon clean, and washing…''

''I don't have any children to watch,'' Tildy said.

Faith stuck her hand in the new sleeve, holding it against the bodice. Except for the bloodstains, the dress would look good as new.

''I must start the biscuits for dinner,'' Faith said.

''Monday,'' Tildy said to Meggie. ''Tell Pete, Monday.''

''We'll see how you feel on Sunday, when you come to church. Right now you can't bear to move your arms. Tossed about in a stagecoach, you'd be crying all the way to Indianapolis.''

''I'll be better Monday,'' Tildy said, wishing it did not hurt to cross her fingers.

Meggie led her home, down the boardwalk in front of the law office and tavern to stay out of the mud in the square.

''I hope you're better, Miss MacIntyre,'' Mr. Ridley said, leaning out the door. ''How fortunate that Lieutenant Hull's books chose that very time to arrive in Muncie. So he might be on hand to rush into the fire and rescue you.'' Looking past Mr. Ridley, she saw Matt bent over a table. Very possibly the side of his face turned faintly red.

*You marry the man you would dash into the fire for.*

And in the opposite case? Did she marry the man who would dash into the fire for her? Even the son of a prostitute?

She composed her features as she and Meggie approached the house, afraid her face might betray her thoughts of Matt Hull, and her anticipation of next Monday. Papa met them at the door.

"Meggie," he said, "go into the kitchen for a moment. I must speak to Matilda alone."

Tildy looked around the sitting room before she stepped across the threshold. What if Mr. Walton...but the room was empty.

"Matilda, circumstances...uh...certain events that have come to my attention...Mr. Walton has shown himself to be less than suitable. A scoundrel, in fact." Tildy's arms came up in automatic surprise. She could say nothing, for she clenched her teeth against the pain that flashed to her right shoulder. Her father seemed not to notice.

"I no longer insist upon the marriage," he said flatly. He hands rose to his vest, dropped. "In fact, I should actively discourage it, if you should be inclined to consider Walton as a husband."

"Consider him as a husband?" Tildy cried. "From the day I met him, I despised him, but you'd not listen to me! Why now?"

Her father's left hand brushed his chest. He forced it down, and hooked his thumb in his belt.

"The news reached my ears...rumors from Muncie...Lieutenant Hull came to me with information suggesting that Walton had designs on this house, my store, to obtain money through mortgages. Rather than possessing wealth, it seems he...he's in need himself."

Her father said more, but she did not hear. *He's in need himself* echoed through her head. Money. Her father would give her to Walton for money. Walton would wed her for money. She walked to the polished, gateleg table against the far wall, picked up the Bible. She shifted it to her left hand, for bending her fingers around the thick binding hurt, and lifting it pulled on her injured tendons. She held the book out with both hands.

"Put your hand on this," she said softly. He eyed the Bible as if she invited him to risk his hand in a box full of snakes. "I wish a promise, a solemn promise." He laid his right hand on the book.

"You will never again, never, never, never, promise me to a man in return for money. You'll never try to force me to marry a man for whom I have no affection," she said. "Say it." He muttered words without meeting her eyes. She did not care whether he said the exact words or not. Just so he understood her demand. He dropped his hand.

"Lieutenant Hull brought you this news?" she asked.

He nodded, cleared his throat. "He spoke to Mr. Boyd on the day of your accident. I left early this morning, found Boyd at his breakfast and asked him bluntly if Walton had approached him asking for a mortgage. He had."

"You must thank Lieutenant Hull. As I will." He nodded again. "On Monday, March sixth, Uncle Jim and Aunt Eliza leave for California. They have asked me to go with them."

"No, Tildy!"

"You and Mama raised me to marry a man of wealth, a man of substance, but no man of that description lives in Pikeston. In California I can find a husband."

"That's not necessary. We can make arrangements...."

"Papa, sell this house, the store, and come along to California!" She nearly said that by selling everything, he would have money to pay his debts, with enough left over to start anew, but she remembered Mama's warning.

"Don't be ridiculous, Matilda! You've spent too much time listening to Meggie, who's weakened her reason reading Captain Frémont's reports. Women's minds can't comprehend the magnitude—"

"Don't tell me what women's minds cannot comprehend!" She rather enjoyed the shock on her father's face.

"I said from the beginning that Mr. Walton was unsuitable to be my husband, and I was right. He fooled you, not me!"

Tildy glared at her father's back as he stumbled into the hall. For a few minutes she stood by the window, savoring her victory. After all her plotting and planning, her rescue had come from an unexpected direction, a simple bit of gossip exchanged in a store in Muncie. So easily did chicanery collapse.

Lies. She told lies, the little ones that were part of being polite, being a lady. Well, from now on she would not play at being a lady, and she would tell the truth. Especially to herself.

The truth would hurt Papa and Mama, for they would expect her to resume her place in the family. The obedient daughter. Except the whole world had shifted on that Sunday of Harvest Home. Mr. Walton had come and gone, but the threat of her father's bankruptcy remained. Half the town talked of going to California, certainly Meggie and Faith would. Half the sewing circle.

Most of all, she had changed.

Tildy leaned against the cold glass and imagined Matt Hull's warm arms encircling her, drawing her to him, leading her up the last step to adulthood. She was in love.

## Chapter Sixteen

From the edge of the clearing Matt watched his father tramp into the woods, followed by John. The boy was small for a twelve-year-old, and he staggered under the weight of the empty jugs. When they were well out of sight, Matt knocked at the cabin door. His mother first looked blank, as if she did not recognize him, then annoyed.

"What do you want?" She stared beyond his head. "Well, you might's well come in. No sense heating the outdoors."

The cabin smelled of sour damp, the air saturated by the steam rising from a tub of hot water. Two little girls huddled under a blanket on the bed in the corner, and a third stirred the water, lifting the gray mass of laundry with a stick.

"That's enough, Martha," his mother said. She lifted out a shirt, twisted it in hands half-raw with chilblains. "What you want?"

"Why does Ira MacIntyre hate me?"

"Lordy! Ask him."

"He said to ask you."

"Ira never was man enough to face his own mistakes. Passes them on to a woman." She concentrated on her

work, wringing the garments, flinging them into an empty
tub. Matt decided silence would be the best response.

"You remember Mark and Luke?" she finally asked.

His brothers? He had only one distinct memory of the
twin babies, crawling in the dooryard. "Yes."

"Not your full brothers, but half. Ira MacIntyre fathered
them." She leaned close to his face and cackled, enjoying
his surprise. He met her stare without blinking. "You look
like he did, tall with a bonny face. I believed his lies when
he brought me here."

"He?"

"Hull. And after you was born, he said he'd go to New
Orleans, and get us money to have a real farm. But he
stayed gone, and Ira came." She laughed under her breath.
"Can't believe it, can you? But I was pretty when I was
seventeen. Looked something like Esther does now. He
said he loved me." Matt tried to imagine this woman, with
her sore hands, wrinkled face and gap-toothed smile, as a
pretty seventeen-year-old.

"Ira'd let himself be bought by that proud woman. She
gave him a daughter, but he thought the sun rose and set
on the twins. He'd found a way to get a pile of money
fast, then we'd go to the Missouri, to the frontier." She
stared at the window. No way she could be looking out,
for it was covered with greased paper that let in light, but
no view. Her eyes misted, far away, eighteen summers ago.
"But the fever came."

Weak limbs, a burning brow. Matt remembered lying on
the bed where the three girls now sat, staring at their
strange elder brother. Another memory, his mother hanging over a double cradle, crying out at fate, cursing God.
It had never before occurred to him to wonder where that
elaborate piece of furniture had come from.

"They died," he said.

"You remember?"

"A little."

She stood in front of him, her hands on her hips, a

bleeding sore staining her shift. "You don't remember how I nursed you to health, I warrant! You don't remember the men I took. That's how I got four bits to buy you soft bread and apples. And when Ira come home, what'd he find? He found a man humping me, and you the only one of three boys above ground!" She emptied a pail of water onto the clothes, turned to the girls. "Martha, go get that full."

"I'll do it," he said, grabbing the pail. The child looked hardly strong enough to tote two gallons of water.

He stepped gingerly onto the slippery rocks at the edge of the river. The bucket barely fit through the hole in the ice. He hacked with the dull ax that hung in a nearby tree, enlarging the hole, and for a moment he felt as if he had never been gone. He bailed out the chunks of floating ice, then filled the pail.

She had kept him alive by selling herself. The money MacIntyre stole—the money to take them to Missouri—had instead built the brick house for the proud woman.

"Do you need more?" he asked after he poured the water in the tub. She shook her head, set about stirring the clothes in the icy water.

"Afterward, Ira came sometimes. Many times. But he paid me, same as the others. And Hull came back about a year later, finally got up the nerve to tackle the river again," she sneered. "He liked the cash I brought in, so he hung about and sometimes found men for me, and built the still."

The temporary nature of her love frightened him. She had loved his father, but when he returned she treated him with contempt. She had loved her son, so much she become a whore, then hated him when she reaped the consequence, and he had lived through years of scorn. The wide-eyed girls asked for nothing, expected nothing.

"Ma," he said, "the children...I've got a bit of money. If I buy clothes for them, would you let them walk into town, go to school?"

"School?" Her cackling laugh grated across his mind, taking with it any sympathy he felt for her. "They'd be jeered out of the schoolhouse. Callom's bastards."

"Is it worse to be jeered than to be ignorant?"

"Ignorant, is it?" She stood up and challenged him again, water dripping from her fists. "That's what you think of your family? And you tempted Esther into leaving, when I need her help, as you can plainly see." She swung a fist in the direction of the washtub. "And she's blinded, thinking that fat man will marry her, and make her a lady." She snorted, and returned to the tub.

"Those men in Pikeston, none of them want the fruit of their sin in town, for fear their wives will see the likeness. You think that schoolmaster wants little Leah there—" she pointed to the youngest with a hand holding a dripping shirt "—sitting in his school, with tumbly hair, just like his own?" She grinned at Matt's discomfort. "Don't believe it, do you? Terrible secretive, he is, and hasty, like most men with book learning." Matt stood up. "Heard enough?" she jeered.

"Yes."

"Just remember, Ira MacIntyre hated being a farmer, then hated storekeeping. He didn't want to stay married to that proud woman. If you'd died, we'd a gone to Missouri. I could've let you die, and been a respectable woman."

"He had a wife. He couldn't marry you."

"If he'd gone west with me, that woman would've got a divorce, Ira said. We would've bred more sons to replace you. I wouldn't be no whore, with Hector Hull asking men down the path from the Muncie road."

Matt plunged out the door, risked falling on the icy patches as he ran down the path along the river. He balanced tenuously on a slick log that bridged a creek flowing into the river. He stopped, out of breath, leaning against a tree. They blamed him. The wrong child had survived. The troublesome child.

Ira MacIntyre had yielded to temptation out of love, but

not love for his wife or her little daughter. He had taken Barman's money, Barman's horses, because he loved two little boys. And came home to find them dead.

Godfroy's tepee loomed through the gray and black poplars. Smoke from his fire drifted to the treetops, where it curled and eddied. Matt watched Godfroy bend a willow branch into a hoop for stretching skins. Long, slender hands he had bequeathed to his daughter. Remembering his woodland manners, Matt called out before he entered the camp. He sat casually on a log, managed to say the trivial words of greeting, while Godfroy bound the hoop with thongs.

"What would you have done if you'd found Belle with another man? What if she got the money for the farm by prostituting herself?"

Godfroy looked up, puzzled. "She'd not do such a thing."

"But if she had?"

"She loved me. We'd pledged ourselves. For Belle and me, love wasn't just being bound at the loins. Our hearts were tied, too."

Love? Was that why it hurt so much to think of Tildy? He closed his eyes, rocked back and forth on the log.

"What's the matter, Matt?" Godfroy's sympathetic voice, the father who taught him to swim, to hold a rifle. Matt had borne the winters of neglect by anticipating Trail Godfroy's summer return. "You got yourself down in love, and she found another man?" Godfroy asked softly.

"She says she'll go to California, to find a husband with money. A man who's the big buck on the lick."

"Tildy MacIntyre?"

"Yes." But he would never stop loving her, even when she married another. "I love her like that smoke. It rises, and you think it will keep on to the sky, but it curls about and sinks, and rises again. No matter what direction I look, there it is."

"You got it bad," Godfroy said, and he followed the

words with a gentle laugh. "Come with us. To California. Try winning her with love."

California, away from his slatternly mother, pimping father. Away from Ira MacIntyre. Leave ice and slush for eternal summer. "And see Tildy marry another man?"

"Then make your move here, before we leave. Seduce her."

"I'm not sure she'd say yes, even naked in my bed."

Godfroy bent another willow branch, slowly forming the hoop. A circle. Everything Matt had learned since returning to Indiana circled and circled, one mystery merging into another. Dancing patterns came in and out of focus—greed, death, blame, hypocrisy—weaving around him, and Matt felt as if he stood alone in the center. He could tell Godfroy what Ira MacIntyre had cost him. That the money from the horses had lined MacIntyre's pockets. That Godfroy and Belle would have been able to marry immediately and go West, away from the spring cough that killed her.

But revenge tasted dry, dust in his mouth, and if he spoke, the circle would shrink and strangle him.

"If she loves you," Godfroy said. Matt waited for the rest, but Godfroy turned back to his work.

He imagined Tildy beside him. He put his arm around her back, to avoid touching her bandaged arms, and together they walked through the boundary of the circle, and the evil dancers rose and spread in the sky with the smoke.

"Get out of my kitchen!" Faith said, lifting a sticky spoon from the mixing bowl and using it to point at the door. A bit of dough spattered on the floor and she moaned. "Pa wants a cake for the company, and I can't mix it properly with you dancing around, trying to steal nuts." Her four brothers dipped their chins and slunk into the sitting room. Matt retreated to a corner. "And don't put your dirty hands on that quilt!" she shouted.

"I didn't mean you. I'm sorry to crowd you," she said, looking up. She dropped the spoon, filled a plate from the skillet on the hearth and cleared a corner of the flour-strewn table. "But Pa asked all the families who might go to California to come here, and we didn't finish the quilting because of Tildy getting hurt, and Rachel and Meggie meant to quilt today." She wiped her arm across her forehead, streaking flour near her hairline. "Maybe Tildy, too, if she's healed enough to hold a needle."

She pried open a small tin box, and the odor of nutmeg filled the kitchen. Matt could almost see the smell, like the smoke of the campfire, rising and eddying. Like love. He watched Faith grate the nutmeg into the bowl. A pretty woman, possibly lovely if she took the mobcap off her blond hair and rested the anxiety out of her eyes. In her own house, with a husband instead of four rambunctious boys, her face would fill out and her cheeks flush. Perhaps he should marry Faith. Except the sensation of smoky love held him in thral[1].

"We're all most grateful for what you did for Tildy," she said. "Not just pulling her from the fire, but telling her father the truth about that awful man."

Matt wiped the final bits of egg from his plate with the last corner of biscuit, swung away from the table to give Faith more room.

"Don't worry about dinner," he said. "You're much too busy."

"No, come ahead. All the women will bring food ready to put on the table."

Ridley had not come in, so Matt settled down with volume three of Blackstone. The law of express contracts. But the words blurred from the effects of a distracted mind. A night of lust he could not satisfy. He had to find a wife.

Faith, Meggie, Rachel and Tildy, the only marriageable young women he knew. Faith the most likely, but not a wife to help his career. Rachel would tie him to Ridley. He and Ridley must inevitably be rivals. Not fair to Rachel, to be torn between an ambitious husband and the uncle who had raised her.

Meggie, lively during the first months of marriage, a bouncy companion. But he had seen women who, as children came, resented the unending duties tying them down. The bright young wives turned sour.

Tildy? His sex surged. All night, in dreams and waking visions, he had burned for her. He cursed Ira MacIntyre for his debts, for his mismanagement of business matters. Irresponsible. One word that described MacIntyre perfectly, from the time he had married the "proud woman" for her money to his decision to sell his daughter.

"Judge Stanley has set the date for the spring court session in Muncie," Ridley said from the doorway. "Too early, end of January, so we've work to be done. Damn unfortunate time, too soon after last session, but he wants it complete before he goes to Indianapolis. Weather's likely to be bad. As the days lengthen, the cold strengthens. If the thaw holds, I'll see Rafferty tomorrow, and tell him if he wants to sue Steward over that boundary fence, we must file soon." He unlocked his desk, riffled through a sheaf of papers to find the ones to be copied. "Then there's Marshall. He's furious about Burdette's words the other night in the tavern, and I assured him we could bring a charge of libel. But Marshall's more likely to settle it with a rifle, I'm afraid. Doesn't profit anyone." He shook his head with profound sadness.

"Perhaps Marshall would hire you to defend him in the murder trial," Matt suggested, keeping the smile off his face and out of his voice.

"No good! Marshall has no cash. But Burdette does, so you see, shooting's not the way to settle the matter."

Matt found his ink bottle very low. Time to mix more. He cranked the bucket of water up and permitted himself a grin into the depths of the well.

Ridley's law differed considerably from the idealism of Blackstone. Manipulation, even a lie here and there for personal profit. Somewhere, in the circuit court, in the state supreme court, there had to be another level of law. Perhaps he should talk to Judge Stanley. When he had first seen the judge in court, he had dismissed the man as a buffoon. Until he heard his penetrating questions, and listened to his lectures on the right and wrong of the cases that came before him. Judge Stanley had not applied cold statutes without thought, but had searched for a reasoned fairness.

"I will be a judge," Matt said to the well.

"Judge...judge...judge," the stone walls echoed back. The black water rippled in irregular turbulence, the turbulence he had suffered last night, lust not love. "Judge..."

Ira MacIntyre had judged his mother. Unfairly. Maybe he had only lusted after her, not loved her. Love forgives. Faith, hope, love...Faith, Meggie, Rachel...and Love.

He forgot why he had gone for water, until he reseated himself at his table and wetted his pen. If he aimed to be a judge, he should court a judge's daughter. Or a supreme court justice. Of a powerful assemblyman. But he loved Tildy.

He did not look up at the rasp of the door hinges.

"Ridley, I need your help." Ira MacIntyre. Matt's pen hung in the air, a drop of ink suspended precariously over the sheet of paper. He moved it away just in time, the drop splattering harmlessly on the blotter.

"All the suckers who've fallen for Godfroy's humbug are over at Tole's. Four, maybe five families. And my daughter! She says she'll go to California with my brother!"

"Without your permission?"

"Of course without my permission! But she's nineteen, and I hesitate to be too strong with her after...what happened this winter. I didn't know a gal could be so stubborn."

Ridley fished about in the disorganized heaps of paper

that spilled from the cubbyholes. He pulled out two sheets of folded newsprint.

"I have a way to end this tomfoolery once and for all. This bit of news—" he struck the paper with his fingertips "—will send Godfroy scuttling off for the frontier alone. His dupes will crawl home with their tails between their legs, with more than second thoughts." Ridley laughed and shook the papers. "Godfroy won't have a ready answer to this, for he doesn't read the newspapers."

Ridley heaved himself out of his chair and reached for his coat and hat. "Want to come, Hull? Tag along, get a lesson in cross-examination of an unwilling witness." MacIntyre's eyes shifted uncertainly. "You don't mind Hull coming?" Ridley asked in a way that made it impossible for MacIntyre to object.

"No, of course not," MacIntyre said through stiff lips. "Come along, Hull."

A spanking new, smallish wagon stood in front of Tole's forge.

"Pete MacIntyre's California wagon," Matt said.

"He'll wish he'd stuck to carriages and farm wagons after I'm done with this crowd," Ridley said.

The sitting room overflowed with men. Jim Mac, Pete, Trail Godfroy, Tole and a number of farmers whom Matt did not know. Tole's four sons hung in at the kitchen door. The quilting frame had been pushed against the far wall, and Meggie, Rachel and Tildy sat with their backs to the men, their heads bent over the quilt. From the kitchen came women's voices, and the clash of pots and pans.

"Mules or oxen, either's fine," Trail was saying. "Oh, howdy, Ridley! Howdy, MacIntyre. Can't tell you to pull up a seat, I'm afraid." Two younger men rose and offered their places on a settee. Ridley took a seat, but MacIntyre declined, stood by the door, staring at Tildy's back. Matt balanced his rear on the sill of the front window.

"Now, as I was saying, either mules or oxen. Three teams for each wagon, and extra animals if you have them.

The boys can drive loose stock behind." He jerked a thumb at Tole's sons.

"How do we feed the animals between here and the Missouri?" a farmer asked. "There's no grass in March."

"You buy hay and grain along the way. I said right off, this is no enterprise for a poor man. You sell your land, anything of value, and bring coin." The farmer looked doubtful. "I'm going to St. Joe in February, by steamboat." Rachel's head turned for an instant. "I'll lay in a supply of hay and grain, so when you folks arrive in April, there's feed to recruit the animals before we set out in May. You give me fifty cents for every animal you'll be bringing, and I guarantee feed will be there waiting."

"That's three dollars for each wagon!"

Trail nodded. "Not an enterprise for a poor man."

"Not an enterprise for any man," Ridley said. "I have notices from the St. Louis paper. Two letters from California that tell the truth about the place, and what you face getting there." He used more time and energy than necessary unfolding the papers. "How do you, Godfroy, account for this statement? 'California, taken altogether, is a most miserable godforsaken country.'" Ridley held out the paper to Godfroy, who regarded it the way a man regards a skunk standing between him and his cabin.

"You skipped over the first words of that letter," Jim Mac said. "We've seen that letter, and you didn't say the man admits he saw little of the country." Ridley snatched the paper against his vest.

"I asked Godfroy," Ridley said. "Not you." He looked from man to man, and Matt realized he was searching for the judge, an authority to force Godfroy's answer.

"The man says there's no game but rattlesnakes and tigers," Ridley said, faltering a little.

"Tell him, Godfroy," Jim Mac said.

"Me and Sampson lived in California last winter on fat deer, and elk, and killed a bear twice as big as what roamed in Indiana during the days of settlement."

"You'll need better evidence than that letter to change our minds," Jim Mac said.

"And I have it! Here!" Ridley flourished the second paper. "A letter from a girl, no more than a child, who saw friends die in the snow of the mountains, saw people eat the—" Ridley glanced at the quilting frame and thought better of his words "—eat flesh forbidden by every statute of humanity."

"Fools!" Godfroy exclaimed.

"Godfroy and Sampson's told us how that happened. The Donners didn't hire an experienced guide. They listened to the lies of a scoundrel, who led them into the salt desert. Hundreds of men and women got over the mountains that year," Jim Mac said.

"According to Trail Godfroy," Ridley sneered. "You accept the word of a man who will profit by your decision?"

" 'It is the greatest country for cattle and horses you ever saw,' " said a clear, womanly voice. The men turned, wondering, toward the quilting frame. Meggie clasped her needle in hands folded against her breast. "That's the very end of the letter you hold in your hand, Mr. Ridley. 'Tell the girls that this is the greatest place for marrying they ever saw, and they must come to California if they want to marry.' " Meggie looked directly at Ira MacIntyre. "And the first letter, Mr. Ridley didn't read the part that says '—the Bay of San Francisco merits all the most enthusiastic have said of it. It is, probably, the finest bay in the world.' Why should you keep a store here, Uncle Ira, when you might come with us and have a business on the finest bay in the world?"

Ridley sprang up, so angry his lips pulled back as though his teeth were hot. He had expected to quiz Godfroy, trip him up by reading unfamiliar letters and make him appear a fool. Instead Ridley faced people who had combed the St. Louis papers for information. He'd been outfoxed. Matt found himself smiling, and then wondered why he should be happy at the outcome.

"Godfroy, did you visit any towns in California?" Ira MacIntyre asked suddenly. "Are there towns?"

"Not so big as Muncie, or Indianapolis. But on the bay at Yerba Buena the Hudson Bay Company has their establishment, and other merchants around it."

"Prosperous merchants? Richer than men here?"

"Men richer'n you, MacIntyre. Richer'n Moffett. At the capital, Monterey, Englishmen and Americans buy and sell goods off American ships, and the steer hides from the ranchos. I met men who emigrated four years ago who've already got fortunes, for the natives don't make so much as a pin for themselves."

"Or wagons," Pete said.

"Why should they need wagons when the land's barren?" Ridley snapped, a last stab at cross-examination.

"Ask John Sutter," Godfroy said.

"Who?" Ridley had been startled into a confession of ignorance, and Matt knew he was beaten.

"The owner of New Helvetia. A kingdom, not a farm, right where the emigrant trail drops out of the mountains. Sutter grows wheat and corn, grapes and peaches, melons and barley. The emigrants buy from him when they arrive, and he helps them get settled, and when their corn patches ripen, or they have skins or furs to trade, they come to his store for pins and powder, calico, such as they need."

"A kingdom, by gum!" exclaimed a farmer. "Glad I got a wife, if women's in short supply. By Jupiter! How about taking two or three old maids?"

"How'd you profit?" asked another farmer. "Can't sell 'em. Women got minds of their own." Ira MacIntyre looked glum.

"When Sampson and I left last spring, Sutter was building a gristmill, so settlers will have a place to grind their grain, and he's planning a sawmill up in the mountains."

"No trees but in the mountains!" Ridley cried. "He's confessed it! No trees for cabins, or fuel—"

"No trees to clear before you plant your first crop," marveled the farmer who dreamed of a kingdom and a market in elderly virgins.

Matt's stomach growled, and he sniffed. Roast meat, and the smell of drippings being thickened into gravy.

"The hell with all of you!" Ridley cried. He threw himself toward the door, crumpling the newspapers. "You'll remember my words when you're trapped in the defiles of the Rocky Mountains—"

"Defiles?" Godfroy asked, astonished. "Why, South Pass has got no more defiles than the road to Muncie." But Ridley did not hear, for he steamed down the street.

"He's going so fast, you could play a game of checkers on his coattails," Godfroy said, leaning to look out the window. Matt sniffed the luscious aromas coming from the kitchen, turned regretfully to the door, for his duty lay with Ridley. He brushed past MacIntyre, who had the look of a man just waking up. MacIntyre shook his head, and followed Matt.

"Suffering Jupiter! The ignoramuses won't listen to reason," Ridley said when they stood in the square. "To the tavern! Ale and whiskey whet the thought processes." Matt turned toward the office. "Come. I'll pay."

"I pledged Mrs. Ridley that—"

"Hell, boy! I pledged her too, but what good is that pledge when she mocks it herself?"

# Chapter Seventeen

"The money they'll take out of this town!" Ridley whispered after his first swallow of whiskey. "And Burdette and Marshall sitting next to each other without so much as a scowl. Burdette must have apologized! Mart Burdette! Apologize! California's pressing good sense out of their skulls!"

Three men entered the tavern and sprawled at a table between them and the door. Matt held his breath, waiting for the first skipped heartbeat, the faint spasm in his lower back.

"Every man in that room's a customer of mine," MacIntyre said. He snarled, and drained his mug of ale.

"Well enough for you," Ridley snapped. "After they've sold their farms, they'll come to your store for supplies. But not one will ask me to file suit for libel."

"They may decide to go by steamboat to Independence, and buy their supplies there," Matt said, a trifle too lightly, he noticed, after the words came out. He had not drunk whiskey for so long, he must watch himself. Two more men joined the party between him and the door. He stiffened his back against the nervous twitches, and found them strangely absent.

MacIntyre snarled again, louder, and poured himself another drink. "I thought if Matilda understood that California's a wilderness, she'd not go. I didn't suppose there'd be towns, with merchants."

"In cross-examining a witness, you should never ask a question you don't know the answer to," Matt said. Neither Ridley nor MacIntyre paid attention.

"And damn Meggie, she had to blabber on about it being a place for marrying. How she can remember such things, word for word, I don't know."

"She remembers everything she reads," Matt said, mostly to distract himself from the noon crowd. "I've heard her quote Captain Frémont, page after page...." No one seemed interested. "Now that I think about it, Meggie would make a great lawyer." No response to this outrageous statement, proving absolutely that neither of the men listened to him.

"We can raise the matter in court—how old is Tildy?" Ridley asked.

"Nineteen."

"Can a girl of nineteen go to California without her father's permission, or must she wait until she's twenty-one?" Ridley mused aloud.

*Why doesn't my back hurt?* No symptoms in the Toles' sitting room, either, Matt mused, and he'd been jammed against the window by a huge, awkward boy.

"Tildy's not going unaccompanied," Matt said. "Her uncle, grown cousins, her aunt and her grandmother."

"Granny?" Ridley asked, so incredulous he put down his freshly poured drink without taking a swallow.

"Yes," MacIntyre said, shaking his head. "She'll die on the plains, of course. And my entire inheritance will consist of a cabin with a broken ridgepole on eighty acres of uncleared land."

Ridley nodded knowingly. "She'll take the cash to California, if she's still got it. A great mistake your father made, turning his cash estate over to his wife, not his sons. Although, Ira, you might have fought for a greater portion of the land than that eighty acres."

"I didn't want land," MacIntyre choked after a great swallow of whiskey. "I figured I'd get my share in cash when the time came to divide Mother's estate. Lord, but I wish someone knew where she keeps it! Now she'll haul it all to California, and squander it investing in some fly-by-night affair, like that sawmill Godfroy boasts of. A sawmill in the wilderness! Sometimes I think…sometimes I think…."

Matt looked at MacIntyre closely. The frantic alarm in his voice hinted at suicide.

"Sometimes I think my brother's right, it's time to head for another frontier. But my wife—"

"You wouldn't, Ira!" Ridley exclaimed, looking far more shocked than when he'd heard of Rachel's ancestry. "You and I, we've wagered our very souls on the future of Pikeston."

"More than my soul. All my wife's money." He drained his glass and refilled it from the bottle left on the table. "A thousand dollars. I married Ravania for the thousand her father offered, so I could open a store and not wallow in the dirt. I hated farming."

Matt's stomach rebelled against the whiskey. Two months of being a teetotaler, and one swallow burned all the way down.

"But being shut in a store—" MacIntyre's words slurred a bit "—not the easy life it's cracked up to be."

Matt recalled he had eaten nothing since that hasty breakfast on the corner of Faith's table. "Excuse me, sir, but I suppose it's time for dinner—"

Ridley waved him away, and continued talking to MacIntyre as Matt went out the door. "Tole says Pikeston's dying, and he's working like hell to make himself a prophet."

Pikeston's dying. If he read day and night, Matt thought he might finish his study of Blackstone before spring, be admitted to the bar and move to a larger town. Indianapolis. Tipple with legislators and judges, maybe with the governor himself. Matt's stomach heaved at the prospect of further tippling, and he detoured into the alley just in case he got sick.

"Naay, naay, stay at home nanny goat!" One group of boys jeered at another. "We're off to California!" Tole's sons yelled at the young MacIntyres, who slunk around the corner.

"Hello, General," said Kit, dragging off his cap. He remembered, slapped the hat back on his head, drew himself erect and saluted, and hit himself in the eye with the piece of pie in his right hand. He stared at the pie, poked it in his mouth. "You joining us on the California trip?" he asked around the mouthful.

"I won't be through my studies until summer. Too late to leave for California."

Swirling skirts filled the Tole kitchen. A man Matt did not know slapped him on the back. "Glad to see you've returned, Lieutenant. The future's in the West!"

"You men get out of the kitchen until we call," ordered a woman. Matt gladly slipped into the sitting room, where Tole and Jim Mac cornered him.

"Now, Hull, you see how things are, just like I told you," said Tole. "Pikeston's no place for a striving young man."

"We'll make you captain," Jim Mac said. "Come along, and I'll see to it you're elected captain."

"Godfroy," Matt said, looking around the room. "Godfroy and Sampson, they're—"

"Guides. Godfroy says we'll pick our own captain, sort of like a governor. Great recommendation for you when we get to California, one of the youngest men along and elected captain. And once we're there, we'll elect you colonel of the local militia, and we'll boost your campaign for the territorial legislature."

"You men lift this table out of the way," a woman ordered. Matt and Jim Mac moved the table so it blocked the way to the door. No flit of his heart. No twitch in his back. What in hell was going on? Ever since he'd run from that fire on the steamboat...

Until he ran into the fire!

"Maybe the lieutenant's not got the nerve for the trail," said a voice at his elbow. The man's head did not reach Matt's shoulder. His narrow, beady eyes challenged, spoiling for a fight. "I knew a man who went to New Orleans, took three years screwing up the courage to come home."

Matt nodded, forced a laugh. "Hector Hull. He didn't know the surest way to get rid of a fright is to run straight at what paled your liver." He smiled into the beady eyes, disappointed eyes. "Sorry, but I haven't time to talk now, but I look forward to making your acquaintance."

"Martin Burdette." The man stuck out a hand, Matt shook it, but turned away as he did so and called through the door, "Faith! Any way I can get a plate of dinner? There's no one in the office, and my stomach's getting ridged flapping against my backbone."

He carried the plate to the office and read Blackstone while he ate, until Ridley tripped over the threshold two hours later.

"What do you think of this California business?" he asked morosely, sitting down rather carefully, as if he feared the chair would roll away. "Why do they want to go?"

"No one reason. Every man, every woman, too, has a different reason."

Ridley shook his head, then held it steady between his hands, as if it threatened to tumble off his shoulders. "Credulous fools, following a liar."

"Jim Mac, he's going because he gets ague every summer, and there's none in California." Ridley stared blankly, but Matt plunged on, talking to himself, fascinated by his sudden revelation. "Jim Mac's wife would sign a contract with the devil himself to make her husband well. Granny and Meggie, they'd set off down the River Styx if the trip promised adventure. Pete, he wants to be rich and there's too many wagon builders in Indiana, and Tole, he knows there's no future in Pikeston for his four boys, that they'll leave home one by one, vanish off to the frontier.''

"Marshall and Burdette, they hate each other," Ridley said thickly.

"They hate those rocky acres that tear up their plows every spring." Burdette. The short man. "And Burdette's a fearful man, always putting other men down to make himself taller. Setting out on an impossible journey proves he's not a coward."

Tildy, he said to himself, will go to find a prosperous husband. A member of the territorial legislature, a judge, someday maybe governor. And in the far distant future, when California grew big enough for statehood, a senator making the long trip back to Washington.

His sex throbbed, swift and complete. If only he could raise a fortune with that speed. Could he, by some miracle, be admitted to the bar before March? Captain of the emigrant party. A quick study of California's political situation, and a plunge into public office. All this before some wealthy merchant tempted her into marriage.

He resented the heavy footsteps on the boardwalk, and the rasp of the hinges. No doubt some idler coming with useless gossip, to interrupt his pleasurable daydreams.

"Mr. Moffett," Ridley cried when the door swung open. "Mr. Walton. Do take a chair. Nearer the stove. Hull, more wood in, right now, these gentlemen must be chilled by their long ride from Muncie. Your hats, sir? Your coats? That muffler's not necessary here, Walton—ha, ha—Hull will have the fire blazing in two shakes of a sheep's tail."

Matt poked at the fire, went out to fetch a new supply of wood. "We intend," Moffett was saying as Matt balanced against the back door, "to sue Ira MacIntyre for breach of promise. My nephew here—" he swung his head toward Walton because his hands were occupied pulling off his tight gloves ''—wants six thousand dollars. Or his bride, of course.''

Matt dropped the wood with a clatter. William Blackstone, volume three. *Some agreements are deemed of so important a nature that they ought not to rest in verbal promise only...any agreement of marriage...*

''Ira MacIntyre made the promise in writing?'' Matt asked, and in return got a hostile glance from Ridley, a glare that warned him to keep his opinions and questions to himself.

Walton pried a letter from between his stomach and the taut fabric of his vest. ''Letter from MacIntyre,'' he puffed. He threw it at Ridley.

''We came to you,'' Moffett said, ''because the next court session's in January.... Afton wants this settled as quickly as possible.'' They came to Ridley so they might preempt the only lawyer in Pikeston. MacIntyre would be forced to find a lawyer in Muncie, an inconvenient, expensive drive away.

''And it shall be settled,'' Ridley said.

Moffett pulled out a little memoranda book. ''How soon can you serve the papers?'' he asked.

''Tomorrow. I'll prepare them tonight, they'll be copied fair tomorrow morning and delivered before the sun's high.'' Ridley rubbed his hands in anticipation, then caught himself and sat unmoved.

''I believe I can convince MacIntyre to let the marriage take place,'' Ridley said in a low voice. ''I'm the only lawyer in Pikeston, so with no one to represent him in court...'' Moffett nodded.

Tildy would run away. The moment she heard of Walton's suit, she would ask Pete to carry her to the stage.

''We must be going,'' Moffett said. ''These dreadful short winter days give little time for necessary work, let alone gadding around the countryside.''

''I'll send my clerk around to MacIntyre with the papers tomorrow, and he'll deliver copies to you, as weather permits.'' Ridley bowed more than once between his desk and the door.

"There! There!'' he said, shutting the door and leaning to the window to watch the buggy pull away. "Pikeston's finished, is it? We'll charge one hundred dollars for writing out a few papers and turning the screws on Ira MacIntyre.'' He patted the letter on his desk. "If you have doubts, Matt, never put anything in writing. If the young lady's father hauls you into court, you can always say the minx misconstrued your jests, or that her father mistook you for another man in the shadows. Be here early in the morning, so we may surprise MacIntyre the moment he opens his store. And, be absolutely tight lipped about this!''

Matt waited impatiently until the clouds sailed over the moon and darkness shrouded the square. He eased his heavy pack out the squat door beneath the eaves. The four volumes of Blackstone did not fit in his pack; he had no alternative but to bind them with string and carry them.

He hugged the building fronts, except where a pool of light spilled from the tavern window. The pack thumped loudly when Matt dropped it on the porch of the brick house. MacIntyre must have heard the thud, for he opened the door only seconds after Matt knocked.

"Who's there?'' He bent forward to stare into the gloom.

"Matt Hull. Walton's bringing a breach of promise suit against you,'' he blurted out. After a few seconds he remembered to say, "sir.''

MacIntyre stepped back from the door, holding it open. "Wait here,'' he said. He closed the door of the sitting room, plunging the hall into darkness. "What's all this?''

Matt gave himself the space of two breaths to organize his thoughts, then summarized the meeting with Moffett and Walton in three sentences. "They have your letter, sir,'' he concluded.

"Six thousand dollars! Good God! No man has money

in that amount lying around! It's blackmail!" Matt agreed, and let silence speak for him. "Why did you come to me?" MacIntyre asked, his voice rough, but not in the way of his hate.

"I cannot...cannot participate in this. I'm leaving Ridley. There comes a time when honor can bear no more." He waited for MacIntyre's mocking laughter at the mention of honor. Nothing.

"Thank you. Thank you for warning me." He opened the door, stood there while Matt heaved the pack on his back. "I'm sorry. I didn't realize you meant to leave Ridley right this moment. Come in. We'll find a place—"

"Godfroy's camped on the river." He did not want to be near Tildy. He did not want to sleep in Tildy's house, even on the floor of the kitchen.

He tramped out of town, cut off the road onto the path along the river, sank into the snowdrifts hanging on the north-facing banks, and stumbled on the flattened briars beneath the poplars.

"Godfroy!" he called. The tepee had to be nearby, but the thickening clouds blocked the starlight. "Trail Godfroy!" His pack caught on a dead branch, wrenched it from the tree with a crack that, in the silence, resonated like a rifle shot.

"Who's there?"

"Me, Matt." He staggered in the direction of the voice, and ran into a tree. "Ouch!"

"Stay where you are." A minute passed, but the swallowing darkness stretched every second to double, triple its length. A lighter patch through the trees, then a flare. Godfroy held up a flaming brand to light the way. He eyed the pack on Matt's back. "So, you're giving up this lawyer business?"

"No. I'll study on my own. I can't stay with Ridley."

"Why not?"

Why not? Ridley's fostering of litigation? His subtle encouragement of quarrels between neighbors? His willingness to accept Walton as a client? His easy assumption that his clerk would do the dirty work?

"I can't stay with Ridley because I'm in love with Tildy MacIntyre." Godfroy nodded. Amazing! He understood. But Matt told himself he should not be surprised, for Godfroy had loved Belle. Still loved her. Love was stronger than death. Therefore, stronger than any other emotion in the world. Matt followed him into the tepee, dropped the books and dumped his pack on the spot vacated for him.

Godfroy disappeared at daybreak to run his trapline, leaving Matt to Blackstone and making plans for his future. He lifted the flap of the tepee a few inches for better light, admitting not only the day's grayness, but an occasional flake of snow. He had intended to study offenses against public justice, but the legal tangle of Walton's suit occupied his mind, and he flipped from page to page, volume to volume, searching for applicable law.

MacIntyre had written a letter accepting Walton's proposal of marriage. But that letter did not stipulate money or property to be given along with Tildy.

Tildy did not wish to marry Walton, and marriage was valid only with the consent of both parties. So in this case the law came into conflict, and how the jury might decide...

"Matt. Matthew." The wind whipped the female voice, making it impossible to distinguish distance or identity. Perhaps his mother had learned he had moved to the river, and had changed her mind about clothes for the children. He lifted the flap.

Tildy stood ten feet away. Snow whitened the hood and shoulders of her dark cloak. A bit fell away, and he saw she was shivering. The mercury had dropped since daybreak, without his noticing. The tepee, with a fire on the central hearth, was so warm he wore nothing but a shirt and pants.

"Get in out of the cold," he said, lifting the flap. She

untied her cloak as she bent to enter; he lifted it from her shoulders and shook the snow away. She wore a dress of dark brown, with white lace sewn in arches over her breasts.

"Matt, we need your help. Desperately."

"The lawsuit?"

"Yes."

"I'm not a lawyer. I've not read all of Blackstone, let alone learned how to file cases and address the court."

"There's no one else, and Papa can't afford to hire a lawyer from Muncie." She arranged her petticoats so she could sit cross-legged on the furs of Godfroy's bed.

"I can't plead a case until I'm admitted to the bar," Matt said, focusing on Tildy's face, so her defined breasts did not tempt him.

"Get admitted to the bar," she said. The heat rising from the hearth distorted his view of her. She came in and out of focus, sensually, eddying, curling. He told himself it had nothing to do with Tildy, that natural law explained rising heat. Sudden tumescence mocked his rationality.

"I don't know enough to be admitted," he protested. "I'm reading volume three of Blackstone, and I'm only that far because I skipped the parts about the king and Parliament. The judge will ask me questions—"

"How many volumes are there?" She leaned forward. Her breasts rose and fell, as if she had run all the way from Pikeston.

Matt pointed to the pile of books. "Four. And I don't study very well alone. I have to read everything three or four times. It was easier when I read aloud at Jim Mac's, and he and Granny and Meggie interrupted me with questions, or saying they didn't understand."

"Read to me!" She crawled around the hearth and grabbed volume three. "We'll read through the books together, and then you go to Judge Stanley in Muncie—Mrs. Stanley is such a nice lady, she'll tell him—"

"Mrs. Stanley doesn't decide."

Tildy hooted. "All men pay attention to their wives."

"I need character references," he said weakly.

She spread the book so it rested on his thigh. And her own. "Papa will give you a reference—"

"Does your father know you're here?"

"Of course. And Uncle Jim and Mr. Tole will write letters testifying to your character."

He shoved the book away, glancing once to make sure it landed free of the fire. He lifted his hands to push her out of danger as well, away from his lust, but she leaned forward, and the rejection turned to embrace. Down, down, into the depths of the fur Godfroy had given him to supplement his blankets.

"The otter skin!" she whispered.

Kisses deep and soft as the fur, her anticipation so energetic he could feel it through the mass of petticoats and her fortress corset. He rolled over, above her, and, resting on his elbows, unfastened the top buttons of her bodice.

"My corset's one of the new ones," she said, with a practicality he found astonishing. "Laces in the back and front fastenings." Her small hands came up to help, small hands marred by a bruise and the scar of a burn. They pushed aside embroidered muslin as he studied the hooks of the corset. Her lungs expanded when it fell open, and hard nipples pushed through a single layer of silk against his expectant palms.

Too damned many clothes. "I didn't put on drawers this morning," she gasped.

Seduced! Seduced by a virgin, who probably did not understand what he would do to her. "You know what happens...between a man and a woman?"

"Granny told me." Bless Granny! He fought the skirt and petticoats while she fumbled at the buttons holding the fall of his trousers. Granny had prepared her. Granny MacIntyre seduced him in the person of her granddaughter. And the moment Tildy came with child, Granny would encourage Jim Mac, Ira, Pete, the whole clan to cock their rifles and come tearing to the river with accusing eyes.

In the bottom of his pack! Unused since Louisiana! He rolled off her, grabbing, searching blindly, his eyes transfixed by the moist immensity of his own erection. The rubberized envelope, within it the limp sheath.

"What's that?" Tildy asked. Granny had not told her about sheaths.

"If a man...wears one..." Where had his breath gone? "There's no babe." The Texas whores had laughed at him, but Major Linder's warning, and the troubles of his companions, had convinced him of the need. "Can you pull off one or two of those petticoats?" She nodded, set to work, taking her eyes away just long enough for him to cover himself.

Still too many clothes, but the wait outdistanced his control. He caressed her thigh, then the moist flower between her legs, a blossom more delicate than her face, demanding gentler touches than the frantic kisses bruising his lips.

"You must not be with child on the trail to California," he whispered.

She framed his face with her hands. "Dear Matt, I love you, but you don't have to marry me. But I thought..."

"What?" Her firm breasts exceeded the span of his hands.

"Papa asked me to ask you, and I thought, maybe if we did what you...we wanted, you'd say yes."

She spread her legs, lay still and submissive, waiting for his thrust. He rolled away. One woman had become a whore to feed him. Now Tildy, to save her father.

"Please, Matt."

"I don't take women as pay. Sex, unwilling sex, isn't my idea of fun."

"It's not unwilling," she whispered, reaching out to him. "I wanted you weeks ago, and you want me, I know, for I felt you when we rode home from Muncie. Please, Matt, make love to me."

He wanted to stroke her, encourage her, but a petticoat got in the way. "Undress. Everything."

Hours passed while she untied the petticoats, stripped off the chemise, unbuttoned her boots. She spread her hands before her breasts and sexual hair, stared down while he undressed. He drew her under the blankets.

So long since he had held a woman this way. No, never had it been like this. Not simply because Tildy was shy, or that each touch gave a new thrill to her. Different, because he loved her.

"I'll be careful," he whispered. "Tell me if you want me to stop." Not too deep the first time. Easy, like the languid snow, except the snow rose to a roar. How did the tepee stand unmoved, with the wind blowing a gale? Erect, hard, stalwart against every force, the tepee, himself, while Tildy drifted like smoke to the treetops... The world came unbound, laces tangled in a pool of heat red as blood. Blood of the virgin beneath him, deeply penetrated, moaning, and he cried out in agony that his lust had hurt her. No delicate flower, but flesh, binding him, and his anguish vanished in cries of relief that matched hers.

# Chapter Eighteen

"We'll go in through the back door," Tildy said, "to avoid Mama, because she doesn't know I went to find you."

"Good idea," Matt said, just as she lifted the latch and came face-to-face with her mother, opening the oven door upon a half-risen cake.

"You must never open the oven while a cake's baking!" Tildy exclaimed.

"How should I know?" her mother said, letting the door slam shut. "I wasn't trained to be a cook. But your father says, things as they are, we might have to give up even Sally." Her chin trembled. "I suppose I should not have turned Rachel away, for she must know how to cook, but to have a half-breed in the house, and one who expects to be treated with respect—"

"Rachel? She came here?"

"Refuge, my dear. Refuge. She absolutely refuses to stay with Mr. Ridley, now that he's taken sides against your father. She told me she'd go to California with that savage who fathered her." She shook her head violently, and looked ready to cry.

"Where's Rachel?" Tildy demanded.

"Why, with James and Eliza, I believe. I suggested they

might take her in." She stared at Matt as if she had just now noticed him. "What are you doing here?"

"Papa asked me to bring him," Tildy said slowly, hoping her mother would listen if she spoke clearly. "He's agreed to help us. We…he read the law of breach of contract, and thinks Walton's case isn't as good as Ridley pretends. Where's Papa?"

"In the sitting room." Her mother's face twisted, not understanding. She left the cake to its fate, and followed them to the sitting room.

"You're not a lawyer," her father said after Matt outlined his plan.

"I have a whole month to study before I present myself to the circuit judge."

"I'll help him," Tildy interrupted, so she, not Matt, raised the issue of them studying together. "He learns easier reading out loud, to someone who questions him."

"Do I have a case?" her father asked, ignoring the fact that she would be with Matt several hours a day. "It seems, no matter which way I turn—"

"I read the letter. You say only that your daughter accepted Walton's proposal. Nothing about a dowry, nothing about Walton controlling your property. He has no letter from Tildy herself, no evidence that she actually agreed to the marriage."

"Because you warned me not to," Tildy said. She smiled her gratitude at Matt, brushed her lower lip with her tongue before she caught herself. She frowned and looked away. Satisfying one's lust had consequences she had not anticipated. Walking home, she had tucked her hand into the crook of his elbow, and found the contact charged. Totally unlike before…

"A marriage requires the consent of both parties," Matt said, fixing a serious expression on his face. "I'll put Tildy on the witness stand, and she can swear that she never agreed to marry Walton, that she had plans to flee before the wedding. Meggie and Pete can testify to the truth of that. And Boyd can give evidence that Walton talked of mortgaging your property.''

"No! Not Matilda on the witness stand!" Mama said breathlessly, holding her hand to her heart. "In front of all those men... Her name would be in the paper. A lady's name appears publicly only three times, at her birth, her marriage—''

"I'm sick of being a lady," Tildy said. "Look at the mess being a lady has got me into.''

Mama's eyes rolled in her head, she fell straight back, but Matt caught her before she hit the floor. Tildy searched through her mother's pocket, found her vial of salts and waved it beneath her nose. She tried to look worried, but Matt's hand grasped hers behind Mama's back, and when his thumb caressed her palm she giggled.

"Mama should be carried upstairs to her bed, to recover from the faint," Tildy managed to say, but she thought about cuddling with Matt on a real bed.

"I could lift her onto the sofa," Matt suggested.

Tildy sat down beside her mother and fanned her with the latest *Godey's*.

"You may study here," Papa said. "I'll warn the boys they're not to barge in and interrupt. And would you please speak to Josh, Lieutenant Hull. This morning he raved about borrowing your revolving pistol and shooting Walton.''

"He'll hang!" sobbed Mama, who opened her eyes and sat up. "What's come over my sweet boy? First California. Now murder!"

"California?" Matt inquired, looking at her father.

"The Tole boys tease my sons every chance they get, how they're bound for adventure in California. Last night Josh and Lewis pestered me, asking why we can't go to California.''

"No woman suffers as I do!" Mama murmured. "How I'll know the spring fashions, I don't understand, for there's no money for *Godey's!*''

"Thank heavens!" Tildy whispered to Matt. She caught herself smiling at him again, and found no reason to stop, because his gray eyes shone like mysterious clouds at sunset, full of adventure. Matt frowned a warning. She straightened her face, but not fast enough.

Her father stared at her, his face lengthening with understanding. He glared at Matt, and his mouth fell open. "Oh, hell! Oh, hell!"

"Don't use such language, Mr. MacIntyre, in front of ladies," her mother scolded. "Whatever called forth such language? You're normally the mildest of men."

Papa threw himself from the room, looked back from the hall, aghast. "Some salt pork to be delivered at the store," he muttered, and fled.

"Mama, shouldn't you check on the cake?"

"I suppose, dear." Mama got to her feet, wandered out of the sitting room. Her skirts rustled on the stairs.

"It's so difficult to keep it a secret," Tildy whispered to Matt. "I want to tell everyone how wonderful you are—"

"Your father guessed," Matt said. "'Oh, hell!' had nothing to do with salted pork."

"I know. But he won't say anything, because you're the only person who will help him. He can't afford to pay a lawyer."

"So I take my fee out in trade. What does that make you?"

His distress pained her. She puckered a noisy kiss to cheer him up. "Your sweet love."

"I must speak to your father, the sooner the—"

She slapped her hand over his mouth with so much force he winced. "I'm sorry. I didn't mean to hurt you. But don't say it, Matt. Don't think you have to marry me. When you go to Papa and ask for my hand, I want you truly to want me as your wife. A proposal out of guilt is almost worse than Walton."

"We must never, ever again...not that I didn't find you

marvelous, you understand, everything about you is perfect, but under the circumstances the impulses—"

"Were wonderful. I'm so glad you were my first time. Now, I think we should look at that cake. If it's not too flat, we might save it by layering it with jam, the way Aunt Eliza rescues her mistakes. And while I clean up the dishes, you explain everything you read this morning."

"Isn't it wonderful," Tildy marveled, "ever since New Year's Day the weather's been more like spring than winter." She consulted the scrap of paper she had tucked in her cuff. "What is malicious mischief?"

"Spring, except the trees have no leaves," Matt said, examining the bare branches overhead. "The trees know it's still winter."

"The ground's thawing, and the breeze smells like spring." Matt had been studying too hard. She must cheer him up.

"Look, by the side of the road, green shoots hidden in the dry grass. And the buds on some of the bushes have swollen—"

"They'll freeze in the next cold spell."

"Do you deny that the weather's been absolutely marvelous?" she snapped. Matt took off his hat and grinned at her. He lifted his face to the sun, and she remembered Harvest Home Sunday, that she had fallen in love with him in a single moment.

"Malicious mischief," he said, returning to the question she thought he had forgotten, "is an injury to private property not done with intent to gain by another's loss, but in a spirit of cruelty or revenge."

"Give me an example," she said. "You must be able to explain how the law applies specifically, not in generalities."

"Your brothers tipped over privies on Hallowe'en in a spirit of wanton cruelty. And the Tole boys blew up your privy in a spirit of revenge."

"Is revenge always malicious mischief?"

"Revenge may be no crime at all, depending upon how it's accomplished." He walked to the top of the low bluff overlooking the river. "One man might murder for revenge. Another may report his enemy's criminal act to the law. The first is a capital crime, and the second praiseworthy."

"Both give satisfaction," she said. "I'd be equally pleased to discover Walton's a thief and inform the sheriff, or shoot him in the head."

"No, you wouldn't. Shooting a man in the head leaves you with nightmares."

"How do you know? Have you done it?" she teased.

"Yes." He extended his hand to her, the fingers stretched wide so she saw the calluses across the top of his palm. She remembered the texture of his touch, when his hand cradled her breast, and prickles sprang out all over in anticipation.

"Shall we walk on to the bridge, or are you ready to go home?" he asked.

"You say you shot a man, and ask if I'd like to turn around and walk home! I want the details."

He stretched his legs, so that to keep up with him she had to run. He leaned against the railing, staring down into the black, roiling water.

"I shot a wounded man, a dying man, in Mexico. We were on the march, no water for at least ten miles, canteens nearly empty, the mules exhausted from simply pulling the guns. His wounds had putrefied. He had no chance. When he saw the men march on, he asked me to end his suffering."

"I had supposed.... Isn't it a matter of honor to carry your wounded with you? That man had fought, perhaps heroically—"

"A woman stabbed him in the stomach. A woman he...raped." She had never heard the word spoken before. She knew its meaning, in a vague, theoretical fashion. Unil Matt, and the hour in Godfroy's lodge, she'd had no experience to conjure up the meaning of rape.

Men did this to women. She must marry, a strong man who would stand between her and other men. But a husband could be cruel as well. A woman must choose very carefully.

She knew Matt cared. Since the Christmas Fair, since he made love to her. But he also lusted. The lust shone from his eyes every day they sat together. He tried to conceal it, but she had seen.

"I went through his knapsack to find his name." The words confused her, until she recalled they were speaking of the dying soldier. "I intended to write his family, tell them. Nothing. No diary, no Bible, no record of any kind. But he carried nearly $150 in silver. Stolen. No soldier would have that much money except by theft."

He grabbed her arm at the very moment she meant to step back from the edge of the bridge. "I kept the money. It brought me home to Indiana. It bought me this winter, a chance to study law, my own copy of Blackstone...." He wrapped his arm about her shoulders and pulled her next to him, against the railing, close to the black, rushing water. "You. It brought you to me."

"Why tell me this? Why tell me? It hurts to think—"

"Because this...this thing, I did for love. I loved the men, they were my responsibility, and I could not burden them. I love you, many, many times more than I ever loved them." She had dreamed of the first time Matt would confess his love. Dreamed of him holding her in his arms, naked, while he said the words.

"You must know what I'm capable of. Granny says I was a troublesome child. The army beat down my impulse to strike out, and I learned to hold it in check myself. But if ever danger threatens you, I might—"

"Kill Mr. Walton?"

"Perhaps. I can't be sure."

"We absolutely must talk about Blackstone, if you're

to see Judge Stanley tomorrow," she said, and the words sounded stilted to her own ears.

She dug in her cuff for the paper, but it had slipped far up her sleeve. She cast about her memory for a topic. "Revenge. What does Blackstone say is permitted as revenge?"

"Nothing. 'Black and diabolical revenge,' he calls it. The law exists for justice, for the community as a whole, not for personal triumph."

She laughed at his idealism. "Justice for everyone?" she mocked. "The law is written for men. What justice is there for me, when next week the judge may bang his gavel and tell me to quit complaining and marry Walton? And if I refuse, my father owes Walton six thousand dollars, which he doesn't have and can't possibly borrow."

He did not respond, but stared into the water. "No justice," he muttered.

"I'm glad you agree."

"Justice for a woman comes first through her father, then through her husband. 'Husband and wife are one, and that one is the husband.' The man she loves brings her justice," he said softly. She turned away from him, walked to the middle of the bridge to avoid the vertigo brought on by the rush of the water.

"Papa's idea of justice gives me little encouragement," she said.

The bridge trembled with the weight of water rumbling against its piers. When she was little, Granny had told her that fairies and gnomes lived in streams. This river held demons. Their roar penetrated the planks of the bridge, shivered through her boots, into her feet. And the shivering reminded her of nakedness, and Matt's weight against her loins.

She wanted Matt to say "I love you," not in the midst of half arguments, but holding her, penetrating her.

"Fathers and husbands worry about justice for their women when they profit from the decision," she said. "A husband judges for his own self-interest, not that of his wife.''

"If he loves her?''

"Do men love that strongly? With such disinterest? Even you! You asked me to marry you simply for the prestige—"

"No!"

"What other reason? That first night behind the livery barn, you said nothing about love.''

He stared at her, shifted his gaze to the sky. "It was not prestige, but revenge. I hated your father, I wanted him to suffer, and taking you as my wife seemed the greatest suffering I could impose.''

"And now?'' She was not sure he heard her trembling words over the roar of the river. He came to her, turned her with a hand on her shoulder, and she spun about lightly, carried by the pounding of water and the sexual desire implicit in its vibrations.

"Revenge has no taste, no flavor but the bitterness behind it,'' he said in a thick voice. He embraced her, but she stiffened against the caress. "Love overwhelms. There is no justice for a woman except as her husband furnishes justice. So a woman must choose wisely, a prosperous man, a man of position, but one who loves her. Lusts after her with love.'' The tightness of his embrace made it hard to breathe.

"Can a woman believe a man's promises? Can a woman trust a man so much that she believes his vow? I vow, I'll follow you to the ends of the earth, work like the very devil—"

"Don't swear by the devil!'' she reproved, but she relaxed in the circle of his arms.

"Work my fingers to the bone, do anything in my power to show I have a magnificent future, if only you'll not accept a proposal for...a year? Give me a year, two years, dear Tildy! Say you'll not marry for two years, and if then I haven't proved myself—"

She reached behind his head, pulled it down so his lips came within reach of her own. Cold, needing the warmth of love. She ran her tongue along his upper lip, and the heat sprang in an instant. He grasped her arm so hard the healing cut protested, but the power of the kiss prevented any retreat. Until he moved his lips to her cheek.

"Will you marry me? Not now, but when I've shown what I can do, what I can be—"

"You've already shown me. I accepted your proposal long ago."

"But you lied."

"Not totally. Not one hundred percent pure lie, because I know now, I loved you at first sight. And after the snow fight, I wanted you to take me into the livery barn and throw me down on the straw."

"Lust. We've satisfied lust. Love is more complicated. After the trial, after I've won. After I've earned the right to you, give me your answer."

"We've not satisfied lust," she said. She presented her lips for a kiss, dropped her hands from his chest and felt his roused sex. "Granny says it's never satisfied, so long as we love each other."

"After the trial," he whispered in her hair, "if I win, I'll ask your father."

"Is Mr. Godfroy at home?" she asked.

He led her the few paces down the river, to the otter skin. Her heart beat with a different rhythm this time, no element of fear or shame as he helped her undress, no shock when he knelt naked beside her. No hesitation in touching the shaft he presented for her approval, nothing but love when his lips closed about her straining nipples and his fingers opened her.

His embrace was slow and close—minutes, hours, days of no importance. She wondered what the soldier had done to the Mexican woman, a sexual force so horrible that she stabbed him. Not at all like Matt's easy prodding. He slid inside her, gentle yet exciting, and he murmured, "I love you, Tildy," over and over again.

She had learned the sequence of passion, and decided to wait until the languid aftermath to explain how much she loved him.

Matt knocked, waited, but no one answered the door. He stepped off the porch, looked up at the peak of the white house. The shutters of the upstairs windows were closed, but those on the ground floor hung open. He heard a thud that echoed deep within the house. He climbed the steps, knocked again, louder. He must talk to Judge Stanley. The circuit court opened in two days.

Another thud. Not in the house, but behind it. Someone splitting wood. From the side yard he saw the axman beyond a disorderly heap of wood. He might know where the judge could be found. The man turned away from the woodpile, and Matt saw his face. Judge Stanley! Matt hurried forward as the judge leaned a log against a chopping block, lifted the ax over his head. At that instant he noticed he had company. He lowered the ax.

"So you've finally come, Burt! By God! When I hire a man to chop wood, I expect him to arrive sooner than midmorning." He held the ax out at arm's length, and after a moment's hesitation, Matt took it.

"This whole pile needs split, for there's cold weather on the way. The ache's in my bones." He examined the high clouds that chilled the sunlight.

"I'm Matthew Hull," Matt began, unsure how to correct the judge's mistake without embarrassing him. "I'll be happy to split your wood, if I might talk to you."

"Not Burt! He said he'd come." He tilted his head. "Did I have an appointment with you?"

"No." Matt lifted the ax, let its weight carry it to the log, which fell into two neat halves. "How small do you need your firewood, sir?"

"Halve those again. What'd you need to see me about?"

"I've been reading law with Ridley, of Pikeston, and I'm ready to be admitted to the bar."

Stanley lifted a section of log on its end and sat down. "You young fellows always want to rush it." He fished about in his coat pocket and produced a pipe. "Where's Ridley? He should accompany you, day after tomorrow. No sense even talking unless you got someone to testify to your character. Who are you?"

"Matthew Hull, lately lieutenant in the U.S. Artillery." Matt leaned the ax against his leg and took the letters from his pocket. "Testimonials of good character from Mr. Ira MacIntyre, Mr. James MacIntyre—two of Pikeston's leading citizens—Mr. Abnet Tole, Mr. Martin Burdette."

"U.S. Army. Not Indiana militia?" asked Stanley as he took the letters.

"No. Regular army."

"An officer and a gentleman, then. By definition." Matt didn't like the grin that followed the words. He nodded, wondering if he'd made the proper response.

"What's perjury?" Stanley snapped. Directly to volume four. Matt heaved another log off the pile, while Tildy's soft voice spoke in his head. Stanley dug into his pocket and extracted a penknife.

"An offense against public justice." Lift the ax, drop it square. "Sir Edward Coke describes perjury as a crime committed when a lawful oath is administered in a judicial proceeding. When a person swears willfully, absolutely and falsely."

Stanley grunted, but gave all his attention to reaming out his pipe. "Malicious mischief?"

Tildy on the bridge. Don't think of what happened next, for he had promised himself, promised her, they would not come together again until they were married.

"Damage done out of spite, or in a spirit of wanton cruelty, or as revenge. It's related to arson." Another log, he paused a moment to catch his breath before lifting the ax.

The questions and the ax settled into a rhythm with puffs from Stanley's pipe. Stealing an heiress. The smoke from the pipe blew away too rapidly to curl and caress. Trespass. Murder as opposed to manslaughter. Slander.

The stack of split wood grew, and Matt blessed his luck. Every piece he added to the pile represented nervous energy, worked off without the judge even suspecting the man he examined was tense as a cornered cat.

The duties of husband and wife. Of parents to their children. Stanley had shifted to volume one. He stretched his boots out straight ahead of him, waggled his rump on the crude seat.

"Describe the power Parliament holds over the king?"

He caught Matt out of rhythm, with the ax overhead. Matt let if fall; the log fell apart. "I don't know, sir. I didn't read the parts of Blackstone that had to do with the king and Parliament."

"Good," said Stanley. "Tainted remnants of feudalism, not important to an American. Never bothered with that part myself. When do you expect to bring your first case to court?"

"The first day of the session in Muncie."

"A client already!" he marveled. "Subject?"

"Breach of promise, sir. Moffett and Walton versus Mr. Ira MacIntyre, in the matter of the marriage of MacIntyre's daughter to Walton."

Stanley nodded with such seriousness, Matt suspected the details of the case had already circulated in Muncie's legal gossip.

"See you in court," said Stanley. "My wife told me about the hurt girl. That you saved her life. She hopes you'll visit us again." He looked at the back of the house, all the shutters closed. "She's in Indianapolis, finding us a new house. The place is mighty empty without her, and

I'm not much of a hand at tea, but we might find a way to boil the coffeepot.''

"Thank you, sir." Matt wished he could take the ax home. He'd hang it on the wall of his office, a trophy. He remembered Meggie's patchwork quilt with the pattern of a double-headed ax. Maybe Tildy would piece one for him.

# *Chapter Nineteen*

Men continued to shove into the courtroom, although every bench had been filled for twenty minutes. They lined the walls two deep. Their bodies heated the room far beyond comfort, and Matt wished he could take off his coat. A tailcoat, borrowed from Ira MacIntyre. Tildy had let out the seams as much as possible, but it still pulled tight across his shoulders. Beneath the vest of striped silk, Matt's shirt clung, wet with sweat.

He looked to the ladies' bench at the back of the room. Tildy sat between Meggie and her mother, dressed in black, as he had ordered. The same dress she had worn to the Christmas Fair. He considered leaving the table for one last word with her, but on second thought sat down. He remembered the effect of Osburn's negligent attitude, the sudden power when he unfolded his long body. Matt slouched in his chair, but his nerves did not relax, and a racket at the back of the room brought him up.

Pete struggled forward, waving a paper. The aisle was clogged; he finally gave up and climbed on a bench. By shoving aside spectators, and stepping from bench to bench, he reached the front.

"You, good fellow, are the luckiest man alive," he said as he leaped over the railing. He thrust the paper into Matt's hands—a letter with the seal broken.

"You read it?" Matt asked.

"Of course! It's from Boston! You don't think I could stand to ride from Pikeston to Muncie without knowing. Good news!"

MacIntyre, who had been slumped in his chair like a possum playing dead, straightened up. "What, what?" Matt held the letter so his client could read along. Good news, indeed. The best. He waved the letter at Tildy, pointing at her, shaking his head. Her mother would be relieved, not to see her daughter on the witness stand.

"Tildy will be awful disappointed if she doesn't get to testify," Pete said. He looked about. "I'm glad I didn't tamper with Walton's gig last fall. If he'd been killed, we wouldn't be having all this fun."

"You...you didn't?"

Pete grinned. "I thought about it, even looked at the axle. It was already cracked, a spiral crack that gave way slowly, and didn't dump him out so fast as to crack his skull. Look at Tildy. She's unhappy she won't get to damn Walton's character."

"But Mrs. MacIntyre will be delighted."

"Oyez, oyez," cried the sheriff, as if Judge Stanley had not been standing behind the bench for the past fifteen minutes. The jury was called, and in the pause while the twelve men made their way to the front of the room, Matt realized he had stopped sweating. The jury made no difference. He could end the case right now by approaching the bench and informing the judge that Walton wasn't Walton. A false identity meant there had been no valid contract.

Then again, Matt thought, sneaking a look at his audience, he needed the practice, and some farmers had driven ten miles through the mud to see the show. He concentrated on looking bored while Ridley lectured the jury on the value of agreements. "Civilization rests upon a foundation of fulfilled contracts," he said in summary.

Matt unfolded himself, resisting the impulse to rush to

the bench with the letter. He fished a few papers from the top hat, new, on account, from MacIntyre's store. "Gentlemen of the jury," he drawled, as if he found the whole affair dull beyond belief, "I quite agree with learned counsel for the plaintiff, that civilization would tumble without respect for contracts. Contracts are like the rope in a three-legged race, binding us to cooperative honesty."

The first laugh of his legal career washed over him, a flood of approval, a guarantee that tonight in the taverns no one would speak of Emma Callom's bastard.

"But a three-legged race works only when the rope is strong and well made. And a contract's only as good as the integrity of the men who concluded it."

He considered mentioning a promise to appear in York, thus flourishing his knowledge of Blackstone. Unnecessary now. He sat down.

"Is that all you're going to say?" MacIntyre hissed. Matt nodded.

Ridley submitted MacIntyre's letter into evidence, proving that he had agreed in writing to the marriage of Miss MacIntyre and Mr. Afton Walton. Moffett was sworn, and testified to the receipt of the letter, and his nephew's delight at the good news. He elaborated on his dear nephew's business plans, based upon the promise of the letter.

"That's all, Your Honor," Ridley said, sitting down.

Matt unfolded himself again, and paced in front of Moffett, passed him three times before he stopped with a half step.

"Had you ever met your nephew, Afton Walton, before he arrived in Muncie in October 1847?"

"No. I corresponded with my sister, naturally, but traveling from Massachusetts to Indiana, that's a grave undertaking."

"Thank you. That's all, Your Honor."

Ridley called Walton, who expressed his dismay at the cancellation of his engagement to Miss MacIntyre. He gazed at the bench where the women sat. Matt supposed he meant his glance to look wistful, but his half-buried eyes looked only dull. Ridley sat down.

Matt walked to the bench, pretended to whisper to the judge, but intentionally spoke loud enough to be overheard by the men in front. "I've seen a better case holding watches." Laughter in the front row.

"What did he say?" bellowed someone in the rear, and the front row turned as one man to inform the row behind, and they turned.... The audience moved like a pond after a rock has been tossed in the center.

"I propose we dismiss," Matt said.

Judge Stanley shook his head. "There's the letter. No denying the letter," he said.

Matt leaned close to Stanley, lowered his voice so only the judge could hear. "Walton will be flattened when I cross-examine. Not embarrassed. Flattened."

"Can't do him any harm," Stanley said lightly. "That chair's about to crack under his weight."

Matt's nerves crackled against his wet shirt. He dispensed with the pacing.

"Mr. Walton, do you understand the meaning of perjury?" he snapped. The crowd swayed again, no rippling wave, but the chaotic movement of a tempest. Did Walton pale?

"Of course I understand perjury."

"In that case, Mr. Walton, what is your true name?" Matt asked slowly. Walton wiggled in the chair. Matt judged he was attempting to draw himself upright in righteous anger.

"You heard when the sheriff swore me. Afton Walton."

"And your birth name?"

"I object, Judge." Laconic words from Ridley. "We've established that the witness is Afton Walton. He's sworn that he's Afton Walton."

"Then why do I possess evidence—written evidence in a letter—that Afton Walton, son of Sarah Moffett Walton, is presently hard at work in his store in Braintree, Massachusetts." Matt fished the letter out of the upturned hat. "A letter from Askew Finlay, of Boston—"

"Oh, God!" exclaimed Walton. "I told him it wouldn't—"

"Shut up!" Ridley yelled, and threw himself between Walton and Matt.

"What's this? What's this?" Moffett cried.

"Your nephew sent a proxy, it seems," Matt replied.

Judge Stanley groaned as he swung his feet off the bench. He banged away with his gavel until the laughter quieted. "Ridley, get back to your place. Now—" he turned to the witness "—who the hell are you?"

Walton had wilted. Matt wondered what happened to his bulk, for about half of him had disappeared.

"Perfect Seawall," he muttered.

"I don't give half a damn whether your seawall's perfect or not," Stanley roared, "what's your name?"

"That's my name," Walton screeched. "Perfect Seawall. Walton said no one in Indiana would guess, that you're all a bunch of stupid Hoosiers with no more sense than to go bankrupt building canals and railroads. I owed him money," he said, and the last word came out in a sob.

Men yelled as a blue disturbance plunged through the crowd, vaulted the railing and flew at Walton. Walton jumped from the chair and tried to take refuge behind the judge, but Esther followed, striking out at random with fists and feet. Walton's size meant that most of her blows found the target.

"You fat bastard!" she screamed. "For more'n two months you been trying to pull my backside in your bed, making promises—" Walton folded his arms over his head and sank to the floor, reminding Matt of Tildy in the sawdust of the flaming tent. Stars in heaven! How could he want her so much and so immediately?

Moffett and the sheriff pulled Esther off Walton—Seawall, Matt reminded himself—but she continued to shriek accusations, and Walton still cowered, as if every curse landed with the force of a barbed arrow. The judge banged his gavel. Matt sent Tildy a smile of triumph, but she did not see him. Her mother leaned against the wall, and Tildy waved salts under her nose.

Esther, finally understanding that her murderous attack was frustrated, threw herself against Moffett and sobbed; Moffett gazed about the room stupidly, as if he had never held a woman in his arms before.

"Your Honor, is this case dismissed?" Moffett asked.

"I believe so, unless there's to be a charge of perjury, or you yourself might want to bring a charge of impersonating—"

"No. I'm sick of lawyers and courts. But don't leave. You see, I never wanted a woman about the house. I thought them too much trouble, so I never married. But then this little gal came, and she's a ray of sunshine, and such a good cook, and maybe it's not too late for me to breed my own heir. That way Afton Walton, the real Afton Walton, the scoundrel, can't claim a cent of my money!" He brushed tears from Esther's face with his fingertips. "Miss Hull, would you be my wife?"

"You?" she gulped. She took less than ten seconds to decide. "Of course, you'll do fine. Better than that—" She gestured to the now empty witness chair. Walton had gained his feet and retreated behind the jury.

"Fine. The judge can marry us right now."

Judge Stanley leaned across the bench and eyed the couple. "This gal don't look anywhere near the age of consent. How old are you?"

"Nearly sixteen."

"Not old enough. Her father out there?" He surveyed the audience.

"Old Hull ain't here," someone called. Matt frowned at the floor, surprised at his disappointment. His father had not been interested enough to attend his first appearance in court.

"Hull's not her father," said a familiar voice at his elbow. Ira MacIntyre walked around the end of the table to approach the judge. "I'm her father. I'll give permission, if she truly wants to marry Moffett."

"You—?" Esther began, but a crash from the back of the room interrupted her. All the women were standing, gathered around in a tight circle.

"Help! Mrs. MacIntyre has swooned quite away!"

"Ma said a gentleman!" Esther cried. "You're nothing but a storekeeper. In Pikeston!" MacIntyre looked guilty, helpless and exhausted. He collapsed in his chair.

"So, a MacIntyre daughter's to control Moffett's Emporium after all," Matt said. "There's bound to be gossip."

"Of no consequence," MacIntyre said. "Last night I talked it over with the boys. I'm selling out and we're going to California. I'll have enough money to start a store in one of those towns on the bay. Where the boys will have a future."

"Your daughter, MacIntyre...would you give permission for the marriage of your daughter...Matilda? I want desperately for Tildy to be my wife."

"And if I say no, I suppose you'll go to the tavern tonight, with those lines you copied from that soldier's diary."

Matt shook his head. "Two nights ago, I burned the paper," he whispered.

"Burned it! You roll me over a barrel, and then throw away—"

"Shut up, MacIntyre! Just leave it. Revenge isn't part of the law. Besides, I'm not sure but what I wouldn't have done the same. Love is a whimsical mistress."

"Better a whimsical wife," MacIntyre said sadly.

"Tildy? I should like your permission—"

"Godfroy says there'll be disputes over land titles in California, since the Spanish got there first," MacIntyre said, "I want my lawyer along."

Six months or more driving a wagon toward the sunset? Matt thought about this as he turned to the men leaning over the railing, hands extended, offering congratulations. He stood, shook again and again, nodded at their words of praise, smiling to cover his confusion.

Jim Mac and Pete, Tole and his sons, the farmers Marshall and Burdette, maybe two or three more. All committed for California. And now Ira MacIntyre would leave. Not much of Pikeston left. Not enough to support two lawyers. And today the slush on the streets had soaked through his boots.

"You mean, if I want to marry Tildy, honestly, with your blessing, I come to California?"

MacIntyre nodded. "Exactly what I mean. Hell, man, Godfroy says in California you'll be a judge before you're twenty-five!"

"Dearly beloved," Judge Stanley intoned.

"Perhaps Tildy and I could be married right now, after the judge finishes with Moffett and Esther."

"No, Matilda's mother expects her wedding to be accomplished with decorum. Friday at the soonest." Friday? Could he wait until Friday? "Ravania will object, of course, that you're no suitable husband for a lady. I'll speak to her the first moment we have alone. Tell me, how did you intend to handle this case if that letter hadn't come?"

"First, I'd quote from Blackstone on the nature of contracts. Then I'd call Boyd as a witness. Tildy next, and she'd weep and cry that her father forced her to agree to the marriage. And I'd quote Blackstone on the validity of forced marriages. Their invalidity, rather."

"Sounds like you meant to put me on trial, not Walton."

"Exactly. I'd put you on trial. Dastardly, unnatural father." Matt smiled to take the sting out of the words.

"You're gonna be a real twisty lawyer," MacIntyre said

mournfully, shaking his head. He brightened. "But you'll be my twisty lawyer."

"Matilda, we must go to Muncie today."

Tildy studied her mother's pale face across the breakfast table. "Are you sure you feel like riding so far?"

"Child, your intended insists that the wedding be tomorrow, and there are things we must, must... Your corsets aren't suitable for a married woman."

"We're leaving in March, Mama. We won't wear fancy corsets on the trail to California."

"Nevertheless..."

The sun was shining, the roads had dried. Why not a ride to Muncie? Matt had gone to help Pete with the wagon they would share with Granny. Perhaps the fresh air would restore her mother's good humor and give her an opportunity to talk her out of wasting money on corsets.

"Not Moffett's, of course," her mother said as she settled in the buggy. "I knew in those days there was another woman, although I never, never suspected Ira would be so decadent.... It's just as well this came out now, with you preparing to marry, so you'll understand...it's best for a wife simply to ignore—"

"Mama, Matt would never do such a thing! His honor—"

Her mother laughed, and her laughter edged into hysteria. "Honor? Matt's no different—"

"I don't believe it." Tildy gripped the reins too tightly.

"And California! A country of degenerate Spaniards, the women all harlots, exposing themselves in chemises. Do you have any idea how out of date *Godey's Lady's Book* will be? Months late! Dresses, bonnets, shawls, all out of style before we ever hear of them!"

"Uncle Jim says the government is establishing mail by sea, through Panama."

"Panama. Another heathen country I've never heard of."

A few cloud shadows drifted over the ground. No more than a mile away a line of bare trees marked the river and concealed Godfroy's tepee…and Friday night, in her very own bed. She shivered.

"You're cold," said her mother. "We'll go first to the hotel—so nice that Muncie has an establishment with a proper ladies' room. A pot of tea will warm you, and then dinner."

"I can't think of one thing I truly need, Mama," Tildy said over the rim of her teacup. "Perhaps some kerchiefs, and a broad hat, but there's kerchiefs in the store at home, and Granny's teaching me to weave straw hats."

"Weaving straw's no occupation for a lady. I would have objected very strongly if I'd known."

"It's a very useful skill."

"It ruins the hands. Look at your hands, Matilda. Once they were soft, proper to a gentle upbringing. No gentleman will look at you until we've soothed away—"

"No gentleman need look at me, Mama. I'm marrying Lieutenant Hull, remember. Tomorrow. Friday." Her mother smiled gently, but her eyes said no. Her daughter would not marry Lieutenant Hull. Not Friday. Not ever.

"Eat, dear. It's almost time to go."

Go? Had they made the journey to Muncie so her mother would have her alone, and argue against her marriage? Tildy had no appetite for the roast pork and potatoes set before them. A distant horn echoed in the street, the herald of the southbound stage. Her mother threw her napkin on the table. "Come, dear, we've wasted time enough here."

The coachman urged the horses to a gallop, flourished his whip and pulled to a dramatic stop before the hotel. Men heaved two trunks off the boardwalk. Tildy blinked against the bright sunlight that reflected from the brass binding and initials.

"Mama, but that's your trunk!"

"Yes, dear. We're going to my brother's. In Virginia."

A man heaved Tildy's trunk into the boot of the coach. "Ladies do not go to California. Not a proper place, even if the streets were paved with gold. Ladies do not marry men like Matthew Hull. In Virginia we'll find people of our own kind, dear. Please help me—" her mother raised her voice, speaking to no one in particular "—my daughter has a weakness of mind, and may resist stepping into the coach."

"Mama, your brother doesn't live in Virginia. He lives in Richmond, Indiana!"

"Richmond, Virginia," her mother said to the men wrestling with the trunks.

"It's Mrs. Ridley who has relatives in Virginia!" Tildy said, desperate, twisting her head, searching for a familiar face.

"Go quietly, miss," a man said to her.

"Mama! You can't do this to me! I'm to be married tomorrow!" A man stepped close to her, so close she could not easily turn away from the stagecoach.

"She has such vivid fancies," her mother said. "Marry! Gentlemen do not propose marriage to women who think their dreams are real."

"So the fire frightened her sense away," said the tall man. "A dreadful experience for a girl. Perhaps she fancies she'll marry the man who carried her away."

The tall man towered above her. "How do you know about the fire?" she asked.

"Why, miss, I stood over you, trying to push the mob away, and before I could snatch you up, a man pulled you from under me, and staggered off into the smoke and dust."

"Thank you, thank you! You saved my life. Now, save it again. I'm not crazy. My mother's confused. We have no relatives in Virginia. Tomorrow I'm to marry the man who carried me out of the fire. Please believe me!"

The tall man wrinkled his forehead in doubt, shifted his eyes to her mother. Tildy ducked beneath his arm. The only clear path led up the steps, into the hotel. She dashed in that direction, felt a tightness on her skirt as a hand grasped her. She turned to jerk her skirt free, saw her mother stepping into the coach. A madwoman! Alone, heading for Indianapolis. From there, where might she go? Tildy dared not leave her mother in the stagecoach alone! She descended the stairs with dignity. The tall man offered his hand.

"Good girl," he said.

"His name is Matthew Hull. In Pikeston. Please send a message to him, tell him I'll come back as soon as possible, after I've settled Mother's fancies. But please tell him I'll come back to him! That I love him!"


"I'm going to California," Matt said. His father did not turn away from stirring the mash in the oak barrels. "Perhaps you and Ma would like to come, too. There's great opportunities—"

"Bah! Opportunities for dying!"

Matt's neck relaxed. He did not want his parents along. But for the sake of the four children in the cabin, he would have been willing.

"You told Emma you'd give money to dress the young'uns," his father said. His fingers moved expectantly.

"Yes, if they'll go to school."

"Give me the money."

"I'll pay the bill at the store," Matt said stubbornly.

"Give me the money. I'll take care of it." Matt knew what care would be taken.

"Let the children come with me. To California. One of the families would take them in."

"Don't trust your father to do right by the kids?"

"No."

"Then get out of here. Highfalutin' lawyer, won his big case. Next won't come so easy, I warrant." He laughed.

"How do you know about the case? You weren't there."

"No, I had better things to do. Got a whole dollar for hauling Miz MacIntyre's trunks to Muncie."

"Mrs. MacIntyre's trunks?" All Matt's senses came to attention.

"She says her daughter's to marry a man in Virginia."

When he'd stopped by the house, Josh had said Tildy and her mother had gone to Muncie. Monday and Thursday, the Indianapolis coach. Matt looked up through the trees, found the sun halfway across the winter sky. He did not look back to yell goodbye. Running, pounding up the trail that led away from the river, cutting across the flattened debris of a wheatfield, losing time to unexpected mud, gaining inches, feet, tenths and quarters of miles on a well-used cow path that cut off a curve in the road.

She would take Tildy away. Tildy would not go. Unless she tricked her.

Walking, breathless, running once more. A mile trotting, a quarter mile plodding. The road out of the little hollow rose like a mountainside. Finally the main street. And the rear of the stagecoach, vanishing in the haze kicked up by three teams and the wheels. He leaned panting against a pillar supporting the veranda roof.

"Did you see a lady? A young lady with her mother?" he gasped.

"You Matthew Hull?"

"Yes."

"The old lady says the young one's loco. Young one says her mother's the crazy. She told me to tell you, she'll be back. Wish I'd been the one to carry her from that tent. Pert girl. Jolly in bed, I would guess."

"I can't say," Matt lied. He pulled in two deep breaths. "We're to be married tomorrow!" The tall man turned away.

Indianapolis? Who in Muncie had a horse he could borrow? Moffett? Moffett might not be anxious to help the lawyer who had argued against him. Then he recalled what still seemed impossible, that Moffett had married Esther and was his brother-in-law!

Moffett welcomed him. Matt found the newlyweds' constant expressions of affection flustering. He rode out of Muncie on a good horse and saddle, with ten crisp banknotes Moffett had pressed upon him, and recurrent fountainings of erotic heat and caustic fear.

## Chapter Twenty

"No lady ever went to California," her mother repeated as the stagecoach rolled past the outskirts of town. "We'll be quite happy in Virginia."

"Hush, Mother," Tildy whispered. "It's been a very exciting day. Lean back and close your eyes."

"I'll crush my hat."

"Take it off and pull your shawl up. There. Rest before we stop for supper."

Tildy leaned back, pretended to close her eyes but actually studied the two men on the opposite seat through her lashes. Could she ask either of them for help? She did not like the way the man on the right stared at her. He leaned to his companion and whispered behind his hand, without taking his eyes off her. The companion laughed softly, but not a laugh to encourage closer acquaintance. Tildy clutched her mother's hat before her like a shield.

Twilight, the coach moving heavily through mud, fleecy clouds in the west behind the line of trees that marked the White River. Long after dark they stopped at a building lit by a single lantern.

"Supper!" the coachman cried. The lantern disappeared along with the hostler who led the tired horses to the barn. The two men made no move to leave the coach.

"Come, Mother," Tildy whispered. Whether or not she ate supper, she could escape their leering eyes.

The landlady served beans and corn bread, and Tildy thought she furnished only a single guttering candle to disguise the condition of the supper.

"Half dollar," said the woman, placing two mugs of coffee on the table with a disrespectful plop. Outrageous, Tildy thought. Fifty cents should buy a feast. But her mother handed her reticule across the table without protest.

"Here, Matilda. Find the proper amount."

Tildy fished about in the small sack, pulled out a vial of salts, a linen handkerchief and several coins.

Twenty-five, thirty cents. She poured all the coins into her palm, stretched her hand to the candle. Less than two dollars!

She gasped with fear, then realized her mother would not be so foolish as to carry her money in her reticule, where it might be snatched. She had sewn a pocket in an underpetticoat, or had a purse strapped to her garter. Tildy picked out half a dollar and laid it on the table.

The coach swayed over the rutted road. Occasionally she dozed, but was jerked to wakefulness whenever the coach dropped into a hole, or rattled over a stretch of corduroy. They made stops at towns she had heard of but never seen. Tildy stared out, curious. Always the same, a pool of lantern light, a covered porch, cursing men leading fresh teams.

Dimly dawn. "Indianapolis!" She heard the thump of trunks on the boardwalk. Through the window she saw they had stopped in front of a hotel.

"Please, Matilda, ask what time the coach for Virginia leaves."

"No, you're exhausted. We'll get a room here, and stay overnight." *And I'll send a message to Papa.*

Mama was loco! Travelers did not take a stage to Virginia, but a steamboat on the Ohio, and canal boats and carriages over the mountains. The night before the trial, when Papa had announced that they would go to California, her mother had not fainted. She had screamed irrationally, accused the whole family of vile crimes.

"If I might be of service..." In the light of morning the man's eyes showed watery blue in red-rimmed slits. Piercing and expectant.

"No, I'll care for my mother...until my father arrives."

The bed and washstand nearly filled the room, and when a boy piled their trunks near the door, Tildy found very little space remained. Particularly since the boy did not leave, but stood before the door, shifting from foot to foot.

"Is there some way we can have a pot of tea? Here in our room?" The boy's eyes brightened, and he dashed away.

A single window overlooked the street. Tildy lifted the sash, pulled the shutters closed and fastened them against the sunrise.

"You didn't give him money," her mother said.

"What? Must I pay for the tea beforehand?"

"He expected money for bringing the trunks up the stairs."

"Why didn't you tell me!"

"I was quite unsure. According to *Godey's*, gentlemen handle the money, and I hadn't thought what we would do, traveling alone."

"Give me the money," Tildy said. Her mother handed over her reticule.

"The rest of your money. From your petticoat pocket, or the purse—"

"The money's in my reticule."

Fear dropped on Tildy's shoulders, and her knees weakened. "Of course," she murmured.

She gave the boy a ten-cent piece, sending him away smiling. One dollar and four cents remaining. And the sign downstairs said the room cost fifty cents per night, with dinner included. And the tea would be extra, she supposed.

Her mother drank half a cup of tea, changed to a nightdress and stretched out on the bed. Tildy searched through her petticoats. No secret pocket. She pawed through her mother's trunk, running her fingers through every pouch on the sides. Nothing.

Her stomach growled. Breakfast would cost at least ten cents, perhaps more. She poured another cup of tea and added sugar until it was a thick syrup. She bathed her face, pushed up her sleeves carefully to avoid pressure on the red scar.

Mrs. Stanley! Matt had not seen her in Muncie, because she had gone house-hunting in Indianapolis. Tildy lifted the latch, determined to run to the courthouse and inquire about Mrs. Stanley. Across the hall a door opened and a disheveled man scuffed out, carrying a razor and dingy towel. She slammed the door. She had forgotten the time. Too early to send a message to Mrs. Stanley.

She removed her shoes, bodice, skirt and petticoats, and stretched out beside her mother. She drifted in and out of a troubling dream, trapped in a box that shook and tumbled. A man with watery eyes offered to free her. She clawed her way to consciousness and swung her legs over the edge of the bed. Her mother sat up behind her.

"What time is it," her mother asked.

"I'm not sure, but I want clean stockings." While she put her mother's trunk onto the bed to open her own, Mama lifted the sash, unlocked the shutters and let in a blast of sunlight.

Tildy stared at the paper wrapping that proclaimed the advantages of La Mode Airproof Bust Improver. She poked at it to convince her unbelieving eyes. Her mother had gone completely, wildly out of her mind!

Matt kept the horse at a walk, and where the road turned muddy, dismounted and walked himself. He inquired at the stations along the way, and learned that two ladies had been passengers on the stage. One young and quite pretty. He pushed on into the night, past midnight, he presumed, so Friday had arrived. His wedding day, with his bride far in advance of him on a muddy road leading to God knows where.

At dawn he got breakfast from a serving girl in a neat house. She brushed the mud from his coat while he wolfed down corn bread and slices of cold pork, and the horse snatched at a few wisps of hay. The sun blazed on his left hand, and he pulled his hat in that direction to block the glare. He followed the wide track of the stagecoach wheels until they were lost in the maze of ruts marking the increased traffic of the capital. He asked directions of a wagon driver, finally found the hotel that displayed the name of the stage line.

"I'm searching for two ladies who came on the stage from the north. Mrs. and Miss MacIntyre," he asked of a bootblacky. The boy beat mud from the sole of the boot he worked on. "Did you see them, by chance?"

"Might have, might not," the lad snarled.

"It's most important. The...the husband of the elder woman...he's concerned—"

"I wager it's not the old nanny you're after," the boy sneered. "Two other gentleman already asked me to send word when the young'un comes down to take dinner. They give me half a dollar." Matt's hopes soared. They had taken a room in this very hotel!

"What's going on, Israel?" A man in a swallowtail coat stood in the doorway.

"This tramp's after the pretty lady what came this morning."

The well-dressed man examined Matt, and his eyes narrowed in disfavor. Matt noticed for the first time that all his clothing, with the exception of his coat, was spattered with mud. And his coat was none too clean.

"This is a respectable hotel, where lady guests find no insult. Be on your way." The gentleman turned his back and disappeared.

"Respectable, except the bootblack can be bribed,"

Matt said to the boy, who simply grinned. "How much, to take a message to the lady?"

"Can't. The two gentleman said they'd give me a whole dollar at dinner, and more'n that if they's *successful*." Matt's chest hollowed out. "They's regulars. Got to put my loyalty somewheres." He went back to the mud on the boot.

Matt slumped on the edge of the boardwalk, propped his chin in his hands. He would get a message to Tildy somehow. The boy would eventually leave to distribute the boots. Perhaps the cook would call him to the kitchen before dinner. He needed only a minute to sneak upstairs and knock on a few doors.

He should send word to MacIntyre, who must be worried sick, coming home in the evening to find his wife and daughter gone. If only the telegraph ran through Pikeston. He could wire Moffett, who would send a messenger the final eight miles on foot or horseback. This evening at the earliest.

"Mother!" The cry came from the heavens. An angel's voice, an angelic direction. "What's this thing doing in my trunk?" Hardly an angelic tone. Matt sprang to his feet. A snake? A trap that caught her fingers?

"Why, dear—" a cultivated voice, a cultivated calmness "—some men look for companions a bit more buxom—"

"Matthew doesn't. Matthew says I'm just fine! Everything about me..."

He jumped across the veranda.

"I told you to be on your way!" shouted the gentleman as Matt ran past him. He hit the stairs before the startled man rounded his counter. The stair twisted past two landings, forcing Matt to hesitate at the top to figure which way led to the front of the building. Which door? Boots pounded behind him.

"Tildy!" he yelled. "Tildy!"

"Mother, sit up! There's no room for you to faint." He

plunged toward her determined voice and pounded on the door.

"Tildy, open the door. I'm here. It's our wedding day!"

She fell into his arms, little whimpering cries of relief and delight. "Thank heavens! How did you know?"

Beyond, Mrs. MacIntyre sprawled on the floor beneath the window, her head and shoulders against the wall. The shutter swung idly, so the beam of sunlight changed shape in a constant rhythm.

"Is your mother sick?" Matt asked after the first long kiss.

"No, she fainted when I said...when I said you liked my bosom, and she realized we hadn't waited to...you know. Let me go, so I can find her salts."

"No," he said. He lifted her onto the bed, the part of the bed not occupied by a trunk. He had the hooks of her corset open when he heard the moan from near the window, and realized her mother would not stay unconscious for more than a few minutes.

"Can we get a marriage license in Indianapolis? And someone to marry us?" she asked from beneath him. Married. Yes, he had promised her. Before they made love again.

Tildy dug about in her trunk and pulled out a yellow dress. While she put on her petticoats, he lifted Mrs. MacIntyre onto the bed.

"How did you know?" Tildy asked. Matt explained his father's errand with the trunks. "Do you have any money?" she asked.

"Ten dollars. Moffett gave it to me, in case—"

"Mr. Moffett! He gave you money?"

"He's my brother-in-law, remember. Besides, he's enormously grateful that I got Perfect Seawall out of his kitchen and store. The man ate up all the profits." Eating? His mouth watered. "Do you want dinner before—"

"The county offices, a judge to marry us, then dinner," Tildy decided. "But hurry, because I'm starved nearly to

death, because the last time I ate was supper at...I don't
remember, but I've always dreamed of having a wedding
breakfast with champagne. So let's get married first.''

Her yellow dress shone as if it had golden depths, the
prettiest thing he had ever seen, with lace across her
breasts, and cascading in long ruffles from her elbows.

"You stay here, Mama," she said, leaning over her
mother to kiss her. "Take a nap."

The well-dressed gentleman stared before he remembered his manners and bowed to the lady.

A filthy buggy stood in front of the hotel. The horse's
head hung nearly to his knees, and the mud-spattered
driver heaved himself wearily to the ground.

"Papa!" Tildy cried.

"Where in h—in this benighted world is your mother?"

"Upstairs. She says she'll take the next stage to Virginia, to live with Uncle Freddie."

"Frederick doesn't live in Virginia! He lives over in
Richmond—"

"I know. I tried to tell her. Maybe she'll believe you."

"I'd better talk to her," he said with a great sigh. "I'm
hungry as a penned hog. Didn't so much as hesitate, except
to let the horse breathe at the top of a hill."

"If you'll wait an hour, sir, we're searching for a judge
to marry us. We'll dine here. Won't you accompany us?"

MacIntyre scrunched his mouth to one side. "Better see
about Ravania. Meet you here in an hour."

Matt carried Tildy across the muddiest of the street corners. The judge had just stepped over the threshold to find
his dinner, but it took very little argument to persuade him
to write out a license and perform a hasty ceremony. Matt
found two sleepy loafers in the recorder's office to serve
as witnesses, and their hooded eyes reminded him he had
not slept the night before.

Leaning against the wall in the dim hallway, Matt wondered if he had the energy to please his bride.

"I'm ready," she called. He pushed open the door, but did not look at her until he dropped the bar against intruders. "I poured clean water in the basin."

He undressed in the semidark, and heard dried mud fall onto the floor. He washed his face, felt the stubble and regretted that he had no means to shave. No means to shave, but worse even than that...

He leaned over her. "Tildy, if I make love to you...I don't have the sheath along. There might be a baby."

"When?" she asked dreamily. Her fingers pressed into his shoulders, one after the other. "February, March...why not until October! We'll be in California by October, won't we?"

She had on no nightdress! As naked as he, ready for him.

"But you'd be expecting on the trip."

"You'll be there to help me. And Rachel and Meggie. Matt, there were two men on the stage, and they frightened me, because they kept staring, like I didn't have a thing on! I'm glad I'm married, and have a husband to stand between me and men like that." She sighed and cradled her head in the notch of his shoulder. He ran his fingers down her right arm, lightly, for fear of the still-tender scar. To her waist, the swell of her hip, her thigh. Tildy took a deep, slow breath, then another. He stopped his fingers' search. Another deep breath. She was asleep. He imagined the ribald comments around a myriad public stoves, if anyone ever found out. *Matt Hull's a poor sort of lover. His bride was so bored, she went to sleep before the plank got planed.*

He would take it as a compliment. She trusted him. After a sleepless night in a rattling stagecoach with two men who frightened her and no company but a crazy woman who thought two dollars sufficient funds to carry her through to Virginia, Tildy deserved her rest.

He drifted off to sleep, oddly happy at the course of this strange wedding night. He woke in pitch black. Tildy moved beside him, her hand reached out to investigate who shared her bed.

"Matt, I'm glad you made love to me before."

"So am I."

A light, misty rain damped the clank of harness chains. Matt watched the three wagons pass through Jim Mac's gate; Pete did not close the gate, knowing the final wagon would follow within a few minutes.

"They're gone?" Granny asked. She stood beside him, holding a sack beneath her cloak. Matt hastily opened the door so she could enter the wagon. Pete had constructed a magnificent wagon for her, with a side opening like a stagecoach, so she need not climb over a tailgate.

"Have you brought your seeds?" he asked. "We'll want you to tell our fortunes once we reach the Missouri."

"Pshaw! You know there's nothing to the seeds," she said. "Of course I have them. Men won't listen to an old woman, unless they think she speaks magic." Her mischievous grin reminded him of Meggie. "There's one more thing," she said from inside the wagon. "The tea caddy. It's too heavy for me."

"Heavy? It's nailed down," he said, remembering the first time he had been in her kitchen, looking for tea to relieve Jim Mac's ague.

"No, it's just heavy. I can't lift it." He walked to the kitchen, doubtful, found that the box moved if he gave it a strong push.

"Can you get it?" Granny asked from the door. Matt heaved the box off the shelf with two hands, lugged it toward the door, his shoulders sagging.

"What's in this thing? You must have an ingot of lead...." The only thing heavier than lead was—he smiled at her as they passed on the porch. "Your money?" She nodded.

In the wagon, before she stowed the box under the floorboards, she unlocked it and lifted out a fitted basket that contained packets of tea. The gold coins shone dully.

"If I die on the plains, divide it among my grandchildren," she said.

"Don't you think you should write a will?"

"Lawyers cost money," she said gruffly. She stared at him, smiled guiltily. "We'll do it tonight, when we stop. If Tildy's expecting, give that child a share, too. I meant for Tildy to be here to see it."

"She went on ahead to get a bag of scraps out of the attic."

"She thinks she'll have time for patchwork!" Granny said, and Matt's face warmed, seeing the twinkle in her eye. "No one else knows where the money is. They gossip about how I gave it away, or buried it in the orchard, or lost it in some speculation. They don't think of a tea caddy."

"I suppose not."

"I've kept it, thinking the day would come when my sons or grandchildren got in a bad scrape. But so far, they've always managed to fend for themselves."

"Tildy? Would you have given the money to Ira, to save Tildy from Walton?"

"Last resort," she muttered, pushing aside a blanket. "Put the box down there. Ira went into debt for foolish things. French corsets and silver spoons. I hated to see my money pay for Ravania's nonsense. Besides, I wanted you to solve the problem for us. And marry her."

"But you thought I was a troublesome child," he protested.

"Troublesome boys are a heartache," she said. "But troublesome men!" Her pale blue eyes misted. "I guess troublesome men can be heartaches, too. But they're usually good in bed."

Pikeston's square, Tildy observed with a critical eye, was not large enough for a courthouse. The eleven wagons took up every bit of space north of the flagpole.

The men drew the double tops of the wagons tight against the rain. Here and there childish fingers pushed at the fabric to spy upon their parents. The side of the Burdette wagon lifted several inches under the hands of three girls and a boy. Childless Mrs. Burdette had wept with joy when Matt proposed they take the children. Mr. Burdette had agreed, so long as no one in the party ever spoke a word that suggested the children were not his own.

Tildy had dreaded the visit to Emma Callom, had been shocked when the woman shrugged and said she supposed it was for the best that the children leave, but she wanted five dollars each. And Tildy knew for a fact that Granny had supplied the twenty dollar goldpiece that rescued Matt's brother and sisters.

Tildy tapped her foot and hung impatiently from under the protection of the livery barn. She clutched the bag of calico and gingham scraps she had rescued from the attic of the brick house. Finally, the twelfth wagon rolled into the square, the dun coats of the oxen dark with wet. The driver's bulky oilcloth coat did not disguise his height, nor the grace with which he moved. She pulled up the hood of her cloak and stepped out to join him.

"Climb in," he said, pointing to the side door. "You'll get wet. And your father says the men will have a meeting in the tavern, where you'll not want to go."

"You think only the men have business?" she teased. "The ladies are meeting in the church."

She stepped close to Matt. He leaned down and searched within the engulfing hood until their lips met. "Don't let Josh sneak whiskey or ale," she said. "Papa's depending on him to drive one of the wagons."

She watched as he directed the oxen to their place, then dashed across the square to the church.

"Have you heard from your mother?" asked Mrs. Fitch the moment Tildy pushed her hood back. Mrs. Fitch shook her head sadly, commenting on both the weakness of Tildy's mother's mind, and her father's insanity in proceeding with the move to California.

"Uncle Freddie wrote. She's quite happy in Richmond, except she complains that she'd expected Virginia to be warmer in the spring."

"I have a letter from Rachel," said Mrs. Ridley sadly. "Mailed when they passed through St. Louis. On the steamboat she met a quilter, who traced out a patchwork pattern. A star. Rachel says it's very complicated, and she can hardly wait until the scrap bags arrive."

Granny entered, her cloak wrapped tightly against the rain. She motioned Tildy aside.

"You understand the men intend to elect Matt captain of the party?" she whispered. Tildy nodded. "This puts a great burden on his shoulders. You understand that? Since he married you, he's had little to do except hover over you and spoil you. That's at an end, the moment he becomes Captain Hull."

"I understand, Granny. He asked last night if he should reject the post. He's a foolish goose of a husband, who thinks I need him dancing attendance every minute. I told him I could do quite well on my own."

"Faith, you and Tildy can have first pick of the scraps," Meggie said, holding out a muslin sack. "They don't matter a pin to me. I won't be sitting in the wagon sewing, but riding ahead with Sampson or Godfroy."

"But when it rains," Faith said, "or in camp, you must at least have a pattern in mind—"

"If I do patchwork, I'll make Wild Geese Flying. It takes only two triangles, and they can be sketched out on a slip of paper, and any color at all will do."

"Is there any particular color you'd like?" Tildy asked Faith. "Have you decided on a pattern?"

"Save me the darkest calicos. I'm making Jacob's Ladder. It's appropriate, since Jacob saw his vision of the ladder to heaven while on a long journey."

"I doubt you'll find Jacob's house of God and the gate of heaven on the road to California," Reverend Fitch said sadly.

"At the end of that journey, Jacob fell in love," Meggie said, eyeing Faith.

"If we arrive in one piece, that will be blessing enough. None of us should expect more," Faith said.

Tildy eyed the scrap bag in Meggie's hand, and decided she should put in her request before another woman mentioned a patchwork project. "If it wouldn't be too much trouble I'd appreciate having any scraps of red and blue."

"Red and blue!" Mrs. Ridley exclaimed. "You're a new bride, dear. A Wedding Ring quilt, that's what you should make, and red and blue aren't appropriate colors."

"I found an appropriate pattern," Tildy said. "Hull's Victory."

"No, dear!" Mrs. Fitch exclaimed. "Men, when they use that word, victory, they quite often mean—" She looked at the unmarried girls and said no more.

"If the men should hear," Mrs. Ridley said, "they'll poke Matt in the ribs, and make…remarks they suppose women don't understand. They'll smirk at you, and…well, think you're not a lady."

"I'm not a lady," Tildy said. "Remember, I married a man who's not a fit husband for a lady. I'm Mrs. Matthew Hull."

\* \* \* \* \*

**Harlequin Historicals presents
an exciting medieval collection**

# THE KNIGHTS OF CHRISTMAS

**With bestselling authors**

Suzanne
**BARCLAY**

Margaret
**MOORE**

Debborah
**SIMMONS**

Available in October
wherever Harlequin Historicals are sold.

# CHRISTMAS MIRACLES

**really can happen, and Christmas
dreams can come true!**

## BETTY NEELS,
### Carole Mortimer and Rebecca Winters

bring you the magic of Christmas in this wonderful
holiday collection of romantic stories intertwined
with Christmas dreams come true.

Join three of your favorite romance authors as they
celebrate the festive season in their own special style!

Available in November at your favorite retail store.

HARLEQUIN®

# WANT WESTERNS?

**Harlequin Historicals has got 'em!**

In October, look for these two
exciting tales:

**WILD CARD by Susan Amarillas**
A lady gambler wanted for murder falls for a
handsome sheriff

**THE UNTAMED HEART by Kit Gardner**
A dashing earl succumbs to a reckless woman
in the American West

In November, watch for
two more stories:

**CADE'S JUSTICE by Pat Tracy**
A schoolteacher heals the soul of the wealthy
uncle of one of her students

**TEMPLE'S PRIZE by Linda Castle**
Two paleontologists battle each other on a dig,
and uncover their hearts

Four new Westerns from four terrific authors!
Look for them wherever Harlequin Historicals
are sold.

**Harlequin® Historical**

# DELTA JUSTICE

**A family dynasty of law and order
is shattered by a mysterious crime
of passion.**

Don't miss the second Delta Justice book
as the mystery unfolds in:

## *Letters, Lies and Alibis*
### by Sandy Steen

Rancher Travis Hardin is determined to right a
sixty-year wrong and wreak vengeance on the Delacroix.
But he hadn't intended to fall in love doing it. Was his
desire for Shelby greater than his need to destroy her
family?

Lawyer Shelby Delacroix never does anything halfway.
She is passionate about life, her work...and Travis. Lost
in a romantic haze, Shelby encourages him to join her in
unearthing the Delacroix family secrets. Little does she
suspect that Travis is keeping a few secrets of his own....

**Available in October
wherever Harlequin books are sold.**

Look us up on-line at: http://www.romance.net

# COMING NEXT MONTH FROM

# HARLEQUIN HISTORICALS